G.A. HENTY
December 8, 1832 --- November 16, 1902

st George For England

A Tale of Cressy & Poitiers by G.A. Henty

Preston
Speed
ublications

Pennsylvania

A note about our name: Preston/Speed Publications
In an age where it has become fashionable to denigrate fathers,
we have decided to honor ours.   Our name is in loving memory
of Preston Louis Schmitt and Speed - Lester Herbert Maynard
("Speed" is a nickname that was earned for prowess in baseball).

This book is printed on acid-free paper, and its binding
materials have been chosen for strength and durability.

Published August 27, 1884 by
BLACKIE & SON, LONDON

Blackie & Son Title Page Date: 1895

Heirloom Hardcover Edition ISBN 1-887159-26-6
Popular Softcover Edition ISBN 1-887159-27-4
Printed in the U.S.A.

PRESTON/SPEED PUBLICATIONS
RR #4, BOX 705
MILL HALL, PENNSYLVANIA   17751
(570) 726-7844
1999

INTRODUCTION:

G. A. Henty's life was filled with exciting adventure. Completing Westminster School, he attended Cambridge University. Along with a rigorous course of study, Henty participated in boxing, wrestling and rowing. The strenuous study and healthy, competitive participation in sports prepared Henty to be with the British army in Crimea, as a war correspondent witnessing Garibaldi fight in Italy, visiting Abyssinia, being present in Paris during the Franco-Prussian war, in Spain with the Carlists, at the opening of the Suez Canal, touring India with the Prince of Wales (later Edward VII) and a trip to the California gold fields. These are only a few of his exciting adventures.

G. A. Henty lived during the reign of Queen Victoria (1837-1901) and began his story telling career with his own children. After dinner, he would spend an hour or two in telling them a story that would continue the next day. Some stories took weeks! A friend was present one day and watched the spell-bound reaction of his children suggesting that he write down his stories so others could enjoy them. He did. Henty wrote approximately 144 books plus stories for magazines and was dubbed as "The Prince of Story-Tellers" and "The Boy's Own Historian." One of Mr. Henty's secretaries reported that he would quickly pace back and forth in his study dictating stories as fast as the secretary could record them.

Henty's stories revolve around a fictional boy hero during fascinating periods of history. His heroes are diligent, courageous, intelligent and dedicated to their country and cause in the face, at times, of great peril. His histories, particularly battle accounts, have been recognized by historian scholars for their accuracy. There is nothing dry in Mr. Henty's stories and thus he removes the drudgery and laborious task often associated with the study of history.

Henty's heroes fight wars, sail the seas, discover land, conquer evil empires, prospect for gold, and a host of other exciting adventures. They meet famous personages like Josephus, Titus, Hannibal, Robert the Bruce, Sir William Wallace, General Marlborough, General Gordon, General Kitchner, Robert E. Lee, Frederick the Great, the Duke of Wellington, Huguenot leader Coligny, Cortez, King Alfred, Napoleon, and Sir Francis Drake just to mention a *few*. The heroes go through the fall of Jerusalem, the Roman invasion of Britain, the Crusades, the Viking invasion of Europe, the Reformation in various countries, the Reign of Terror, etc. In short, Henty's heroes live through tumultuous historic eras meeting the leaders of that time. Understanding the culture of the time period becomes second nature as well as comparing/contrasting the society of various European and heathen cultures.

Preston/Speed Publications is delighted to offer again the works of G. A. Henty. Action-packed exciting adventure awaits adults and a whole new generation. The books have been reproduced with modern type-setting. However, the original grammar, spellings and punctuation remains the same as the original versions.

Attempted assassination of Sir Walter.

PREFACE.

MY DEAR LADS,

You may be told perhaps that there is no good to be obtained from tales of fighting and bloodshed,—that there is no moral to be drawn from such histories. Believe it not. War has its lessons as well as Peace. You will learn from tales like this that determination and enthusiasm can accomplish marvels, that true courage is generally accompanied by magnanimity and gentleness, and that if not in itself the very highest of virtues, it is the parent of almost all the others, since but few of them can be practised without it. The courage of our forefathers has created the greatest empire in the world around a small and in itself insignificant island; if this empire is ever lost, it will be by the cowardice of their descendants.

At no period of her history did England stand so high in the eyes of Europe as in the time whose events are recorded in this volume. A chivalrous king and an even more chivalrous prince had infected the whole people with their martial spirit, and the result was that their armies were for a time invincible, and the most astonishing successes were gained against numbers which would appear overwhelming. The victories of Cressy and Poitiers may be to some extent accounted for by superior generalship and discipline on the part of the conquerors; but this will not account for the great naval victory over the Spanish fleet off the coast of Sussex, a victory even more surprising and won against greater odds than was that gained in the same waters centuries later over the Spanish Armada. The historical facts of the story are all drawn from Froissart and other contemporary historians, as collated and compared by Mr. James in his carefully written history. They may therefore be relied upon as accurate in every important particular.

Yours sincerely,

G. A. HENTY.

CONTENTS

ILLUSTRATIONS

ST. GEORGE FOR ENGLAND

CHAPTER I
A WAYFARER

It was a bitterly cold night in the month of November, 1330. The rain was pouring heavily, when a woman, with a child in her arms, entered the little village of Southwark. She had evidently come from a distance, for her dress was travel-stained and muddy. She tottered rather than walked, and when, upon her arrival at the gateway on the southern side of London Bridge, she found that the hour was past and the gates closed for the night, she leant against the wall with a faint groan of exhaustion and disappointment.

After remaining, as if in doubt, for some time, she feebly made her way into the village. Here were many houses of entertainment, for travellers like herself often arrived too late to enter the gates, and had to abide outside for the night. Moreover, house rent was dear within the walls of the crowded city, and many, whose business brought them to town, found it cheaper to take up their abode in the quiet hostels of Southwark rather than to stay in the more expensive inns within the walls. The lights came out brightly from many of the casements, with sounds of boisterous songs and laughter. The woman passed these without a pause. Presently she stopped before a cottage, from which a feeble light alone showed that it was tenanted.

She knocked at the door. It was opened by a pleasant-faced man of some thirty years old.

"What is it?" he asked.

"I am a wayfarer," the woman answered feebly. "Canst take me and my child in for the night?"

1

"You have made a mistake," the man said; "this is no inn. Further up the road there are plenty of places where you can find such accommodation as you lack."

"I have passed them," the woman said, "but all seemed full of roisterers. I am wet and weary, and my strength is nigh spent. I can pay thee, good fellow, and I pray you as a Christian to let me come in and sleep before your fire for the night. When the gates are open in the morning I will go; for I have a friend within the city who will, methinks, receive me."

The tone of voice, and the addressing of himself as good fellow, at once convinced the man that the woman before him was no common wayfarer.

"Come in," he said; "Geoffrey Ward is not a man to shut his doors in a woman's face on a night like this, nor does he need payment for such small hospitality. Come hither, Madge!" he shouted; and at his voice a woman came down from the upper chamber. "Sister," he said; "this is a wayfarer who needs shelter for the night; she is wet and weary. Do you take her up to your room and lend her some dry clothing; then make her a cup of warm posset, which she needs sorely. I will fetch an armful of fresh rushes from the shed and strew them here: I will sleep in the smithy. Quick, girl," he said sharply; "she is fainting with cold and fatigue." And as he spoke he caught the woman as she was about to fall, and laid her gently on the ground. "She is of better station than she seems," he said to his sister; "like enough some poor lady whose husband has taken part in the troubles; but that is no business of ours. Quick, Madge, and get these wet things off her; she is soaked to the skin. I will go round to the Green Dragon and will fetch a cup of warm cordial, which I warrant me will put fresh life into her."

So saying, he took down his flat cap from its peg on the wall and went out, while his sister at once proceeded to remove the drenched garments and to rub the cold hands of the guest until she recovered consciousness. When Geoffrey Ward returned, the woman was sitting in a settle by the fireside, dressed in a warm woollen garment belonging to his sister.

Madge had thrown fresh wood on the fire, which was blazing brightly now. The woman drank the steaming beverage which her host brought with him. The colour came faintly again into her cheeks.

"I thank you, indeed," she said, "for your kindness. Had you not taken me in I think I would have died at your door, for indeed I could go no further; and though I hold not to life, yet would I fain live until I have delivered my boy into the hands of those who will be kind to him, and this will, I trust, be to-morrow."

"Say nought about it," Geoffrey answered; "Madge and I are right glad to have been of service to you. It would be a poor world indeed if one could not give a corner of one's fireside to a fellow-creature on such a night as this, especially when that fellow creature is a woman with a child. Poor little chap ! he looks right well and sturdy, and seems to have taken no ill from his journey."

"Truly, he is well and sturdy," the mother said, looking at him proudly; "indeed I have been almost wishing to-day that he were lighter by a few pounds, for in truth I am not used to carry him far, and his weight has sorely tried me. His name is Walter, and I trust," she added, looking at the powerful figure of her host, "that he will grow up as straight and as stalwart as yourself." The child, who was about three years old, was indeed an exceedingly fine little fellow, as he sat, in one scanty garment, in his mother's lap, gazing with round eyes at the blazing fire; and the smith thought how pretty a picture the child and mother made. She was a fair, gentle-looking girl some two-and-twenty years old, and it was easy enough to see now from her delicate features and soft shapely hands that she had never been accustomed to toil.

"And now," the smith said, "I will e'en say good night. The hour is late, and I shall be having the watch coming along to know why I keep a fire so long after the curfew. Should you be a stranger in the city, I will gladly act as your guide in the morning to the friends whom you seek, that is, should they be known to me; but if not, we shall doubtless find them without difficulty."

So saying, the smith retired to his bed of rushes in the smithy, and soon afterwards the tired visitor, with her baby, lay down on the rushes in front of the fire, for in those days none of the working or artisan class used beds, which were not indeed, for centuries afterwards, in usage by the common people.

In the morning Geoffrey Ward found that his guest desired to find one Giles Fletcher, a maker of bows.

"I know him well," the smith said. "There are many who do a larger business, and hold their heads higher; but Giles Fletcher is well esteemed as a good workman, whose wares can be depended upon. It is often said of him that did he take less pains he would thrive more; but he handles each bow that he makes as if he loved it, and finishes and polishes each with his own hand. Therefore he doeth not so much trade as those who are less particular with their wares, for he hath to charge a high price to be able to live. But none who have ever bought his bows have regretted the silver which they cost. Many and many a gross of arrow-heads have I sold him, and he is well-nigh as particular in their make as he is over the spring and temper of his own bows. Many a friendly wrangle have I had with him over their weight and finish, and it is not many who find fault with my handiwork, though I say it myself; and now, madam, I am at your service."

During the night the wayfarer's clothes had been dried. The cloak was of rough quality, such as might have been used by a peasant woman; but the rest, though of sombre colour, were of good material and fashion. Seeing that her kind entertainers would be hurt by the offer of money, the lady contented herself with thanking Madge warmly, and saying that she hoped to come across the bridge one day with Dame Fletcher; then, under the guidance of Geoffrey, who insisted on carrying the boy, she set out from the smith's cottage. They passed under the outer gate and across the bridge, which later on was covered with a double line of houses and shops, but was now a narrow structure. Over the gateway across the river, upon pikes, were a number of heads and human limbs. The lady shuddered as she looked up.

"It is an ugly sight," the smith said, "and I can see no warrant for such exposure of the dead. There are the heads of Wallace, of three of Robert Bruce's brothers, and of many other valiant Scotsmen who fought against the king's grandfather some twenty years back. But after all they fought for their country, just as Harold and our ancestors against the Normans under William, and I think it a foul shame that men who have done no other harm should be beheaded, still less that their heads and limbs should be stuck up there gibbering at all passers-by. There are over a score of them, and every fresh trouble adds to their number; but pardon me," he said suddenly as a sob from the figure by his side called his attention from the heads on the top of the gateway, "I am rough and heedless in speech, as my sister Madge does often tell me, and it may well be that I have said something which wounded you."

"You meant no ill," the lady replied; "it was my own thoughts and troubles which drew tears from me; say not more about it, I pray you."

They passed under the gateway, with its ghastly burden, and were soon in the crowded streets of London. High overhead the houses extended, each story advancing beyond that below it until the occupiers of the attics could well-nigh shake hands across. They soon left the more crowded streets, and turning to the right, after ten minutes walking, the smith stopped in front of a bowyer shop near Aldgate.

"This is the shop," he said, "and there is Giles Fletcher himself trying the spring and pull of one of his bows. Here I will leave you, and will one of these days return to inquire if your health has taken ought of harm by the rough buffeting of the storm of yester-even."

So saying he handed the child to its mother, and with a wave of the hand took his leave, not waiting to listen to the renewed thanks which his late guest endeavoured to give him.

The shop was open in front, a projecting pent-house sheltered it from the weather; two or three bows lay upon a wide shelf in front, and several large sheaves of arrows tied together stood by the wall. A powerful man of some forty years old was standing in the middle of the shop with a bent bow in his arm, taking aim at a spot in the wall. Through an open door three men could be seen in an inner workshop cutting and shaping the wood for bows. The bowyer looked round as his visitor entered the shop, and then, with a sudden exclamation, lowered the bow.

"Hush, Giles!" the lady exclaimed; "it is I, but name no names; it were best that none knew me here."

The craftsman closed the door of communication into the inner room. "My Lady Alice," he exclaimed in a low tone, "you here, and in such a guise?"

"Surely it is I," the lady sighed, "although sometimes I am well-nigh inclined to ask myself whether it be truly I or not, or whether this be not all a dreadful dream."

"I had heard but vaguely of your troubles," Giles Fletcher said, "but hoped that the rumours were false. Ever since the Duke of Kent was executed the air has been full of rumours. Then came news of the killing of Mortimer and of the imprisonment of the king's mother, and it was said that many who were thought to be of her party had been attacked and slain, and I heard—" and there he stopped.

"You heard rightly, good Giles, it is all true. A week after the slaying of Mortimer a band of knights and men-at-arms arrived at our castle and demanded admittance in the king's name. Sir Roland refused, for he had news that many were taking up arms, but it was useless. The castle was attacked, and after three days' fighting, was taken. Roland was killed, and I was cast out with my child. Afterwards they repented that they had let me go, and searched far and wide for me; but I was hidden in the cottage of a wood-cutter.

6

They were too busy in hunting down others whom they proclaimed to be enemies of the king, as they had wrongfully said of Roland, who had but done his duty faithfully to Queen Isabella, and was assuredly no enemy of her son, although he might well be opposed to the weak and indolent king, his father. However, when the search relaxed I borrowed the cloak of the good man's wife and set out for London, whither I have travelled on foot, believing that you and Bertha would take me in and shelter me in my great need."

"Ay, that will we willingly," Giles said. "Was not Bertha your nurse ? and to whom should you come if not to her? But will it please you to mount the stairs, for Bertha will not forgive me if I keep you talking down here. What a joy it will be to her to see you again!"

So saying, Giles led the way to the apartment above. There was a scream of surprise and joy from his wife, and then Giles quietly withdrew down-stairs again, leaving the women to cry in each other's arms.

A few days later Geoffrey Ward entered the shop of Giles Fletcher.

"I have brought you twenty score of arrow-heads, Master Giles," he said. "They have been longer in hand than is usual with me, but I have been pressed. And how goes it with the lady whom I brought to your door last week?"

"But sadly, Master Ward, very sadly, as I told you when I came across to thank you again in her name and my own for your kindness to her. She was but in poor plight after her journey; poor thing, she was little accustomed to such wet and hardship, and doubtless they took all the more effect because she was low in spirit and weakened with much grieving. That night she was taken with a sort of fever, hot and cold by turns, and at times off her head. Since then she has lain in a high fever and does not know even my wife; her thoughts ever go back to the storming of the castle, and she cries aloud and begs them to spare her lord's life. It is pitiful to hear her. The leech gives but small hope for her life, and in troth, Master Ward, methinks that God would deal most gently with her were He to take her. Her heart is already in her husband's grave, for she was ever of a most loving and faithful nature. Here there would be little comfort for her— she would fret that her boy would never inherit the lands of his father; and although she knows well enough that she would be always welcome here, and that Bertha would serve her as gladly and faithfully as ever she did when she was her nurse, yet she could not but greatly feel the change. She was tenderly brought up, being, as I told you last week, the only daughter of Sir Harold Broome. Her brother, who but a year ago became lord of Broomecastle at the death of his father, was one of the queen's men, and it was he, I believe, who brought Sir Roland Somers to that side. He was slain on the same night as Mortimer, and his lands, like those of Sir Roland, have been seized by the crown. The child upstairs is by right heir to both estates, seeing that his uncle died unmarried. They will doubtless be conferred upon those who have aided the young king in freeing himself from his mother's domination, for which, indeed, although I lament that Lady Alice should have suffered so sorely in the doing of it, I blame him not at all. He is a noble prince and will make us a great king, and the doings of his mother have been a shame to us all. However, I meddle not in politics. If the poor lady dies, as methinks is well-nigh certain, Bertha and I will bring up the boy as our own. I have talked it over with my wife, and so far she and I are not of one mind. I think it will be best to keep him in ignorance of his birth and lineage, since the knowledge cannot benefit him, and will but render him discontented with his lot and make him disinclined to take to my calling, in which he might otherwise earn a living and rise to be a respected citizen. But Bertha hath notions. You have not taken a wife to yourself, Master Geoffrey, or you would know that women oft have fancies which wander widely from hard facts, and she says she would have him brought up as a man-at-arms, so that he may do valiant deeds, and win back some day the title and honour of his family."

Geoffrey Ward laughed. "Trust a woman for being romantic," he said. "However, Master Fletcher, you need not for the present trouble about the child's calling, even should its mother die. At anyrate, whether he follows your trade, or whether the blood in his veins leads him to take to martial deeds, the knowledge of arms may well be of use to him, and I promise you that such skill as I have I will teach him when he grows old enough to wield sword and battle-axe. As you know I may, without boasting, say that he could scarce have a better master, seeing that I have for three years carried away the prize for the best sword-player at the sports. Methinks the boy will grow up into a strong and stalwart man, for he is truly a splendid lad. As to archery, he need not go far to learn it, since your apprentice, Will Parker, last year won the prize as the best marksman in the city bounds. Trust me, if his tastes lie that way we will between us turn him out a rare man-at-arms. But I must stand gossiping no longer; the rumours that we are likely ere long to have war with France, have rarely bettered my trade. Since the wars in Scotland men's arms have rusted somewhat, and my two men are hard at work mending armour and fitting swords to hilts, and forging pike-heads. You see I am a citizen though I dwell outside the bounds, because house rent is cheaper and I get my charcoal without paying the city dues. So I can work somewhat lower than those in the walls, and I have good custom from many in Kent, who know that my arms are of as good temper as those turned out by any craftsman in the city."

Giles Fletcher's anticipations as to the result of his guest's illness turned out to be well founded. The fever abated, but left her prostrate in strength. For a few weeks she lingered; but she seemed to have little hold of life, and to care not whether she lived or died. So, gradually she faded away.

"I know you will take care of my boy as if he were your own, Bertha," she said one day; "and you and your husband will be far better protectors for him than I should have been had I lived. Teach him to be honest and true. It were better, methinks, that he grew up thinking you his father and mother, for otherwise he may grow discontented with his lot; but this I leave with you, and you must speak or keep silent according as you see his disposition and mind. If he is content to settle down to a peaceful life here, say nought to him which would unsettle his mind; but if Walter turn out to have an adventurous disposition, then tell him as much as you think fit of his history, not encouraging him to hope to recover his father's lands and mine, for that can never be, seeing that before that time can come they would have been enjoyed for many years by others; but that he may learn to bear himself bravely and gently as becomes one of good blood."

A few days later Lady Alice breathed her last, and at her own request was buried quietly and without pomp, as if she had been a child of the bowman, a plain stone, with the name "Dame Alice Somers", marking the grave.

The boy grew and throve until at fourteen years old there was no stronger or sturdier lad of his age within the city bounds. Giles had caused him to be taught to read and write, accomplishments which were common among the citizens, although they were until long afterwards rare among the warlike barons. The greater part of his time, however, was spent in sports with lads of his own age in Moorfields beyond the walls. The war with France was now raging, and, as was natural, the boys in their games imitated the doings of their elders, and mimic battles, ofttimes growing into earnest, were fought between the lads of the different wards. Walter Fletcher, as he was known among his play-fellows, had by his strength and courage won for himself the proud position of captain of the boys of the ward of Aldgate.

Geoffrey Ward had kept his word, and had already begun to give the lad lessons in the use of arms. When not engaged otherwise Walter would, almost every afternoon, cross London Bridge and would spend hours in the armourer's forge. Geoffrey's business had grown, for the war had caused a great demand for arms, and he had now six men working in the forge. As soon as the boy could handle a light tool

Walter in the armourer's forge.

Geoffrey allowed him to work, and although not able to wield the heavy sledge Walter was able to do much of the finer work. Geoffrey encouraged him in this, as, in the first place, the use of the tools greatly strengthened the boy's muscles, and gave him an acquaintance with arms. Moreover, Geoffrey was still a bachelor, and he thought that the boy, whom he as well as Giles had come to love as a son, might, should he not take up the trade of war, prefer the occupation of an armourer to that of a bowmaker, in which case he would take him some day as his partner in the forge. After work was over and the men had gone away, Geoffrey would give the lad instructions in the use of the arms at which he had been at work, and so quick and strong was he that he rapidly acquired their use, and Geoffrey foresaw that he would one day, should his thoughts turn that way, prove a mighty man-at-arms.

It was the knowledge which he acquired from Geoffrey which had much to do with Walter's position among his comrades. The skill and strength which he had acquired in wielding the hammer, and by practice with the sword rendered him a formidable opponent with the sticks, which formed the weapons in the mimic battles, and indeed not a few were the complaints which were brought before Giles Fletcher of bruises and hurts caused by him.

"You are too turbulent, Walter," the bowyer said one day when a haberdasher from the ward of Aldersgate came to complain that his son's head had been badly cut by a blow with a club from Walter Fletcher. "You are always getting into trouble, and are becoming the terror of other boys. Why do you not play more quietly? The feuds between the boys of different wards are becoming a serious nuisance, and many injuries have been inflicted. I hear that the matter has been mentioned in the Common Council, and that there is a talk of issuing an order that no boy not yet apprenticed to a trade shall be allowed to carry a club, and that any found doing so shall be publicly whipped."

A WAYFARER

"I don't want to be turbulent," Walter said; "but if the Aldersgate boys will defy us, what are we to do? I don't hit harder than I can help, and if Jonah Harris would leave his head unguarded I could not help hitting it."

"I tell you it won't do, Walter," Giles said. "You will be getting yourself into sore trouble. You are growing too masterful altogether, and have none of the quiet demeanour and peaceful air which becomes an honest citizen. In another six months you will be apprenticed, and then I hope we shall hear no more of these doings."

"My father is talking of apprenticing me, Master Geoffrey," Walter said that evening. "I hope that you will, as you were good enough to promise, talk with him about apprenticing me to your craft rather than to his. I should never take to the making of bows, though, indeed, I like well to use them; and Will Parker, who is teaching me says that I show rare promise; but it would never be to my taste to stand all day sawing, and smoothing, and polishing. One bow is to me much like another, though my father holds that there are rare differences between them; but it is a nobler craft to work on iron, and next to using arms the most pleasant thing surely is to make them. One can fancy what good blows the sword will give and what hard knocks the armour will turn aside; but some day, Master Geoffrey, when I have served my time, I mean to follow the army. There is always work there for armourers to do, and sometimes at a pinch they may even get their share of fighting."

Walter did not venture to say that he would prefer to be a man-at-arms, for such a sentiment would be deemed as outrageous in the ears of a quiet city craftsman as would the proposal of the son of such a man nowadays to enlist as a soldier. The armourer smiled; he knew well enough what was in Walter's mind. It had cost Geoffrey himself a hard struggle to settle down to a craft, and deemed it but natural that with the knightly blood flowing in Walter's veins he should long to distinguish himself in the field. He said nothing of this, however, but renewed his promise to speak to Giles Fletcher, deeming that a few years passed in his forge would be the best preparation which Walter could have for a career as a soldier.

CHAPTER II
THE HUT IN THE MARSHES

A WEEK later a party of knights and court gallants, riding across the fields without the walls, checked their horses to look at a struggle which was going on between two parties of boys. One, which was apparently the most powerful, had driven the other off from a heap of rubbish which had been carried without the walls. Each party had a flag attached to a stick, and the boys were armed with clubs such as those carried by the apprentice boys. Many of them carried mimic shields made of wood, and had stuffed their flat caps with wool or shavings, the better to protect their heads from blows. The smaller party had just been driven from the heap, and their leader was urging them to make another effort to regain it.

"That is a gallant-looking lad, and a sturdy, my Lord de Vaux," a boy of about ten years of age said. "He bears himself like a young knight, and he has had some hard knocks, for, see, the blood is streaming down his face. One would scarcely expect to see these varlets of the city playing so roughly."

"The citizens have proved themselves sturdy fighters before now, my prince," the other said; "they are ever independent, and hold to their rights even against the king. The contingent which the city sends to the wars bears itself as well as those of any of the barons."

"See!" the boy interrupted, "they are going to charge again. Their leader has himself seized the flag and has swung his shield behind him, just as a knight might do if leading the stormers against a place of strength. Let us stop till we see the end of it."

With a shout of "Aldgate! Aldgate!" the leader of the assailants dashed forward, followed by his comrades, and with a rush reached the top of the heap.

"Well done!" the young prince exclaimed, clapping his hands. "See how he lays about him with that club of his. There, he has knocked down the leader of the defenders as if his club had been a battle-axe. Well done, young sir, well done! But his followers waver. The others are too strong for them. Stand, you cowards, rally round your leader!" and in his enthusiasm the young prince urged his horse forward to the scene of conflict.

But the assailants were mastered; few of them could gain the top of the heap, and those who did so were beaten back from it by the defenders. Heavy blows were exchanged, and blood flowed freely from many of their heads and faces, for in those days boys thought less than they do now of hard knocks, and manliness and courage were considered the first of virtues. Their leader, however, still stood his ground on the crest, though hardly pressed on all sides, and used his club both to strike and parry with a skill which aroused the warmest admiration on the part of the prince. In vain his followers attempted to come to his rescue; each time they struggled up the heap they were beaten back again by those on the crest.

"Yield thee prisoner," the assailants of their leader shouted, and the prince in his excitement echoed the cry. The lad, however, heard or heeded them not. He still kept his flag aloft in his left hand. With a sudden spring he struck down one of his opponents, plucked up their flag from the ground, and then fought his way back through his foes to the edge of the battleground; then a heavy blow struck him on the temple, and, still holding the flags, he rolled senseless to the foot of the heap. The defenders with shouts of triumph were rushing down when the prince urged his horse forward.

"Cease!" he said authoritatively. "Enough has been done, my young masters, and the sport is becoming a broil."

16

THE HUT IN THE MARSHES

Hitherto the lads, absorbed in their strife, had paid but little heed to the party of onlookers; but at the word they at once arrested their arms, and, baring their heads, stood still in confusion.

"No harm is done," the prince said, "though your sport is of the roughest; but I fear that your leader is hurt, he moves not; lift his head from the ground." The boy was indeed still insensible. "My lords," the prince said to the knights who had now ridden up, "I fear that this boy is badly hurt; he is a gallant lad, and has the spirit of a true knight in him, citizen's son though he be. My Lord de Vaux, will you bid your squire ride at full speed to the Tower and tell Master Roger, the leech, to come here with all haste, and to bring such nostrums as may be needful for restoring the boy to life."

The Tower was but half a mile distant, but before Master Roger arrived Walter had already recovered consciousness, and was just sitting up when the leech hurried up to the spot.

"You have arrived too late, Master Roger," the prince said; "but I doubt not that a dose of cordials may yet be of use, for he is still dazed, and the blow he got would have cracked his skull had it been a thin one."

The leech poured some cordial from a vial into a small silver cup and held it to the boy's lips. It was potent and nigh took his breath away; but when he had drunk it he struggled to his feet, looking ashamed and confused when he saw himself the centre of attention of so many knights of the court.

"What is thy name, good lad?" the prince asked.

"I am known as Walter Fletcher."

"You are a brave lad," the prince said, "and if you bear you as well as a man as you did but now, I would wish no better to ride beside me in the day of battle. Should the time ever come when you tire of the peaceable life of a citizen and wish to take service in the wars, go to the Tower and ask boldly for the Prince of Wales, and I will enroll you among my own men-at-arms, and I promise you that you shall have your share of fighting as stark as that of the assault of yon heap. Now, my lords, let us ride on; I crave your pardon for having so long detained you."

Walter was some days before he could again cross London Bridge to inform his friend Geoffrey of the honour which had befallen him of being addressed by the Prince of Wales. During the interval he was forced to lie abed, and he was soundly rated by Master Giles for again getting into mischief. Geoffrey was far more sympathetic, and said "Well, Walter, although I would not that Gaffer Giles heard me say so, I think you have had a piece of rare good fortune. It may be that you may never have cause to recall the young prince's promise to him; but should you some day decide to embrace the calling of arms, you could wish for nothing better than to ride behind the Prince of Wales. He is, by all accounts, of a most noble and generous disposition, and is said, young as he is, to be already highly skilled in arms. Men say that he will be a wise king and a gallant captain, such a one as a brave soldier might be proud to follow; and as the king will be sure to give him plenty of opportunities of distinguishing himself, those who ride with him may be certain of a chance of doing valorous deeds. I will go across the bridge to-morrow, and will have a talk with Master Fletcher. The sooner you are apprenticed, the sooner you will be out of your time; and since Madge married eight years since I have been lonely in the house and shall be glad to have you with me."

Geoffrey Ward found his friend more ready to accede to his request, that Walter should be apprenticed to him, than he had expected. The bowyer, indeed, was a quiet man, and the high spirits and somewhat turbulent disposition of his young charge gave him so much uneasiness, that he was not sorry the responsibility of keeping him in order should be undertaken by Geoffrey. Moreover, he could not but agree with the argument, that the promise of the Prince of Wales offered a more favourable opportunity for Walter to enter upon the career of arms and so, perhaps, someday to win his way back to rank and honours than could have been looked for. Therefore, on the following week Walter was indentured to the armourer, and, as was usual at the time, left his abode in Aldgate and took up his residence with his master. He threw himself with his whole heart into the work, and by the time he was fifteen was on the way to become a skilful craftsman. His frame and muscles developed with labour, and he was now able to swing all save the very heaviest hammers in the shop. He had never abated in his practice at arms, and every day when work was over, he and his master had a long bout together with cudgel or quarter-staff, sword or axe; Walter of course used light weapons, but so quick was he with them that Geoffrey Ward acknowledged that he needed to put out all his skill to hold his own with his pupil. But it was not alone with Geoffrey that Walter had an opportunity of learning the use of arms. Whenever a soldier, returned from the wars, came to have a weapon repaired by the armourer, he would be sure of an invitation to come in in the evening and take a stoup of ale, and tell of the battles and sieges he had gone through, and in the course of the evening would be asked to have a bout of arms with the young apprentice, whom Geoffrey represented as being eager to learn how to use the sword as well as how to make it.

Thus Walter became accustomed to different styles of fighting, but found that very few, indeed, of their visitors were nearly so well skilled with their arms as his master. Some of the soldiers were mortified at finding themselves unable to hold their own with a boy; others would take their reverses in good part and would come again, bringing with them some comrade known to be particularly skilled with his weapons, to try the temper of the armourer's apprentice. At the age of fifteen Walter had won the prize at the sports, both for the best cudgel play and the best sword-and-buckler play among the apprentices, to the great disgust of many who had almost reached the age of manhood and were just out of their time.

On Sundays Walter always spent the day with Giles Fletcher and his wife, going to mass with them and walking in the fields, where, after service, the citizens much congregated. Since Walter had gone to work he had taken no part in the fights and frolics of his former comrades; he was in fact, far too tired at the end of his day's work to have any desire to do aught but to sit and listen to the tales of the wars, of the many old soldiers who pervaded the country. Some of these men were disabled by wounds or long service, but the greater portion were idle scamps, who cared not for the hard blows and sufferings of a campaign, liking better to hang about taverns drinking, at the expense of those to whom they related fabulous tales of the gallant actions they had performed. Many, too, wandered over the country, sometimes in twos or threes, sometimes in large bands, robbing and often murdering travellers or attacking lonely houses. When in one part or another their ill deeds became too notorious, the sheriffs would call out a posse of men and they would be hunted down like wild beasts. It was not, however, easy to catch them, for great tracts of forests still covered a large portion of the country and afforded them shelter.

In the country round London these pests were very numerous, for here, more than anywhere else, was there a chance of plunder. The swamps on the south side of the river had an especially evil reputation. From Southwark to Putney stretches a marshy country over which, at high tides, the river frequently flowed. Here and there were wretched huts, difficult of access and affording good hiding-places for those pursued by justice, since searchers could be seen approaching a long way off, and escape could be made by paths across the swamp known only to the dwellers there, and where heavily-armed men dared not follow. Further south, in the wild country round Westerham, where miles of heath and forest stretched away in all directions, was another noted place where the robber vagrants mustered thickly, and the Sheriff of Kent had much trouble with them.

The laws in those days were extremely severe, and death was the penalty of those caught plundering. The extreme severity of the laws, however, operated in favour of its breakers, since the sympathy of the people who had little to lose was with them, and unless caught red-handed in the act they could generally escape, since none save those who had themselves been robbed would say aught that would place the pursuers on their traces, or give testimony which would cost the life of a fellow-creature. The citizens of London were loud in their complaints against the discharged soldiers, for it was upon them that the loss mainly fell, and it was on their petitions to the king that the sheriffs of Middlesex and Hertford, Essex, Surrey, and Kent, were generally stirred up to put down the ill-doers.

Sometimes these hunts were conducted in a wholesale way, and the whole posse of a county would be called out. Then all found within its limits who had not land or visible occupation were collected. Any against whom charges could be brought home were hung without more ado, and the rest were put on board ship and sent across the sea to the army. Sometimes, when they found the country becoming too hot for them, these men would take service with some knight or noble going to the war, anxious to take with him as strong a following as might be, and not too particular as to the character of his soldiers.

Walter, being of an adventurous spirit, was sometimes wont of a summer evening, when his work was done, to wander across the marshes, taking with him his bow and arrows, and often bringing home a wild duck or two which he shot in the pools. More than once surly men had accosted him, and had threatened to knock him on the head if they again found him wandering that way; but Walter laughed at their threats, and seeing, that though but an apprentice lad, he might be able to send an arrow as straight to the mark as another, they were content to leave him alone.

One day when he was well-nigh in the heart of the swamp of Lambeth he saw a figure making his way across. The hour was already late and the night was falling, and the appearance of the man was so different from that of the usual denizens of the swamp that Walter wondered what business there might be. Scarcely knowing why he did so, Walter threw himself down among some low brushwood and watched the approaching figure. When he came near he recognized the face, and saw, to his surprise, that it was a knight who had but the day before stopped at the armourer's shop to have two rivets put in his hauberk. He had particularly noticed him because of the arrogant manner in which he spoke. Walter had himself put in the rivets, and had thought, as he buckled on the armour again, how unpleasant a countenance was that of its wearer. He was a tall and powerful man, and would have been handsome had not his eyes been too closely set together; his nose was narrow, and the expression of his face reminded Walter of a hawk. He had now laid aside his helmet, and his figure was covered with a long cloak.

"He is up to no good," Walter said to himself, "for what dealings could a knight honestly have with the ruffians who haunt these swamps. It is assuredly no business of mine, but it may lead to an adventure, and I have had no real fun since I left Aldgate. I will follow and see if I can get to the bottom of the mystery."

When he came close to the spot where Walter was lying the knight paused and looked round as if uncertain of his way. For four or five minutes he stood still, and then gave a shout of "Humphrey" at the top of his voice. It was answered by a distant "Hallo!" and looking in the direction from which the answer had come, Walter saw a figure appear above some bushes some four hundred yards distant. The knight at once directed his steps in that direction, and Walter crept cautiously after him.

"A pest upon these swamps and quagmires," the knight said angrily as he neared the other. "Why didst not meet me and show me the way through, as before?"

"I thought that as you had come once you would be able to find your way hither again," the man said. "Had I thought that you would have missed it I would have come ten times as far, rather than have had my name shouted all over the country. However, there is no one to hear, did you shout thrice as loud, so no harm is done."

"I thought I saw a figure a short time since," the knight said.

The man looked round in all directions.

THE HUT IN THE MARSHES

"I see none," he said, "and you may have been mistaken, for the light is waning fast. It were ill for anyone I caught prying about here. But come in, sir knight; my hovel is not what your lordship is accustomed to, but we may as well talk there as here beneath the sky."

The two men disappeared from Walter's sight. The latter in much surprise crept forward, but until he reached the spot where he had last seen the speakers he was unable to account for their disappearance. Then he saw that the spot, although apparently a mere clump of bushes no higher than the surrounding country, was really an elevated hummock of ground. Anyone might have passed close to the bushes without suspecting that aught lay among them. In the centre, however, the ground had been cut away, and a low doorway, almost hidden by the bushes, gave access into a half subterranean hut; the roof was formed of an old boat turned bottom upwards, and this had been covered with brown turf. It was an excellent place of concealment, as searchers might have passed within a foot of the bushes without suspecting that aught lay concealed within them.

"A clever hiding-place," Walter thought to himself. "No wonder the posse search these swamps in vain. This is the lowest and wettest part of the swamp, and would be but lightly searched, for none would suspect that there was a human habitation among these brown ditches and stagnant pools."

To his disappointment the lad could hear nothing of the conversation which was going on within the hut. The murmur of voices came to his ear, but no words were audible; however, he remained patiently, thinking that perhaps as they came out a word might be said which would give him a clue to the object of the mysterious interview between a knight and one who was evidently a fugitive from justice.

His patience was rewarded. In the half hour which he waited the night had fallen, and a thick fog which was rising over the swamps rendered it difficult to discern anything at the distance of a few paces.

"You are quite sure that you can manage it?" a voice said as the two men issued from the hut.

"There is no difficulty in managing it," the other replied, "if the boat is punctual to the hour named. It will be getting dusk then, and if one boat runs into another no one need be surprised. Such accidents will happen."

"They will be here just before nightfall," the other said, "and you will know the boat by the white mantle the lady will wear. The reward will be fifty pieces of gold, of which you have received ten as earnest. You can trust me, and if the job be well done I shall take no count of the earnest money."

"You may consider it as good as done," the other replied. "If the boat is there the matter is settled. Now I will lead you back across the swamps. I would not give much for your life if you tried to find the way alone. Who would have thought when you got me off from being hung, after that little affair at Bruges, that I should be able to make myself useful to your worship?"

"You may be sure," the knight replied, "that it was just because I foresaw that you might be useful that I opened the doors of your cell that night. It is always handy in times like these to be able to lay one's hand on a man whom you can hang if you choose to open your mouth."

"Did it not strike you, sir knight, that it might enter my mind that it would be very advisable for me to free myself from one who stands towards me in that relation?"

"Certainly it did," the knight replied; "but as I happen to be able to make it for your interest to serve me, that matter did not trouble me. I knew better than to bring money into this swamp of yours, when I might be attacked by half a dozen ruffians like yourself; and I took the precaution of informing Peter, the captain of my men-at-arms, of the spot to which I was going, bidding him, in case I came not back, to set a hue and cry on foot and hunt down all who might be found here, with the especial description of your worthy self."

Walter could hear no more; he had taken off his shoes and followed them at a distance, and their voices still acted as a guide to him through the swamp. But he feared to keep too close, as, although the darkness would conceal his figure, he might at any moment tread in a pool or ditch, and so betray his presence. Putting his foot each time to the ground with the greatest caution, he moved quietly after them. They spoke little more, but their heavy footsteps on the swampy ground were a sufficient guidance for him. At last these ceased suddenly. A few words were spoken, and then he heard returning steps. He drew aside a few feet and crouched down, saw a dim figure pass through the mist, and then resumed his way. The ground was firmer now, and, replacing his shoes, he walked briskly on. As he neared the higher ground along which the road ran he heard two horsemen galloping away in the distance. He now turned his face east, and after an hour's walking he reached the armourer's.

"Why, Walter, you are late," the smith said. "The men are in bed this hour or more, and I myself can scarce keep awake. Where hast thou been, my boy?"

"I have been in the swamps and lost my way," Walter replied.

"It is a bad neighbourhood, lad, and worse are the people who live there. If I had my way the whole posse should be called out, and the marshes searched from end to end, and all found there should be knocked on head and thrown into their own ditches. There would be no fear of any honest man coming to his end thereby; but now to bed, lad. You can tell me all about it to-morrow; but we have a rare day's work before us, and the fire must be alight at daybreak."

On his way back Walter had debated with himself whether to inform his master of what had happened. He was, however, bent upon having an adventure on his own account, and it was a serious thing in those days for an apprentice lad to bring an accusation against a noble. The city would not indeed allow even an apprentice to be overridden, and although Geoffrey Ward's forge stood beyond the city walls it was yet within the liberties, the city allowing its craftsmen to open shops just outside the gates, and to enjoy the same privileges as if dwelling actually within the walls.

On the following afternoon Walter asked leave to cease work an hour earlier than usual, as he wished to go across into the city. The armourer was surprised, since this was the first time that such a thing had happened since the lad had worked for him.

"What are you up to, Walter?—some mischief, I will be bound. Go, lad; you have worked so steadily that you have well earned more than an hour's holiday should you want it."

Walter crossed the bridge, and seeking out four or five of his old companions, begged them to bring their bows and clubs and rejoin him at the stairs by London Bridge. To their laughing inquiries whether he meant to go a-shooting of fish, he told them to ask no questions until they joined him. As soon as work was over the boys gathered at the steps, where Walter had already engaged a boat. There were some mocking inquiries from the watermen standing about as to where they were going shooting. Walter answered with some light chaff, and, two of the party taking oars, they started up the river.

"Now I will tell you what we are bent on," Walter said. "From some words I overheard I believe that some of the ruffians over in the marshes are this evening going to make an attack upon a boat with a lady in it coming down the river. We will be on the spot, and can give them a reception such as they do not expect."

"Do you know who the lady is, Walter?"

"I have not the least idea. I only caught a few words, and may be wrong; still, it will do no harm should I be mistaken."

The tide was running down strongly, for there had been a good deal of rain during the preceding week, and all night it had poured heavily. It was fine now, but the stream was running down thick and turbid, and it needed all the boys' efforts to force the wherry against it. They rowed by turns; all were fairly expert at the exercise, for in those days the Thames was at once the great highway and playground of London. To the wharves below the bridge ships brought the rich merchandise of Italy and the Low Countries; while from above, the grain, needed for the wants of the great city was floated down in barges from the west.

Passing the Temple, the boys rowed along by the green banks and fields as far as Westminster, which at that time was almost a rival of the city, for here were the abbey and great monastery; here were the king's palace and court, and the houses of many of his nobles. Then they went along by the low shores of Millbank, keeping a sharp look-out for boats going down with the stream. It was already getting dark, for Walter had not allowed for the strength of the stream, and he was full of anxiety lest he should arrive too late.

CHAPTER III
A THWARTED PLOT

A BOAT was rowing rapidly down the stream. It had passed the village of Chelsea, and the men were doing their best to reach their destination at Westminster before nightfall. Two men were rowing; in the stern sat a lady with a girl about eleven years old. A woman, evidently a servant, sat beside the lady, while behind, steering the boat, was an elderly retainer.

"It is getting dark," the lady said; "I would that my cousin James had not detained us so long at Richmond, and then after all he was unable to accompany us. I like not being out on the river so late."

"No, indeed, my lady," the woman replied; "I have heard tell lately much of the doings of the river pirates. They say that boats are often picked up stove in and broken, and that none know what had become of their occupants, and that bodies, gashed and hewn, are often found floating in the river."

"How horrible," the girl said; "your tale makes me shiver, Martha; I would you had said nothing about it till we were on land again."

"Do not be afraid, Edith," the lady said cheerfully; "we shall soon be safe at Westminster."

There were now only two or three boats to be seen on the river. They were nearing the end of their journey now, and the great pile of the Abbey could be seen through the darkness. A boat with several men in it was seen rowing across the river towards the Lambeth side. It was awkwardly managed.

A THWARTED PLOT

"Look out!" the steersman of the boat coming down stream shouted; "you will run into us if you don't mind."

An order was given in the other boat, the men strained to their oars, and in an instant the boat ran with a crash into the side of the other, cutting it down to the water's edge. For a minute there was a wild scene of confusion; the women shrieked, the watermen shouted, and, thinking that it was an accident, strove, as the boat sank from under them, to climb into that which had run them down. They were speedily undeceived. One was sunk by a heavy blow with an oar, the other was stabbed with a dagger, while the assailants struck fiercely at the old man and the women.

At this moment, however, a third boat made its appearance on the scene, its occupants uttering loud shouts. As they rowed towards the spot their approach was heralded by a shower of arrows. Two of the ruffians were struck—one fell over mortally wounded, the other sank down into the boat.

"Row, men, row," their leader shouted, "or we shall all be taken."

Again seizing their oars, the rowers started at full speed towards the Lambeth shore. The arrows of their pursuers still fell among them, two more of their number being wounded before they reached the opposite shore. The pursuit was not continued, the new-comers ceasing to row at the spot where the catastrophe had taken place. Walter stood up in the boat and looked round. A floating oar, a stretcher, and a sheep-skin which had served as a cushion, alone floated.

Suddenly there was a choking cry heard a few yards down stream, and Walter leapt into the river. A few strokes took him to the side of the girl, and he found, on throwing his arm round her, that she was still clasped in her mother's arms. Seizing them both, Walter shouted to his comrades. They had already turned the boat's head, and in a minute were alongside.

It was a difficult task to get the mother and child on board, as the girl refused to loose her hold. It was, however, accomplished, and the child sat still and quiet by Walter's side, while his comrades endeavoured to stanch the blood which was flowing from a severe wound in her mother's head. When they had bound it up they rubbed her hands, and by the time they had reached the steps at Westminster the lady opened her eyes. For a moment she looked bewildered, and then, on glancing round, she gave a low cry of delight at seeing her child sitting by Walter's side.

On reaching the steps the boys handed her over to the care of the watermen there, who soon procured a litter and carried her, she being still too weak to walk, to the dwelling of the Earl of Talbot, where she said she was expected. The apprentices rowed back to London Bridge, elated at the success of their enterprise, but regretting much that they had arrived too late to hinder the outrage, or to prevent the escape of its perpetrators.

Walter on his return home related the whole circumstance to his master.

"I would you had told me, Walter," the latter said, "since we might have taken precautions which would have prevented this foul deed from taking place. However, I can understand your wanting to accomplish the adventure without my aid; but we must think now what had best be said and done. As the lady belongs to the court, there is sure to be a fine pother about the matter, and you and all who were there will be examined touching your share of the adventure, and how you came to be upon the spot. The others will, of course, say that they were there under your direction; and we had best think how much of your story you had better tell."

"Why should I not tell it all?" Walter asked indignantly.

"You should never tell a lie, Walter; but in days like these it is safer sometimes not to tell more than is necessary. It is a good rule in life, my boy, to make no more enemies than may be needful. This knight, who is doubtless a great villain, has maybe powerful friends, and it is as well, if it can be avoided, that you should not embroil yourself with these. Many a man has been knocked on head or stabbed on a dark night, because he could not keep his tongue from wagging. 'Least said, the sooner mended,' is a good proverb; but I will think it over to-night, and tell you in the morning."

When they met again in the workshop the armourer said: "Clean yourself up after breakfast, Walter, and put on your best clothes. I will go with you before the mayor, and then you shall tell him your story. There is sure to be a stir about it before the day is done. As we walk thither we can settle how much of your story it is good to tell."

On their way over the bridge Geoffrey told Walter that he thought he had better tell the whole story exactly as it had occurred, concealing only the fact that he had recognized the knight's face. "You had best too," he said, "mention nought about the white cloak. If we can catch the man of the hut in the swamp, likely enough the rack will wring from him the name of his employer, and in that case, if you are brought up as a witness against him you will of course say that you recognize his face; but 'tis better that the accusation should not come from you. No great weight would be given to the word of a 'prentice boy as against that of a noble. It is as bad for earthen pots to knock against brass ones, as it is for a yeoman in a leathern jerkin to stand up against a knight in full armour."

"But unless the lady knows her enemy she may fall again into his snares."

"I have thought of that," Geoffrey said, "and we will take measures to prevent it."

"But how can we prevent it?" Walter asked, surprised.

"We must find out who this knight may be, which should, methinks, not be difficult. Then we will send to him a message that his share in this night's work is known to several, and that if any harm should ever again be attempted against the lady or her daughter, he shall be denounced before King Edward himself as the author of the wrong. I trust, however, that we may capture the man of the swamp, and that the truth may be wrung from him."

By this time they had arrived at the Guildhall, and making their way into the court, Geoffrey demanded private speech with the Lord Mayor.

"Can you not say in open court what is you business?" the Lord Mayor asked.

"I fear that if I did it would defeat the ends of justice."

Retiring with the chief magistrate into an inner room, Geoffrey desired Walter to tell his story. This he did, ending by saying that he regretted much that he had not at once told his master what he had heard; but that, although he deemed evil was intended, he did not know that murder was meant, and thought it but concerned the carrying off of some damsel, and that this he had intended, by the aid of his comrades, to prevent.

"You have done well, Master Walter, since that be your name," the magistrate said. "That you might have done better is true, for had you acted otherwise you might have prevented murder from being done. Still, one cannot expect old heads upon young shoulders. Give me the names of those who were with you, for I shall doubtless receive a message from Westminster this morning to know if I have heard aught of the affair. In the meantime we must take steps to secure these pirates of the marsh. The ground is across the river, and lies out of my jurisdiction."

"It is for that reason," Geoffrey said, "that I wished that the story should be told to you privately, since the men concerned might well have sent a friend to the court to hear if aught was said which might endanger them."

"I will give you a letter to a magistrate of Surrey, and he will despatch some constables under your guidance to catch these rascals. I fear there have been many murders performed by them lately besides that in question, and you will be doing a good service to the citizens by aiding in the capture of these men."

"I will go willingly," the smith assented.

A THWARTED PLOT

"I will at once send off a messenger on horseback," the Lord Mayor said, after a moment's thought. "It will be quicker; I will tell the justice that if he will come to the meeting of the roads on Kennington Common, at seven this evening, you will be there with your apprentice to act as a guide."

"I will," the armourer said, "and will bring with me two or three of my men who are used to hard blows, for, to tell you the truth, I have no great belief in the valour of constables, and we may meet with a stout resistance."

"So be it," the Lord Mayor said; "and luck be with you, for these men are the scourges of the river."

That evening the armourer shut up his shop sooner than usual, and accompanied by Walter and four of his workmen, and all carrying stout oaken cudgels, with hand-axes in their girdles, started along the lonely road to Kennington. Half an hour after their arrival the magistrate, with ten men, rode up. He was well pleased at the sight of the reinforcement which awaited him, for the river pirates might be expected to make a desperate resistance. Geoffrey advised a halt for a time until it should be well-nigh dark, as the marauders might have spies set to give notice should strangers enter the marsh.

They started before it was quite dark, as Walter doubted whether he should be able to lead them straight to the hut after the night had completely fallen. He felt, however, tolerably sure of his locality, for he had noticed that two trees grew on the edge of the swamp just at the spot where he had left it. He had no difficulty in finding these, and at once led the way. The horses of the magistrate and his followers were left in charge of three of their number.

"You are sure you are going right?" the magistrate said to Walter. "The marsh seems to stretch everywhere, and we might well fall into a quagmire, which would swallow us all up."

"I am sure of my way," Walter answered; "and see, yonder clump of bushes, which you can just observe above the marsh, a quarter of a mile away, is the spot where the house of their leader is situated."

With strict injunctions that not a word was to be spoken until the bush was surrounded, and that all were to step noiselessly and with caution, the party moved forward. It was now nearly dark, and as they approached the hut sounds of laughter and revelry were heard.

"They are celebrating their success in a carouse," Geoffrey said. "We shall catch them nicely in a trap."

When they came close a man who was sitting just at the low mouth of the hut suddenly sprang to his feet and shouted, "Who goes there?" He had apparently been placed as sentry, but had joined in the potations going on inside, and had forgotten to look round from time to time to see that none were approaching.

At his challenge the whole party rushed forward, and as they reached the hut the men from within came scrambling out, sword in hand. For two or three minutes there was a sharp fight, and had the constables been alone they would have been defeated, for they were outnumbered and the pirates were desperate.

The heavy clubs of the armourers decided the fight. One or two of the band alone succeeded in breaking through, the rest were knocked down and bound; not, however, until several severe wounds had been inflicted on their assailants.

When the fray was over, it was found that nine prisoners had been captured. Some of these were stunned by the blows which the smiths had dealt them, and two or three were badly wounded; all were more or less injured in the struggle. When they recovered their senses they were made to get on their feet, and with their hands tied securely behind them were marched between a double line of their captors off the marsh.

"Thanks for your services," the justice said when they had gained the place where they had left their horses. "Nine of my men shall tie each one of these rascals to their stirrups by halters round their necks, and we will give them a smart run into Richmond, where we will lodge them in the jail. To-morrow is Sunday; on Monday they will be brought before me, and I shall want the evidence of Master Walter Fletcher and of those who were in the boat with him as to what took place on the river. Methinks the evidence on that score, and the resistance which they offered to us this evening, will be sufficient to put a halter round their necks; but from what I have heard by the letter which the Lord Mayor sent me, there are others higher in rank concerned in the affair; doubtless we shall find means to make these ruffians speak."

Accordingly, at the justice's orders, halters were placed round the necks of the prisoners, the other ends being attached to the saddles, and the party set off at a pace which taxed to the utmost the strength of the wounded men. Geoffrey and his party returned in high spirits to Southwark.

On the Monday Walter went over to Richmond, accompanied by the armourers and by the lads who had been in the boat with him. The nine ruffians, strongly guarded, were brought up in the justice room. Walter first gave his evidence, and related how he had overheard a portion of the conversation, which led him to believe that an attack would be made upon the boat coming down the river.

"Can you identify either of the prisoners as being the man whom you saw at the door of the hut?"

"No," Walter said. "When I first saw him I was too far off to make out his face. When he left the hut it was dark."

"Should you know the other man, the one who was addressed as sir knight, if you saw him again?"

"I should," Walter replied. He then gave an account of the attack upon the boat, but said that in the suddenness of the affair and the growing darkness he noticed none of the figures distinctly enough to recognize them again. Two or three of the other apprentices gave similar testimony as to the attack.

A gentleman then presented himself, and gave his name as Sir William de Hertford. He said that he had come at the request of the Lady Alice Vernon, who was still suffering from the effects of the wound and immersion. She had requested him to say that at some future occasion she would appear to testify, but that in the confusion and suddenness of the attack she had noticed no faces in the boat which assailed them, and could identify none concerned in the affair.

The justice who had headed the attack on the hut then gave his evidence as to that affair, the armourer also relating the incidents of the conflict.

"The prisoners will be committed for trial," the justice said. "At present there is no actual proof that any of them were concerned in this murderous outrage beyond the fact that they were taken in the place where it was planned. The suspicion is strong that some at least were engaged in it. Upon the persons of all of them were valuable daggers, chains, and other ornaments, which could not have been come by honestly, and I doubt not that they form part of the gang which has so long been a terror to peaceful travellers alike by the road and river, and it may be that some who have been robbed will be able to identify the articles taken upon them. They are committed for trial: firstly, as having been concerned in the attack upon Dame Alice Vernon; secondly, as being notorious ill-livers and robbers; thirdly, as having resisted lawful arrest by the king's officers. The greatest criminal in the affair is not at present before me, but it may be that from such information as Dame Vernon may be able to furnish, and from such confessions as justice will be able to wring from the prisoners, he will at the trial stand beside his fellows."

Walter returned to town with his companions. On reaching the armourer's they found a retainer of the Earl of Talbot awaiting them, with the message that the Lady Alice Vernon wished the attendance of Walter Fletcher, whose name she had learned from the Lord Mayor as that of the lad to whom she and her daughter owed their lives, at noon on the following day, at the residence of the Earl of Talbot.

"That is the worst of an adventure," Walter said crossly, after the retainer had departed. "One can't have a bit of excitement without being sent for, and thanked, and stared at. I would rather fight the best swordsman in the city than have to go down to the mansion of Earl Talbot with my cap in my hand."

Geoffrey laughed. "You must indeed have your cap in your hand, Walter; but you need not bear yourself in that spirit. The 'prentice of a London citizen may have just as much honest pride and independence as the proudest earl at Westminster; but carry not independence too far. Remember that if you yourself had received a great service you would be hurt if the donor refused to receive your thanks; and it would be churlish indeed were you to put on sullen looks, or to refuse to accept any present which the lady whose life you have saved may make you. It is strange, indeed, that it should be Dame Vernon, whose husband, Sir Jasper Vernon, received the fief's of Westerham and Hyde."

"Why should it be curious that it is she?" Walter asked.

"Oh!" Geoffrey said, rather confusedly. "I was not thinking—that is—I mean that it is curious because Bertha Fletcher was for years a dependant on the family of Sir Roland Somers, who was killed in the troubles when the king took the reins of government in his hands, and his lands, being forfeit, were given to Sir Jasper Vernon, who aided the king in that affair."

"I wish you would tell me about that," Walter said. "How was it that there was any trouble as to King Edward having kingly authority?"

"It happened in this way," Geoffrey said. "King Edward II., his father, was a weak prince, governed wholly by favourites, and unable to hold in check the turbulent barons. His queen, Isabella of France, sister of the French king, a haughty and ambitious woman, determined to snatch the reins of power from the indolent hands of her husband, and after a visit to her brother she returned with an army from Hainault in order to dethrone him. She was accompanied by her eldest son, and after a short struggle the king was dethroned. He had but few friends, and men thought that under the young Edward, who had already given promise of virtue and wisdom, some order might be introduced into the realm. He was crowned Edward III., thus, at the early age of fifteen, usurping the throne of his father. The real power, however, remained with Isabella, who was president of the council of regency, and who, in her turn, was governed by her favourite Mortimer. England soon found that the change which had been made was far from beneficial. The government was by turns weak and oppressive. The employment of foreign troops was regarded with the greatest hostility by the people, and the insolence of Mortimer alienated the great barons. Finally, the murder of the dethroned king excited throughout the kingdom a feeling of horror and loathing against the queen.

"All this feeling, however, was confined to her, Edward, who was but a puppet in her hands, being regarded with affection and pity. Soon after his succession the young king was married to our queen, Philippa of Hainault, who is as good as she is beautiful, and who is loved from one end of the kingdom to the other. I can tell you, the city was a sight to see when she entered with the king. Such pageants and rejoicing were never known. They were so young, he not yet sixteen, and she but fourteen, and yet to bear on their shoulders the weight of the state. A braver looking lad and a fairer girl mine eyes never looked on. It was soon after this that the events arose which led to the war with France, but this is too long a tale for me to tell you now. The Prince of Wales was born on the 15th of June, 1330, two years after the royal marriage.

"So far the king had acquiesced quietly in the authority of his mother, but he now paid a visit to France, and doubtless the barons around him there took advantage of his absence from her tutelage to shake her influence over his mind; and at the same time a rising took place at home against her authority. This was suppressed, and the Earl of Kent, the king's uncle, was arrested and executed by Isabella. This act of severity against his uncle, no doubt, hastened the prince's determination to shake off the authority of his haughty mother and to assume the reins of government himself. The matter, however, was not easy to accomplish. Mortimer having the whole of the royal revenue at his disposal, had attached to himself by ties of interest a large number of barons, and had in his pay nearly two hundred knights and a large body of men-at-arms. Thus it was no easy matter to arrest him. It was determined that the deed should be done at the meeting of the parliament at Nottingham. Here Mortimer appeared with Isabella in royal pomp. They took their abode at the castle, while the king and other members of the royal family were obliged to content themselves with an inferior place of residence.

"The gates of the castle were locked at sunset, and the keys brought by the constable, Sir William Eland, and handed to the queen herself. This knight was a loyal and gallant gentleman, and regarded Mortimer with no affection, and when he received the king's commands to assist the barons charged to arrest him he at once agreed to do so. He was aware of the existence of a subterranean communication leading from the interior of the castle to the outer country, and by this, on the night of the 19th of October, 1330, he led nine resolute knights—the Lords Montague, Suffolk, Stafford, Molins, and Clinton, with three brothers of the name of Bohun, and Sir John Nevil—into the heart of the castle. Mortimer was found surrounded by a number of his friends. On the sudden entry of the knights known to be hostile to Mortimer his friends drew their swords, and a short but desperate fight took place. Many were wounded, and Sir Hugh Turpleton and Richard Monmouth were slain. Mortimer was carried to London, and was tried and condemned by parliament, and executed for felony and treason. Several of his followers were executed, and others were attacked in their strongholds and killed; among these was Sir Roland Somers.

"Queen Isabella was confined in Castle Risings where she still remains a prisoner. Such, Walter, were the troubles which occurred when King Edward first took up the reins of power in this realm; and now, let's to supper, for I can tell you that my walk to Kingston has given me a marvellous appetite. We have three or four hours' work yet before we go to bed, for that Milan harness was promised for the morrow, and the repairs are too delicate for me to entrust it to the men. It is good to assist the law, but this work of attending as a witness makes a grievous break in the time of a busy man. It is a pity, Walter, that your mind is so set on soldiering, for you would have made a marvellous good craftsman. However, I reckon that after you have seen a few years of fighting in France, and have got some of your wild blood let out, you will be glad enough to settle down here with me; as you know, our profits are good, and work plentiful; and did I choose I might hold mine head higher than I do among the citizens; and you, if you join me, may well aspire to a place in the common council, ay, and even to an alderman's gown, in which case I may yet be addressing you the very worshipful my Lord Mayor."

"Pooh!" Walter laughed; "a fig for your lord Mayors! I would a thousand times rather be a simple squire in the following of our young prince."

CHAPTER IV
A KNIGHT'S CHAIN

The following morning Walter put on the sober russet dress which he wore on Sundays and holidays, for gay colours were not allowed to the apprentices, and set out for Westminster. Although he endeavoured to assume an air of carelessness and ease as he approached the dwelling of Earl Talbot, he was very far from feeling comfortable, and wished in his heart that his master had accompanied him on his errand. Half a dozen men-at-arms were standing on the steps of the mansion, who looked with haughty surprise at the young apprentice.

"Dame Alice Vernon has sent to express her desire to have speech with me," he said quietly, "and I would fain know if she can receive me."

"Here, Dikon," one of the men cried to another within the hall. "This is the lad you were sent to fetch yesterday. I wondered much who the city apprentice was, who with such an assured air, marched up to the door; but if what thou sayest be true, that he saved the life of Dame Vernon and her little daughter, he must be a brave lad, and would be more in place among men and soldiers than in serving wares behind the counter of a fat city tradesman."

"I serve behind no counter," Walter said indignantly. "I am an armourer, and mayhap can use arms as well as make them."

There was a laugh among the men at the boy's sturdy self-assertion, and then the man named Dikon said:

"Come along, lad. I will take you to Dame Vernon at once. She is expecting you; and, my faith, it would not be safe to leave you standing here long, for I see you would shortly be engaged in splitting the weasands of my comrades."

There was another roar of laughter from the men, and Walter, somewhat abashed, followed his conductor into the house. Leading him through the hall and along several corridors, whose spaciousness and splendour quite overpowered the young apprentice, he handed him over to a waiting woman, who ushered him into an apartment where Dame Vernon was reclining on a couch. Her little daughter was sitting upon a low stool beside her, and upon seeing Walter she leapt to her feet, clapping her hands.

"Oh! mother, this is the boy that rescued us out of the river."

The lady looked with some surprise at the lad. She had but a faint remembrance of the events which occurred between the time when she received a blow from the sword of one of her assailants and that when she found herself on a couch in the abode of her kinsman; and when she had been told that she had been saved by a city apprentice she had pictured to herself a lad of a very different kind to him who now stood before her.

Walter was now nearly sixteen years old. His frame was very powerful and firmly knit. His dark-brown hair was cut short, but, being somewhat longer than was ordinary with the apprentices, fell with a slight wave back on his forehead. His bearing was respectful, and at the same time independent. There was none of that confusion which might be expected on the part of a lad from the city in the presence of a lady of rank. His dark, heavy eyebrows, resolute mouth, and square chin gave an expression of sternness to his face, which was belied by the merry expression of his eyes and the bright smile when he was spoken to.

"I have to thank you, young sir," she said, holding out her hand, which Walter, after the custom of the time, raised to his lips, bending upon one knee as he did so, "for the lives of myself and my daughter, which would surely have been lost had you not jumped over to save us."

"I am glad that I arrived in time to be of aid," Walter said frankly; "but indeed I am rather to be blamed than praised, for had I, when I heard the plotting against the safety of the boat, told my master of it, as I should have done, instead of taking the adventure upon mine own shoulders, doubtless a boat would have been sent up in time to prevent the attack from taking place. Therefore, instead of being praised for having arrived a little too late, I should be rated for not having come there in time."

Dame Vernon smiled.

"Although you may continue to insist that you are to blame, this does not alter the fact that you have saved our lives. Is there any way in which I can be useful to you? Are you discontent with your state? for, in truth, you look as if Nature had intended you for a gallant soldier rather than a city craftsman. Earl Talbot, who is my uncle, would, I am sure, receive you into his following should you so choose it, and I would gladly pay for the cancelling of your indentures."

"I thank you, indeed, lady, for your kind offices," Walter said earnestly; "for the present I am well content to remain at my craft, which is that of an armourer, until, at any rate, I have gained such manly strength and vigour as would fit me for a man-at-arms, and my good master, Geoffrey Ward, will, without payment received, let me go when I ask that grace of him."

"Edith, go and look from the window at the boats passing along the river; and now," she went on, as the girl had obeyed her orders, "I would fain ask you more about the interview you overhead in the marshes. Sir William de Hertford told me of the evidence that you had given before the justice. It is passing strange that he who incited the other to the deed should have been by him termed 'Sir Knight'. Maybe it was merely a nickname among his fellows."

ST. GEORGE FOR ENGLAND

"Before I speak, lady," Walter said quietly, "I would fain know whether you wish to be assured of the truth. Sometimes, they say, it is wiser to remain in ignorance; at other times forewarned is forearmed. Frankly, I did not tell all I know before the court, deeming that peradventure you might wish to see me, and that I could then tell the whole to your private ear, should you wish to know it, and you could then bid me either keep silence or proclaim all I knew when the trial of these evil-doers comes on."

"You seem to me to be wise beyond your years, young sir," the lady said.

"The wisdom is not mine, lady, but my master's. I took counsel with him, and acted as he advised me."

"I would fain know all," the lady said. "I have already strange suspicions of one from whom assuredly I looked not for such evil designs. It will grieve me to be convinced that the suspicions are well founded; but it will be better to know the truth than to remain in a state of doubt."

"The person then was a knight, for I had seen him before when he came in knightly harness into my master's shop to have two rivets put into his hauberk. I liked not his face then, and should have remembered it anywhere. I knew him at once when I saw him. He was a dark-faced knight, handsome, and yet with features which reminded me of a hawk."

Dame Vernon gave a little exclamation, which assured the lad that she recognized the description.

"You may partly know, lady, whether it is he whom you suppose, for he said that he would detain your boat so that it should not come along until dark, and, moreover, he told them that they would know the boat since you would be wrapt in a white mantle."

The lady sat for some time with her face hidden in her hands.

"It is as I feared," she said at last, "and it grieves me to the heart to think that one who, although not so nearly related in blood, I regarded as a brother, should have betrayed me to death. My mind is troubled indeed, and I know not what course I shall take, whether to reveal this dreadful secret or to conceal it."

"I may say, madam," Walter said earnestly, "that should you wish the matter to remain a secret, you may rely upon it that I will tell no more at the trial than I revealed yesterday; but I would remind you that there is a danger that the leader of yon ruffians, who is probably alone acquainted with the name of his employer, may, under the influence of the torture, reveal it."

"That fear is for the present past, since a messenger arrived from Kingston but a few minutes since, saying that yester-even, under the threat of torture, the prisoners had pointed out the one among their number who was their chief. This morning, however, it was found that the warder who had charge of them had been bribed; he was missing from his post, and the door of the cell wherein the principal villain had been immured, apart from the others, was opened, and he had escaped."

"Then," Walter said, "it is now open to you to speak or be silent as you will. You will pardon my forwardness if I say that my master, in talking the matter over with me, suggested that this evil knight might be scared from attempting any future enterprise against you were he informed that it was known to several persons that he was the author of this outrage, and that if any further attempts were at any time made against you, the proofs of his crime would be laid before the king."

"Thanks, good lad," the lady said, "for your suggestion. Should I decide to keep the matter secret, I will myself send him a message to that effect, in such guise that he would not know whence it comes. And now, I would fain reward you for what you have done for us; and," she went on, seeing a flush suddenly mount upon the lad's face, as he made a half-step backwards, "before I saw you, had thought of offering you a purse of gold, which, although it would but poorly reward your services, would yet have proved useful to you when the time came for you to start as a craftsman on your own account; but now that I have seen you, I feel that although there are few who think themselves demeaned by accepting gifts of money in reward for services, you would rather my gratitude took some other form. It can only do that of offering you such good services that I can render with Earl Talbot, should you ever choose the profession of arms; and in the meantime, as a memento of the lives you have saved, you will, I am sure, not refuse this chain," and she took a very handsome one of gold from her neck; "the more so since it was the gift of her majesty, our gracious queen to myself. She will, I am sure, acquit me of parting with her gift when I tell her that I transferred it to one who had saved the lives of myself and my daughter, and who was too proud to accept other acknowledgment."

Colouring deeply, and with tears in his eyes at the kindness and thoughtful consideration of the lady, Walter knelt on one knee before her, and she placed round his neck the long gold chain which she had been wearing.

"It is a knight's chain," the lady said, smiling, "and was part of the spoil gained by King Edward from the French. Maybe," she added kindly, "it will be worn by a knight again. Stranger things have happened, you know."

Walter flushed again with pleasure.

"Maybe, lady," he said modestly, "even apprentices have their dreams, and men-at-arms may always hope, by deeds of valour, to attain a knight's spurs even though they may not be of noble blood or have served as page and squire to a baron; but whether as a 'prentice or soldier, I hope I shall never do discredit to your gift."

"Edith, come here," Dame Vernon said, "I have done talking now. And what are you going to give this brave knight of ours who saved us from drowning."

The girl looked thoughtfully at Walter. "I don't think you would care for presents," she said; "and you look as if a sword or a horse would suit you better than a girl's gift. And yet I should like to give you something, such as ladies give

"Take this gage as a reward of your valour."

their knights who have done brave deeds for them. It must be something quite my own, and you must take it as a keepsake. What shall it be, mamma?"

"Give him the bracelet which your cousin gave you last week," her mother said; "I would rather that you did not keep it, and I know you are not very fond of him."

"I can't bear him," the girl said earnestly, "and I wish he would not kiss me; he always looks as if he were going to bite, and I will gladly give his bracelet to this brave boy."

"Very well, Edith, fetch the bracelet from that coffer in the corner."

The girl went to the coffer and brought out the little bracelet, then she approached Walter.

"You must go down on your knee," she said; "true knights always do that to receive their lady's gifts. Now hold out your hand. There," she went on in a pretty imperious way, "take this gage as a reward of your valour, and act ever as a true knight in the service of your lady."

Bending down she dropt a kiss upon Walter's glowing cheek, and then, half frightened at her own temerity, ran back to her mother's side.

"And now," Dame Vernon went on, "will you thank your five comrades for their service in the matter, and give them each two gold pieces to spend as they will."

"He is a noble lad," Dame Vernon had said to herself when Walter had taken his leave. "Would he had been the son of one of the nobles of the court! It might have been then, if he distinguished himself in war, as he would surely do, that the king might have assigned Edith to him. As her lord and guardian he is certain to give her hand as a reward for valour in the field, and it may well be to a man with whom she would be less happy than with this 'prentice lad; but there, I need not be troubling myself about a matter which is five or six years distant yet. Still the thought that Edith is a ward of the crown, and that her hand must go where the king wills, often troubles me. However, I have a good friend in the queen, who will, I know, exert what influence she has in getting me a good husband for my child. But even for myself I have some fears, since the king hinted, when last he saw me, that it was time I looked out for another mate, for that the vassal of Westerham and Hyde needed a lord to lead them in the field. However, I hope that my answer that they were always at his service under the leading of my cousin James will suffice for him. Now, what am I to do in that matter? Who would have thought that he so coveted my lands that he would have slain me and Edith to possess himself of them? His own lands a thrice as broad as mine, though men say that he has dipped deeply into them and owes much money to the Jews. He is powerful and has many friends, and although Earl Talbot would stand by me, yet the unsupported word of an apprentice boy were but poor evidence on which to charge a powerful baron of such a crime as this. It were best, methinks, to say nought about it, but to bury the thought in my own heart. Nevertheless, I will not fail to take the precaution which the lad advised, and to let Sir James know that there are some who have knowledge of his handiwork. I hear he crosses the seas to-morrow to join the army, and it may be long ere he return. I shall have plenty of time to consider how I had best shape my conduct towards him on his return; but assuredly he shall never be friendly with me again, or frighten Edith with his kisses."

"Well, Walter, has it been such a dreadful business as you expected?" the armourer asked the lad when he re-entered the shop. "The great folks have not eaten you at anyrate."

"It has not been dreadful," Walter replied with a smile, "though I own that it was not pleasant when I first arrived at the great mansion; but the lady put me quite at my ease, and she talked to me for some time, and finally she bestowed on me this chain, which our lady, the queen, had herself given her."

"It is a knight's chain and a heavy one," Geoffrey said, examining it, "of Genoese work, I reckon, and worth a large sum. It will buy you harness when you go to the wars."

"I would rather fight in the thickest mêlée in a cloth doublet," Walter said indignantly, "than part with a single link of it."

"I did but jest, Walter," Geoffrey said laughing; "but as you will not sell it, and you cannot wear it, you had best give it me to put aside in my strong coffer until you get of knightly rank."

"Lady Vernon said," the lad replied, "that she hoped one day it might again belong to a knight; and if I live," he added firmly, "it shall."

"Oh! she has been putting these ideas into your head; nice notions truly for a London apprentice! I shall be laying a complaint before the lord mayor against Dame Vernon, for unsettling the mind of my apprentice, and setting him above his work. And the little lady, what said she? Did she give you her colours and bid you wear them at a tourney?"

Walter coloured hotly.

"Ah! I have touched you," laughed the armourer; "come now, out with the truth. My lad," he added more gravely, "there is no shame in it; you know that I have always encouraged your wishes to be a soldier, and have done my best to render you as good a one as any who draws sword 'neath the king's banner, and assuredly I would not have taken all these pains with you did I think that you were always to wear an iron cap and trail a pike. I too, lad, hope some day to see you a valiant knight, and have reasons that you wot not of, for my belief that it will be so. No man rises to rank and fame any the less quickly because he thinks that bright eyes will grow brighter at his success."

"But, Geoffrey, you are talking surely at random. The Lady Edith Vernon is but a child; a very beautiful child," he added reverently, "and such that when she grows up, the bravest knight in England might be proud to win. What folly for me, the son of a city bowyer, and as yet but an apprentice, to raise mine eyes so high!"

"The higher one looks the higher one goes," the armourer said sententiously. "You aspire some day to become a knight, you may well aspire also to win the hand of Mistress

Edith Vernon. She is five years younger than yourself, and you will be twenty-two when she is seventeen. You have time to make your way yet, and I tell you, though why it matters not, that I would rather you set your heart on winning Mistress Edith Vernon than any other heiress of broad lands in merry England. You have saved her life, and so have made the first step and a long one. Be ever brave, gentle, and honourable, and, I tell you, you need not despair; and now, lad, we have already lost too much time in talking; let us to our work."

That evening Walter recalled to Geoffrey his promise to tell him the causes which had involved England in so long and bloody a war with France.

"It is a tangled skein," Geoffrey said, "and you must follow me carefully. First, with a piece of chalk I will draw upon the wall the pedigree of the royal line of France from Phillip downwards, and then you will see how it is that our King Edward and Phillip of Valois came to be rival claimants to the throne of France.

"Now, you see that our King Edward is nephew of Charles le Bel, the last King of France, while Phillip of Valois is only nephew of Phillip le Bel, the father of Charles. Edward is consequently in the direct line, and had Isabella been a man instead of a woman his right to the throne would be unquestionable. In France, however, there is a law called the 'Salic' law, which excludes females from the throne; but it is maintained by many learned in the law, that although a female is held to be incompetent to reign because from her sex she cannot lead her armies to battle, yet she no ways forfeits otherwise her rights, and that her son is therefore the heir to the throne. In this contention, which is held by all English jurists, and by many in France also, be well founded, Edward is the rightful King of France. Phillip of Valois contends that the 'Salic law' not only bars a female from ascending the throne, but also destroys all her rights, and that the succession goes not to her sons but to the next heir male; in which case, of course, Phillip is rightful king. It is not for me to say which view is the right one, but certainly the great majority of those who have been consulted have decided that, according to ancient law and usage, the right lies with Edward. But in these matters 'right is not always might.' Had Isabella married a French noble instead of an English king it is probable that her son's claim to the throne would have been allowed without dispute, but her son is King of England, and the French nobles prefer being ruled by one of themselves to becoming united with England under one king.

"At the time of the death of the last king, Edward was still but a boy under the tuition of his mother, Phillip was a man, and upon the spot, therefore he was able to win support by presence and promises, and so it came that the peers of France declared Phillip of Valois to be their rightful monarch. Here in England, at parliament held at Northampton, the rights of Edward were discussed and asserted, and the Bishops of Worcester and Coventry were despatched to Paris to protest against the validity of Phillip's nomination. As, however, the country was not in a position to enforce the claim of their young king by arms, Phillip became firmly seated as King of France, and having shown great energy in at once marching against and repressing the people of Flanders, who were in a state of rebellion against their count, one of the feudatories of the French crown, the nobles were well satisfied with their choice, and no question as to his right was ever henceforth raised in France. As soon as the rebellion in Flanders was crushed, Phillip summoned the King of England to do homage for Aquitaine, Ponthieu and Montreuil, fiefs held absolutely from the crown of France. Such a proceeding placed Edward and his council in a great embarrassment. In case of a refusal the whole of the possessions of the crown in France might be declared forfeited and be seized, while England was in no condition to defend them; on the other hand, the fact of doing homage to Phillip of Valois would be a sort of recognition of his right to the throne he had assumed. Had Edward then held the reins of power in his hands, there can be little doubt that he would at once have refused, and would have called out the whole strength of England to enforce his claim. The influence of Isabella and Mortimer was, however, all powerful, and it was agreed that Edward should do homage as a public act, making a private reservation in secret to his own councillors, taking exception to the right of Phillip.

"Edward crossed to France and journeyed to Amiens, where Phillip with a brilliant court awaited him, and on the appointed day they appeared together in the cathedral. Here Edward, under certain protestations, did homage for his French estates, leaving certain terms and questions open for the consideration of his council. For some time the matter remained in this shape; but honest men cannot but admit that King Edward did, by his action at the time, acknowledge Phillip to be King of France, and that he became his vassal for his estates there; but, as has happened scores of times before, and will no doubt happen scores of times again, vassals, when they become powerful enough, throw off their allegiance to their feudal superiors, and so the time came to King Edward.

"After the death of Mortimer and the imprisonment of Isabella, the king gave rein to his taste for military sports. Tournaments were held at Dartford and other places, one in Westcheape. What a sight was that, to be sure! For three days the king, with fourteen of his knights, held the list against all comers, and in the sight of the citizens and the ladies of the court, jousted with knights who came hither from all parts of Europe. I was there each day and the sight was a grand one, though England was well-nigh thrown into mourning by an accident which took place. The gallery in which the queen and her attendants were viewing the sports had been badly erected, and in the height of the contests it gave way. The queen and her ladies were in great peril, being thrown from a considerable height, and a number of persons were severely injured. The king, who was furious at the danger to which the queen had been exposed, would have hung upon the spot the master workman whose negligence had cause the accident, but the queen went on her knees before him and begged his life of the king. The love of Edward for warlike exercises caused England to be regarded as the most chivalrous court in Europe, and the frequent tournaments aroused to the utmost the spirits of the people and prepared them for the war with France. But of the events of that war I will tell you some other night. It is time now for us to betake us to our beds."

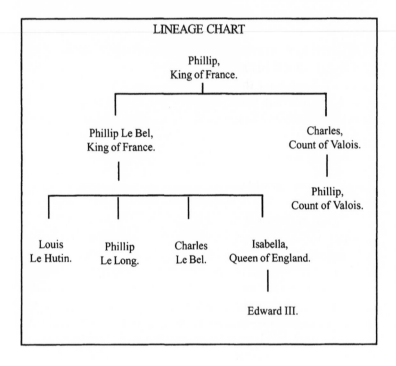

LINEAGE CHART

Phillip, King of France.

Phillip Le Bel, King of France.

Charles, Count of Valois.

Phillip, Count of Valois.

Louis Le Hutin.

Phillip Le Long.

Charles Le Bel.

Isabella, Queen of England.

Edward III.

CHAPTER V
THE CITY GAMES

THE next evening the armourer, at Walter's request, continued his narrative.

"Soon after the tournament we began to fight again with Scotland. For some years we had had peace with that country, and under the regency a marriage was made between David, King of Scotland, son of Robert the Bruce, and the Princess Joan, sister to our king, and a four years' truce was agreed to."

"But why should we always be fighting with Scotland?" Walter asked.

"That is more than I can tell you, Walter. We were peaceful enough with them until the days of Edward I.; but he set up some claim to the throne of Scotland, the rights of which neither I nor anyone else, so far as I know, have ever been able to make out. The fact was he was strong, and thought that he could conquer Scotland. The quarrels between her nobles—most of them were allied by blood with our own and held possessions in both kingdoms—gave Edward an excuse to interfere. Scotland was conquered easily enough, but it was a hard task to hold it. Sir William Wallace kept the country in a turmoil for many years, being joined by all the common people. He inflicted one heavy defeat upon us at Stirling, but receiving no support from the nobles he was defeated at Falkirk, and some years afterwards was captured and executed here. His head you may see any day over London Bridge. As he fought only for his country and had ever refused allegiance to our king, it seems to me that his fate was a cruel one. Then when all appeared quiet, Robert Bruce raised Scotland again, and was crowned king. There was war for many years, but at last, at Bannockburn he inflicted such a defeat upon us as we have never had before. After that there were skirmishes and excursions, but Edward II. was a weak prince, and it seem that the marriage of David and the Princess Joan would bring about a permanent peace between the two countries; but it was not to be so.

"Many of the English nobles held claims by marriage or grants upon lands in Scotland. They had, of course, been driven from these when the English were turned out by Bruce. By the terms of the marriage treaty in 1328 it was agreed that they should be reinstated. It was a foolish clause, because it was plain that the King of Scotland could not take these lands again from the Scotch nobles who had possession of them, many of them being well-nigh as powerful as himself. At this time Edward Baliol, son of the great rival of Robert Bruce, was in England. He still claimed the throne of Scotland as his right. Round him gathered a number of the English nobles who claimed lands in Scotland. The king offered no hindrance to the gathering of this force, for I doubt not that he was glad to see dissension in Scotland, which might give him some such pretext for interference as that which Edward I. had seized to possess himself of that country. At first Baliol was successful, and was crowned at Scone, but he was presently defeated and driven out of Scotland. The Scots now made an eruption across the frontier as a retaliation for Edward's having permitted Baliol to gather a force here for his war against Bruce. King Edward was on the point of starting for Ireland, and he at once hastened north. He defeated the Scots at Halidon Hill, captured Berwick, and placed Baliol upon the throne. Bruce fled to France, where he was supported and encouraged by the French king.

"The ill feeling between Edward and Phillip of Valois had gone on increasing ever since the former had been compelled to take the oath of allegiance to the latter, but outwardly the guise of friendship was kept up, and negotiations went on between the two courts for a marriage between the little Prince of Wales and Joanna, daughter of the French king.

"The aid which Phillip gave to Bruce increased the bad feeling, and Edward retaliated for Phillip's patronage of Bruce by receiving with the greatest honour and courtesy Robert of Artois, a great feudatory of France, who had been banished by King Phillip. For a time, although both countries were preparing for war, peace was not broken, as Edward's hands were full in Scotland, where Baliol having bestowed immense possessions upon the English nobles who had assisted him, the country again rose in favour of Bruce. During the three years that followed King Edward was obliged several times to go to Scotland to support Baliol, who held the crown as his feudal vassal. He was always successful in the field, but directly his army recrossed the frontier the Scotch rose again. In 1330 a new crusade was preached, and in October of that year King Phillip solemnly received the cross and collected an immense army nominally for the recovery of Jerusalem. Whether his intentions were honest or not I cannot say, but certainly King Edward considered that Phillip's real aim in creating so great an army was to attack England. Whether this was so or not would need a wiser head than mine, Walter, to tell. Certainly Phillip of Valois invited Edward to co-operate with him in the crusade. The king in reply stated his belief that the preparations were intended for war in Europe rather than in Asia; but that if the King of France would agree to conclude a firm league of amity between the two countries, to restore the castles and towns of Aquitaine, whose surrender had been frequently promised but never carried out, and would bind himself by oath to give no assistance, direct or indirect, to Scotland, he would join him in his war for the delivery of the Holy Land.

"I must say that King Edward's demands were reasonable, for it was clear that he could not march away from England with his whole force and leave Baliol unsupported against the assaults of his Scotch enemies, aided by France. Phillip was willing to accede to the first two conditions; but in regard to the third positively declined treating until David Bruce should be restored to the throne of his father. Now, had the French king openly supported Bruce from the first, none could have said that his conduct in befriending a dethroned monarch was aught but noble and generous; but he had all along answered Edward's complaints of the aid afforded by Frenchmen to the Bruce by denials that he himself supported him; and this declaration in his favour now certainly seemed to show that he had at last determined openly to throw off the veil, and that his great army was really collected against England. Robert of Artois craftily seized a moment when the king's indignation against Phillip was at the highest. At a great banquet held by King Edward, at which all his warlike nobles were present, Robert entered, preceded by two noble maidens carrying a heron, which, as you know, Walter, is considered the most cowardly of birds. Then in loud tones he called upon the knights present each to swear on the bird to perform some deed of chivalrous daring. First he presented it to King Edward himself, giving him to understand that he regarded him but as little braver than the heron for resigning without a blow the fair heritage of France.

"The moment was well chosen, for Edward was smarting under the answer he had just received from Phillip. He at once rose and took an oath to enter France in arms; to wait there a month in order to give Phillip time to offer him battle, and to accept the combat, even should the French outnumber him ten to one. Every knight present followed the example of the king, and so the war with France, which had been for years a mere question of time, was at last suddenly decided upon. You yourself, Walter, can remember the preparations which were made throughout England: men were enrolled and arms prepared. We armourers were busy night and day, and every man felt that his own honour, as well as that of the country, was concerned in winning for King Edward the heritage of which he had been unlawfully robbed by the King of France.

THE CITY GAMES

"On the 17th of March, 1337, at the parliament at Westminster, the king created the little prince, then seven years of age, Duke of Cornwall; and the prince immediately, in exercise of his new dignity, bestowed upon twenty of the most distinguished aspirants the honour of knighthood. Immense supplies were voted by the parliaments held at Nottingham, Westminster, and Northamton. Half the wool shorn in the summer following was granted to the king, with a variety of other taxes, customs, and duties. The revenues of all the foreign priories in England, a hundred and ten in number, were appropriated to the crown. Provisions of bacon, wheat, and oats were granted, and the king pawned his own jewels, and even the crown itself, to hire soldiers, and purchase him allies on the Continent. So great did the scarcity of money become in the country that all goods fell to less than half their value. Thus a vast army was raised, and with this King Edward prepared to try his strength with France.

"Phillip on his part was making great preparations. While Edward had purchased the assistance of many of the German nobles Phillip raised large armaments in the maritime states of Italy. Spain also contributed a number of naval adventurers, and squadrons were fitted out by his vassals on the sea-coasts of Normandy, Brittany, and Picardy. King Edward had crossed over into Belgium, and after vast delays in consequence of the slowness of the German allies, at last prepared to enter France at the end of September, 1339. Such, my lad, is the story, as far as I know, of the beginning of that war with France which is now raging, and whose events you know as well as I do, seeing that they are all of late occurrence. So far, although the English have had the best of it, and have sorely mauled the French both in the north and south, we have not gained any such advantages as would lead to a belief that there is any likelihood of an early termination, or that King Edward will succeed for a long time in winning back his inheritance of the throne of France.

ST. GEORGE FOR ENGLAND

"There is no doubt that the war weighs heavily upon the people at large. The taxes are doubled, and the drain of men is heavy. We armourers, of course, have a busy time of it, and all trades which have to do with the furnishing of an army flourish exceedingly. Moreover, men of metal and valour have an opportunity of showing what they are composed of, and England rings with the tales of martial deeds. There are some, Walter, who think that peace is the greatest of blessings, and in some ways, lad, they are no doubt right; but there are many compensations in war. It brings out the noble qualities; it raises men to think that valour and fortitude and endurance and honour are qualities which are something above the mere huckstering desire for getting money, and for ignoble ease and comfort. Some day it may be that the world will change, and that war may become a thing of the past; but to my mind, boy, I doubt whether men will be any happier or better for it. The priests, no doubt, would tell you otherwise; but then you see I am an armourer, and so perhaps am hardly a fair judge on the matter, seeing that without wars my craft would come to an end."

Walter remained in thought for some time. "It seems to me, Master Geoffrey, that while wars may suit strong and courageous men, women would rejoice were such things to be at an end."

"Women suffer most from wars, no doubt," Geoffrey said, "and yet do you mark that they are more stirred by deeds of valour and chivalry than are we men; that they are ever ready to bestow their love upon those who have won honour and glory in war, even although the next battle may leave them widows. This has been always somewhat of a marvel to me; but I suppose that it is human nature, and that admiration for deeds of valour and bravery is ingrained in the heart of man, and will continue until such times come that the desire for wealth, which is ever on the increase, has so seized all men that they will look with distaste upon everything which can interfere with the making of money, and will regard the man who amasses gold by trading as a higher type than he who does valiant deeds in battle."

THE CITY GAMES

"Surely that can never be," Walter said indignantly.

"There is no saying," the armourer answered; "at any rate, Walter, it will matter little to you or to me, for many generations must pass before such a state of things can come about."

Two days later Walter, who had been across into the city, returned in a state of excitement.

"What do you think, Geoffrey? The king, with the Prince of Wales and all his court, are coming to the games next month. They say that the king himself will adjudge the prizes; and there is to be a grand assault-at-arms between ten of the 'prentices with a captain, and an equal number of sons of nobles and knights."

"That will be rare," Geoffrey Ward exclaimed; "but there will be some broken limbs, and maybe worse. These assaults-at-arms seldom end without two or three being killed. However, you youngsters will not hit as hard as trained knights; and if the armour be good, no great damage should be done."

"Do you think that I shall be one of the ten?" Walter asked anxiously.

"Just as if you did not know you would," Geoffrey replied, laughing. "Did you not win the prize for swordplay last year ? and twelve months have added much to the strength of your arm, to say nothing of your skill with weapons. If you win this year again—and it will be strange if you do not—you are like enough to be chosen captain. You will have tough fighting, I can tell you, for all these young aspirants to knighthood will do their best to show themselves off before the king and queen. The fight is not to take place on horseback, I hope; for if so, it will be settled as soon as it begins."

"No, it is to be on foot; and the king himself is to give orders as to the fighting."

"You had best get out that helmet and coat of mail of yours," Geoffrey said, "I warrant me that there will be none of finer make or of truer metal in the tourney, seeing that I made them specially for you. They are light, and yet strong enough to withstand a blow from the strongest arm. I tried them hard, and will warrant them proof, but you had best see to the rivets and fastenings. They had a rough handling last year, and you have not worn them since. There are some other pieces that I must put in hand at once, seeing that in such a mêlée you must be covered from head to foot."

For the next week nothing was talked of in London but the approaching sports, and the workmen were already engaged in the erection of the lists and pavilions in the fields between the walls and Westminster. It was reported that the king would add valuable prizes to those given to the winners by the city; that there would be jousting on horseback by the sons of the court nobles, and that the young Prince of Wales would himself ride.

The king had once before taken part in the city sports, and with ten of the citizens had held his own against an equal number of knights. This was at the commencement of his reign; but the accident to the queen's stand had so angered him that he had not again been present at the sports, and his reappearance now was considered to be an act of approval of the efforts which the city had made to aid him in the war, and as an introduction of the young prince to the citizens.

When the day arrived there was a general flocking out of the citizens to the lists. The scene was a picturesque one; the weather was bright and warm; the fields were green; and Westminster, as well as London, sent out large numbers to the scene. The citizens were all in their best; their garments were for the most part of somber colours—russet, murrey, brown, and gray. Some, indeed, of the younger and wealthier merchants adopted somewhat of the fashion of the court, wearing their shoes long and pointed, and their garments parti-coloured. The line of division was down the centre of the body; one leg, arm, and half the body would be blue, the other half russet or brown. The ladies' dresses were similarly divided. Mingling with the citizens, as they strolled to and fro upon the sward, were the courtiers. These wore the brightest colours, and their shoes were so long that the points were looped up to the knees with little gold chains to enable them to walk. The ladies wore head-dresses of prodigious height, culminating in two points; and from these fell, sweeping to the ground, streamers of silk or lighter material. Cloths of gold and silver, rich furs, silks, and velvets, were worn both by men and women.

None who saw the nobles of the court walking in garments so tight that they could scarce move, with their long parti-coloured hose, their silk hoods buttoned under the chin, their hair braided down their back, would have thought that these were the most warlike and courageous of knights, men whose personal prowess and gallantry were the admiration of Europe. Their hair was generally cut close upon the forehead, and the beard was suffered to grow, but was kept trimmed a moderate length. Many of the ladies had the coat-of-arms of their family embroidered upon their dresses, giving them the appearance of heralds' tabards. Almost all wore gold or silver girdles, with embroidered pouches, and small daggers.

Thus the appearance of the crowd who moved about among the fields near the lists was varied and brilliant indeed. Their demeanour was quiet, for the London merchants deemed a grave demeanour to belong to their calling, and the younger men and apprentices restrained their spirits in the presence of their superiors. For their special amusement, and in order, perhaps, to keep them from jostling too freely against the court gallants and ladies, the city authorities had appointed popular sports such as pleased the rougher classes; and bull-baiting, cock-fighting, wrestling for a ram, pitching the bar, and hand-ball, were held in a field some distance away. Here a large portion of the artisans and apprentices amused themselves until the hour when the king and queen were to arrive at their pavilion, and the contests were to commence.

Presently a sound of trumpets was heard, and the royal procession was seen moving up from Westminster. Then the minor sports were abandoned; the crowd gathered round the large fenced-in space, and those who, by virtue of rank or position in the city, had places in the various stands, took their places there.

There was a flourish of trumpets as the king and queen appeared in front of the pavilion, accompanied by the Prince of Wales and many of the nobles of the court, and a shout of welcome arose from the crowd. The shooting at a mark at once began. The preliminary trials had been shot off upon the preceding day, and the six chosen bowmen now took their places.

Walter had not entered for the prizes at archery. He had on previous years shot well; but since he had fully determined to become a man-at-arms he had given up archery, for which, indeed, his work at the forge and his exercises at arms when the fires were out, left him but little time. The contest was a close one, and when it was over the winner was led by the city marshal to the royal pavilion, where the queen bestowed upon him a silver arrow, and the king added a purse of money. Then there were several combats with quarter-staff and broadsword between men who had served among the contingents sent by the city to aid the king in his wars. Some good sword-play was shown and many stout blows exchanged, two or three men were badly hurt, and the king and all present were mightily pleased with the stoutness with which they fought.

The apprentices then came forward to compete for the prizes for sword-play. They wore light iron caps and shirts of thickly quilted leather, and fought with blunted swords, for the city fathers deemed wisely that with these weapons they could equally show their skill, and that with sharpened swords not only would severe wounds be given, but bad blood would be created between the apprentices of the various wards. Each ward sent its champion to the contest, and as these fought in pairs, loud was the shouting which rose from their comrades at each blow given or warded, and even the older citizens joined sometimes in the shouting and took a warm interest in the champions of their respective wards.

THE CITY GAMES

The iron caps had stout cheek-pieces which defended the sides of the face and neck, for even a blunted sword can deliver a terrible blow if it fall upon the naked flesh. It took a long time to get through the combats; the pairs were drawn by lot, and fought until the king decided which was the superior. Some were speedily beaten, at other times the contests were long and severe. It was generally thought by the apprentices that the final contest lay between Walter Fletcher of Aldgate and Ralph Smith of Ludgate. The former was allowed to be superior in the use of his weapon, but the latter was also skilful, was two years older, and greatly superior in strength. He had not taken part in the contest in the preceding year, as he had been laid up with a hurt in his hand which he had got in his employment as a smith, and the lads of Ludgate were confident that he would turn the tables upon the champion of the eastern ward. Both had defeated with ease the various opponents whom they had met, but it chanced that they had not drawn together until the last round, when they remained alone to struggle for the first and second prizes.

The interest in the struggle had increased with each round, and wagers were freely laid upon the result. According to custom the two champions had laid aside their leathern shirts and had donned mail armour, for it was considered that the crowning contest between the two picked young swordsmen of the city would be a severe one, and greater protection to the limbs was needed.

Before taking their places they were led up to the royal pavilion, where they were closely inspected by the king and his nobles.

"You are sure that this man is still an apprentice?" the king asked the Lord Mayor, who was seated next to him; "he has the appearance of a man-at-arms, and a stout one too; the other is a likely stripling, and is, as I have seen, marvellously dexterous with his sword, but he is but a boy while the other is a grown man."

"He is an apprentice, my liege, although his time will be up in a few days, while the other has yet three years to serve, but he works for an armourer, and is famed through the city, boy as he is, for his skill with weapons."

After a few words to each, exhorting them to do their best in the sight of the queen and her ladies, the king dismissed them.

"I know the young one now!" the Prince of Wales said, clapping his hands as the apprentices turned away to take their places. "My Lord Talbot, I will wager a gold chain with you upon the smaller of the two."

"I will take your wager," the noble answered; "but I am by no means sure that I shall win it, for I have watched your champion closely, and the downright blows which he struck would seem to show that he has the muscle and strength of a man though still but a boy."

The event justified the Prince of Wales's confidence; at the commencement of the struggle Ralph Smith tried to beat down his opponent by sheer strength as he had done his prior opponents, but to his surprise he found that all his efforts could not break down his opponent's guard. Walter indeed did not appear to take advantage of his superior lightness and activity, but to prefer to prove that in strength as well as skill he was equal to his antagonist. In the latter respect there was no comparison, for as soon as the smith began to relax his rain of blows Walter took the offensive and with a sweeping blow given with all his strength broke down his opponent's guard and smote him with such force upon his steel cap that, blunted as the sword was, it clove through the iron, and stretched the smith senseless on the ground. A loud shout broke from the assemblage. The marshal came up to Walter, and removing his helmet, led him to the royal pavilion, while Ralph was carried to a tent near, where a leech attended his wound.

CHAPTER VI
THE MÊLÉE

Y ou have won your prize stoutly and well, sir 'prentice,"
the king said. "I should not have deemed it possible
that one of your age could have smitten such a blow,
and right glad should I be of a few hundred lads of your
mettle to follow me against the French. What is your calling?"

"I am an armourer, my liege," Walter answered.

"And you are as good at mending armour as you are at
marring it," the king said, "you will be a rare craftsman one
of these days. 'Tis a rare pity so promising a swordsman
should be lost to our army. Wouldst like to change your
calling, boy, and take to that of arms?"

"It is my hope to do so, sir," Walter answered modestly,
"and his grace the Prince of Wales has already promised me
that I shall some day ride behind him to the wars."

"Ah! Edward," the king ejaculated, "how is this? Have
you been already enlisting a troop for the wars?"

"No, sir," the young prince replied, "but one day, now
some four years since, when I was riding with my Lord Talbot
and others in the fields near the Tower I did see this lad lead
his play-fellows to the assault of an earthen castle held by
others, and he fought so well and gallantly that assuredly no
knight could have done better, until he was at last stricken
senseless, and when he recovered I told him that should he
choose to be a man-at-arms I would enlist him in my following
to the wars."

The king laughed.

"I deemed not that the lads of the city indulged in such
rough sports; but I wonder not, seeing that the contingent
which my good city of London furnishes me is ever one of

the best in my army. We shall see the lad at work again to-morrow and will then talk more of it. Now let us bestow upon him the prize that he has so well earned."

Walter bent on one knee, and the queen handed to him a sword of the best Spanish steel, which was the prize given by the city to the victor. The king handed him a heavy purse of gold pieces, saying:

"This may aid in purchasing your freedom."

Walter bowed deeply and murmured some words of thanks, and was then led off by the marshal. After this many of the young nobles of the court jousted on horseback, ran at the ring, and performed other feats of knightly exercise to the great pleasure of the multitude. The marshal on leading Walter away said to him, "You will be captain of the city band to-morrow, and I must therefore tell you what the king purports. He has prepared a surprise for the citizens, and the present show will be different to anything ever before seen in London. Both to show them somewhat of the sieges which are taking place on the borders of France and the Low Countries, in which Sir Walter Manny and many other gallant knights have so greatly distinguished themselves, and as an exercise for the young nobles, he has determined that there shall be a castle erected. It will be built of wood, with battlements and towers, with a moat outside. As soon as the lists are over a large number of workmen will commence its erection; the pieces are all sawn and prepared. There will be machines, ladders, and other appliances. The ten champions on either side will fight as knights; you will have a hundred apprentices as men-at-arms, and the court party will have an equal number of young esquires. You, as winner of to-day's tourney, will have the choice of defence or attack. I should advise you to take the defence, since it is easier and requires less knowledge of war, and many of the other party have accompanied their fathers and masters in the field and have seen real sieges carried out."

"Can you show me a plan of the castle," Walter said, "if it be not contrary to the rules, in order that I may think over to-night the plan of fighting to-morrow?"

"Here it is," the marshal said. "You see that the walls are 200 feet long, they are 12 feet in height, with a tower at the end and one over the gateway in the centre six feet high. There is a drawbridge defended by an outwork of palisades six feet high. The moat will be a dry one, seeing that we have no means of filling it with water, but it will be supposed to be full, and must be crossed on planks or bridges. Two small towers on wheels will be provided, which may be run up to the edge of the moat, and will be as high as the top of the towers.

"Surely they cannot make all this before morning?" Walter said.

"They will do so," the marshal replied. "The castle has been put together in the king's courtyard, and the pieces are all numbered. Two hundred carpenters will labour all night at it, besides a party of labourers for the digging of the moat. It will be a rare show, and will delight both the citizens and the ladies of the court, for such a thing has never before been attempted. But the king grudges not the expense which it will cost him, seeing that spectacles of this kind do much to arouse the warlike spirit of the people. Here is a list of the various implements which will be provided, only it is understood that the mangonels and arblasts will not be provided with missiles, seeing that many would assuredly be killed by them. They will be employed, however, to show the nature of the work, and parties of men-at-arms will be told off to serve them. Crossbows and arrows will be used, but the weapons will be blunted. You will see that there are ladders, planks for making bridges, long hooks for hauling men down from the wall, beams for battering down the gate, axes for cutting down the palisades, and all other weapons. The ten who will serve under you as knights have already been nominated, and the city will furnish them with full armour. For the others, the apprentices of each ward will choose sufficient representatives to make up the hundred, who will fight as men-at-arms; these will wear steel caps and breastpieces, with leather jerkins, and vizors to protect their faces, for even a blunted arrow or wooden quarrel might well kill if it struck true."

On leaving the marshal Walter joined Giles Fletcher and Geoffrey Ward, who warmly congratulated him upon his success. He informed them of the spectacle which the king had prepared for the amusement of the citizens on the morrow.

"In faith," Geoffrey said, "the idea is a good one, and promises rare sport, but it will be rough, and we may expect many broken limbs, for it be no joke to be thrown down with a ladder from a wall even twelve feet high, and there will be the depth of the moat besides."

"That will only be two feet," Walter said, "for so it is marked on the plan."

"And which do you mean to take, Walter, the attack or the defence? Methinks the king has erred somewhat in making the forces equal, for assuredly the besiegers should outnumber the besieged by fully three to one to give them a fair chance of success."

"I shall take the assault," Walter answered; "there is more to be done that way than in the defence. When we get home, Geoffrey, we will look at the plans, and see what may be the best manner of assault."

Upon examining the plan that evening they found that the wall was continued at an angle at either end for a distance of some twenty feet back so as to give a postern gate behind each of the corner towers through which a sortie might be made. Geoffrey and Walter talked the matter over, and together contrived a plan of operation for the following day.

"You will have one great advantage," Geoffrey said. "The apprentices are all accustomed to the use of the bow, while the young nobles will know but little of that weapon; therefore your shooting will be far straighter and truer, and even a blunt-headed arrow drawn from the shoulder will hit so smart a blow that those on the wall will have difficulty in withstanding them."

After the talk was ended Walter again crossed London Bridge, and made his way to Ludgate, where he found his late antagonist, whose head had been plastered up, and was little the worse for the conflict.

"There is no ill-will between us, I hope," Walter said, holding out his hand.

"None in the world," the young smith said frankly. He was a good-tempered-looking young giant, with closely-cropped hair, light-blue eyes, and a pleasant but somewhat heavy face.

"My faith ! but what a blow was that you gave me; why, one would think that your muscles were made of steel. I thought that I could hit a good downright blow, seeing that I have been hammering at the anvil for the last seven years; but strike as I would I could not beat down your guard, while mine went down, as if it had been a feather, before yours. I knew, directly that I had struck the first blow, and felt how firm was your defence, that it was all up with me, knowing that in point of skill I had no chance whatever with you."

"I am glad to see that you bear no malice, Ralph," Walter said, "and hope that we shall be great friends henceforth, that is, if you will take me as such, seeing that you are just out of your apprenticeship, while I am not yet half through mine. But I have come to talk to you about to-morrow. Have you heard that there is to be a mimic siege?"

"I have heard about it," Ralph said. "The city is talking of nothing else. The news was published at the end of the sports. It will be rare fun, surely."

"It will be pretty rough fun," Walter replied; "and I should not be much surprised if some lives are lost; but this is always so in a tournament; and if knights and nobles are ready to be killed, we apprentices need not fear to hazard our lives. But now as to to-morrow. I, as the winner to-day, am to be the leader of the party, and you, as second, will of course be captain under me. Now I want to explain to you exactly what I propose to do, and to arrange with you as to your share in the business."

The young smith listened attentively to Walter's explanation, and, when he had done, exclaimed admiringly: "Why, Walter, you seem to be made for a general. How did it all come to you, lad? I should never have thought of such a scheme."

"I talked it over with my master," Walter said, "and the idea is his as much as mine. I wonder if it will do."

"It is sure to do," the smith said enthusiastically. "The castle is as good as taken."

The next day all London poured out to the scene of the sports, and the greatest admiration and wonder were expressed at the castle, which had risen, as if by magic, in the night. It was built at one end of the lists, which had been purposely placed in a hollow, so that a great number of people besides those in the pavilions could obtain a view from the surrounding slopes. The castle was substantially built of heavy timber painted gray, and looked at a little distance as if constructed of stone. A flag floated from the central tower, and the building looked so formidable that the general opinion was freely expressed that the task of the assailants, whoever they might be—for at present this was unknown—was quite impossible. At ten o'clock the king and his court arrived. After they had taken their places the two bands, headed by their leaders, advanced from the lower end of the lists, and drew up in front of the royal pavilion. The leaders took their places in front. Behind them stood, ten chosen followers, all of whom, as well as their chiefs, were encased in full armour. Behind, on one side, were 100 apprentices, on the other 100 esquires, all attired as men-at-arms. The court party were led by Clarence Aylmer, son of the Earl of Pembroke. His companions were all young men of noble family, aspirants for the order of knighthood. They were, for the most part, somewhat older than the apprentices, but as the latter consisted chiefly of young men nearly out of their term the difference was not great. Walter's armour was a suit which the armourer had constructed a year previously for a young knight who had died before the armour could be delivered. Walter had wondered more than once why Geoffrey did not endeavour to sell it elsewhere, for, although not so decorated and inlaid as many of the suits of Milan armour, it was constructed of the finest steel, and the armourer had bestowed special care upon its manufacture, as the young knight's father had long been one of his best customers. Early that morning Geoffrey had brought it to his room and had told him to wear it instead of that lent by the city.

"But I fear it will get injured," Walter had urged. "I shall not spare myself, you know, Geoffrey, and the blows will be hard ones."

"The more need for good armour, Walter. These city suits are made for show rather than use. You may be sure that young Pembroke and his band will fight their hardest rather than suffer defeat at the hands of those whom they consider a band of city varlets."

Before issuing from the tent where he and his companions had put on their mail Walter carefully fastened in the front of his helmet a tiny gold bracelet. Upon taking their places before the pavilion the king ordered the two leaders to advance, and addressed them and the multitude in the following words:

"Brave leaders, and you, my people, I have contrived the pastime to-day that I may show you on a mimic scale the deeds which my brave soldiers are called upon to perform in France. It is more specially suited for the combatants of to-day, since one party have had but small opportunity of acquiring skill on horseback. Moreover, I wish to teach the lesson that fighting on foot is as honourable as fighting on horseback, for it has now been proved, and sometimes to our cost, in Scotland, that footmen can repulse even the bravest chivalry. To-day each party will fight his best. Remember that, even in the heat of conflict, matters must not be carried to an extreme. Those cut off from their friends will be accounted prisoners, as will those who, being overpowered, throw down their arms. Any wounded on either side will not be accounted as prisoners, but may retire with honour from the field. You," he said, looking at Walter, "as the conqueror of yesterday, have the choice of either the attack or defence; but I should advise you to take the latter, seeing it is easier to defend a fortress than to assault it. Many of your opponents have already gained credit in real warfare, while you and your following are new to it. Therefore, in order to place the defence on fair terms with the assault, I have ordered that both sides shall be equal in numbers."

"If your liege will permit me," Walter said bowing, "I would fain take the assault. Methinks that, with my following, I could do better thus than in defence."

The king looked somewhat displeased.

"As you will," he said coldly; "but I fear this will somewhat mar the effect of the spectacle seeing that you will have no chance whatever against an equal force, more accustomed to war than your party, and occupying so superior a position. However," he went on, seeing that Walter made no sign of changing his mind, "as you have chosen, so be it; and now it is for you to choose the lady who shall be queen of the tourney and shall deliver the prizes to the victors. Look round you; there are many fair faces, and it is for you to choose among them."

Smiles passed between many of the courtly dames and ladies at the choice that was to be made among them by the apprentice lad; and they thought that he would be sorely puzzled at such a duty. Walter, however, did not hesitate an instant. He ran his eye over the crowd of ladies in the royal gallery, and soon saw the object of his search.

"Since I have your majesty's permission," he said, "I choose, as queen of the tournament, Mistress Edith Vernon."

There was a movement of surprise and a general smile. Perhaps to all who thought that they had a chance of being chosen the selection was a relief, as none could be jealous of the pretty child, who, at the king's order, made her way forward to the front, and took her seat in a chair placed between the king and queen. The girl coloured brightly; but she had heard so much of tourneys and jousts that she knew what was her duty. She had been sitting far back on the previous day, and the apprentice, when brought up before the king, was too far below for her to see his features. She now recognized him.

"Sir Knights," she said in a loud, clear, childish voice, "you will both do your duty to-day and show yourselves worthy cavaliers. Methinks that, as queen of the tourney, I should be neutral between you, but as one of you carries my gage in his helm, my good wishes must needs go with him; but bright eyes will be fixed on you both, and may well stir you to deeds of valour."

So saying, she resumed her seat with a pretty air of dignity.

"Why, sweetheart," the king said, "how is it that this 'prentice lad knows your name, and how is it that he wears your gage, for I know that the young Pembroke wears the glove of the Earl of Surrey's daughter?"

"He saved my life, sir, mine and my mother's," the child said, "and I told him he should be my true knight, and gave him my bracelet, which you see he wears in his helm."

"I recall somewhat of the story," the king said, "and will question my Lady Vernon further anon; but see, the combatants are filing off to their places."

With flags flying and trumpets blowing young Pembroke led his forces into the castle. Each of his ten knights was followed by an esquire bearing his banner, and each had ten men-at-arms under his immediate order. Two of them, with twenty men, remained in the outwork beyond the drawbridge. The rest took their station on the walls, and towers, where a platform had been erected, running along three feet below the battlements. The real men-at-arms with the machines of war now advanced, and for a time worked the machines, which made pretence at casting great stones and missiles at the walls. The assailants then moved forward and, unslinging their bows, opened a heavy fire of arrows at the defenders, who, in turn, replied with arrows and cross-bows.

"The 'prentices shoot well," the king said; "by our lady, it would be hot work for the defenders were the shafts but pointed! Even as it is the knocks must be no child's play, for the arrows, although not pointed, are all tipped with iron, without which, indeed, straight shooting would be impossible."

The return fire from the walls was feeble, and the king said, laughing, "So far your knight, fair mistress, has it all his own way. I did not reckon sufficiently upon the superiority of shooting of the London lads, and, indeed, I know not that I ought not in fairness to order some of the defenders off the walls, seeing, that in warfare, their numbers would be rapidly thinned. See, the assailants are moving up to the two towers under shelter of the fire of the archers."

By this time Aylmer, seeing that his followers could make no effectual reply to the arrow fire, had ordered all, save the leaders in full armour, to lie down behind the parapet. The assailants now gathered thickly round each tower, as if they intended to attempt to cross by the bridges, which could be let down from an opening in the tower level with the top of the wall, while archers upon the summit shot fast and thick among the defenders who were gathering to oppose them.

"If the young Pembroke is wise," the king said, "he will make a strong sally now and fall upon one or other of the parties."

As he spoke there was a sudden movement on the part of the assailants, who, leaving the foot of the towers, made a rush at the outwork in the centre. The instant they arrived they fell to work with axes upon the palisades. Many were struck down by the blows dealt them by the defenders, but others caught up the axes and in less than a minute several of the palisades were cut down and the assailants poured in. The defenders fought gallantly, but they were overpowered by numbers. Some were struck down, others taken prisoners by main force, and the rest driven across the drawbridge, just as the gates were opened and Pembroke, at the head of the defenders, swarmed out to their assistance.

THE MÊLÉE

There was a desperate fight on the bridge, and it was well that the armour was stout, and the arms that wielded the weapons had not yet attained their full strength. Several were knocked off the bridge into the moat, and these were, by the rules, obliged at once to retire and take no further part in the contest. Walter and Ralph the smith, fought in front of their men, and hard as Pembroke and his followers struggled, they could not drive them back a foot. The court party were galled by the heavy fire of arrows kept up by the apprentices along the side of the moat, and finding all his efforts to regain the earth-work useless, Pembroke withdrew his forces into the castle, and in spite of the efforts of the besiegers managed to close the gates in their faces. The assailants, however, succeeded in severing the chains of the drawbridge before it could be raised.

From the tower above, the defenders now hurled over great stones, which had been specially placed there for the purpose of destroying the drawbridge should the earthwork be carried. The boards were soon splintered, and the drawbridge was pronounced by the Earl of Talbot, who was acting as judge, to be destroyed. The excitement of the spectators was worked up to a great pitch while the conflict was going on, and the citizens cheered lustily at the success of the apprentices.

"That was gallantly done," the king said to Queen Philippa, "and the leader of the assailants is a lad of rare mettle. Not a captain of my army, no, not Sir Walter Manny himself, could have done it more cleverly. You see, by placing his forces at the ends of the wall he drew all the garrison thither to withstand the assaults from them, and thus by his sudden movement he was able to carry the outwork before they could recover from their surprise, and come down to its aid. I am curious to know what he will do next. What thinkst thou, Edward?" he asked his son, who was standing by his side.

"He will win the day," the young prince said; "and in faith, although the others are my comrades, I should be glad to see it. He will make a gallant knight, sir, one of these days, and remember he is engaged to follow my banner, so you must not steal him from me. See, my liege, they are taking planks and ladders to the outwork."

"They are doing wrongly then," the king said, "for even should they bridge the moat where the drawbridge is, they cannot scale the wall there, since the tower defends it, and the ladders are but long enough to reach the lower wall. No, their leader has changed his mind, they are taking the planks along the edge of the moat towards the tower on the left, and will aid the assault by its bridge by a passage of the moat there."

It seemed, indeed, that this was the plan. While some of the assailants kept up the arrow fire on the wall others mounted the tower, while a party prepared to throw a bridge of planks across the moat. The bridge from the tower was now lowered; but a shout of triumph rose from the defenders when it was seen that by some mistake of the carpenters this was too short, and when lowered did not reach within six feet of the wall.

"All the better," the king said, while the prince gave an angry exclamation. "Accidents of this kind will happen, and give an opportunity to a leader to show his resources. Doubtless he will carry planks up to the tower and so connect the bridge and the wall."

This, indeed, was what the assailants tried to do, while a party threw planks across the moat, and rushing over placed ladders against the wall and strove to climb. They strove in vain, however. The ladders were thrown down as fast as they were placed, while the defenders, thickly clustered on the walls, drove back those who tried to cross from the tower.

"I do not see the leader of the assailants," the prince said.

"He has a white plume, but it may have been shorn off," the king said. "Look, the young Pembroke is making a sortie!"

From the sortie gate behind the tower the defenders now poured out, and running down to the edge of the moat fell upon the stormers. These, however, received them with great steadiness, and while some continued the attack the rest turned upon the garrison, and, headed by Ralph the smith, drove them gradually back.

"They fight well and steadily," the king said. "One would have thought that they had reckoned on the sortie, so steadily did they receive it."

As only a portion of the garrison had issued out they were unable to resist long the pressure of the apprentices, who drove them back step by step to the sally-port, and pressing them hard endeavoured to force their way in at their heels.

CHAPTER VII
THE YOUNG ESQUIRE

WHILE the attention of the whole of the spectators and combatants was fixed upon the struggle at the right-hand angle of the castle, a party of twenty 'prentices suddenly leapt to their feet from among the broken palisades of the outwork. Lying perdu there they had escaped the attention of the spectators as well as of the defenders. The reason why the assailants carried the planks and ladders to this spot was now apparent. Only a portion had been taken on to the assault of the right-hand tower; those who now rose to their feet lifted with them planks and ladders, and at a rapid pace ran towards the left angle of the castle, and reached that point before the attention of the few defenders who remained on the wall there was attracted to them, so absorbed were they in the struggle at the other angle. The moment that they saw the new assailants they raised a shout of alarm, but the din of the combat, the shouts of the leaders and men were so loud, that their cries were unheard. Two or three then hurried away at full speed to give the alarm, while the others strove to repel the assault. Their efforts were in vain. The planks were flung across the moat, the ladders placed in position, and led by Walter the assailants sprang up and gained a footing on the wall before the alarm was fairly given. A thundering cheer from the spectators greeted the success of the assailants. Springing along the wall they drove before them the few who strove to oppose them, gained the central tower, and Walter, springing up to the top, pulled down the banner of the defenders and placed that of the city in its place. At this moment the defenders, awakened too late to the ruse which had been played upon them, came swarming back along the wall and strove to regain the central tower. In the confusion the assault by the flying tower of the assailants was neglected, and at this point also they gained footing on the wall. The young nobles of the court, furious at being outwitted, fought desperately to regain their lost laurels. But the king rose from his seat and held up his hand. The trumpeter standing below him sounded the arrest of arms, which was echoed by two others who accompanied Earl Talbot, who had taken his place on horseback close to the walls. At the sound swords dropt and the din abruptly ceased, but the combatants stood glaring at each other, their blood too heated to relinquish the fray readily.

Already much damage had been done. In spite of armour and mail many serious wounds had been inflicted, and some of the combatants had already been carried senseless from the field. Some of the assailants had been much shaken by being thrown backward from the ladders into the moat, one or two were hurt to death; but as few tourneys took place without the loss of several lives, this was considered but a small amount of damage for so stoutly fought a mêlée, and the knowledge that many were wounded, and some perhaps dying, in no way damped the enthusiasm of the spectators, who cheered lustily for some minutes at the triumph which the city had obtained. In the galleries occupied by the ladies and nobles of the court there was a comparative silence. But brave deeds were appreciated in those days, and although the ladies would far rather have seen the victory incline the other way, yet they waved their handkerchiefs and clapped their hands in token of their admiration at the success of an assault which, at the commencement, appeared well-nigh hopeless.

Lord Talbot rode up to the front of the royal pavilion.

"I was about to stop the fight, sire, when you gave the signal. Their blood was up, and many would have been killed had the combat continued. But the castle was fairly won, the central tower was taken and the flag pulled down, a footing had been gained at another point of the wall, and the assailants had forced their way through the sally-port. Further resistance was therefore hopeless, and the castle must be adjudged as fairly and honourably captured."

A renewed shout greeted the judge's decision. The king now ordered the rival hosts to be mustered before him as before the battle, and when this was done Earl Talbot conducted Walter up the broad steps in front of the king's pavilion. Geoffrey Ward, who had, after fastening on Walter's armour in the tent, before the sports began, taken his place among the guards at the foot of the royal pavilion, stept forward and removed Walter's helmet at the foot of the steps.

"Young sir," the king said, "you have borne yourself right gallantly to-day, and have shown that you possess the qualities which make a great captain. I do my nobles no wrong when I say that not one of them could have better planned and led the assault than you have done. Am I not right, sirs?" and he looked round. A murmur of assent rose from the knights and nobles, and the king continued: "I thought you vain and presumptuous in undertaking the assault of a fort held by an equal number, many of whom are well accustomed to war, while the lads who followed you were all untrained in strife, but you have proved that your confidence in yourself was not misplaced. The Earl of Talbot has adjudged you victor, and none can doubt what the end of the strife would have been. Take this chain from your king, who is glad to see that his citizens of London are able to hold their own even against those of our court, than whom we may say no braver exist in Europe. Kneel now to the queen of the tourney, who will bestow upon you the chaplet which you have so worthily earned."

Walter bent his knee before Edith Vernon. She rose to her feet, and with an air of pretty dignity, placed a chaplet of laurel leaves, wrought in gold and clasped with a valuable ruby, on his head.

"I present to you," she said, "the chaplet of victory, and am proud that my gage should have been worn by one who has borne himself so bravely and well. May a like success rest on all your undertakings, and may you prove a good and valiant knight!"

"Well said, Mistress Edith," Queen Philippa said smiling. "You may well be proud of your young champion. I too must have my gift," and drawing a ring set with brilliants from her finger she placed it in Walter's hand.

The lad now rose to his feet. "The prince my son," the king said, "has promised that you shall ride with his men-at-arms when he is old enough to take the field. Should you choose to abandon your craft and do so earlier I doubt not that one of my nobles, the brave Sir Walter Manny, for example, will take you before that time."

"That will I readily enough," Sir Walter said, "and glad to have so promising a youth beneath my banner."

"I would that you had been of gentle blood," the king said.

"That makes no difference, sire," Sir Walter replied. "I will place him among the young gentlemen, my pages and esquires, and am sure that they will receive him as one of themselves."

Geoffrey Ward had hitherto stood at the foot of the steps leading to the royal pavilion, but doffing his cap he now ascended. "Pardon my boldness, sire," he said to the king, "but I would fain tell you what the lad himself has hitherto been ignorant of. He is not, as he supposes, the son of Giles Fletcher, citizen and bowmaker, but is the lawfully born son of Sir Roland Somers, erst of Westerham and Hythe, who was killed in the troubles at the commencement of your majesty's reign. His wife, Dame Alice, brought the child to Giles Fletcher, whose wife had been her nurse, and dying left him in her care. Giles and his wife, if called for, can vouch for the truth of this, and can give you proofs of his birth."

Walter listened with astonishment to Geoffrey's speech. A thrill of pleasure rushed through his veins as he learned that he was of gentle blood and might hope to aspire to a place among the knights of King Edward's court. He understood now the pains which Geoffrey had bestowed in seeing that he was perfected in warlike exercises, and why both he and Giles had encouraged rather than repressed his love for martial exercises and his determination to abandon his craft and become a man-at-arms when he reached man's estate.

"Ah ! is it so?" the king exclaimed. "I remember Sir Roland Somers, and also that he was slain by Sir Hugh Spencer, who, as I heard on many hands, acted rather on a private quarrel than, as he alleged, in my interest, and there were many who avowed that the charges brought against Sir Roland were unfounded. However, this matter must be inquired into, and my High Justiciar shall see Master Giles and his wife, hear their evidence, and examine the proofs which they may bring forward. As to the estates, they were granted to Sir Jasper Vernon and cannot be restored. Nevertheless I doubt not that the youth will carve out for himself a fortune with his sword. You are his master, I suppose? I would fain pay you to cancel his apprenticeship. Sir Walter Manny has promised to enrol him among his esquires."

"I will cancel his indentures willingly, my liege," the armourer answered, "and that without payment. The lad has been to me as a son, and seeing his high spirit, and knowing the gentle blood running in his veins, I have done my best so to teach him and so to put him in the way of winning back his father's rank by his sword."

"He hath gone far towards it already," the king said, "and methinks may yet gain some share in his father's inheritance," and he glanced at little Mistress Edith Vernon and then smiled at the queen. "Well, we shall see," he went on. "Under Sir Walter Manny he will have brave chances of distinguishing himself, and when my son takes the field he shall ride with him. But I am keeping the hosts waiting. Bring hither," he said to Earl Talbot, "Clarence Aylmer."

The young noble was led up to the king. "You have done well, Clarence; though you have been worsted you fought bravely, but you were deceived by a ruse which might have taken in a more experienced captain. I trust that you will be friends with your adversary, who will be known to you henceforth as Walter Somers, son of Sir Roland of that name, and who will ride to the wars, whither you also are shortly bound, under the standard of Sir Walter Manny."

The cloud which had hung over the face of the young noble cleared. It had indeed been a bitter mortification to him that he, the son of one of the proudest of English nobles, should have been worsted by a London apprentice, and it was a relief to him to find that his opponent was one of knightly blood. He turned frankly to Walter and held out his hand. "I greet you as a comrade, sir," he said, "and hope some day that in our rivalry in the field I may do better than I have done to-day."

"That is well spoken," the king said. Then he rose and in a loud voice addressed the combatants, saying, that all had borne themselves well and bravely, and that he thanked them, not only for the rare pastime which they had made, but for the courage and boldness which had been displayed on both sides. So saying, he waved his hand as a token that the proceedings were ended, and returned with the court to Westminster; while the crowd of spectators overflowed the lists, those who had friends in the apprentice array being anxious to know how they had fared. That evening there was a banquet given by the lord-mayor. Walter was invited to be present, with Giles and Geoffrey, and many complimentary things were said to him, and he was congratulated on the prospects which awaited him. After dinner all the 'prentices who had taken part in the sports filed through the hall and were each presented with a gold piece by the lord-mayor, in the name of the corporation, for having so nobly sustained the renown of the city.

ST. GEORGE FOR ENGLAND

After the entertainment was over Walter returned with Geoffrey to the bowyer's house, and there heard from his two friends and Bertha the details of his mother's life from the time that she had been a child, and the story of her arrival with him, and her death. He had still difficulty in believing that it was all true, that Giles and Bertha, whom he had so long regarded as father and mother, were only his kind guardians, and that he was the scion of two noble families. Very warmly and gratefully he thanked his three friends for the kindness which they had shown to him, and vowed that no change of condition should ever alter his feelings of affection towards them. It was not until the late hour of nine o'clock that he said good-bye to his foster parents, for he was next day to repair to the lodging of Sir Walter Manny, who was to sail again before the week was out for the Low Countries, from which he had only returned for a few days to have private converse with the king on the state of matters there. His friends would have delivered to him his mother's ring and other tokens which she had left, but thought it better to keep these, with the other proofs of his birth, until his claim was established to the satisfaction of the lord justiciaries.

The next morning early, when Walter descended the stairs, he found Ralph Smith waiting for him. His face was strapped up with plaster and he wore his arm in a sling, for his armour had been twice cut through as he led his party in through the sally-port.

"How goes it with you, Ralph?" Walter said. "Not much the worse, I hope, for your hard knocks?"

"Not a whit," Ralph replied cheerfully, "and I shall be all right again before the week is out; but the leech made as much fuss over me as if I had been a girl, just as though one was not accustomed to hard knocks in a smithy. Those I got yesterday were not half so hard as that which you gave me the day before. My head rings yet with the thought of it. But I have not come to talk about myself. Is the story true which they tell of you, Master Walter, that you are not the son of Giles the bowyer, but of a great noble?"

THE YOUNG ESQUIRE

"Not of a great noble, Ralph, but of a gallant knight, which is just as good. My father was killed when I was three years old, and my mother brought me to Bertha, the wife of Giles the bowyer, who had been her nurse in childhood. I had forgotten all that had passed, and deemed myself the son of the good citizen, but since I have heard the truth my memory has awakened somewhat, and I have a dim recollection of a lordly castle and of my father and mother."

"And they say, Walter, that you are going with Sir Walter Manny, with the force which is just sailing to the assistance of Lady De Montford."

"That is so, Ralph, and the good knight has taken me among his esquires, young as I am, although I might well have looked for nothing better than to commence, for two years at least, as a page, seeing that I am but eighteen now. Now I shall ride with him into the battles and shall have as good a chance as the others of gaining honour and winning my spurs."

"I have made up my mind that I will go with you, Master Walter, if you will take me; each squire has a man-at-arms who serves him, and I will give you good and faithful service if you will take me with you. I spoke to the smith, my master, last night when I heard the news, and as my apprenticeship is out next week he was willing enough to give me the few days which remain. Once out of my apprenticeship I may count to be a man, and seeing that I am nineteen, and as I may say well grown of my years, methinks I am fit for service as a man-at-arms, and I would rather fight behind you than labour all my life in the smithy."

"I shall be glad indeed, Ralph, to have you with me if such be really your wish, and I do not think that Sir Walter Manny will say nay, for they have been beating up for recruits through the kingdom, and we proved yesterday that you have courage as well as strength. If he will consent I should be glad indeed to have so brave a comrade with me, so we may consider that settled, and if you will come down to

Westminster, to Sir Walter Manny's lodging, this afternoon, I will tell you what he says touching the matter. You will, of course, need arms and armour."

"I can provide that," Ralph replied, "seeing that his worshipful the lord-mayor bestowed upon me yesterday five gold pieces as the second in command in the sports. I have already a steel cap and breast and back pieces, which I have made for myself in hours of leisure, and warrant will stand as hard a knock as the Frenchmen can give them."

Going across into the city with Geoffrey, Walter purchased, with the contents of the purse which the king had given him, the garments suited for his new position. He was fortunate in obtaining some which fitted him exactly. These had been made for a young esquire of the Earl of Salisbury; but the tailor, when he heard from Geoffrey for whom they were required, and the need for instant despatch, parted with them to Walter, saying that he for whom they were made could well wait a few days, and that he would set his journeymen to work at once to make some more of similar fit and fashion.

Walter felt strange in his new attire, and by no means relished the tightness of the garments, which was strictly demanded by the fashion of the day. His long hose, one of which was of a deep maroon, the other a bright yellow, came far up above the knee, then came a short pair of trunks of similar colours divided in the middle. The tight-fitting doublet was short and circled at the waist by a buff belt mounted in silver, and was of the same colours as the hose and trunks. On his head was a cap, peaked in front; this was of maroon, with a short erect feather of yellow. The long-pointed shoes matched the rest of the costume. There were three other suits similar in fashion, but different in colour; two like the first were of cloth, the third was of white and blue silk, to be worn on grand occasions.

"You look a very pretty figure, Walter," Geoffrey said, "and will be able to hold your own among the young gallants of the court. If you lack somewhat of courtly manners it will matter not at all, since you are leaving so soon for the wars.

The dress sets off your figure, which is fully two years in advance of your age, seeing that hard work has widened you out and thickened your muscles. I need not tell you, lad, not to be quarrelsome, for that was never your way; but just at first your companions may try some jests with you, as is always the manner of young men with new-comers, but take them in a good spirit and be sure that, seeing the strength of arm and skill which you showed yesterday and the day before, none will care to push matters with you unduly."

One of the journeymen accompanied Walter to Westminster to carry up from the boat the valise with his clothes and the armour which he had worn in the sports. Sir Walter received the lad with much kindness and introduced him to his future companions. They were five in number; the eldest was a man of some thirty years old, a Hainaulter, who had accompanied Sir Walter Manny to England at the time when the latter first came over as a young squire in the suite of the Princess Philippa. He was devotedly attached to the knight, his master, and although he might several times have received the rank of knighthood for his bravery in the field, he preferred remaining in his position as esquire and faithful friend of his master.

The other four were between the ages of nineteen and twenty-one, and all belonged to the families of the highest nobility of England, it being deemed a distinguished honour to be received as a squire by the most gallant knight at the court of England. Their duties were, as Walter soon learned, almost nominal, these being discharged almost exclusively by John Mervaux. Two of the young esquires, Richard Coningsby and Edward Clifford, had fought in the mêlée, having been among the ten leaders under Clarence Aylmer. They bore no malice for the defeat, but received Walter with cordiality and kindness, as did the other young men. Walter on his arrival acquainted the knight with Ralph's wish to follow him, and requested permission for him to do so. This was readily granted, Sir Walter Manny telling the lad that although esquires were supposed to wait entirely upon themselves, to groom their horses, and keep their armour and arms bright and in good order, yet, in point of fact, young men of good families had the greater part of these duties performed for them by a retainer who rode in the ranks of their master's following as a man-at-arms.

"The other esquires have each one of their father's retainers with them, and I am glad that you should be in the same position. After you have taken your midday meal you had best go across to the Earl of Talbot's and inquire for the Lady Vernon, who is still staying with him. She told me at the king's ball last night that she wished to have speech with you, and I promised to acquaint you with her desire. By the way, dost know aught of riding?"

"I have learnt to sit on a horse, Sir Walter," the lad answered. "My good friend Geoffrey, the armourer, advised that I should learn, and frequently hired from the horse-dealer an animal for my use. I have often backed half-broken horses which were brought up by graziers from Kent and Sussex for use in the wars. Many of them abode at the hostels at Southwark, and willingly enough granted me permission to ride their horses until they were sold. Thus I have had a good deal of practice, and that of a rough kind; and seeing that latterly the horses have, for the most part, found it difficult to fling me when sitting barebacked across them, I think I could keep my seat in the high-peaked saddles on the most vicious, but I have had no practice at tilting, or at the ring, or other knightly exercises."

"That matters not at all," the knight said. "All these knightly exercises which you speak of are good in time of peace, for they give proficiency and steadiness, but in time of war he who can sit firmly in his saddle and wield sword and battle-axe lustily and skilfully is equal to the best; but never fear, when this expedition is over, and we have time for such things, I will see that you are instructed in them. One who has achieved so much martial skill as you have done at so early an age will have little difficulty in acquiring what may be termed the pastime of chivalry."

THE YOUNG ESQUIRE

Ralph arrived just as Walter was setting out. The latter presented him to the knight, who spoke with praise of the gallantry which he had displayed on the previous day, and then handed him over to John Mervaux, with instructions to enrol him as a man-at-arms among his followers, to inform him of his duties, and to place him with those who attended upon the other esquires.

After seeing Ralph disposed of, Walter went across to the Earl of Talbot and was again conducted to the presence of Dame Vernon.

"You have changed since we met last, young sir," she said with a smile, "though it is but a month since. Then you were a 'prentice boy, now you are an esquire of Sir Walter Manny, and on the highway to distinction. That you will win it I am well assured, since one who risked his life to rescue a woman and child whose very names were unknown to him is sure to turn out a noble and valiant knight. I little thought when my daughter called you her knight, that in so short a time you might become an aspirant to that honour. I hope that you do not look askance at us, now that you know I am in possession of the lands of your parents. Such changes of land, you know, often occur, but now I know who you are, I would that the estates bestowed upon Sir Jasper had belonged to some other than you; however, I trust that you will hold no grudge against us, and that you may win as fair an estate by the strength of your arm and the king's favour."

"Assuredly I feel no grudge, madam," Walter replied, "and since the lands were forfeited, am pleased that of all people they should have gone to one so kind and so fair as yourself."

"What, learning to be a flatterer already!" Dame Vernon laughed. "You are coming on fast, and I predict great things from you. And now, Edith, lay aside that sampler you are pretending to be so busy upon and speak to this knight of yours."

Edith laid down her work and came forward. She was no longer the dignified little queen of the tournament, but a laughing, bright-faced girl.

"I don't see that you are changed," she said, "except in your dress. You speak softly and naturally, just as you used to do, and not a bit like those little court fops, Uncle Talbot's pages. I am afraid you will not want to be my knight any more, now that you are going to get great honours at the war; for I heard my Uncle Talbot tell my lady mother that he was sure you would gain great credit for yourself."

"I shall be always your knight," Walter said earnestly; "I told you I should, and I never break my word. That is," he went on, colouring, "if Dame Vernon makes no objection, as she well might."

"If I did not object before, Walter," she said smiling, "why should I do so now?"

"It is different, my lady; before, it was somewhat of a jest, a sort of childish play on the part of Mistress Edith, though so far as I was concerned it was no play, but sober earnest."

"It needs no permission from me," Dame Vernon replied, "for you to wear my daughter's colours. Any knight may proclaim any lady he chooses the mistress of his heart, and a reigning beauty will often have a dozen young knights who wear her colours. However, I am well content that one who has done me such great service and who has shown such high promise should be the first to wear the gage of my little daughter, and if in after years your life fulfils the promise of your youth, and you remain true to her gage, there is none among all the youths of the court whom I would so gladly see at her feet. Remember," she said, as Walter was about to speak, "her hand will not be at my disposal, but at that of the king. His majesty is wont to bestow the hands of his wards upon those who most distinguish themselves in the field. You have already attracted his royal attention and commendation. Under Sir Walter Manny you will be sure of opportunities of distinguishing yourself, and the king may well be glad some day at once to reward your services and to repair a cruel injustice by bestowing upon you the hand of the heiress of your father's lands. If I mistake not, such a thought has even now crossed his majesty's mind, unless I misinterpreted a glance which yesterday passed between him and our sweet queen. I need not tell you to speak of your hopes to none, but let them spur you to higher exertions and nobler efforts. Loving my little Edith as I do, I naturally consider the prize to be a high one. I have often been troubled by the thought that her hand may be some day given to one by years or temper unsuited for her, and it will be a pleasure to me henceforth to picture her future connected with one who is, I am sure, by heart and nature fitted for her. And now, farewell, young sir. May God protect you in the field, and may you carry in the battle which awaits you the gage of my daughter as fairly and successfully as you did in the mimic fray of yesterday!"

CHAPTER VIII
OFF TO THE WARS

Two days later Walter started with Sir Walter Manny, with a large number of knights, squires, men-at-arms, and archers, for the Orwell. Walter was mounted, as were the other squires and men-at-arms, and indeed many of the archers. Ralph Smith, in the attire of a man-at-arms, rode behind.

Walter was in the highest spirits. A brilliant career was open to him under the most favourable circumstances; he had already distinguished himself, and had gained the attention of the highest personages in the realm, his immediate lord was one of the bravest and most chivalrous knights in Europe, and he had to sustain and encourage him the hopes that Lady Vernon had given him, of regaining some day the patrimony of his father. It was a satisfaction to him that he was as well born as those who surrounded him, and his purse was well lined as any in the company. Although he had spent the largess which had been bestowed upon him at the tournament in procuring clothes fitted for his rank, he was yet abundantly supplied with money, for both Geoffrey Ward and Giles Fletcher, having no children of their own and being both well-to-do men, had insisted upon his accepting a sum which would enable him to make a good appearance with the best.

A large number of squires followed the banner of Sir Walter Manny. The records of the time show that the barons were generally accompanied in the field by almost as many squires as men-at-arms. The former were men of good family, sons of knights and nobles, aspirants for the honour of knighthood, and sons of the smaller gentry. Many were there from pure love of a life of excitement and adventure, others in fulfilment of the feudal tenure by which all land was then held, each noble and landowner being obliged to furnish so many knights, squires, men-at-arms, and archers, in accordance with the size of his holding. The squires fought in the field in the front rank of the men-at-arms, save those who, like Walter, were attached to the person of their leader, and who in the field fought behind him or bore his orders to the companies under his banner.

In the field all drew pay, and it may be interesting in the present day to know what were the rates for which our forefathers risked their lives. They were as follows:—each horse archer received 6 deniers, each squire 12 deniers or 1 sol, each knight 2 sols, each knight banneret 4 sols. 20 sols went to the pound, and although the exact value of money in those days relative to that which it bears at the present time is doubtful, it may be placed at twelve times the present value. Therefore each horse archer received an equivalent to 6s. a day, each squire 12s., each knight 24s., and each knight banneret 48s. per day.

Upon their arrival at the Orwell, where many troops from other parts had been gathered, the expedition at once embarked on board the numerous ships which had been collected. As that in which Sir Walter sailed also carried several of his knights there was not room for all his young esquires, and Walter and the three other juniors were told off into another ship. She was a smaller vessel than most of those which composed the expedition, and only carried twelve men-at-arms and as many archers, together with the four young squires, and a knight, Sir John Powis, who was in command of the whole.

"Your craft is but a small one," the knight said to the captain.

"She is small, but she is fast," the latter answered. "She would sail round and round the best part of the fleet. I had her built according to my own fancy. Small though she be, I warrant you she will be one of the first to arrive at Hennebon, and the sooner the better say I, since I am but paid by the trip, and would fain be back again at my regular work. It pays better carrying merchants' goods between London and Holland than taking his majesty's troops over to France."

"Your speed will not be of much avail," Sir John Powis said, "seeing that the fleet will keep together."

"Yes, I know that is the order," the captain answered; "but accidents happen sometimes, you know"—and his eye twinkled. "Vessels get separated from fleets. If they happen to be slow ones so much the worse for those on board; if they happen to be fast ones so much the better, seeing that those they carry will arrive long before their comrades, and may be enabled to gain credit and renown while the others are whistling for a wind in mid-ocean. However, we shall see."

The next morning the fleet sailed from the Orwell. It contained 620 men-at-arms, among whom were many of the noblest and bravest of the country, and 6000 picked archers in the pay of the king. The whole were commanded by Sir Walter. The scene was a very gay one. The banners of the nobles and knights floated from the lofty poops, and the sun shone on bright armour and steel weapons. Walter, who had never seen the sea before, was delighted. The wind was fair, and the vessels glided smoothly along over the sea. At evening the knight and his four young companions gathered in the little cabin, for it was in the first week in March, and the night was cold.

"Will you please tell me, Sir John," Walter said to the knight, "the merits of this quarrel in which we are going to fight? I know that we are going in aid of the Countess of Montford; but why she is in a sore strait I know not."

"The matter is a mixed one, Walter, and it requires a herald to tell you all the subtleties of it. John III., Duke of Brittany, was present with his liege lord, Phillip of Valois, in the last war with England, on the border of the low country. When the English retired from before Tournay Phillip dismissed his nobles. The Duke of Burgundy was taken ill, and died at Caen, in Normandy, on the 30th of April, 1341. Arthur II., his father, had been twice married. By his first wife he had three sons, John, Guy, and Peter. John and Peter left no issue. Guy, who is also dead, left a daughter, Joan. By his second wife, Jolande de Dieux, Duke Arthur had one son, John, Count of Montford. Thus it happened, that when Duke John died, his half-brother, the Count of Montford, and Joan, daughter of his second brother Guy, were all that survived of the family. These were the rival claimants for the vacant dukedom. In England we have but one law of succession, which rules through the whole land. In France it is different. There the law of succession depends entirely upon the custom of the county, dukedom, or lordship, which is further affected both by the form of grant by which the territory was conveyed to its first feudal possessors and by the mode in which the province had been acquired by the kings of France. This is important, as upon these circumstances alone it depended whether the son or the grand-daughter of Arthur II. should inherit the dukedom.

"Joan claimed the duchy as the daughter of the elder brother. The Salic law of France, which barred females from the right of succession, and in virtue of which Phillip of Valois succeeded to the throne instead of King Edward, certainly did not obtain in Brittany. Duke John regarded Joan as his heiress, and married her to Charles of Blois, nephew of the King of France, thus strengthening her in her position; and he also induced the provincial parliament of Brittany to acknowledge her husband as his successor in the dukedom. Altogether it would seem that right is upon Joan's side; but, on the other hand, the Count of Montford the son of Jolande, a great heiress in Brittany. He is an active and energetic noble. The Bretons love not too close a connection with France, and assuredly prefer to be ruled by a duke whom they regard as one of themselves rather than by Charles of Blois, nephew of the French king. Directly Duke John was dead the Count of Montford claimed the inheritance. Assuming the title of duke he rode to Nantes, where the citizens did him homage, and then proceeded to Limoges with a large train of men-at-arms, and there took possession of the immense treasures which the late duke had accumulated in the course of a long and tranquil reign. With these sinews of war at his command he turned to Nantes, where he had left his wife the countess, who was a sister of the Count of Flanders. He immediately invited the nobility of Brittany to a grand banquet, but only one knight of any renown presented himself at the feast, the rest all holding aloof. With the wealth of which he had possessed himself he levied large forces and took the field. He first marched against Brest, where the garrison, commanded by Walter de Clisson, refused to acknowledge him. After three days' hard fighting the place was taken. Rennes was next besieged, and presently surrendered. Other towns fell into his hands, and so far as Brittany was concerned all opposition, except in one or two fortresses, ceased. In the meanwhile Charles of Blois sought assistance from his uncle the King of France; the Count de Montford, therefore, crossed to England and besought the aid of King Edward, and did homage to him as King of France. Edward, on his part, promised to assist him. The fact that Phillip was sure to espouse the opposite side was in itself sufficient to decide him; besides which, the dukes of Brittany have always been in a special way connected with England and bear the English title of Earls of Richmond.

"Believing that his journey, which had been a secret one, was unknown to the King of France, De Montford went boldly to Paris, where he had been summoned by the king to an assembly of peers called to decide upon the succession. He found, however, that Phillip had already obtained news of his journey to England. His manner convinced De Montford that it was unsafe to remain in Paris, and he secretly made his escape. Fifteen days afterwards the peers gave judgment in favour of Charles of Blois. The Dukes of Normandy, Burgundy, and Bourbon, the Counts of Alençon, Eu, and Guisnes, and many other French nobles, prepared to lead an army into the field to support Charles, and the king added a body of 3000 Genoese mercenaries in his pay.

OFF TO THE WARS

"Knowing the storm that was preparing to break upon him, De Montford put every town and castle in a state of defence. He himself, confiding in the affection of the inhabitants of Nantes, remained in that city, while his wife repaired to Rennes.

"The Duke of Normandy advanced from Angiers with an army of 5000 men-at-arms and a numerous infantry, and after capturing the castle of Chantoceaux marched to Nantes and laid siege to the city. A sortie was made by the besieged, led by Henry de Leon, but, being attacked by the whole of the French army, they were driven back into the town, a great many of the citizens being killed. A warm altercation took place between Henry de Leon and De Montford, who attributed to him the evil result of the sortie. The result was that a large number of the citizens whose friends had been captured by the French conspired to deliver up the place to Charles of Blois, and Henry de Leon also entered into private negotiations with the Duke of Normandy. De Montford, finding that he could rely neither upon the citizens nor the soldiers, surrendered to the duke on condition that his life was spared. He was sent to Paris, where he still remains a prisoner. Winter was coming on, and after putting Nantes in a fresh state of defence and leaving Charles of Blois there, the Duke of Normandy dismissed his forces, engaging them to reassemble in the spring. Had he pushed on at once he would have experienced no resistance, so great was the panic which the surrender of Nantes and the capture of De Montford had caused among the latter's partisans.

"In Rennes, especially, the deepest despondency was felt. The countess, however, showed the greatest courage and firmness. Showing herself, with her infant in her arms, she appealed to the citizens, and by her courageous bearing inspired them with new hopes. Having restored heart at Rennes she travelled from garrison to garrison throughout the province, and filled all with vigour and resolution. Feeling, however, the hopelessness of her struggle against all France, she despatched Sir Almeric de Clisson, who had lately joined her party, to England, to ask the aid which the king had promised. He arrived a month since, and, as you see, our brave king has not been long in despatching us to her aid; and now, youngsters, to bed, for methinks that the sea is rougher than it was and that the wind is getting up."

"Ay, that is it," the captain, who heard the knight's closing words, exclaimed. "We are in for a storm, and a heavy one, or my name is not Timothy Martin, and though with plenty of sea-room the *Kitty* makes not much ado about a storm more or less, it's a very different thing in the middle of a fleet of lubbery craft, which may run one down at any time. I shall edge out of them as soon as I can, you may be sure."

Before morning a serious gale was blowing, and for the next three or four days Walter and his companions knew nothing of what was going on. Then the storm abated, and they staggered out from their cabin. The sea was still high, but the sun shone brightly overhead. In front of them the land was visible. They looked round, but to their astonishment not a sail was in sight.

"Why, where is the fleet?" Walter exclaimed in astonishment.

"Snug in the Thames, I reckon," the captain said. "Soon after the storm came on one of the sailors pretended he saw the lights of recall on the admiral's ship; but I was too busy to look that way, I had enough to do to look after the safety of the ship. Anyhow, I saw no more of them."

"And what land is that ahead?" Walter asked.

"That is Brittany, young sir, and before nightfall we shall be in the port of Hennebon; as to the others, it may be days and it may be weeks before they arrive."

The lads were not sorry at the chance which had taken them to their destination before their companions and had given them a chance of distinguishing themselves. Late in the afternoon the ship dropped anchor off the castle of Hennebon, and Sir John Powis and his following were conveyed in the ship's boats to shore. The countess received them most graciously, and was delighted at the news that so strong a force was on its way to her aid.

OFF TO THE WARS

"In the absence of Sir Walter Manny, madam, I place myself and my men at your orders. Our horses will be landed the first thing in the morning, and we will then ride whithersoever you may bid us."

"Thanks, Sir John," the countess replied. "In that case I would that you ride by Rennes, towards which the army of the Duke of Normandy is already advancing. The garrison there is commanded by Sir William of Caddoudal, a good and valiant knight."

The horses were landed on the following morning, and accompanied by the four young squires and the men-at-arms, and followed by the twenty archers on foot, Sir John Powis set out for Rennes. They arrived there, but just in time, for the assailants were closing round the city. They were received with the greatest cordiality by the governor, who assigned apartments to Sir John and the squires, and lodged the men-at-arms and archers near them.

In a day or two the whole of the French army came up, and the siege commenced. Sir John Powis, at his own request, was posted with his men for the defence of a portion of the wall which was especially open to the assaults of the enemy. These soon commenced in earnest, and the Genoese and Spanish mercenaries endeavoured to carry the place by assault. Sometimes one point would be attacked, at others points far distant. Covered by the fire of the French crossbowmen, the Spaniards and Germans came on to the assault, carrying ladders, with which they strove to climb the walls, but the defenders plied them so vigorously with quarrels from their cross-bows and flights of arrows that they frequently desisted before reaching the walls. When they pushed on, and strove to ascend, their luck was no better. Great stones were hurled down, and boiling oil poured upon them. The ladders were flung back, and many crushed by the fall, and in none of the assaults did they gain any footing in the town. Machines were used, but these were not sufficiently powerful to batter down the walls, and at the end of April the city was as far from being captured as it was on the day of the commencement of the siege.

The citizens prepare to defend Hennebon.

OFF TO THE WARS

Walter bore his full share in the fighting, but he had no opportunity of especially distinguishing himself, although Sir John several times commended him for his coolness when the bolts of the crossbow-men and the stones from the machines were flying most thickly. But although as yet uninjured by the enemy's attacks, the prospect of the city holding out was not bright. The burghers, who had at first fought valiantly, were soon wearied of the strife, and of the hardships it entailed upon them. The siege had continued but a short time when they began to murmur loudly. The force under the command of the governor was but a small one, and it would have been impossible for him to resist the will of the whole population. For a time his exhortations and entreaties were attended with success, and the burghers returned to their positions on the walls; but each time the difficulty became greater, and it was clear to Caddoudal and Sir John Powis that ere long the citizens would surrender the place in spite of them. The English knight was furious at the cowardliness of the citizens, and proposed to the governor to summon twenty of the leading burghers, and to hang them as a lesson to the others; but the governor shook his head.

"I have but two hundred men on whom I can rely, including your following, Sir John. We could not keep down the inhabitants for an hour; and were we to try to do so, they would open the gates and let in the French. No; I fear that we must await the end."

The following morning Sir John was awoke with the news that in the night Caddoudal had been seized and thrown into prison by the burghers, and that a deputation of citizens had already gone out through the gate to treat with the Duke of Normandy for the surrender of the city.

The English knight was furious, but with his little band he could do nothing, especially as he found that a strong guard of burghers had been placed at the door of the apartments occupied by him and the esquires, and he was informed that he must consider himself a prisoner until the conclusion of the negotiations.

ST. GEORGE FOR ENGLAND

Cowardly and faithless as the burghers of Rennes showed themselves to be, they nevertheless stipulated with the Duke of Normandy, as one of the conditions of the surrender, that Caddoudal, Sir John Powis, and the troops under them should be permitted to pass through the French lines and go whithersoever they would. These terms were accepted. At mid-day the governor was released, and he with his men-at-arms and the band of Englishmen filed out from the city gate, and took their way unmolested through the lines of the French army to Hennebon.

They had been for a month in ignorance of all that had passed outside the walls, and had from day to day been eagerly looking for the arrival of Sir Walter Manny with his army to their relief. Once past the French lines they inquired of the peasantry, and heard to their surprise that the English fleet had not yet arrived.

"We were in luck indeed," Walter said to his companions, "that Captain Timothy Martin was in a hurry to get back to his tradings with the Flemings. Had he not been so, we should all this time have been kicking our heels and fretting on board a ship."

On nearing Hennebon, Sir William Caddoudal, with Sir John Powis and the squires, rode forward and met the countess. They were the first bearers of the news of the surrender of Rennes, and the countess was filled with consternation at the intelligence. However, after her first burst of indignation and regret had passed, she put a brave face on it.

"They shall meet with another reception at Hennebon," she said. "This is but a small place, and my garrison here, and the soldiers you have brought, will well-nigh outnumber the burghers; and we need have no fear of such faintheartedness as that which has given Nantes and Rennes into the hands of my enemy. The English aid cannot tarry long. Until it come we can assuredly hold the place."

All was now bustle in Hennebon. Sir John Powis took charge of a part of the walls, and busied himself with his men in placing the machines in position, and in preparing for defence. The countess, attired in armour, rode through the streets haranguing the townspeople. She urged the men to fight till the last, and bade the women and girls cut short their dresses so that they could the better climb the steps to the top of the walls, and that one and all should carry up stones, chalk, and baskets of lime to be cast down upon the assailants. Animated by her words and gestures, the townspeople set to work, and all vied with each other, from the oldest to the youngest, in carrying up stores of missiles to the walls. Never did Hennebon present such a scene of life and bustle. It seemed like an ant-hill which a passer-by has disturbed.

Absorbed in their work, none had time to think of the dangers which threatened them, and a stranger would rather have thought from their cheerful and animated countenances that they were preparing for a great fête than for a siege by an army to which the two chief towns in Brittany had succumbed.

Ere long the French army was seen approaching. The soldiers, who had been labouring with the rest, buckled on their armour. The citizens gathered on the walls to hurl down the piles of stones which had been collected, and all prepared for the assault.

"Sir John Powis," the countess said, "I pray you to grant me one of your esquires, who may attend me while I ride about, and may bear my messages for me. He will not be idle, nor will he escape his share of the dangers; for, believe me, I do not intend to hide myself while you and your brave soldiers are fighting for me."

"Willingly, lady," Sir John answered. "Here is Walter Somers, the son of a good knight, and himself brave and prudent beyond his years; he will, I am sure, gladly devote himself to your service."

The French, encouraged by their successes, thought that it would be a comparatively easy task to capture so small a place as Hennebon, and as soon as their camp was pitched they moved forward to the attack.

"Come with me, Master Somers," the countess said. "I will mount to one of the watch-towers, where we may see all that passes."

Walter followed her, and marvelled to see the lightness and agility with which the heroic countess, although clad in armour, mounted the rickety ladders to the summit of the watch-tower. The French bowmen opened a heavy fire upon the walls, which was answered by the shafts of the little party of English bowmen. These did much execution, for the English archers shot far harder and straighter than those of France, and it was only the best armour which could keep out their cloth-yard shafts. So small a body, however, could not check the advance of so large a force, and the French swarmed up to the very foot of the walls.

"Well done, my men!" the countess exclaimed, clapping her hands, as a shower of heavy rocks fell among the mass of the assailants, who were striving to plant their ladders, crushing many in their fall; "but you are not looking, Master Somers. What is it that you see in yonder camp to withdraw your attention from such a fight?"

"I am thinking, Countess, that the French have left their camp altogether unguarded, and that if a body of horse could make a circuit and fall upon it, the camp, with all its stores, might be destroyed before they could get back to save it."

"You are right, young sir," the countess exclaimed, "and it shall be done forthwith."

So saying, she descended the stairs rapidly and mounted her horse, which stood at the foot of the tower; then riding through the town, she collected a party of about three hundred men, bidding all she met mount their horses and join her at the gate on the opposite side to that on which the assault was taking place. Such as had no horses she ordered to take them from those in her own stables. Walter was mounted on one of the best of the count's charges. Immediately the force was collected, the gate was opened and the countess rode forth at their head. Making a considerable detour, the party rode without being observed into the rear of the French camp. Here only a few servants and horse-boys were found, these were at once killed or driven out; then all dismounting, set fire to the tents and stores; and ere the French were aware of what was going on, the whole of their camp was in flames. As soon as the conflagration was perceived, the French commanders drew off their men from the attack, and all ran at full speed towards the camp.

"We cannot regain the town," the countess said; "we will ride to Auray at full speed, and re-enter the castle when best we may."

Don Louis of Spain, who with a considerable following was fighting in the French ranks, hearing from the flying camp followers that the countess herself was at the head of the party which had destroyed the camp, instantly mounted, and with a large number of horsemen set off in hot pursuit. A few of the countess's party who were badly mounted were overtaken and slain, but the rest arrived safely at Auray, when the gates were shut in the face of their pursuers.

The blow was a heavy one for the besiegers, but they at once proceeded to build huts, showing that they had no intention of relinquishing the siege. Spies were sent from Auray, and these reported that the new camp was established on the site of the old one, and that the French evidently intended to renew the attack upon the side on which they had first commenced, leaving the other side almost unwatched.

Accordingly, on the fifth day after leaving the town, the countess prepared to return. Except Walter, none were informed of her intention, as she feared that news might be taken to the French camp by friends of Charles of Blois; but as soon as it was nightfall, and the gates were shut, the trumpet sounded to horse. In a few minutes the troop assembled in the market-place, and the countess, accompanied by Walter, placing herself at their head, rode out from the town. The strictest silence was observed. On nearing the town all were directed to dismount, to tear up the horse-cloths, and to muffle the feet of their horses. Then the journey was resumed, and so careless was the watch kept by the French that they passed through the sentries unobserved, and reached in safety the gate from which they had issued. As they neared it they were challenged from the walls, and a shout of joy was heard when Walter replied that the countess herself was present. The gates were opened and the party entered. The news of their return rapidly ran through the town, and the inhabitants, hastily attiring themselves, ran into the streets, filled with joy. Much depression had been felt during her absence, and few had entertained hopes that she would be able to re-enter the town. She had brought with her from Auray two hundred men, in addition to the party that had sallied out.

CHAPTER IX
THE SIEGE OF HENNEBON

THE besiegers of Hennebon were greatly discouraged at the success of the enterprise of the countess. They had already attempted several desperate assaults, but had each time been repulsed with very heavy loss. They now sent to Rennes for twelve of the immense machines used in battering walls, which had been left behind there on a false report of the weakness of Hennebon. Pending the arrival of these, Charles of Blois, with one division of the army, marched away to attack Auray, leaving Don Louis to carry on the siege with a force considered amply sufficient to compel its surrender after the arrival of the battering machines.

In a few days these arrived and were speedily set to work, and immense masses of stone were hurled at the walls.

Walter continued to act as the countess's especial squire. She had informed Sir William Caddoudal and Sir John Powis that it was at his suggestion that she had made the sudden attack upon the French camp, and he had gained great credit thereby.

The effect of the new machines was speedily visible. The walls crumbled under the tremendous blows, and although the archers harassed by their arrows the men working them, the French speedily erected screens which sheltered them from their fire. The spirits of the defenders began to sink rapidly, as they saw that in a very short time great breaches would be made in the walls, and that all the horrors and disasters of a city taken by assault awaited them. The Bishop of Quimper who was within the walls, entered into secret negotiations with his nephew, Henry de Leon, who had gone over to the enemy after the surrender of Nantes, and was now with the besieging army. The besiegers, delighted to find an ally within the walls who might save them from the heavy losses which an assault would entail upon them, at once embraced his offers, and promised him a large recompense if he would bring over the other commanders and nobles. The wily bishop set to work, and the consequences were soon visible. Open grumbling broke forth at the hardships which were endured, and at the prospect of the wholesale slaughter which would attend a storm when all hope of a successful resistance was at an end.

"I fear, Walter," Sir John said one morning, "that the end is at hand. On all sides submission is spoken of, and all that I can say to keep up their spirits is useless. Upon our own little band we can rely, but I doubt if outside them a single determined man is to be found in the town. In vain do I speak of the arrival of Sir Walter Manny. Nearly ninety days have elapsed since we sailed, and all hope of his coming is gone. I point out to them that contrary winds have been blowing, and that at any moment he may arrive; but they will not hear me. The bishop has gained over the whole of them by his promises that none shall be molested in property or estate should they surrender."

"It is sad to see the countess," Walter replied; "she who has shown such high spirit throughout the siege now does nothing but weep, for she knows that with her and her child in the hands of the French the cause of the count is lost. If she could carry off the child by sea she would not so much care for the fall of the town, but the French ships lie thick round the port, and there is no hope of breaking through."

Two days later the conspiracy came to a head, and the people, assembling round the countess's house, clamoured for surrender. The breaches were open, and the enemy might pour in at any time and put all to the sword. The countess begged for a little further delay, but in vain, and withdrew to the turret where she had for so many weary weeks watched the horizon, in hopes of seeing the sails of the approaching fleet. Walter was at the time with Sir John Powis on the walls.

Presently a large body of French were seen approaching headed by Henry de Leon, who summoned the town to surrender. Many standing on the walls shouted that the gates should be thrown open; but Sir John returned for answer that he must consult the countess, and that upon her answer must depend whether he and his men would defend the breach until the last.

"Come with me, Walter," he said, "we must fain persuade the countess. If she says no, we Englishmen will die in the breach; but though ready to give my life for so brave a lady, I own that it is useless to fight longer. Save our own little band not one in the town will lift a sword again. Such resistance as we can offer will but inflame them to fury, and all the horrors of a sack will be inflicted upon the inhabitants. There she is, poor lady, on the turret, gazing, as usual, seaward."

Suddenly they saw her throw up her arms, and then, turning towards the city, she cried, as she perceived the English knight: "I see them! I see them! The English fleet are coming!"

"Run up, Walter," Sir John exclaimed, "maybe the countess is distraught with her sorrows."

Walter dashed up to the turret, and looking seaward beheld rising over the horizon a number of masts.

"Hurrah ! Sir John," he shouted, "we are saved, the English fleet is in sight."

Many others heard the shout, and the tidings ran like lightning through the town. In wild excitement the people ran to the battlements and roofs, and with cheering and clapping of hands hailed the appearance of the still far-distant fleet. The church bells rang out joyfully and the whole town was wild with excitement.

The Bishop of Quimper, finding that his plans were frustrated, gathered around him some of those who had taken a leading part in the intrigue. These, leaving the city by a gate at which they had placed some of their own faction to open it to the French, issued out and made their way to the assailants' camp, to give news of the altered situation. Don

Louis at once ordered an attack to be made with his whole force, in hopes of capturing the place before the arrival of the English succour. But, animated by their new hopes, those so lately despondent and ready to yield manned the breaches and repulsed with great slaughter all attempts on the part of the French to carry them. While the struggle was still going on, the countess, aided by the wives of the burghers, busied herself in preparing a sumptuous feast in honour of her deliverers who were fast approaching, their ships impelled by a strong and favourable breeze. The vessels of the French hastily drew off, and the English fleet sailed into the port hailed by the cheers of the inhabitants. The countess herself received Sir Walter Manny on his landing, and the townspeople vied with each other in offering hospitality to the men-at-arms and archers.

"Ah! Sir John Powis," Sir Walter exclaimed, "what, are you here? I had given you up for lost. We thought you had gone down in the gale the night you started."

"We were separated from the fleet, Sir Walter, but the master held on, and we arrived here four days after we put out. We took part in the siege of Rennes, and have since done our best to aid the countess here."

"And their best has been much," the countess said; "not to say how bravely they have fought upon the walls, it is to Sir John and his little band that I owe it that the town was not surrendered days ago. They alone remained steadfast when all others fell away, and it is due to them that I am still able, as mistress of this town, to greet you on your arrival. Next to Sir John himself, my thanks are due to your young esquire, Walter Somers, who has cheered and stood by me, and to whose suggestions I owe it that I was able at the first to sally out and destroy the French camp while they were attacking the walls, and so greatly hindered their measures against the town. And now, sir, will you follow me? I have prepared for you and your knights such a banquet of welcome as our poor means will allow, and my townspeople will see that good fare is set before your soldiers."

THE SIEGE OF HENNEBON

That evening there was high feasting in the town, although the crash of the heavy stones cast by the French machines against the walls never ceased. Early the next morning Sir Walter Manny made a survey of the place and of the disposition of the enemy, and proposed to his knights to sally forth at once and destroy the largest of the enemy's machines, which had been brought up close to the walls. In a few minutes the knights were armed and mounted. Three hundred knights and esquires were to take part in the sortie, they were to be followed by a strong body of men-at-arms.

As soon as the gates were opened a number of archers issued out, and taking their place at the edge of the moat, poured a rain of arrows upon the men working the machine and those guarding it. Most of these took to flight at once, the remainder were cut down by the men-at-arms, who at once proceeded to hew the machine in pieces with the axes with which they were provided. Sir Walter himself and his mounted companions dashed forward to the nearer tents of the French camps, cut down all who opposed them, and setting fire to the huts retired towards the city.

By this time the French were thoroughly alarmed, and numbers of knights and men-at-arms dashed after the little body of English cavalry. These could have regained the place in safety, but in the chivalrous spirit of the time they disdained to retire without striking a blow. Turning their horses, therefore, and laying their lances in rest, they charged the pursuing French.

For a few minutes the conflict was desperate and many on both sides were overthrown; then, as large reinforcements were continually arriving to the French, Sir Walter called off his men and retired slowly. On reaching the moat he halted his forces. The knights wheeled and presented a firm face to the enemy, covering the entrance of their followers into the gate. The French chivalry thundered down upon the little body, but were met by a storm of arrows from the archers lining the moat. Many knights were struck through the bars of their vizors or the joints of their mail. The horses, though defended by iron trappings, fell dead under them, or, maddened by pain, dashed wildly through the ranks, carrying confusion with them, and the French commanders, seeing how heavy were their losses, called off their men from the assault. Sir Walter Manny with his party remained without the gate until the enemy had re-entered their camp, and then rode into the town amid the acclamations of the inhabitants, the countess herself meeting her deliverers at the gate and kissing each, one after the other, in token of her gratitude and admiration.

The arrival of the reinforcements and the proof of skill and vigour given by the English leader, together with the terror caused by the terrible effect of the English arrows, shook the resolution of Don Louis and his troops. Deprived of half their force by the absence of Charles of Blois, it was thought prudent by the leaders to withdraw at once, and the third morning after the arrival of Sir Walter Manny the siege was raised, and the French marched to join Charles of Blois before the Castle of Auray.

Even with the reinforcements brought by Sir Walter Manny, the forces of the Countess of Montford were still so greatly inferior to those of the divisions of the French army that they could not hope to cope with them in the field until the arrival of the main English army, which the King of England himself was to bring over shortly. Accordingly the French laid siege to and captured many small towns and castles. Charles of Blois continued the siege of Auray, and directed Don Louis with his division to attack the town of Dinan. On his way the Spaniard captured the small fortress of Conquet and put the garrison to the sword. Sir Walter Manny, in spite of the inferiority of his force, sallied out to relieve it, but it was taken before his arrival, and Don Louis had marched away to Dinan, leaving a small garrison in Conquet. It was again captured by Sir Walter, but finding it indefensible he returned with the whole of his force to Hennebon. Don Louis captured Dinan and then besieged Guerande. Here he met with a vigorous resistance, but carried it by storm, and gave it up to be pillaged by his soldiers. He now sent back to Charles of Blois the greater part of the French troops who accompanied him, and embarked with the Genoese and Spanish, 8000 in number, and sailed to Quimperlé, a rich and populous town in Lower Brittany.

Anchoring in the River Leita, he disembarked his troops, and leaving a guard to protect the vessels marched to the interior, plundering and burning, and from time to time despatching his booty to swell the immense mass which had brought in his ships from the sack of Guerande.

Quimperlé lies but a short distance from Hennebon, and Sir Walter Manny with Almeric de Clisson, a number of English knights, and a body of English archers, in all three thousand men, embarked in the ships in the port, and entering the Leita captured the enemy's fleet and all his treasure. The English then landed, and dividing into three bodies, set out in search of the enemy.

The English columns marched at a short distance apart so as to be able to give each other assistance in case of attack. The news of the English approach soon reached the Spaniards, who were gathered in a solid body, for the enraged country people, armed with clubs and bills, hung on their flanks and cut off any stragglers who left the main body. Don Louis at once moved towards the sea-coast, and coming in sight of one of the English divisions, charged it with his whole force.

The English fought desperately, but the odds of seven to one were too great, and they would have been overpowered had not the other two divisions arrived on the spot and fallen upon the enemy's flanks. After a severe and prolonged struggle the Genoese and Spaniards were completely routed. The armed peasantry slew every fugitive they could overtake, and of the 7000 men with whom Don Louis commenced the battle only 300 accompanied him in his flight to Rennes, the troops of Sir Walter and de Clisson pursuing him to the very gates of that city. Sir Walter marched back with his force to the ships, but finding the wind unfavourable returned to Hennebon by land, capturing by the way the castle of Goy la Forèt. Their return was joyfully welcomed, not only for the victory which they had achieved, but because the enemy was again drawing near to the town. Auray had fallen. The brave garrison, after existing for some time upon the flesh of their horses, had endeavoured to cut their way through the besiegers. Most of them were killed in the attempt, but a few escaped and made their way to Hennebon.

Vannes, an important town, and Carhaix quickly surrendered, and the French force was daily receiving considerable reinforcements. This arose from the fact that large numbers of French nobles and knights had, with their followers, taken part with Alfonso, King of Castile and Leon, in his war with the Moors. This had just terminated with the expulsion of the latter from Spain, and the French knights and nobles on their way home for the most part joined at once in the war which their countrymen were waging in Bretagne.

Seeing the great force which was gathering for a fresh siege of Hennebon, Sir Walter Manny and the Countess of Montford sent an urgent message to King Edward for further support. The king was not yet ready, but at the beginning of August he despatched a force under the command of the Earl of Northampton and Robert of Artois. It consisted of twenty-seven knights bannerets and 2000 men-at-arms. Before, however, it could reach Hennebon the second siege of that city had begun. Charles of Blois had approached it with a far larger army than that with which he had on the first occasion sat down before it. Hennebon was, however, much better prepared than at first for resistance. The walls had been repaired, provisions and military stores laid up, and machines constructed. The garrison was very much larger, and was commanded by one of the most gallant knights of the age, and the citizens beheld undaunted the approach of the great French army.

Four days after the French had arrived before Hennebon they were joined by Don Louis, who had been severely wounded in the fight near Quimperé, and had lain for six weeks at Rennes. Sixteen great engines at once began to cast stones against the walls, but Sir Walter caused sandbags to be lowered, and so protected the walls from the attack that little damage was done. The garrison confident in their powers to resist, taunted the assailants from the walls, and specially enraged the Spaniards and Don Louis by allusions to the defeat at Quimperlé.

So furious did the Spanish prince become that he took a step unprecedented in those days of chivalry. He one morning entered the tent of Charles of Blois, where a number of French nobles were gathered, and demanded a boon in requital of all his services. Charles at once assented, when, to his surprise and horror, Prince Louis demanded that two English knights, Sir John Butler and Sir Hubert Frisnoy, who had been captured in the course of the campaign and were kept prisoners at Faouet, should be delivered to him to be executed. "These English," he said, "have pursued, discomforted, and wounded me, and have killed the nephew whom I loved so well, and as I have none other mode of vengeance I will cut off their heads before their companions who lie within those walls."

Charles of Blois and his nobles were struck with amazement and horror at the demand, and used every means in their power to turn the savage prince from his purpose, but in vain. They pointed out to him that his name would be dishonoured in all countries where the laws of chivalry prevailed by such a deed, and besought him to choose some other boon. Don Louis refused to yield, and Charles of Blois, finding no alternative between breaking his promise and delivering his prisoners, at last agreed to his request.

The prisoners were sent for, and were informed by Don Louis himself of their approaching end. At first they could not believe that he was in earnest, for such a proceeding was so utterly opposed to the spirit of the times that it seemed impossible to them. Finding that he was in earnest they warned him of the eternal stain which such a deed would bring upon his name. The Spaniard, however, was unmoved either by their words or by the entreaties of the French nobles but told them that he would give them a few hours to prepare for death, and that they should be executed in sight of the walls after the usual dinner hour of the army.

In those days sieges were not conducted in the strict manner in which they are at present, and non-combatants passed without difficulty to and fro between town and camp. The news, therefore, of what was intended speedily reached the garrison, whom it filled with indignation and horror. A council was immediately called, and Sir Walter Manny proposed a plan, which was instantly adopted.

Without loss of time Almeric de Clisson issued forth from the great gate of Hennebon, accompanied by 300 men-at-arms and 1000 archers. The latter took post at once along the edge of the ditches. The men-at-arms rode straight for the enemy's camp, which was undefended, the whole army being within their tents at dinner. Dashing into their midst the English and Breton men-at-arms began to overthrow the tents and spear all that were in them. Not knowing the extent of the danger or the smallness of the attacking force, the French knights sprang up from table, mounted, and rode to encounter the assailants.

For some time these maintained their ground against all assaults until, finding that the whole army was upon them, Almeric de Clisson gave order for his troop to retire slowly upon the town. Fighting every step of the ground and resisting obstinately the repeated onslaught of the French, Clisson approached the gate. Here he was joined by the archers, who with bent bows prepared to resist the advance of the French. As it appeared that the garrison were prepared to give battle outside the walls, the whole French army prepared to move against them.

In the meantime Sir Walter Manny, with 100 men-at-arms and 500 horse archers, issued by a sally-port on the other side of the town, and with all speed rode round to the rear of the French camp. There he found none to oppose him save servants and camp-followers, and making his way straight to the tent of Charles of Blois, where the two knights were confined, he soon freed them from their bonds. They were mounted without wasting a moment's time upon two spare horses, and turning again the whole party rode back towards Hennebon, and had reached the postern gate before the fugitives from the camp reached the French commanders and told them what had happened.

Seeing that he was now too late, because of De Clisson's sortie, Charles of Blois recalled his army from the attack, in which he could only have suffered heavily from the arrows of the archers and the missiles from the walls. The same day, he learned from some prisoners captured in the sortie, of the undiminished spirit of the garrison, and that Hennebon was amply supplied with provisions brought by sea. His own army was becoming straitened by the scarcity of supplies in the country round, he therefore determined at once to raise the siege, and to besiege some place where he would encounter less serious resistance.

Accordingly, next morning he drew off his army and marched to Carhaix.

Shortly afterwards the news came that the Earl of Northampton and Robert of Artois, with their force, had sailed, and Don Louis, with the Genoese and other Italian mercenaries, started to intercept them with a large fleet. The fleets met off the island of Guernsey, and a severe engagement took place, which lasted till night. During the darkness a tremendous storm burst upon them and the combatants separated. The English succeeded in making their way to Brittany and landed near Vannes. The Spaniards captured four small ships which had been separated in the storm from their consorts, but did not succeed in regaining the coast of Brittany, being driven south by the storm as far as Spain. The Earl of Northampton at once laid siege to Vannes, and Sir Walter Manny moved with every man that could be spared from Hennebon to assist him.

As it was certain that the French army would press forward with all speed to relieve the town, it was decided to lose no time in battering the walls, but to attempt to carry it at once by assault. The walls, however, were so strong that there seemed little prospect of success attending such an attempt, and a plan was therefore determined upon by which the enemy might be thrown off their guard. The assault commenced at three points in the early morning and was continued all day. No great vigour, however, was shown in these attempts which were repulsed at all points.

At nightfall the assailants drew off to their camp, and Oliver de Clisson, who commanded the town, suffered his weary troops to quit the walls and to seek for refreshment and repose. The assailants, however, did not disarm, but after a sufficient time had elapsed to allow the garrison to lay aside their armour two strong parties attacked the principal gates of the town, while Sir Walter Manny and the Earl of Oxford moved round to the opposite side with ladders for an escalade. The plan was successful. The garrison, snatching up their arms, hurried to repel their attack upon the gates, every man hastening in that direction. Sir Walter Manny with his party were therefore enabled to mount the walls unobserved and make their way into the town; here they fell upon the defenders in the rear, and the sudden onslaught spread confusion and terror among them. The parties at the gates forced their way in and joined their friends, and the whole of the garrison were killed or taken prisoners, save a few, including Oliver Clisson, who made their escape by sally-ports. Robert of Artois, with the Earl of Stafford, was left with a garrison to hold the town. The Earl of Salisbury, with four thousand men, proceeded to lay siege to Rennes, and Sir Walter Manny hastened back to Hennebon.

Some of Sir Walter's men formed part of the garrison of Vannes, and among these was Sir John Powis with a hundred men-at-arms.

The knight had been so pleased with Walter's coolness and courage at the siege at Hennebon that he requested Sir Walter to leave him with him at Vannes. "It is possible," he said to Walter, "that we may have fighting here. Methinks that Sir Walter would have done better to leave a stronger force. The town is a large one, and the inhabitants ill-disposed towards us. Oliver Clisson and the French nobles will feel their honour wounded at the way in which we outwitted them, and will likely enough make an effort to regain the town. However, Rennes and Hennebon are not far away, and we may look for speedy aid from the Earl of Salisbury and Sir Walter should occasion arise."

Sir John's previsions were speedily verified. Oliver Clisson and his friends were determined to wipe out their defeat, and scattered through the country raising volunteers from among the soldiery in all the neighbouring towns and castles, and a month after Vannes was taken they suddenly appeared before the town with an army of 12,000 men, commanded by Beaumanoir, marshal of Bretagne for Charles of Blois. The same reasons which had induced the Earl of Northampton to decide upon a speedy assault instead of the slow process of breaching the walls, actuated the French in pursuing the same course, and, divided into a number of storming parties, the army advanced at once to the assault on the walls. The little garrison prepared for the defence.

"The outlook is bad, Walter," Sir John Powis said. "These men approach with an air of resolution which shows that they are bent upon success. They outnumber us by twelve to one, and it is likely enough that the citizens may rise and attack us in the rear. They have been ordered to bring the stones for the machines to the walls, but no one has laid his hand to the work. We must do our duty as brave men, my lad, but I doubt me if yonder is not the last sun which we shall see. Furious as the French are at our recent success here you may be sure that little quarter will given."

CHAPTER X
A PLACE OF REFUGE

THE French, excited to the utmost by the exhortations of their commanders, and by their desire to wipe out the disgrace of the easy capture of Vannes by the English, advanced with ardour to the assault, and officers and men vied with each other in the valour which they displayed. In vain did the garrison shower arrows and cross-bow bolts among them, and pour down burning oil and quicklime upon them as they thronged at the foot of the wall. In vain were the ladders, time after time, hurled back loaded with men upon the mass below. The efforts of the men-at-arms to scale the defences were seconded by their archers and crossbow-men, who shot such a storm of bolts that great numbers of the defenders were killed. The assault was made at a score of different points, and the garrison was too weak to defend all with success. Sir John Powis and his party repulsed over and over again the efforts of the assailants against that part of the wall entrusted to them, but at other points the French gained a footing, and swarming up rushed along the walls, slaying all whom they encountered.

"All is lost," Sir John exclaimed; "let us fall back to the castle and die fighting there."

Descending from the wall the party made their way through the streets. The French were already in the town; every house was closed and barred, and from the upper windows the burghers hurled down stones and bricks upon the fugitives, while parties of the French soldiers fell upon them fiercely. Many threw down their arms and cried for quarter, but were instantly slain.

A PLACE OF REFUGE

For a while the streets were a scene of wild confusion; here and there little knots of Englishmen stood together and defended themselves until the last, others ran through the streets chased by their exulting foes, some tried in vain to gain shelter in the houses. Sir John Powis's band was soon broken and scattered, and their leader slain by a heavy stone from a housetop. Walter fought his way blindly forward towards the castle although he well knew that no refuge would be found there. Ralph Smith kept close beside him, levelling many of his assailants with the tremendous blows of a huge mace. Somehow, Walter hardly knew how, they made their way through their assailants and dashed in at the castle gate. A crowd of their assailants were close upon their heels. Walter glanced round; dashing across the courtyard he ran through some passages into an inner yard, in which, as he knew, was the well. The bucket hung at the windlass.

"Catch hold, Ralph!" he exclaimed; "there is just a chance, and we may as well be drowned as killed." They grasped the rope and jumped off. The bucket began to descend with frightful velocity. Faster and faster it went and yet it seemed a long time before they plunged into the water, which was nigh a hundred feet below the surface. Fortunately the rope was considerably longer than was necessary, and they sank many feet into the water, still retaining their hold. Then clinging to the rope they hauled themselves to the surface.

"We cannot hold on here five minutes," Ralph exclaimed, "my armour is dragging me down."

"We will soon get rid of that," Walter said.

"There go our helmets; now I will hold on with one hand and help you to unbuckle your breast and back pieces; you do the same for me."

With great efforts they managed to rid themselves of their armour, and then held on with ease to the rope. They hauled the bucket to the surface and tied a knot in the slack of the rope, so that the bucket hung four feet below the level of the water. Putting their feet in this, they were able to stand with their heads above the surface without difficulty.

"This is a nice fix," Ralph exclaimed. "I think it would have been just as well to have been killed at once. They are sure to find us here, and if they don't we shall die of cold before to-morrow morning."

"I don't think they will find us," Walter said cheerfully. "When they have searched the castle thoroughly it may occur to some of them that we have jumped down the well, but it will be no particular business of anyone to look for us, and they will all be too anxious to get at the wine butts to trouble their heads about the matter; besides, it must be a heavy job to wind up this bucket, and it is not likely there will be such urgent need of water that anyone will undertake the task."

"But we are no better off if they don't," Ralph remarked, "for we must die here if we are not hauled out. I suppose you don't intend to try and climb that rope. I might do twenty feet or so on a pinch, but I could no more get up to the top there than I could fly."

"We must think it over," Walter rejoined; "where there is a will there is a way, you know. We will take it by turns to watch that little patch of light overhead; if we see anyone looking down we must leave the bucket and swim to the side without making the least noise. They may give a few turns of the windlass to see if anyone has hold of the rope below; be sure you do not make the slightest splashing or noise, for the sound would be heard above to a certainty."

Ten minutes later they saw two heads appear above, and instantly withdrew their feet from the bucket and made a stroke to the side, which was but four feet distant, being careful as they did that no motion was imparted to the rope. Then though it was too dark to see anything, they heard the bucket lifted from the water. A minute later it fell back again with a splash, then all was quiet.

"We are safe now, and can take our place in the bucket. They are satisfied that if we did jump down here we are drowned. And now we must think about climbing up."

"Ay, that will require a good deal of thinking," Ralph grumbled.

A PLACE OF REFUGE

For some time there was silence; then Walter said, "The first thing to do is to cut off the slack of the rope, there are some twelve feet of it. Then we will unwind the strands of that. There are five or six large strands as far as I can feel; we will cut them up into lengths of about a couple of feet and we ought to be able to tie these to the rope in such a way as not to slip down with our weight. If we tie them four feet apart we can go up step by step; I don't see much difficulty about that."

"No," Ralph said much more cheerfully, "I should think that we could manage that."

They at once set to work. The rope was cut up and unravelled, and the strands cut into pieces about two feet long. They then both set to work trying to discover some way of fastening it by which it would not slip down the rope. They made many fruitless attempts; each time that a strand was fastened with a loop large enough for them to pass a leg through, it slid down the rope when their weight was applied to it. At last they succeeded in finding out a knot which would hold. This was done by tying a knot close to one end of a piece of the strand, then sufficient was left to form the loop, and the remainder was wound round the rope in such a way that the weight only served to tighten its hold.

"Shall we begin at once?" Ralph said, when success was achieved.

"No, we had better wait until nightfall. The vibration of the rope when our weight once gets on it might be noticed by anyone crossing the courtyard."

"Do you think we have sufficient bits of rope," Ralph asked.

"Just enough, I think," Walter replied; "there were six strands, and each has made six pieces, so we have thirty-six. I know the well is about a hundred feet deep, for the other day I heard some of the soldiers who were drawing water grumbling over the labour required. So if we put them three feet apart it will take thirty-three of them, which will leave three over; but we had better place them a little over a yard so as to make sure."

In a short time the fading brightness of the circle of light far overhead told them that twilight had commenced, and shortly afterwards they attached the first strand to the rope some three feet above the water.

"Now," Walter said, "I will go first, at anyrate for a time. I must put one leg through the loop, and sit, as it were, while I fasten the one above, as I shall want both hands for the work. You will find it a good deal easier to stand with your foot in the loop. If I get tired I will fasten another loop by the side of that on which I am resting, so you can come up and pass me. There is no hurry. It ought not to take up above an hour, and it will not do for us to get to the top until the place becomes a little quiet. To-night they are sure to be drinking and feasting over their victory until late."

They now set to work, and step by step mounted the rope. They found the work less arduous than they had expected. The rope was dry, and the strands held tightly to it. Two or three times they changed places, resting in turn from the work; but in less than two hours from the time they made the first loop Walter's head and shoulders appeared above the level of the courtyard. He could hear sounds of shouting and singing within the castle, and knew that a great feast was going on. Descending a step or two he held parley with Ralph.

"I think, perhaps, it will be better to sally out at once. Everyone is intent on his own pleasure, and we shall have no difficulty in slipping out of the castle unnoticed. All will be feasting and riot in the town, and so long as we do not brush against any one so that they may feel our wet garments we are little likely to be noticed; besides, the gates of the town will stand open late, for people from the villages round will have come in to join in the revels."

"I am ready to try it, Master Walter," Ralph replied, "for I ache from head to foot with holding on to this rope. The sooner the better, say I."

A PLACE OF REFUGE

In another minute both stood in the courtyard. It was a retired spot, and none were passing. Going along the passage they issued into the main yard. Here great fires were blazing, and groups of men sat round them drinking and shouting. Many lay about in drunken sleep.

"Stay where you are in the shade, Ralph. You had best lie down by the foot of the wall. Anyone who passes will think that you are in a drunken sleep. I will creep forward and possess myself of the steel caps of two of these drunkards, and if I can get a couple of cloaks so much the better."

There was no difficulty about the caps, and by dint of unbuckling the cloaks and rolling their wearers gently over, Walter succeeded at last in obtaining two of them. He also picked up a sword for Ralph—his own still hung in its sheath—and then he joined his companion, and the two putting on the steel caps and cloaks walked quietly to the gate. There were none on guard, and they issued unmolested into the town. Here all was revelry. Bonfires blazed in the streets. Hogsheads of wine, with the heads knocked out, stood before many of the houses for all to help themselves who wished. Drunken soldiers reeled along shouting snatches of songs, and the burghers in the highest state of hilarity thronged the ways.

"First of all, Ralph, we will have a drink of wine, for I am chilled to the bone."

"Ay, and so am I," Ralph replied. "I got hot enough climbing that rope, but now the cold has got hold of me again, and my teeth are chattering in my head."

Picking up one of the fallen vessels by a cask they dipped it in and took a long draught of wine; then, turning off from the principal streets, they made their way by quiet lanes down to one of the gates. To their dismay they found that this was closed. The French commanders knew that Sir Walter Manny or Salisbury might ere this be pressing forward to relieve the town, and that, finding that it had fallen, they might attempt to recapture it by a sudden attack. While permitting therefore the usual licence, after a successful assault, to the main body of their forces, they had placed a certain number of their best troops on the walls, giving them a handsome largess to make up for their loss of the festivities.

At first Walter and his friend feared that their retreat was cut off for the night, but several other people presently arrived, and the officer on guard said, coming out, "You must wait a while; the last batch have only just gone, and I cannot keep opening and closing the gate; in half an hour I will let you out."

Before that time elapsed some fifty or sixty people, anxious to return to their villages, gathered round the gate.

"Best lay aside your steel cap, Ralph, before we join them," Walter said. "In the dim light of that lamp none will notice that we have head-gear, but if it were to glint upon the steel cap the officer might take us for deserters and question us as to who we are."

Presently the officer came out from the guard-room again. There was a forward movement of the little crowd, and Walter and Ralph closed in to their midst. The gates were opened, and without any question the villagers passed out, and the gates were shut instantly behind them.

Walter and his comrade at once started at a brisk pace and walked all night in the direction of Hennebon. Their clothes soon dried, and elated at their escape from danger they struggled on briskly. When morning broke they entered a wood, and lay there till evening, as they feared to continue their journey lest they might fall into the hands of some roving band of French horse. They were, too, dog-tired, and were asleep a few minutes after they lay down. The sun was setting when they awoke, and as soon as it was dark they resumed their journey.

"I don't know what you feel, Master Walter, but I am well-nigh famished. It is thirty-six hours since I swallowed a bit of food, just as the French were moving to the attack. Hard blows I don't mind—I have been used to it; but what with fighting, and being in the water for five or six hours, and climbing up that endless rope, and walking all night on an empty stomach, it does not suit me at all."

"I feel ravenous too, Ralph, but there is no help for it. We shall eat nothing till we are within the walls of Hennebon, and that will be by daylight to-morrow if all goes well. Draw your belt an inch or two tighter, it will help to keep out the wolf."

They kept on all night, and in the morning saw to their delight the towers of Hennebon in the distance. It was well that it was no further, for both were so exhausted from want of food that they could with difficulty drag their legs along.

Upon entering the town Walter made his way at once to the quarters of the leader. Sir Walter had just risen, and was delighted at the sight of his esquire.

"I had given you up for dead," he exclaimed. "By what miracle could you have escaped? Are you alone?"

"I have with me only my faithful follower Ralph Smith, who is below; but, Sir Walter, for mercy's sake order that some food be placed before us, or we shall have escaped from the French only to die of hunger here. We have tasted nought since the attack on Vannes began. Have any beside us escaped?"

"Lord Stafford contrived, with two or three others, to cut their way out by a postern-gate, bringing with them Robert of Artois, who is grievously wounded. None others, save you and your man-at-arms, have made their way here."

In a few minutes a cold capon, several manchets of bread, and a stoop of wine were placed before Walter, while Ralph's wants were attended to below. When he had satisfied his hunger the young esquire related his adventures to Sir Walter and several other knights and nobles, who had by this time gathered in the room.

"In faith, Master Somers, you have got well out of your scrape," Sir Walter exclaimed. "Had I been in your place I should assuredly have perished, for I would a thousand times rather meet death sword in hand, than drop down into the deep hole of that well. And your brains served you shrewdly in devising a method of escape. What say you, gentlemen?"

All present joined in expressions of praise at the lad's coolness and presence of mind.

"You are doing well, young sir," the English leader went on, "and have distinguished yourself on each occasion on which we have been engaged. I shall be proud when the time comes to bestow upon you myself the order of knighthood if our king does not take the matter off my hands."

A little later Robert of Artois died of his wounds and disappointment at the failure of his hopes.

In October King Edward himself set sail with a great army, and landing in Brittany early in November marched forward through the country and soon reduced Ploermel, Malestrail, Redon, and the rest of the province in the vicinity of Vannes, and then laid siege to that town. As his force was far more than sufficient for the siege, the Earls of Norfolk and Warwick were despatched in the direction of Nantes to reconnoitre the country and clear it of any small bodies of the enemy they might encounter. In the meantime Edward opened negotiations with many of the Breton lords, who, seeing that such powerful aid had arrived for the cause of the Countess of Montford, were easily persuaded to change sides. Among them were the lords of Clisson, Moheac, Machecoul, Retz, and many others of less importance.

The Count of Valentinois, who commanded the garrison of Vannes, supported the siege with great courage and fortitude, knowing that Charles of Blois and the King of France were collecting a great army for his relief. Uniting their forces they advanced towards the town. Before the force of the French, 40,000 strong, the Earl of Norfolk had fallen back and rejoined the king, but even after this junction the French forces exceeded those of Edward fourfold. They advanced towards Vannes and formed a large entrenched camp near that of the English, who thus, while still besieging Vannes, were themselves enclosed by a vastly superior force. The King of France himself arrived at the French camp. The French, although so greatly superior, made no motion toward attacking the English, but appeared bent upon either starving them out or forcing them to attack the strongly entrenched position occupied by the French.

A PLACE OF REFUGE

Provisions were indeed running short in the English camp, and the arrival of supplies from England was cut off by a strong fleet under Don Louis, which cruised off the coast and captured all vessels arriving with stores. At this moment two legates, the Cardinal Bishop of Preneste and the Cardinal Bishop of Tusculum, arrived from the pope and strove to mediate between the two sovereigns and to bring about a cessation of hostilities, pointing out to them the scandal and desolation which their rivalry caused in Christendom, the waste of noble lives, the devastation of once happy provinces, and the effusion of innocent blood. Going from camp to camp they exhorted, prayed, and reproached the rival sovereigns, urging that while Christians were shedding each other's blood in vain, the infidels were daily waxing bolder and more insolent. Their arguments would have been but of little use had either of the monarchs felt sure of victory. King Edward, however, felt that his position was growing desperate, for starvation was staring him in the face, and by a victory over an immensely superior force in a strongly entrenched position could he extricate himself. Upon the part of the French, however circumstances were occurring which rendered them anxious for a release from their position, for they were not without their share of suffering. While the English army lay on a hill the French camp was pitched on low ground. An unusually wet season had set in with bitterly cold wind. The rain was incessant, a pestilence had destroyed a vast number of their horses, and their encampment was flooded. Their forces were therefore obligated to spread themselves over the neighbouring fields, and a sudden attack by the English might have been fatal.

Thus distress pressed upon both commanders, and the pope's legates found their exertions at last crowned with success. A suspension of hostilities was agreed to, and the Dukes of Burgundy and Bourbon on the one side and the Earls of Lancaster, Northampton, and Salisbury on the other, met as commissioners and agreed to a convention by which a general truce was to be made from the date of the treaty to the following Michaelmas, and to be prolonged from that day for the full term of three years. It was agreed that the truce should embrace not only the sovereigns, but all the adherents of each of them. The truce was to hold good in Brittany between all parties, and the city of Vannes was to be given into the hands of the cardinals to dispose of as they chose. It was specially provided that in the case of any of the adherents of either party in the Duchies of Gascony and Brittany waging war against each other, neither of the monarchs should either directly or indirectly meddle therewith, nor should the truce be at all broken thereby.

Immediately the treaty was signed, on the 19th of January, 1343, the King of France dismissed his army, and Edward sailed for England with the greater part of his troops. The Countess of Montford and her son accompanied him, and the possessions of her husband in Brittany were left to the guardianship of her partisans, with a small but choice body of English troops.

The towns which had fallen into their hands and still remained were Brest, Quimper-Corentin, Quimperlé, Redon, and Guerande; Vannes was handed over to them by the cardinals, and Hennebon, of course, remained in their possession.

Walter returned to England with Sir Walter Manny, and on reaching London was received with delight by his old friends Geoffrey Ward and Giles Fletcher, who were never tired of listening to his tales of the wars. Dame Vernon also received him with great kindness, and congratulated him warmly upon the very favourable account which Sir Walter Manny had given of his zeal and gallantry.

The time now for a while passed very quietly. Walter and the other young squires practised diligently, under the instructions of Sir Walter, at knightly exercises. Walter learned to bear himself well on horseback and to tilt in the ring. He was already a skilful swordsman, but he spared no pains to improve himself with his weapons. The court was a gay one, and Walter, as a favoured esquire of one of the foremost knights there, was admitted to all that took place. His courtly education, of course, included dancing, and when he went down, as he often did, for a long chat with his old friends, Geoffrey often said, laughing, that he was growing such a fine gentleman that he hardly liked to sit in his presence; but although changed in manner, Walter continued to be, as before, a frank, manly young fellow, and free from the affectations which were so general among the young men of the court.

CHAPTER XI
A STORMY INTERVIEW

SOON after Walter's return from France Dame Vernon returned to her country estate, and a year passed before he again saw her. During this time the truce which had been established between England and France had remained unbroken. It was certain, however, that ere long the two powers would again come to blows. The King of England had honourably observed the terms of the treaty. Upon his return home he had entirely disbanded his army and had devoted his whole attention to increasing the trade and prosperity of the country. The measures which he took to do this were not always popular with the people of England, for seeing how greatly they excelled the English manufacturers Edward encouraged large numbers of Flemings and other foreign workmen to settle in London, and gave them many privileges to induce them to do so; this the populace strongly resented. There was a strong ill feeling against the Flemings and serious popular riots took place, for the English traders and workmen considered that these foreigners were taking the bread from their mouths. The king, however, was wiser than his people, he saw that although the English weavers were able to produce coarse cloths, yet that all of the finer sort had to be imported from the Continent. He deemed that in time the Flemings would teach their art to his subjects, and that England would come to vie with the Low Countries in the quality of her produce. Such was indeed afterwards the case, and England gained greatly by the importation of the industrious Flemings, just as she afterwards profited from the expulsion from France of tens of thousands of Protestant workmen who brought here many of the manufactures of which France had before the monopoly. The relations between England and the Flemings were at this time very close, for the latter regarded England as her protector against the ambition of the King of France.

But while King Edward had laid aside all thought of war, such was not the case with Phillip of Valois. He had retired after the signature of the treaty full of rage and humiliation; for hitherto in all their struggles his English rival had had the better of him, and against vastly superior forces had foiled all his efforts and had gained alike glory and military advantage. King Edward had hardly set sail when Phillip began to break the terms of truce by inciting the adherents of Charles of Blois to attack those of De Montford, and by rendering assistance to them with money and men. He also left no means untried to detach Flanders from its alliance with England. Several castles and towns in Brittany were wrested from the partisans of De Montford, and King Edward, after many remonstrances at the breaches of the conditions of the truce, began again to make preparations for taking the field. Several brilliant tournaments were held and every means were taken to stir up the warlike spirit of the people.

One day Walter had attended his lord to the palace and was waiting in the anteroom with many other squires and gentlemen, while Sir Walter, with some other noblemen, was closeted with the king, discussing the means to be adopted for raising funds for a renewal of a war with France, when a knight entered whom Walter had not previously seen at court.

"Who is that?" he asked one of his acquaintances; "methinks I know his face, though it passes my memory to say where I have seen it."

"He has been away from England for some two years," his friend answered. "That is Sir James Carnegie; he is a cousin of the late Sir Jasper Vernon; he left somewhat suddenly a short time after Dame Vernon had that narrow escape from drowning that you wot of; he betook himself then to Spain, where he has been fighting the Moors; he is said to be a valiant knight, but otherwise he bears but an indifferent good reputation."

Walter remembered the face now; it was that of the knight he had seen enter the hut of the river pirate on the Lambeth marshes. When released from duty he at once made his way to the lodging of Dame Vernon. Walter was now nineteen, for a year had elapsed since the termination of the French war, and he was in stature and strength the match of most men, while his skill at knightly exercises, as well as with the sword, was recognized as pre-eminent among all the young esquires of the court.

After the first greeting he said to Dame Vernon: "I think it right to tell you, lady, that I have but now, in the king's anteroom, seen the man who plotted against your life in the hut at Lambeth. His face is a marked one and I could not mistake it. I hear that he is a cousin of yours, one Sir James Carnegie, as you doubtless recognized from my description of him. I came to tell you in order that you might decide what my conduct should be. If you wish it so I will keep the secret in my breast; but if you fear aught from him I will openly accuse him before the king of the crime he attempted, and shall be ready to meet him in the ordeal of battle should he claim it."

"I have seen Sir James," Lady Vernon said. "I had a letter writ in a feigned hand telling him that his handiwork in the plot against my life was known, and warning him that, unless he left England, the proofs thereof would be laid before justice. He at once sailed for Spain, whence, he has returned but a few days since. He does not know for certain that I am aware of his plottings against us; but he must have seen by my reception of him when he called that I no longer regard him with the friendship which I formerly entertained. I have received a message from him that he will call upon me this evening, and that he trusts he will find me alone, as he would fain confer with me on private matters. When I have learned his intentions I shall be the better able to judge what course I had best adopt. I would fain, if it may be, let the matter rest. Sir James has powerful interest, and I would not have him for an open enemy if I can avoid it; besides, all the talk and publicity which so grave an accusation against a knight, and he of mine own family, would entail, would be very distasteful to me; but should I find it necessary for the sake of my child, I shall not shrink from it. I trust, however, that it will not come to that; but I shall not hesitate, if need be, to let him know that I am acquainted with his evil designs towards us. I will inform you of as much of our interview as it is necessary that you should know."

That evening Sir James Carnegie called upon Dame Vernon. "I would not notice it the other day, fair cousin," he said, in return for her stiff and ceremonious greeting; "but methinks that you are mightily changed in your bearing towards me. I had looked on my return from my long journeying for something of the sisterly warmth with which you once greeted me, but I find you as cold and hard as if I had been altogether a stranger to you. I would fain know in what way I have forfeited your esteem."

"I do not wish to enter into bygones, Sir James," the lady said, "and would fain let the past sleep if you will let me. Let us then turn without more ado to the private matters concerning which you wished to speak with me."

"If such is your mood, fair dame, I must needs fall in with it, though in no way able to understand your allusion to the past, wherein my conscience holds me guiltless of aught which could draw upon me your disfavour. I am your nearest male relative, and as such would fain confer with you touching the future of young Mistress Edith, your daughter. She is now nigh thirteen years of age, and is the heiress of broad lands; is it not time that she were betrothed to one capable of taking care of them for her, and leading your vassals to battle in these troubled times?"

"Thanks, Sir James, for your anxiety about my child," Dame Vernon said coldly. "She is a ward of the king. I am in no way anxious that an early choice should be made for her; but our good Queen Philippa has promised that, when the time shall come, his Majesty shall not dispose of her hand without my wishes being in some way consulted; and I have no doubt that when the time shall come that she is of marriageable age—and I would not that this should be before she has gained eighteen years, for I like not the over young marriages which are now in fashion—a knight may be found for her husband capable of taking care of her and her possessions; but may I ask if, in so speaking to me, you have anyone in your mind's eye as a suitor for her hand?"

"Your manner is not encouraging, certes; but I had my plan, which would, I hoped, have met with your approval. I am the young lady's cousin, and her nearest male relative; and although we are within the limited degrees, there will be no difficulty in obtaining a dispensation from Rome. I am myself passably well off, and some of the mortgages which I had been forced to lay upon my estates have been cleared off during my absence. I have returned home with some reputation, and with a goodly sum gained in the wars with the Moors. I am older than my cousin certainly; but as I am still but thirty-two, this would not, I hope, be deemed an obstacle, and methought that you would rather entrust her to your affectionate cousin than to a stranger. The king has received me very graciously, and would, I trust, offer no opposition to my suit were it backed by your good-will."

"I suppose, Sir James," Dame Vernon said, "that I should thank you for the offer which you have made; but I can only reply, that while duly conscious of the high honour you have done my daughter by your offer, I would rather see her in her grave than wedded to you."

The knight leapt from his seat with a fierce exclamation. "This is too much," he exclaimed, "and I have a right to know why such an offer on my part should be answered by disdain, and even insolence."

"You have a right to know," Dame Vernon answered quietly, "and I will tell you. I repeat that I would rather see my child in her grave than wedded to a man who attempted to compass the murder of her and her mother."

"What wild words are these?" Sir James asked sternly. "What accusation is this that you dare to bring against me?"

A STORMY INTERVIEW

"I repeat what I said, Sir James," Dame Alice replied quietly. "I know that you plotted with the water pirates of Lambeth to upset our boat as we came down the Thames; that you treacherously delayed us at Richmond in order that we might not reach London before dark; and that by enveloping me in a white cloak you gave a signal by which I might be known to your creatures."

The knight stood for a moment astounded. He was aware that the fact that he had had some share in the outrage was known, and was not surprised that his cousin was acquainted with the secret; but that she should know all the details with which but one besides himself was, as he believed, acquainted, completely stupefied him. He rapidly, however, recovered himself.

"I recall now," he said scornfully, "the evidence which was given before the justices by some ragged city boy, to the effect that he had overheard a few words of a conversation between some ruffian over in the Lambeth marshes, and an unknown person; but it is new to me indeed that there was any suspicion that I was the person alluded to, still less that a lady of my own family, in whose affection I believed, should credit so monstrous an accusation."

"I would that I could discredit it, Sir James," Dame Vernon said sadly; "but the proofs were too strong for me. Much more of your conversation than was narrated in court was overheard, and was at my request that the ragged boy, as you call him, kept silence."

"And is it possible," the knight asked indignantly, "that you believed the word of a fellow like this to the detriment to your kinsman? Why, in any court of law the word of such a one as opposed to that of a knight and gentleman of honour would not be taken for a moment."

"You are mistaken, sir," Dame Vernon said haughtily. "You may remember, in the first place, that the lad who overheard this conversation risked his life to save me and my daughter from the consequences of the attack which he heard planned; in the second place, he was no ragged lad, but the apprentice of a well-known citizen; thirdly, and this

139

Dame Alice reveals Sir James' villainy.

is of importance, since he has recognized you since your return, and is ready should I give him the word, to denounce you. He is no mere apprentice boy, but is of gentle blood, seeing that he is the son of Sir Roland Somers, the former possessor of the lands which I hold, and that he is in high favour with the good knight Sir Walter Manny, whose esquire he now is, and under whom he distinguished himself in the wars in France, and is, as Sir Walter assured me, certain to win his spurs ere long. Thus you see his bare word would be of equal value to your own, beside the fact that his evidence does not rest upon mere assertion; but that the man in the hut promised to do what you actually performed, namely, to delay me at Richmond, and to wrap me in a white cloak in order that I might be recognized by the river pirates."

Sir James was silent. In truth, as he saw, the evidence was overwhelmingly strong against him. After a while he stammered out, "I cannot deny that I was the man in question; but I swear to you that this boy was mistaken, and that the scoundrel acted altogether beyond my instructions, which were simply that he should board the boat and carry you and your daughter away to a safe place."

"And with what object, sir," Dame Vernon said contemptuously, "was I to be thus taken away?"

"I do not seek to excuse myself," the knight replied calmly, having now recovered his self-possession, "for I own I acted wrongly and basely; but in truth I loved you, and would fain have made you my wife. I knew that you regarded me with only the calm affection of a kinswoman; but I thought that were you in my power you would consent to purchase your freedom with your hand. I know now that I erred greatly. I acknowledge my fault, and that my conduct was base and unknightly, and my only excuse is the great love I bore you."

"And which," the lady said sarcastically, "you have now transferred to my daughter. I congratulate you, Sir James, upon the possession of a ready wit and an invention which does not fail you at a pinch, and of a tongue which repeats unfalteringly any fable which your mind may dictate. You do not, I suppose, expect me to believe the tale. Still, I own that it is a well-devised one, and might, at a pinch, pass muster; but fear not, Sir James. As hitherto I have kept silence as to the author of the outrage committed upon me, so I have no intention of proclaiming the truth now unless you force me to do so. Suffice that both for myself and for my daughter I disclaim the honour of your hand. So long as you offer no molestation to us, and abstain from troubling us in any way, so long will my mouth be sealed; and I would fain bury in my breast the memory of your offence. I will not give the world's tongue occasion to wag by any open breach between kinsfolk, and shall therefore in public salute you as an acquaintance, but under no pretence whatever will I admit you to any future private interview. Now leave me, sir, and I trust that your future life will show that you deeply regret the outrage which in your greed for my husband's lands you were tempted to commit."

Without a word Sir James turned and left the room, white with shame and anger, but with an inward sense of congratulation at the romance which he had, on the spur of the moment, invented, and which would, he felt sure, be accept by the world as probable, in the event of the share he had in the matter being made public, either upon the denunciation of Dame Vernon or in any other manner.

One determination, however, he made, and swore, to himself, that he would bitterly avenge himself upon the youth whose interference had thwarted his plans, and whose report to his kinswoman had turned her mind against him. He, at any rate, should be put out of the way at the first opportunity, and thus the only witness against himself be removed; for Lady Vernon's own unsupported story would be merely her word against his, and could be treated as the malicious fiction of an angry woman.

The following day Dame Vernon sent for Walter, and informed him exactly what had taken place.

"Between Sir James and me," she said, "there is, you see, a truce. We are enemies, but, we agree to lay aside our arms for the time. But, Walter, you must be on your guard.

know as well as I do how dangerous this man is, and how good a cause he has to hate you. I would not have divulged your name had I not known that the frequency of your visits here and the encouragement which I openly give you as the future suitor of my daughter, would be sure to come to his ears, and he would speedily discover that it was you who saved our lives on the Thames and gave your testimony before the justices as to the conversation in the hut on the marshes. Thus I forestalled what he would in a few days have learnt."

"I fear him not, lady," Walter said calmly. "I can hold mine own, I hope, against him in arms, and having the patronage and friendship of Sir Walter Manny I am above any petty malice. Nevertheless I will hold myself on my guard. I will, so far as possible, avoid any snare which he may, as 'tis not unlikely, set for my life, and will, so far as I honourably can, avoid any quarrel with which he may seek to saddle me."

A few days later Walter again met Sir James Carnegie in the king's anteroom, and saw at once, by the fixed look of hate with which he had regarded him, that he had already satisfied himself of his identity. He returned the knight's stare with a cold look of contempt. The knight moved towards him, and in a low tone said, "Beware, young sir, I have a heavy reckoning against you, and James Carnegie never forgets debts of that kind!"

"I am warned, Sir James," Walter said calmly, but in the same low tone, "and, believe me, I hold but very lightly the threats of one who does not succeed even when he conspires against the lives of women and children."

Sir James started as if he had been struck. Then, with a great effort he recovered his composure, and, repeating the word "Beware!" walked across to the other side of the chamber. The next day Walter went down the river and had a talk with his friend Geoffrey.

"You must beware, lad," the armourer said when he told him of the return of Sir James Carnegie and the conversation which had taken place between them. "This man is capable of anything, and careth not where he chooseth his instruments. The man of the hut at Lambeth has never been caught since his escape from Richmond Jail—thanks, doubtless, to the gold of his employer—and, for aught we know, may still be lurking in the marshes there, or in the purlieus of the city. He will have a grudge against you as well as his employer, and in him Sir James would find a ready instrument. He is no doubt connected, as before, with a gang of water pirates and robbers, and is not one sword alone that you would have to encounter. I think not that you are in danger just at present, for he would know that, in case of your murder, the suspicions of Dame Vernon and of any others who may know the motive which he has in getting rid of you would be excited, and he might be accused of having had a share in your death. Still, it would be so hard to prove aught against him, that he may be ready to run the risk in order to rid himself of you. Look here, Walter. What think you of this?" and the smith drew out from a coffer a shirt of mail of finer work than Walter had ever before seen.

"Ay, lad, I knew you would be pleased," he said in answer to Walter's exclamation at the fineness of the workmanship. "I bought this a month ago from a Jew merchant who had recently come from Italy. How he got it I know not, but I doubt if it were honestly, or he would have demanded a higher price than I paid him. He told me that it was made by the first armourer in Milan, and was constructed especially for a cardinal of the church, who had made many enemies by his evil deeds and could not sleep for fear of assassination. At his death it came as the Jew said, into his possession. I suppose some rascally attendant took it as a perquisite, and, knowing not of its value, sold it for a few ducats to the Jew. However, it is of the finest workmanship. It is, as you see, double, and each link is made of steel so tough that no dagger or sword-point will pierce it. I put it on a block and tried the metal myself, and broke one of my best daggers on it without a single link giving. Take it, lad. You are welcome to it. I bought it with a special eye to you, thinking that you might wear it under your armour in battle without greatly adding to the weight; but for such dangers as threaten you now it is invaluable. It is so light and soft that none will dream that you have it under your doublet, and I warrant me it will hold you safe against the daggers of Sir James's ruffians.

Walter did not like taking a gift so valuable, for his apprenticeship as an armourer had taught him the extreme rarity and costliness of so fine a piece of work. Geoffrey, however, would not hear of his refusal, and insisted on his then and there taking off his doublet and putting it on. It fitted closely to the body, descending just below the hips, and coming well up on the neck, while the arms extended to the wrists.

"There!" the smith said with delight. "Now you are safe against sword or dagger, save for a sweeping blow at the head, and that your sword can be trusted to guard. Never take it off, Walter, save when you sleep; and except when in your own bed, at Sir Walter Manny's, I should advise you to wear it even at night. The weight is nothing, and it will not incommode you. So long as this caitiff knight lives, your life will not be safe. When he is dead you may hang up the shirt of mail with a light heart."

CHAPTER XII
JACOB VAN ARTEVELDE

KING EDWARD found no difficulty in awakening the war spirit of England anew, for the King of France, by an act of infamous treachery, in despite of the solemn terms of the treaty, excited against himself the indignation not only of England but of all Europe. Oliver de Clisson, with fourteen other nobles of Brittany and Normandy, were arrested by his order, taken to Paris, and without form of trial there decapitated. This act of treachery and injustice aroused disgust and shame among the French nobles, and murmurs and discontent spread throughout the whole country.

In Brittany numbers of the nobles fell off from the cause of Charles of Blois, and King Edward hastened his preparations to avenge the butchery of the adherents of the house of Montford. Phillip, however, in defiance of the murmurs of his own subjects, of the indignant remonstrances of Edward, and even those of the pope, who was devoted to his cause, continued the course he had begun, and a number of other nobles were seized and executed. Godfrey of Harcourt alone, warned by the fate of his companions, refused to obey the summons of the king to repair to Paris, and fled to Brabant. His property in France was at once seized by Phillip; and Godfrey, finding that the Duke of Brabant would be unable to shield him from Phillip's vengeance, fled to the English court, and did homage to Edward.

JACOB VAN ARTEVELDE

On the 24th of April, 1345, Edward determined no longer to allow Phillip to continue to benefit by his constant violations of the truce, and accordingly sent a defiance to the King of France.

De Montford, who had just succeeded in escaping from his prison in Paris, arrived at this moment in England, and shortly afterwards set sail with a small army under the command of the Earl of Northampton for Britanny, while the Earl of Derby took his departure with a larger force for the defence of Guienne.

King Edward set about raising a large army, which he determined to lead himself, but before passing over to France he desired to strengthen his hold of Flanders. The constant intrigues of Phillip there had exercised a great effect. The count of that country was already strongly in his interest, and it was only the influence of Jacob van Artevelde which maintained the alliance with England. This man had, by his talent and energy, gained an immense influence over his countrymen; but his commanding position and ability had naturally excited the envy and hatred of many of his fellow-citizens, among whom was the dean of the weavers of Ghent, one Gerard Denis. The weavers were the most powerful body in this city, and had always been noted for their turbulence and faction; and on a Monday in the month of May, 1345, a great battle took place in the market-place between them and the fullers, of whom 1500 were slain. This victory of the weavers strengthened the power of the party hostile to Artevelde and the English connection; and the former saw that unless he could induce his countrymen to take some irretrievable step in favour of England they would ultimately fall back into the arms of France. Accordingly he invited Edward to pass over with a strong force into Flanders, where he would persuade the Flemings to make the Prince of Wales their duke. King Edward at once accepted the offer, and sailing from Sandwich on the 3d of July arrived in safety at Sluys. His intention had been kept a profound secret, and his arrival created the greatest surprise throughout Flanders. He did not disembark, but received on board a ship with great honour and magnificence the burgomasters of the various towns who appeared to welcome him. The king had brought with him the Prince of Wales, now fifteen years old, who wore a suit of black armour, and was therefore called "the Black Prince."

Walter Somers was on board the royal vessel. The Prince of Wales had not forgotten the promise which he had six years before made to him, and had asked Sir Walter Manny to allow him to follow under his banner.

"You are taking my most trusty squire from me, Prince," the knight said; "for although I have many brave young fellows in my following, there is not one whom I value so much as Walter Somers. It is but fair, however, that you should have him, since you told me when I first took him that he was to follow your banner when you were old enough to go to the wars. You can rely upon him implicitly. He cares not for the gaieties of which most young men of his age think so much. He is ever ready for duty, and he possesses a wisdom and sagacity which will some day make him a great leader."

Walter was sorry to leave his patron, but the step was of course a great advancement, and excited no little envy among his companions, for among the young esquires of the Prince of Wales were the sons of many of the noblest families of England.

Sir Walter presented him on leaving with a heavy purse. "Your expenses will be large," he said, "among so many young gallants, and you must do credit to me as well as to yourself. The young prince is generous to a fault, and as he holds you in high favour, both from his knowledge of you and from my report, you will, I know, lack nothing when you are once fairly embarked in his service; but it is needful that when you first join you should be provided with many suits of courtly raiment, of cloth of gold and silk, which were not needed while you were in the service of a simple knight like myself, but which must be worn by a companion of the heir of England."

Walter had hoped that Sir James Carnegie would have accompanied the forces of either the Earls of Northampton or Derby, but he found that he had attached himself to the royal army.

Ralph of course followed Walter's fortunes, and was now brilliant in the appointments of the Prince of Wales's chosen body-guard of men-at-arms.

The councils of all the great towns of Flanders assembled at Sluys, and for several days great festivities were held. Then a great assembly was held, and Van Artevelde rose and addressed his countrymen. He set forth to them the virtues of the Prince of Wales, whose courtesy and bearing had so captivated them; he pointed out the obligations which Flanders was under towards King Edward, and the advantages which would arise from a nearer connection with England. With this he contrasted the weakness of their count, the many ills which his adherence to France had brought upon the country, and the danger which menaced them should his power be ever renewed. He then boldly proposed to them that they should at once cast off their allegiance to the count and bestow the vacant coronet upon the Prince of Wales, who, as Duke of Flanders, would undertake the defence and government of the country with the aid of a Flemish council. This wholly unexpected proposition took the Flemish burghers by surprise. Artevelde had calculated upon his eloquence and influence carrying them away, but his power had diminished, and many of his hearers had already been gained to the cause of France. The burgher councils had for a long time had absolute power in their own towns, and the prospect of a powerful prince at their head foredoomed a curtailment of those powers. When Artevelde ceased, therefore, instead of the enthusiastic shouts with which he hoped his oration would be greeted, a confused murmur arose. At last several got up and said that, greatly attached as they were to the king, much as they admired the noble young prince proposed for their acceptance, they felt themselves unable to give an answer upon an affair of such moment without consulting their fellow-countrymen and learning their opinions. They therefore promised that they would return on a certain day and give a decided answer.

The Flemish burghers then took their leave. Van Artevelde, after a consultation with the king, started at once to use his influence among the various towns.

After leaving the king he bade adieu to the Prince of Wales. "Would you like," the young prince said, "that one of my esquires should ride with you? His presence might show the people how entirely I am with you; and should you have tidings to send me he could ride hither with them. I have one with me who is prudent and wise, and who possesses all the confidence of that wise and valiant knight, Sir Walter de Manny."

"I will gladly take him, your royal highness," Van Artevelde said, "and hope to despatch him to you very shortly with the news that the great towns of Flanders all gladly receive you as their lord."

In a few minutes Walter had mounted his horse, accompanied by Ralph, and, joining Van Artevelde, rode to Bruges. Here and at Ypres Van Artevelde's efforts were crowned with success. His eloquence carried away the people with him, and both these cities agreed to accept the Prince of Wales as their lord; but the hardest task yet remained. Ghent was the largest and most powerful of the Flemish towns, and here his enemies were in the ascendant. Gerard Denis and the weavers had been stirring up the people against him. All kinds of accusations had been spread, and he was accused of robbing and selling his country. The news of the hostile feeling of the population reached Van Artevelde, and he despatched Walter with the request to the king for a force of five hundred English soldiers as a guard against his enemies.

Had Artevelde asked for a large force, Edward would have disembarked his army and marched at their head into Ghent. As the rest of the country was already won, there can be little doubt that this step would at once have silenced all opposition, and would have annexed Flanders to the British crown. Van Artevelde, however, believed himself to be stronger than he really was, and thought with a small party of soldiers he could seize his principal opponents, and that the people would then rally round him.

Upon the arrival of the five hundred men he started for Ghent; but as he feared that the gates would be shut if he presented himself with an armed force, he left the soldiers in concealment a short distance from the town and entered it, accompanied only by his usual suite. At his invitation, however, Walter, followed of course by Ralph, rode beside him. No sooner was he within the gates than Van Artevelde saw how strong was the popular feeling against him. He had been accustomed to be received with bows of reverence; now men turned aside as he approached, or scowled at him from their doors.

"Methinks, sir," Walter said, "that it would be wiser did we ride back, and, joining the soldiers, enter at their head, or as that number would be scarce sufficient should so large a town rise in tumult, to send to King Edward for a larger force and await their coming. Even should they shut the gates, we can reduce the town, and as all the rest of Flanders is with you, surely a short delay will not matter."

"You know not these Flemings as well as I do," Van Artevelde replied; "they are surly dogs, but they always listen to my voice, and are ready enough to do my bidding. When I once speak to them you will see how they will smooth their backs and do as I ask them."

Walter said no more, but as he saw everywhere lowering brows from window and doorway as they rode through the streets he had doubts whether the power of Van Artevelde's eloquence would have the magical potency he had expected from it.

When the party arrived at the splendid dwelling of the great demagogue, messengers were instantly sent out to all his friends and retainers. A hundred and forty persons soon assembled, and while Van Artevelde was debating with them as to the best steps to be taken, Walter opened the casement and looked out into the street. It was already crowded with the people, whose silent and quiet demeanor seemed to bode no good. Arms were freely displayed among them, and Walter saw men passing to and fro evidently giving instructions.

"I am sorry to disturb you, Master Artevelde," he said, returning to the room where the council was being held, "but methinks that it would wise to bar the doors and windows, and to put yourself in a posture of defence, for a great crowd is gathering without, for the most part armed, and as it seems to me with evil intentions."

A glance from the windows confirmed Walter statements, and the doors and windows were speedily barricaded. Before many minutes had elapsed the tolling of bells in all parts of the town was heard, and down the different streets leading towards the building large bodies of armed men were seen making their way.

"I had rather have to do with a whole French army, Master Walter," Ralph said, as he stood beside him at an upper window looking down upon the crowd, "than with these citizens of Ghent. Look at those men with bloody axes and stained clothes. Doubtless those are the skinners and butchers. Didst ever see such a ferocious band of savages? Listen to their shouts. Death to Van Artevelde! Down with the English alliance! I thought our case was a bad one when the French poured over the walls into Vannes but methinks it is a hundred times worse now."

"We got out of that scrape, Ralph, and I hope we shall get out of this, but, as you say, the prospect is black enough. See, the butchers are hammering at the door with their pole-axes. Let us go down and aid in the defence."

"I am ready," Ralph said, "but I shall fight with a lighter heart if you could fix upon some plan for us to adopt when the rabble break in. That they will do so I regard as certain, seeing that the house is not built for purposes of defence, but has numerous broad windows on the ground-floor by which assuredly they will burst their way in."

"Wait a moment then, Ralph; let us run up to the top storey and see if there be any means of escape along the roofs."

The house stood detached from the others, but on one side was separated from that next to it only by a narrow lane, and as the upper storeys projected beyond those below, the windows were but six feet distant from those on the opposite side of the way.

"See," Water said, "there is a casement in the room to our left there which is open; let us see if it is tenanted."

Going into the next room they went to the window and opened it. It exactly faced the casement opposite, and so far as they could see the room was unoccupied.

"It were easy to put a plank across," Ralph said.

"We must not do that," Walter answered. "The mob are thick in the lane below—what a roar comes up from their voices!—and a plank would be surely seen, and we should be killed there as well as here. No, we must get on to the sill and spring across; the distance is not great, and the jump would be nothing were it not that the casements are so low. It must be done as lightly and quickly as possible, and we may not then be seen from below. Now leave the door open that we may make no mistake as to the room, and come along, for by the sound the fight is hot below."

Running down the stairs Walter and Ralph joined in the defence. Those in the house knew that they would meet with no mercy from the infuriated crowd, and each fought with the bravery of despair. Although there were many windows to be defended, and at each the mob attacked desperately, the assaults were all repulsed. Many indeed of the defenders were struck down by the pikes and pole-axes, but for a time they beat back the assailants whenever they attempted to enter. The noise was prodigious. The alarm-bells of the town were all ringing and the shouts of the combatants were drowned in the hoarse roar of the surging crowd without.

Seeing that however valiant was the defence the assailants must in the end prevail, and feeling sure that his enemies would have closed the city gates and thus prevented the English without from coming to his assistance, Van Artevelde ascended to an upper storey and attempted to

153

address the crowd. His voice was drowned in the roar. In vain he gesticulated and made motions imploring them to hear him, but all was useless, and the courage of the demagogue deserted him and he burst into tears at the prospect of death. Then he determined to try and make his escape to the sanctuary of a church close by, and was descending the stairs when a mighty crash below, the clashing of steel, shouts, and cries, told that the mob had swept away one of the barricades and were pouring into the house.

"Make for the stair," Walter shouted, "and defend yourselves there." But the majority of the defenders, bewildered by the inrush of the enemy, terrified at their ferocious aspect and terrible axes, had no thought of continuing the resistance. A few, getting into corners, resisted desperately to the end; others threw down their arms and dropping on their knees cried for mercy, but all were ruthlessly slaughtered.

Keeping close together Walter and Ralph fought their way to the foot of the stairs, and closely pursued by a band of the skinners headed by Gerard Denis, ran up. Upon the first landing stood a man paralysed with terror. On seeing him a cry of ferocious triumph rose from the mob. As nothing could be done to aid him Walter and his follower rushed by without stopping. There was a pause in the pursuit, and glancing down from the upper gallery Walter saw Van Artevelde in the hands of the mob, each struggling to take possession of him; then a man armed with a great axe pushed his way among them, and swinging it over his head struck Van Artevelde dead to the floor. His slayer was Gerard Denis himself.

Followed by Ralph, Walter sprang through the open door into the chamber they had marked, and closed the door behind them. Then Walter, saying, "I will go first, Ralph, I can help you in should you miss your spring," mounted on the sill of the casement. Short as was the distance the leap was extremely difficult, for neither casement was more than three feet high. Walter was therefore obliged to stoop low and to hurl himself head forwards across the gulf. He succeeded in the attempt, shooting clear through the casement on to the floor beyond. Instantly he picked himself up and went to Ralph's assistance. The latter, taller and more bulky, had greater difficulty in the task, and only his shoulder arrived through the window. Walter seized him, and aided him at once to scramble in, and they closed the casement behind them.

"It was well we took off our armour, Ralph; its pattern would have been recognized in an instant."

Walter had thrown off his helmet as he bounded up the stairs, and both he and his companion had rid themselves of their heavy armour.

"I would give a good deal," he said, "for two bourgeois jerkins, even were they as foul as those of the skinners. This is a woman's apartment," he added, looking round, "and nothing here will cover my six feet of height, to say nothing of your four inches extra. Let us peep into some of the other rooms. This is, doubtless, the house of some person of importance, and in the upper floor we may find some clothes of servants or retainers."

They were not long in their search. The next room was a large one, and contained a number of pallet beds, and hanging from pegs on walls were jerkins, mantles, and other garments, evidently belonging to the retainers of the house. Walter and Ralph were not long in transmogrifying their appearance, and had soon the air of two respectable serving-men in a Flemish household.

"But how are we to descend?" Ralph asked. "We can hardly hope to walk down the stairs and make our escape without being seen, especially as the doors will all be barred and bolted, seeing the tumult which is raging outside."

"It all depends whether our means of escape are suspected," Walter replied, "I should scarce think that they would be. The attention of our pursuers was wholly taken up by Van Artevelde, and some minutes must have passed before they followed us. No doubt they will search every place in the house, and all within it will by this time have been slaughtered. But they will scarce organize any special search for us. All will be fully occupied with the exciting events which have taken place, and as the casement by which we entered is closed it is scarcely likely to occur to any one that we have escaped by that means. I will listen first if the house is quiet. If so, we will descend and take refuge in some room below, where there is a better chance of concealment than here. Put the pieces of armour into that closet so that they may not catch the eye of any who may happen to come hither. The day is already closing. In half an hour it will be nightfall. Then we will try and make our way out."

Listening at the top of the stairs they could hear voices below; but as the gallery was quiet and deserted they made their way a floor lower, and seeing an open door entered it. Walter looked from the window.

"There is a back-yard below," he said, "with a door opening upon a narrow lane. We are now upon the second storey, and but some twenty-five feet above the ground. We will not risk going down through the house, which could scarce be accomplished without detection, but will at once tear up into strips the coverings of the bed, and I will make a rope by which we may slip down into the courtyard as soon as it is dark. We must hope that none will come up before that time; but, indeed, all will be so full of the news of the events which have happened that it is scarce likely that any will come above at present."

The linen sheets and coverings were soon cut up and knotted together in a rope. By the time that this was finished the darkness was closing in, and after waiting patiently for a few minutes they lowered the rope and slid down into the yard. Quietly they undid the bolts of the gate and issued into the lane. The mantles were provided with hoods, as few of the lower class of Flemings wore any other head-covering.

Drawing these hoods well over their heads so as to shade their faces the two sallied out from the lane. They were soon in one of the principal streets, which was crowded with people. Bands of weavers, butchers, skinners, and others were parading the streets shouting and singing in honour of their victory and of the downfall and death of him whom they had but a few days before regarded as the mainstay of Flanders. Many of the better class of burghers stood in groups in the streets and talked in low and rather frightened voices of the consequences which the deed of blood would bring upon the city. On the one hand Edward might march upon it with his army to avenge the murder of his ally. Upon the other hand they were now committed to France. Their former ruler would return, and all the imposts and burdens against which they had rebelled would again be laid upon the city.

"What shall we do now?" Ralph asked, "for assuredly there will be no issue by the gates."

"We must possess ourselves of a length of rope if possible, and make our escape over the wall. How to get one I know not, for the shops are all closed, and even were it not so I could not venture in to purchase any, for my speech would betray us at once. Let us separate, and each see whether he can find what we want. We will meet again at the entrance to this church in an hour's time. One or other of us may find what we seek."

Walter searched in vain. Wherever he saw the door of a yard open he peered in, but in no case could he see any signs of rope. At the end of the hour he returned to their rendezvous. Ralph was already there.

"I have found nothing, Ralph. Have you had better fortune?"

"That have I, Master Walter, and was back nigh an hour since. Scarce had I left you when in a back street I came upon a quiet hostelry, and in the courtyard were standing half a dozen teams of cattle. Doubtless their owners had brought hay or corn into the city, and when the tumult arose and the gates were closed found themselves unable to escape. The masters were all drinking within, so without more ado I cut off the ropes which served as traces for the oxen, and have them wound round my body under my mantle. There must be twenty yards at least, and as each rope is strong enough to hold double our weight there will be no difficulty in lowering ourselves from the walls."

"You have done well indeed, Ralph," Walter said. "Let us make our way thither at once. Everyone is so excited in the city, that, as yet, there will be but few guards upon the wall. The sooner, therefore, that we attempt to make our escape the better."

CHAPTER XIII
THE WHITE FORD

THEY made their way without interruption to the wall. This they found, as they expected, entirely deserted, although, no doubt, guards had been posted at the gates. The Flemings, however, could have felt no fear of an attack by so small a force as the five hundred English whom they knew to be in the neighbourhood.

Walter and his companion soon knotted the ropes together and lowered themselves into the moat. A few strokes took them to the other side, and scrambling out, they made their way across the country to the spot where the English had been posted. They found the Earl of Salisbury, who commanded, in a great state of uneasiness. No message had reached him during the day. He had heard the alarmbells of the city ring, and a scout who had gone forward returned with the news that the gates were closed and the drawbridges raised, and that a strong body of men manned the walls.

"Your news is indeed bad," he said, when Walter related to him the events which had taken place in the town. "This will altogether derange the king's plans. Now that his ally is killed I fear that his hopes of acquiring Flanders for England will fall to the ground. It is a thousand pities that he listened to Van Artevelde and allowed him to enter Ghent alone. Had his majesty landed, as he wished, and made a progress through the country, the prince receiving the homage of all the large towns, we could then very well have summoned Ghent as standing alone against all Flanders. The citizens then would, no doubt, have gladly opened their gates and received the prince, and if they had refused we would have made short work of them. However, as it has turned out, it is as well that we did not enter the town with the Fleming, for against so large and turbulent a population we should have had but little chance. And now, Master Somers, we will march at once for Sluys and bear the news to the king, and you shall tell me as we ride thither how you and your man-at-arms managed to escape with whole skins from such a tumult."

The king was much grieved when he heard of the death of Artevelde, and held a council with his chief leaders. At first, in his indignation and grief, he was disposed to march upon Ghent and to take vengeance for the murder of his ally, but after a time calmer counsels prevailed.

The Flemings were still in rebellion against their count, who was the friend of France. Were the English to attack Ghent they would lose the general good-will of the Flemings, and would drive them into the arms of France, while, if matters were left alone, the effect of the popular outburst which had caused the death of Artevelde would die away, and motives of interest and the fear of France would again drive them into the arms of England. The expedition therefore returned to England, and there the king, in a proclamation to his people, avoided all allusion to the death of his ally, but simply stated that he had been waited upon by the councils of all the Flemish towns, and that their faithful obedience to himself as legitimate King of France, was established upon a firmer basis than ever.

This course had the effect which he had anticipated from it. The people of Flanders perceived the danger and disadvantage which must accrue to their trade from any permanent disagreement with England. They were convinced by the events which soon afterwards happened in France that the King of England had more power than Phillip of Valois, and could, if he chose, punish severely any breach of faith towards him. They therefore sent over commissioners to express their grief and submission. The death of Artevelde was represented as the act of a frantic mob, and severe fines were imposed upon the leaders of the party who slew him, and although the principal towns expressed their desire still to remain under the rule of the Count of Flanders, they suggested that the ties which bound them to England should be strengthened by the marriage of Louis, eldest son of the count, to one of Edward's daughters. More than this, they offered to create a diversion for the English forces acting in Guienne and Gascony by raising a strong force and expelling the French garrisons still remaining in some parts of the country. This was done. Hugo of Hastings was appointed by the king captain-general in Flanders, and with a force of English and Flemings did good service by expelling the French from Termond and several other towns.

The character of Jacob van Artevelde has had but scant justice done to it by most of the historians of the time. These, living in an age of chivalry, when noble blood and lofty deeds were held in extraordinary respect, had little sympathy with the brewer of Ghent, and deemed it contrary to the fitness of things that the chivalry of France should have been defied and worsted by mere mechanics and artisans. But there can be no doubt that Artevelde was a very great man. He may have been personally ambitious, but he was a true patriot. He had great military talents. He completely remodelled and wonderfully improved the internal administration of the country, and raised its commerce, manufactures, and agriculture to a pitch which they had never before reached. After his death his memory was esteemed and revered by the Flemings, who long submitted to the laws he had made, and preserved his regulations with scrupulous exactitude.

Edward now hastened to get together a great army. Every means were adopted to raise money and to gather stores, and every man between sixteen and sixty south of the Trent was called upon to take up arms and commanded to assemble at Portsmouth in the middle of Lent. A tremendous tempest, however, scattered the fleet collected to carry the expedition, a great many of the ships were lost, and it was not until the middle of July, 1346, that it sailed from England.

It consisted of about 500 ships and 10,000 sailors, and carried 4000 men-at-arms, 10,000 archers, 12,000 Welsh, and 6000 Irish.

This seems but a small army considering the efforts which had been made; but it was necessary to leave a considerable force behind for the defence of the Scottish frontier, and England had already armies in Guienne and Brittany. Lionel, Edward's second son, was appointed regent during his father's absence. On board Edward's own ship were Godfrey of Harcourt and the Prince of Wales. Walter, as one of the personal squires of the prince, was also on board.

The prince had been greatly interested in the details of Walter's escape from Van Artevelde's house, the king himself expressed his approval of his conduct, and Walter was generally regarded as one of the most promising young aspirants to the court. His modesty and good temper rendered him a general favourite, and many even of the higher nobles noticed him by their friendly attentions, for it was felt that he stood so high in the good-will of the prince that he might some day become a person of great influence with him, and one whose good-will would be valuable.

It was generally supposed, when the fleet started, that Guienne was their destination, but they had not gone far when a signal was made to change the direction in which they were sailing and to make for La Hogue in Normandy. Godfrey of Harcourt had great influence in that province, and his persuasions had much effect in determining the king to direct his course thither. There was the further advantage that the King of France, who was well aware of the coming invasion, would have made his preparations to receive him in Guienne. Furthermore, Normandy was the richest and most prosperous province in France. It had for a long time been untouched by war, and offered great abundance of spoil. It had made itself particularly obnoxious to the English by having recently made an offer to the King of France to fit out an expedition and conquer England with its own resources.

THE WHITE FORD

The voyage was short and favourable, and the expedition landed at La Hogue, on the small peninsula of Cotentin, without opposition. Six days were spent at La Hogue disembarking the men, horses, and stores, and baking bread for the use of the army on the march. A detachment advanced and pillaged and burnt Barfleur and Cherbourg and a number of small towns and castles.

In accordance with custom, at the commencement of the campaign a court was held, at which the Prince of Wales was dubbed a knight by his father. A similar honour was bestowed upon a number of other young aspirants, among whom was Walter Somers, who had been highly recommended for that honour to the king by Sir Walter Manny.

The force was now formed into three divisions—the one commanded by the king himself, the second by the Earl of Warwick, and the third by Godfrey of Harcourt. The Earl of Arundel acted as Lord High Constable, and the Earl of Huntingdon, who was in command of the fleet, followed the army along the sea-coast. Valognes, Carentan, and St. Lo were captured without difficulty, and the English army advanced by rapid marches upon Caen, plundering the country for six or seven leagues on each side of the line of march. An immense quantity of booty was obtained. As soon as the news of Edward's landing in Normandy reached Paris, Phillip despatched the Count d'Eu, Constable of France, with the Count of Tankerville and 600 men-at-arms, to oppose Edward at Caen. The Bishop of Bayeux had thrown himself into that city, which was already garrisoned by 300 Genoese. The town was not defensible, and the only chance of resistance was by opposing the passage of the river Horn, which flowed between the suburbs and the city. The bridge was barricaded, strong wooden towers were erected, and such was the confidence of the inhabitants and their leaders that Edward's promise of protection for the person and property of the citizens was rejected with scorn, and the whole male population joined the garrison in the defence of the bridge. Marching through the deserted suburbs the

English army attacked the bridge with such vehemence that although the enemy defended the barricades gallantly they were speedily forced, and the English poured into the town. Before the first fury of the attack was over near 5000 persons were slain. The Count of Tankerville, 140 knights, and as many squires were made prisoners. The plunder was so enormous as to be sufficient to cover the whole expenses of the expedition, and this with the booty which had been previously acquired was placed on board ship and despatch to England, while the king marched forward with his army. At Lisieux he was met by two cardinals sent by the pope to negotiate a truce; but Edward had learned the fallacy of truces made with King Phillip, and declined to enter into negotiations. Finding that Rouen had been placed in a state of defence and could not be taken without a long siege he left it behind him and marched along the valley of the Eure, gathering rich booty at every step.

But while he was marching forward a great army was gathering in his rear. The Count of Harcourt brother of Godfrey, called all Normandy to arms. Every feudal lord and vassal answered to the summons, and before Edward reached the banks of the Seine a formidable army had assembled.

The whole of the vassals of France were gathering by the orders of the king at St. Denis. The English fleet had now left the coast, and Edward had only the choice of retreating through Normandy into Brittany or of attempting to force the passage of the Seine, and to fight his way through France to Flanders. He chose the latter alternative, and marched along the left bank of the river towards Paris, seeking in vain to find a passage. The enemy followed him step by step on the opposite bank, and all the bridges were broken down and the fords destroyed.

Edward marched on, burning the towns and ravaging the country until he reached Poissy. The bridge was as usual destroyed, but the piles on which it stood were still standing, and he determined to endeavour to cross here. He accordingly halted for five days, but despatched troops in all directions, who burned and ravaged to the very gates of Paris. The villages of St. Germain, St. Cloud, Bourg la Reine, and many others within sight of the walls were destroyed, and the capital itself thrown into a state of terror and consternation. Godfrey of Harcourt was the first to cross the river, and with the advance guard of English fell upon a large body of the burghers of Amiens, and after a severe fight defeated them, killing over five hundred. The king himself with his whole force passed on the 16th of August.

Phillip, with his army, quitted St. Denis, when he heard that the English army had passed the Seine, and by parallel marches endeavoured to interpose between it and the borders of Flanders. As his force was every hour increasing he despatched messengers to Edward offering him battle within a few days on condition that he would cease to ravage the country; but Edward declined the proposal, saying that Phillip himself by breaking down the bridges had avoided a battle as long as he could, but that whenever he was ready to give battle he would accept the challenge. During the whole march the armies were within a few leagues of each other, and constant skirmishes took place between bodies detached from the hosts.

In some of these skirmishes Walter took part, as he and the other newly made knights were burning to distinguish themselves. Every day the progress of the army became more difficult, as the country people everywhere rose against them, and several times attempted to make a stand but were defeated with great loss. The principal towns were found deserted, and even Poix, which offered great capabilities of defence, had been left unguarded. Upon the English entering, the burghers offered to pay a large ransom to save the town from plunder. The money was to be delivered as soon as the English force had withdrawn, and Walter Somers was ordered by the king to remain behind with a few men-at-arms to receive the ransom.

No sooner had the army departed than the burghers, knowing that the French army was close behind, changed their minds, refused to pay the ransom, and fell upon the little body of men-at-arms. Although taken quite by surprise by the act of treachery Walter instantly rallied his men although several had been killed at the first onslaught. He, with Ralph and two or three of the stanchest men, covered the retreat of the rest through the streets, making desperate charges upon the body of armed burghers pressing upon them. Ralph fought as usual with a mace of prodigious weight, and the terror of his blows in no slight degree enabled the party to reach the gate in safety, but Walter had no idea of retreating further. He despatched one of his followers to gallop at full speed to overtake the rear-guard of the army, which was still but two miles distant, while with the rest he formed a line across the gate and resisted all the attempts of the citizens to expel them.

The approach to the gate was narrow, and the overwhelming number of the burghers were therefore of little avail. Walter had dismounted his force and all fought on foot, and although sorely pressed they held their ground until Lords Cobham and Holland, with their followers, rode up. Then the tide of war was turned, the town was plundered and burnt, and great numbers of the inhabitants slain. Walter gained great credit for holding the gate, for had he been driven out, the town could have resisted, until the arrival of Louis, all assaults of the English.

The river Somme now barred the passage of Edward. Most of the bridges had been destroyed, and those remaining were so strongly fortified that they could not be forced.

The position of the English was now very critical. On one flank and in front were impassable rivers. The whole country was in arms against them, and on their rear and flank pressed a hostile army fourfold their strength. The country was swampy and thinly populated, and flour and provisions were only obtained with great difficulty. Edward, on finding from the reports of his marshals who had been sent to examine the bridges, that no passage across the river could be found, turned and marched down the river towards the sea, halting for the night at Oisemont.

THE WHITE FORD

Here, a great number of peasantry attempted a defence, but were easily defeated and a number of prisoners taken. Late in the evening the Earl of Warwick, who had pushed forward as far as Abbeville and St. Valery, returned with the news that the passages at those places were as strongly guarded as elsewhere, but he had learnt from a peasant that a ford existed somewhere below Abbeville, although the man was himself ignorant of its position.

Edward at once called the prisoners belonging to that part of the country before him, and promised to any one who would tell him where the ford lay his freedom and that of twenty of his companions. A peasant called Gobin Agase stepped forward and offered to show the ford, where at low tide twelve men could cross abreast. It was, he said, called "La Blanche Tache".

Edward left Oisemont at midnight and reached the ford at daylight. The river, however, was full and the army had to wait impatiently for low tide. When they arrived there no enemy was to be seen on the opposite bank, but before the water fell sufficiently for a passage to be attempted, Sir Godemar du Fay with 12,000 men, sent by King Phillip, who was aware of the existence of the ford, arrived on the opposite side.

The enterprise was a difficult one indeed, for the water, even at low tide, is deep. Godemar du Fay, however, threw away part of his advantage by advancing into the stream. The English archers lined the banks, and poured showers of arrows into the ranks of the enemy, while the Genoese bowmen on their side were able to give comparatively little assistance to the French.

King Edward shouted to his knights, "Let those who love me follow me," and spurred his horse into the water. Behind him followed his most valiant knights, and Walter riding close to the Prince of Wales was one of the foremost.

The French resisted valiantly and a desperate battle took place on the narrow ford, but the impetuosity of the English prevailed, and step by step they drove the French back to the other side of the river. The whole army poured after their leaders, and the French were soon entirely routed and fled, leaving two thousand men-at-arms dead on the field.

King Edward, having now freed himself from the difficulties which had encompassed him on the other side of the river, prepared to choose a ground to give battle to the whole French army.

Louis had advanced slowly, feeling confident that the English would be unable to cross the river, and that he should catch them hemmed in by it. His mortification and surprise on finding, when he approached La Blanche Tache, that twelve thousand men had been insufficient to hold a ford by which but twelve could cross abreast, and that his enemy had escaped from his grasp, were great. The tide had now risen again, and he was obliged to march on to Abbeville and cross the river there.

King Edward now advanced into the Forest of Cressy.

Hugh de le Spencer, with a considerable force, was despatched to Crotoy, which he carried by assault after a severe conflict, in which four thousand of the French men-at-arms were slain. The capture of this city removed all danger of want from the army, for large stores of wine and meal were found there, and Sir Hugh at once sent off a supply to the tired army in the field.

The possession of Crotoy and the mouth of the Somme would have now rendered it easy for the English monarch to have transported his troops to England, and to have returned triumphant after the accomplishment of his extraordinary and most successful march through France. The army, however, was elated by the many great successes it had won, he was now in Ponthieu, which was one of his own fiefs, and he determined to make a stand in spite of the immense superiority of the enemy.

Next morning, then—Friday the 25th of August, 1346— he despatched the Earl of Warwick with Godfrey of Harcourt and Lord Cobham, to examine the ground and choose a site for a battle.

THE WHITE FORD

The plan of the fight was drawn out by the king and his councillors, and the king yielded to the Black Prince the chief place of danger and honour placing with him the Earl of Warwick, Sir John Chandos, and many of his best knights.

The ground which had been chosen for the battle was an irregular slope between the forest of Cressy and the river Maie near the little village of Canchy. The slope looked towards the south and east, from which quarters the enemy was expected to arrive, and some slight defences were added to the natural advantages of the ground.

On the night of the 25th all the principal leaders of the British host were entertained by King Edward. Next morning, Mass was celebrated, and the king, the prince, and many knights and nobles received the Sacrament, after which the trumpet sounded, and the army marched to take up its position. Its numbers are variously estimated, but the best account puts it at about 30,000 men which, considering that 32,000 had crossed the Channel to La Hogue, is probably about the force which would have been present allowing that 2000 had fallen in the various actions or had died from disease.

The division of the Black Prince consisted of 800 men-at-arms, 4000 archers, and 6000 Welsh foot. The archers, as usual, were placed in front, supported by the light troops of Wales and the men-at-arms; on his left was the second division, commanded by the Earls of Arundel and Northampton; its extreme left rested on Canchy and the river, and it was further protected by a deep ditch; this corps was about 7000 strong.

The king himself took up his position on a knoll of rising ground surmounted by a windmill, and 12,000 men under his personal command were placed here in reserve.

In the rear of the Prince's division an enclosure of stakes was formed; in this, guarded by a small body of archers, were ranged the wagons and baggage of the army, together with all the horses, the king having determined that the knights and men-at-arms on his side should fight on foot.

ST.GEORGE FOR ENGLAND

When the army had taken up its position, the king, mounted on a small palfrey, with a white staff in his hand, rode from rank to rank exhorting his soldiers to do their duty gallantly. It was nearly noon before he had passed through all the lines, and permission was then given to the soldiers to fall out from their ranks and to take refreshments while waiting for the coming of the enemy. This was accordingly done, the men eating and drinking at their ease and lying down in their ranks on the soft grass with their steel caps and their bows or pikes beside them.

In the meantime the French had, on their side, been preparing for the battle. Phillip had crossed the Somme at Abbeyville late on Thursday afternoon, and remained there next day marshalling the large reinforcements which were hourly arriving. His force now considerably exceeded 100,000 men, the number with which he had marched from Amiens three days previously.

Friday was the festival of St. Louis, and that evening Phillip gave a splendid banquet to the whole of the nobles of his army.

On the following morning the king, accompanied by his brother the Count d'Alençon, the old King of Bohemia and his son, the King of Rome, the Duke of Lorraine, the Count of Blois, the Count of Flanders, and a great number of other feudal princes, heard Mass at the Abbey, and then marched with his great army towards Cressy. He moved but slowly in order to give time to all the forces scattered over the neighbourhood to come up, and four knights, headed by one of the King of Bohemia's officers, went forward to reconnoitre the English position. They approached within very short distance of the English lines and gained a very exact knowledge of the position, the English taking no measures to interrupt the reconnaissance. They returned with the information they had gathered, and the leader of the party, Le Moyne de Basele, one of the most judicious officers of his time, strongly advised the king to halt his troops, pointing out that as it was evident the English were ready to give battle, and as they were fresh and vigorous while the French were wearied and hungry, would be better to encamp and give battle the next morning.

Phillip saw the wisdom of the advice and ordered his two marshals the Lord of St. Venant and Charles de Montmorency to command a halt. They instantly spurred off, one to the front and the other to the rear, commanding the leaders to halt their banners. Those in advance at once obeyed, but those behind still pressed on, declaring that they would not halt until they were in the front line. All wanted to be first, in order to obtain their share of the honour and glory of defeating the English. Those in front, seeing the others still coming on, again pressed forward, and thus, in spite of the efforts of the king and his marshals, the French nobles with their followers pressed forward in confusion, until, passing through a small wood, they found themselves suddenly in the presence of the English army.

CHAPTER XIV
CRESSY

THE surprise of the French army at finding themselves in the presence of the English was so great that the first line recoiled in confusion. Those marching up from behind imagined that they had been already engaged and repulsed by the English, and the disorder spread through the whole army, and was increased by the common people, who had crowded to the field in immense numbers from the whole country round to see the battle and share in the plunder of the English camp.

From King Edward's position on the rising ground he could see the confusion which prevailed in the French ranks, and small as were his forces he would probably have obtained an easy victory by ordering a sudden charge upon them. The English, however, being dismounted, but small results would have followed the scattering of the great host of the French. The English army therefore remained immovable, except that the soldiers rose from the ground, and taking their places in the ranks, awaited the onslaught of the enemy.

King Phillip himself now arrived on the field and his hatred for the English led him at once to disregard the advice which had been given him and to order the battle to commence as soon as possible.

The army was divided into four bodies, of which Phillip commanded one, the Count D'Alençon on the second, the King of Bohemia the third, and the Count of Savoy the fourth. Besides these were a band of 15,000 mercenaries, Genoese crossbow-men, who were now ordered to pass between the ranks of cavalry and to clear the ground of the English archers, who were drawn up in the usual form in which they fought—namely, in very open order, line behind line, the men standing alternately, so that each had ample room to use his bow and to fire over the heads of those in front. The formation was something that of a harrow, and, indeed, exactly resembled that in which the Roman archers fought, and was called by them a quincunx.

The Genoese had marched four leagues beneath a hot sun loaded with their armour and heavy cross-bows, and they remonstrated against the order, urging that they were in no condition to do good service without some repose. The Count D'Alençon, furious at their hesitation, ordered them up, but as they advanced a terrible thunderstorm, with torrents of rain, broke over the armies, and wetting the cords of the crossbows rendered many of them unserviceable. At length the crossbow-men were arranged in front, while behind them were the vast body of French cavalry, and the order was given for the battle to begin.

The Genoese advanced with loud shouts but the English archers paid no attention to the noise, but waited calmly for the attack. At this moment the sun, now approaching the west, shone out brightly between the clouds behind the English, its rays streaming full in the faces of the French. The Genoese were now within distance, and began to discharge their quarrells at their impassive enemies, but as they opened fire the English archers drew their bows from the cases which had protected them from the rain, and stepping forward poured their arrows among the Genoese. The crossbow-men were smitten as with a storm, numbers were struck in the face and other unprotected parts, and they were instantly thrown into confusion, and casting away their cross-bows they recoiled in disorder among the horsemen behind them.

Phillip, passionate and cruel as ever, instead of trying to rally the Genoese, ordered the cavalry behind them to fall upon them, and the men-at-arms at once plunged in among the disordered mass of the crossbow-men, and a wild scene of carnage and confusion ensued, the English archers continuing to pour their unerring arrows into the midst.

The Count D'Alençon, who was behind, separated his division into two bodies, and swept round on one side himself, while the Count of Flanders did the same on the other to attack the Prince of Wales in more regular array. Taking a circuitous route, D'Alençon appeared upon a rising ground on the flank of the archers of the Black Prince, and thus, avoiding their arrows, charged down with his cavalry upon the 800 men-at-arms gathered round the Black Prince, while the Count of Flanders attacked on the other flank. Nobly did the flower of English chivalry withstand the shock of the French, and the prince himself and the highest nobles and simple men-at-arms fought side by side. None gave away a foot.

In vain the French, with impetuous charges, strove to break through the mass of steel. The spear-heads were cleft off with sword and battle-axe, and again and again men and horses recoiled from the unbroken line. Each time the French retired the English ranks were formed anew, and as attack followed attack a pile of dead rose around them. The Count D'Alençon and the Duke of Lorraine were among the first who fell. The young Count of Blois, finding that he could not ride through the wall of steel, dismounted with his knights and fought his way on foot towards the banner of the Prince of Wales. For a time the struggle was desperate, and the young prince, with his household knights, was for a time well-nigh beaten back.

Walter, fighting close beside the prince, parried more than one blow intended for him, and the prince himself slew the Count of Blois, whose followers all fell around him. The Count of Flanders was also slain, and confusion began to reign among the assailants, whose leaders had now all fallen. Phillip himself strove to advance with his division into the fight, but the struggle between the Genoese and the men-at-arms was still continuing, and the very multitude of his troops in the narrow and difficult field which the English had chosen for the battle embarrassed his movements.

CRESSY

Charles of Luxembourg, King of the Romans, and afterwards Emperor of Germany, son of the old King of Bohemia, with a large body of German and French cavalry, now assailed the English archers, and in spite of their flights of arrows came to close quarters, and cutting their way through them joined in the assault upon the men-at-arms of the Black Prince. Nearly 40,000 men were now pressing round the little body, and the Earls of Northampton and Arundel moved forward with their divisions to his support, while the Earl of Warwick, who was with the prince, despatched Sir Thomas of Norwich to the king, who still remained with his powerful reserve, to ask for aid.

"Sir Thomas," demanded the king, "is my son killed, overthrown, or wounded beyond help?"

"Not so, sire," replied the knight, "but he is in a rude fight, and much needs your aid."

"Go back, Sir Thomas, to those who sent you and tell them from me that whatsoever happens they require no aid from me so long as my son is in life. Tell them also that I command them to let the boy win his spurs, for, God willing, the day shall be his, and the honour shall rest with him and those into whose charge I have given him."

The prince and those around him were filled with fresh ardour when they received this message. Each man redoubled his efforts to repel the forces that were incessantly poured down upon them by the French. On all sides these pressed around them, striving desperately, but ever in vain, to break through the solid ranks of the English. The French men-at-arms suffered, moreover, terribly from the attacks of the Welsh infantry. These men, clad in thick leather jerkins, nimble of foot, accustomed to a life of activity, were armed with shortened lances and knives, mingled fearlessly among the confused mass of French cavalry, creeping beneath the horses' bellies, standing up when they got a chance, and stabbing horses and men with their knives and pikes. Many were trampled upon or struck down, but numbering, as they did, 6000, they pervaded the whole mass of the enemy, and did terrible execution, adding in no small degree to the confusion caused by the shower of arrows from the archers within the circle of the men-at-arms. That instant a French knight fell, struck from his horse with a battle-axe or arrow, or by the fall of a wounded steed, the half-wild Welsh were upon him, and slew him before he could regain his feet.

The slaughter was immense. The Count of Harcourt, with his nephew the Count D'Aumale and his two gallant sons, fell together, and at last Charles of Luxembourg, seeing his banner down, his troops routed, his friends slain, and the day irreparably lost, and being himself severely wounded in three places, turned his horse and fled, casting off his rich emblazoned surcoat to avoid recognition. In the meantime Prince Charles's father, the veteran King of Bohemia, once one of the most famous warriors of Europe, but now old and blind, sat on horseback at a little distance from the fight; the knights around him told him the events as they happened, and the old monarch soon saw that the day was lost. He asked them for tidings of his son Charles of Luxembourg, but they were forced to reply that the banner of the King of the Romans was no longer in sight, but that, doubtless, he was somewhere engaged in the mêlée.

"Lords," said the old man, "you are my vassals, my friends, and my companions, and on this day I command and beseech you to lead me forward so far that I may deal one blow of my sword in the battle."

His faithful friends obeyed him, a number of knights arranged themselves around him, and lest they should lose him in the fight they tied their horses together by the bridles and charged down into the fray. Advancing directly against the banner of the Prince of Wales, the blind monarch was carried into the midst of the thickest strife.

There the little group of knights fought gallantly, and after the battle was over, the bodies of the king and his friends were found lying together their dead horses still linked by the bridles.

During this terrible battle, which had been raging since three o'clock, Phillip had made strenuous efforts to aid his troops engaged in the front by continually sending fresh bodies to the assault. It was now growing dark, terror and confusion had already spread among the French, and many were flying in all directions, and the unremitting showers of English arrows still flew like hail among their ranks. As the king made his way forward, surrounded by his personal attendants to take part himself in the fight, his followers fell thick around him, and his horse was slain by an arrow. John of Hainault, who had remained by his side during the whole day, mounted upon a fresh horse and urged him to fly, as the day was lost. Phillip, however, persisted, and made his way into the mêlée, where he fought for some time with extreme courage, until almost all around him were slain, the royal standard bearer killed, and himself wounded in two places. John of Hainault then seized his bridle exclaiming "Come away, sire, it is full time; do not throw your life away foolishly; if you have lost this day you will win another," and so almost forced the unwilling king from the field. Phillip, accompanied by the lords of Montmorency, Beaujeu, Aubigny, and Mansault, with John of Hainault, and sixty men-at-arms, rode to the Castle of Broye, and there halted for a few hours. At midnight he again set out, and in the morning arrived safely at Amiens.

The Black Prince held his station until night without yielding a single step to all the efforts of the French. Gradually, however, the assailants became less and less numerous, the banners disappeared, and the shouts of the leaders and the clang of arms died away, and the silence which prevailed over the field at once announced that the victory was complete and the enemy in full flight. An immense number of torches were now lighted through the English lines, and the king, quitting for the first time his station on the hill, came down to embrace his gallant son. Edward and his host rejoiced in a spirit of humility over the victory. No songs of triumph, no feastings or merriment were permitted, but a solemn service of the church was held, and the king and his soldiers offered their thanks to God for the victory He had given them. The English army lay all night under arms, and a number of scattered parties of the French, wandering about in the darkness, entered the lines and were slain or taken prisoners.

The dawn of the next morning was thick and foggy, and intelligence coming in that a large body of the enemy were advancing upon them, the Earls of Northampton, Warwick, and Norfolk, with 500 men-at-arms and 2000 archers, went out to reconnoitre, and came in the misty twilight upon an immense force composed of the citizens of Beauvais, Rouen, and some other towns, led by the Grand Prior of France and the Archbishop of Rouen, who were approaching the field.

By some extraordinary accident they had not met any of the fugitives flying from Cressy, and were ignorant that a battle had been fought. The English charged them at once. Their advance-guard, consisting of burghers, was easily overthrown. The second division, which was composed of men-at-arms, fought bravely, but was unable to withstand the charge of the triumphant English, and was completely broken and defeated. The Grand Prior was killed and a vast number of his followers slain or captured. During the whole of the morning detached parties from Edward's army scoured the country, dispersing and slaughtering bands of French who still remained together, and towards night the Earl of Northampton returned to the camp with the news that no enemy remained in the vicinity that could offer a show of resistance to the English force.

It is said that a far greater number of French were killed upon the second day than upon first. This can be accounted for by the fact that on the first day but a small portion of the English army were engaged, and that upon the second the English were fresh and vigorous, and their enemy exhausted and dispirited.

The greater number of the French nobles and knights who fell, died in their attempts to break through the Black Prince's array. Besides the King of Bohemia, nine sovereign princes and eighty great nobles were killed, with 1200 knights,

1500 men-at-arms, and 30,000 foot; while on the English side only three knights and a small number of men-at-arms and infantry were killed.

The body of the King of Bohemia and those of the other great leaders were carried in solemn pomp to the Abbey of Maintenay. Edward himself and his son accompanied them as mourners. On the Monday following Edward marched with his army against Calais, and summoned the town to surrender. John of Vienne, who commanded the garrison, refused to comply with the demand. The fortifications of the town were extremely strong and the garrison numerous, and Edward perceived that an assault would be very unlikely to succeed, and would entail great loss, while a repulse would have dimmed the lustre of the success which he had gained. He therefore determined to reduce it by famine, and the troops were set to work to build huts. So permanently and strongly were these constructed that it seemed to the enemy that King Edward was determined to remain before Calais even should he have to stay there for ten years.

Proclamations were issued in England and Flanders inviting traders to establish stores and to bring articles of trade of all kinds, and in a short time a complete town sprang up which was named by Edward "New-Town the Bold". The English fleet held complete possession of the sea, cutting off the besieged from all succour by ship, and enabling abundant supplies for the army to be brought from England and Flanders. Strong parties were sent out in all directions. The northern provinces of France were scoured, and the army was amply provided with necessaries and even luxuries.

After the first terrible shock caused by the crushing defeat of Cressy, King Phillip began at once to take measures for the relief of Calais, and made immense efforts again to put a great army in the field. He endeavoured by all means in his power to gain fresh allies. The young Count of Flanders, who, at the death of his father at Cressy, was sixteen years of age, was naturally even more hostile to the English than the late prince had been, and he strove to win over his subjects to the French alliance, while Phillip made them magnificent offers if they would join him. The Flemings, however, remained stanch to the English alliance, and held their prince in duresse until he at last consented to marry the daughter of Edward. A week before the date fixed for the nuptials, however, he managed to escape from the vigilance of his guards when out hawking, and fled to the court of France.

In Scotland Phillip was more successful, and David Bruce, instead of employing the time given him by the absence of Edward with his armies in driving out the English garrisons from the strong places they still held in Scotland, raised and an army of 50,000 men and marched across the border into England plundering and ravaging. Queen Philippa, however, raising an army, marched against him, and the Scotch were completely defeated at Neville's Cross, 15,000 being killed and their king himself taken prisoner.

Walter's conduct at the battle of Cressy gained him still further the favour of the Black Prince. The valour with which he had fought was conspicuous even on a field where all fought gallantly, and the prince felt that more than once he would have been smitten down had not Walter's sword interposed. Ralph too had fought with reckless bravery, and many French knights and gentlemen had gone down before the tremendous blows of his heavy mace, against which the stoutest armour availed nothing. After the battle the prince offered to make him an esquire in spite of the absence of gentle blood in his veins, but Ralph declined the honour.

"An it please you, Sir Prince," he said, "but I should feel more comfortable among the men-at-arms, my fellows. In the day of battle I trust that I should do no discredit to my squirehood, but at other times I should feel woefully out of my element, and should find nought for my hands to do, therefore if it so pleases your Royal Highness, I would far rather remain a simple man-at-arms."

Ralph did not, however, refuse the heavy purse which the prince gave him, although indeed he, as well as all the soldiers, was well supplied with money, so great were the spoils which the army had gathered in its march before Cressy, and which they now swept off in their raids among the northern provinces of France.

One evening Walter was returning from a banquet at the pavilion of the Prince of Wales, with Ralph as usual following at a little distance, when from a corner of the street a man darted suddenly out and struck a dagger with all his force between his shoulders. Well was it for Walter that he had taken Geoffrey's advice, and had never laid aside the shirt of mail, night or day. Fine as was its temper, two or three links of the outer fold were broken, but the point did not penetrate the second fold, and the dagger snapped in the hand of the striker. The force of the sudden blow, however, hurled Walter to the ground. With a loud cry Ralph rushed forward. The man instantly fled. Ralph pursued him but a short distance and then hastened back to Walter.

"Are you hurt, Sir Walter?" he exclaimed.

"In no way, Ralph, thanks to my shirt of mail. Well, indeed, was it for me that I was wearing it, or I should assuredly have been a dead man. I had almost begun to forget that I was a threatened man; but I shall be on guard for the future."

"I wish I had followed the fellow," Ralph said. "I would not have slain him could I have helped it, but would have left it for the hangman to extort from him the name of his employer; but, in truth, he struck so hard, and you fell so straight before the blow, that I feared the mail had given way, and that you were sorely wounded if not killed. You have oft told me that I was over-careful of you, but you see that I was not careful enough, however, you may be assured that if another attempt be made those who attempt it shall not get off scot free. Do you think of laying a complaint before the provost against him you suspect?"

"It would be useless, Ralph. We may have suspicion of the man from whom the blow came, but have no manner of proof. It might have been done by any ruffian camp-follower who struck the blow only with the hope of carrying off my chain and purse. The camp swarms with such fellows, and we have no clue which could lead to his detection, unless," he added, stooping and picking a piece of steel which lay at his feet, "this broken dagger may some day furnish us with one. No; we will say nought about it. Sir James Carnegie is not now in camp, having left a week since on business in England. We exchange no words when we meet, but I heard that he had been called away. Fortunately the young prince likes him not, and I therefore have seldom occasion to meet him. I have no doubt that he credits me with disfavour in which he is held by the prince; but I have never even mentioned his name before him, and the prince's misliking is but the feeling which a noble and generous heart has, as though by instinct, against one who is false and treacherous. At the same time we must grant that this traitor knight is a bold and fearless man-at-arms; he fought well at La Blanche Tache and Cressy, and he is much liked and trusted by my lord of Northampton, in whose following he mostly rides; 'tis a pity that one so brave should have so foul and treacherous a heart. Here we are at my hut, and you can sleep soundly to-night, Ralph, for there is little fear that the fellow, who has failed to-night, will repeat his attempt for some time. He thinks, no doubt, that he has killed me, for with a blow so strongly struck he would scarcely have felt the snapping of the weapon, and is likely enough already on board one of the ships which ply to and fro from England on his way to acquaint his employer that I am removed from his path."

The next morning Walter mentioned to the Black Prince the venture which had befallen him, and the narrow escape he had had of his life. The prince was extremely exasperated, and gave orders that an inquisition should be made through the camp, and that all men found there not being able to give a good account of themselves as having reasonable and lawful calling there should be forthwith put on board ship and sent to England. He questioned Walter closely whether he deemed that the attack was for the purpose of plunder only, or whether he had any reason to believe that he had private enemies.

"There is a knight who is evilly disposed toward me, your highness," Walter said; "but seeing that I have no proof whatever that he had a hand in this affair, however strongly I may suspect it, I would fain, with your leave, avoid mentioning his name."

"But think you that there is any knight in this camp capable of so foul an action?"

"I have had proofs, your highness, that he is capable of such an act; but in this matter my tongue is tied, as the wrong he attempted was not against myself, but against others who have so far forgiven him that they would fain the matter should drop. He owes me ill-will, seeing that I am aware of his conduct, and that it was my intervention which caused his schemes to fail. Should this attempt against me be repeated it can scarce be the effect of chance, but would show premeditated design, and I would then, both in defence of my own life, and because I think that such deeds should not go unpunished, not hesitate to name him to you, and if proof be wanting to defy him to open combat."

"I regret, Sir Walter, that your scruples should hinder you from at once denouncing him; but seeing how grave a matter it is to charge a knight with so foul a crime, I will not lay stress upon you; but be assured that should any repetition of the attempt be made I shall take the matter in hand, and will see that this caitiff knight receives his deserts."

A short time afterwards Walter accompanied the prince in an excursion which he made with a portion of the army, sweeping the French provinces as far as the river Somme. Upon their way back they passed through the village of Près, hard by which stood a small castle. It was situated some forty miles from Calais, and standing upon rising ground, it commanded a very extensive view over the country.

"What say you, Sir Walter?" the prince said to the young knight who was riding near him. "That castle would make a good advanced post, and a messenger riding in could bring news of any large movements of the enemy." Walter assented. "Then, Sir Walter, I name you chatelain. I shall be sorry to lose your good company; but the post is one of peril, and I know that you are ever longing to distinguish yourself. Take forty men-at-arms and sixty archers. With that force you may make shift to resist any attack until help reaches you from camp. You may be sure that I shall not be slack in spurring to your rescue should you be assailed."

Walter received the proposal with delight. He was weary of the monotony of life in New Town, and this post in which vigilance and activity would be required was just to his taste; so, taking the force named by the prince, with a store of provision, he drew off from the column and entered the castle.

CHAPTER XV
THE SIEGE OF A FORTALICE

WALTER'S first step on assuming the command was to examine thoroughly into the capabilities of defence of the place, to see that the well was in good order, and the supply of water ample, and to send out a foraging party, which, driving in a number of beasts and some cart-loads of forage, would supply his garrison for some time. The castle he found was less strong than it looked. The walls were lightly built, and were incapable of withstanding any heavy battering. The moat was dry, and the flanking towers badly placed, and affording little protection to the faces of the walls; however, the extent of the defences was small, and Walter felt confident that with the force at his command he could resist any sudden attack, unless made in overwhelming force, so that all the faces of the wall could be assaulted at the same time. He had a large number of great stones brought in to pile against the gate, while others were brought into the central keep, similarly to defend the door should the outer wall be carried. He appointed Ralph as his lieutenant, and every day, leaving him in charge of the castle, rode through the country for many miles round, with twenty men-at-arms, to convince himself that no considerable force of the enemy were approaching. These reconnaissances were not without some danger and excitement, for several times bodies of the country people, armed with scythes, axes, and staves, tried to intercept them on their return to the castle, and once or twice Walter and his men had to fight their way through their opponents. Contrary to the custom of the times, Walter gave orders to his men not to slay any when resistance had ceased.

"They are but doing what we ourselves should do did French garrisons hold our castles at home, and I deem them in no way to be blamed for the efforts which they make to slay us. In self-defence, of course, we must do our best, and must kill in order that we may not ourselves be slain; but when they are once routed, let them go to their homes. Poor people, the miseries which this war has brought upon them are great, and there is no wonder that they hate us."

This leniency on Walter's part was not without good effect. When the country people found that the garrison of the castle of Près did not carry fire and sword through the villages around, that they took only sufficient for their needs, and behaved with courtesy to all, their animosity to a great extent subsided. No longer did the women and children of the little villages fly to the woods when they saw the gleam of Walter's approaching spears, but remained at their avocations, and answered willingly enough the questions which he asked them as to whether they had heard aught of the movements of French troops. So far as possible, Walter refrained from seizing the cattle or stores of grain of the poorer classes, taking such as he needed from the lands of the wealthy proprietors, all of whom had left the country, and were either with the French army or sheltering in Paris. Five of his best mounted men Walter chose as messengers, and one rode each day to New Town with the news which had been gathered, returning on the following day, and then resting his horse for three days before again setting out.

Night and day sentries were placed on the walls, for although Walter heard nothing of any body gathering in his immediate vicinity, a force might at any moment issue from Amiens and appear suddenly before the place. Such was indeed what really took place, and at daybreak one morning Walter was aroused by the news that the sentinels saw a large body of men rapidly approaching. The horse of the messenger next on duty stood, as usual, saddled and bridled in readiness, and without a moment's delay Walter ordered the man to mount and ride to the prince, and to give news that the castle was assailed, but by how large a force he could not as yet say.

The instant the messenger had started through the gates Walter ascended to the walls; he saw at once that the party was a strong one; for although still at some distance, and but dimly seen in the gray morning light, he judged that it must contain at least a thousand men-at-arms. At this moment a call from the sentry on the other side of the castle was heard, and hastening thither, Walter saw that another body nearly as numerous as the first were approaching from the side of Calais, having made a detour so as to place themselves between the castle and the army, to which news would naturally be sent of their coming. Walter watched his messenger, who had now ridden half a mile towards the approaching body. Suddenly he saw him turn his horse and ride off at right angles to the road.

"He sees them," he said, "and is going to try to ride round them. I fear that there is but little hope of his escaping, seeing that they are between him and Calais, and that assuredly some among them must be as well or better mounted than himself." As he spoke a party of horsemen were seen to detach themselves from the flank of the French column and to gallop off at full speed to intercept the messenger; the latter diverged more and more from his course, but he was constantly headed off by his pursuers, and at last, seeing the impossibility of getting through them, he again turned his horse's head and galloped off towards the castle, which he reached a few hundred yards only in advance of his foes.

"I could not help it, Sir Walter," he said, as he galloped in at the gate. "I found that although Robin is fast, some of those horsemen had the turn of speed of me, and that it was impossible that I could get through; so deeming that I should do more service by coming to strike a blow here than by having my throat cut out in the fields, I made the best of my way back."

"Quite right, Martin!" Walter said. "I should have been grieved had you thrown your life away needlessly. I saw from the first that your escape was cut off. And now, men, each to his place; but first pile up the stones against the gate, and then let each man take a good meal, for it is like enough to be long before we get a chance of doing so again."

Again ascending to the walls Walter saw that the first body of men-at-arms he had perceived was followed at a distance by a strong force of footmen having with them some large wagons.

"I fear," he said to Ralph, "that they have brought machines with them from Amiens, and in that case they will not be long in effecting a breach, for doubtless they know that the walls are but weak. We shall have to fight stoutly, for it may be days before the news of our leaguer reaches the camp. However, I trust that the prince will, by to-morrow night, when he finds that two days have elapsed without the coming of my usual messenger, suspect that we are besieged and will sally forth to our assistance. And now let us to breakfast, for we shall need all our strength to-day, and you may be sure that French will lose no time in attacking, seeing that assistance may shortly arrive from Calais."

There were but few preparations to be made. Each man had had his post assigned to him on the walls in case of an attack, and piles of stones had been collected in readiness to cast down upon the heads of those attempting an assault. Cauldrons were carried up to the walls and filled with water, and great fires were lighted under them. In half an hour the French infantry had reached the spot, but another two hours elapsed before any hostile movement was made, the leaders of the assailants giving their men that time to rest after their long march. Then a stir was visible among them, and they were seen to form in four columns, each about a thousand strong, which advanced simultaneously against opposite sides of the castle. As soon as their intentions were manifest Walter divided his little force, and these, gathering in four groups upon the walls, prepared to resist the assault. To four of his most trusty men-at-arms he assigned the command of these parties, he himself and Ralph being thus left free to give their aid where it was most needed.

The assailants were well provided with scaling-ladders, and advanced with a number of crossbow-men in front, who speedily opened a hot fire on the walls. Walter ordered his archers to bide their time, and not to fire a shot till certain that every shaft would tell. They accordingly waited until the French arrived within fifty yards of the wall, when the arrows began to rain among them with deadly effect, scarce one but struck its mark—the face of an enemy. Even the closed vizors of the knights and chief men-at-arms did not avail to protect their wearers; the shafts pierced between the bars or penetrated the slits left open for sight, and many fell slain by the first volley. But their numbers were far too great to allow the columns being checked by the fire of so small a number of archers; the front ranks, indeed, pressed forward more eagerly than before, being anxious to reach the foot of the wall, where they would be in comparative shelter from the arrows.

The archers disturbed themselves in no way at the reaching of the wall by the heads of the columns; but continued to shoot fast and true into the mass behind them, and as these were, for the most part, less completely armed than their leaders, numbers fell under the fire of the sixty English bowmen. It was the turn of the men-at-arms now. Immediately the assailants poured into the dry moat and sought to raise their ladders the men-at-arms hurled down the masses of stones piled in readiness, while some poured buckets of boiling water over them. In spite of the loss they were suffering the French raised their ladders, and, covering their heads with their shields, the leaders strove to gain the walls. As they did so, some of the archers took post in the flanking towers, and as with uplifted arms the assailants climbed the ladders, the archers smote them above the joints of their armour beneath the arm-pits, while the men-at-arms with pike and battle-axe hewed down those who reached the top of the ladders. Walter and Ralph hastened from point to point encouraging the men and joining in the defence where the pressure was hottest; and at last, after two hours of vain effort and suffering great loss, the assailants drew off and the garrison had breathing time.

"Well done, my men!" Walter said, cheeringly; "they have had a lesson which they will remember, and if so be that they have brought with them no machines we may hold out against them for any time."

It was soon manifest, however, that along with the scaling-ladders the enemy had brought one of their war-machines. Men were seen dragging massive beams of timber towards the walls, and one of the wagons was drawn forward and upset on its side at a distance of sixty yards from the wall, not, however, without those who drew it suffering much from the arrows of the bowmen. Behind the shelter thus formed the French began to put together the machine, whose beams soon raised themselves high above the wagon.

In the meantime groups of men dragged great stones laid upon a sort of hand sledge to the machine, and late in the afternoon it began to cast its missiles against the wall. Against these Walter could do little. He had no sacks, which, filled with earth, he might have lowered to cover the part of the walls assailed, and beyond annoying those working the machines by flights of arrows shot high in the air, so as to descend point downwards among them, he could do nothing.

The wall crumbled rapidly beneath the blows of the great stones, and Walter saw that by the following morning a breach would be effected. When night fell he called his men together and asked if any would volunteer to carry news through the enemy to the prince. The enterprise seemed well-nigh hopeless, for the French, as if foreseeing that such an attempt might be made, had encamped in a complete circle round the castle, as was manifest by the position of their fires. Several men stepped forward, and Walter chose three light and active men—archers—to attempt the enterprise. These stripped off their steel caps and breastpieces, so that they might move more quickly, and when the French fires burned low and all was quiet save the creak of the machine and the dull heavy blows of the stones against the wall, the three men were lowered by ropes at different points, and started on their enterprise. A quarter of an hour later the garrison heard shouts and cries, and knew that a vigilant watch had been set by the French, and that one, if not all, of their friends had fallen into their hands. All night long the machine continued to play.

An hour before daylight, when he deemed that the enemy's vigilance would be relaxed, Walter caused himself with Ralph and twelve of his men-at-arms to be lowered by ropes from the wall. Each rope had a loop at the bottom in which one foot was placed, and knots were tied in order to give a better grasp for the hands. They were lowered at a short distance from the spot at which the machine was at work; all were armed with axes, and they made their way unperceived until within a few yards of the wagon. Then there was a cry of alarm, and in a moment they rushed forward among the enemy. The men working the machine were instantly cut down, and Walter and his party fell upon the machine, cutting the ropes and smashing the wheels and pulleys and hewing away at the timber itself. In a minute or two, however, they were attacked by the enemy, the officer in command having bade a hundred men lie down to sleep close behind the machine in case the garrison should attempt a sortie. Walter called upon Ralph and four of the men-at-arms to stand beside him while the others continued their work of destruction. The French came up in a tumultuous body, but, standing so far apart that they could wield their axes, the English dealt such destruction among their first assailants that these for a time recoiled. As fresh numbers came up, encouraged by their leader they renewed the attack, and in spite of the most tremendous efforts Walter and his party were driven back. By this time, however, so much damage had been done to the machine that it would be some hours before it could be repaired, even if spare ropes and other appliances had been brought with it from Amiens; so that, reinforced by the working party, Walter was again able to hold his ground, and after repulsing a fresh onslaught of the enemy he gave the word for his men to retire at full speed.

The French were so surprised by the sudden disappearance of their foes that it was a moment or two before they started in pursuit, and Walter and his men had gained some thirty yards before the pursuit really commenced.

The night was a dark one, and they considerably increased this advantage before they reach the foot of the wall, where the ropes were hanging.

"Has each of you found his rope?" Walter asked.

As soon as an affirmative answer was given he placed his foot in the loop and shouted to the men above to draw up, and before the enraged enemy could reach the spot the whole party were already some yards above their heads. The archers opened fire upon the French, doing, in spite of the darkness, considerable execution, for the men had snatched up their arms at the sudden alarm, and had joined the fray in such haste that many of them had not had time to put on their steel caps. There was noise and bustle in the enemy's camp, for the whole force were now under arms, and in their anger at the sudden blow which had been struck them some bodies of men even moved forward towards the walls as if they intended to renew the assault of the previous day; but the showers of arrows with which they were greeted cooled their ardour and they presently retired out of reach of bowshot. There was a respite now for the besiegers. No longer every few minutes did a heavy stone strike the walls.

The morning's light enabled the defenders of the castle to see the extent of the damage which the battering machine had effected. None too soon had they put a stop to its work, for had it continued its operations another hour or two would have effected a breach.

Already large portions of the wall facing it had fallen, and other portions were so seriously damaged that a few more blows would have levelled them.

THE SIEGE OF A FORTALICE

"At anyrate," Walter said to Ralph, "we have gained a respite; but even now I fear that if the Black Prince comes not until to-morrow he will arrive too late."

The French, apparently as well aware as the garrison of the necessity for haste, laboured at the repair of the machine. Bodies of men started to cut down trees to supply the place of the beams which had been rendered useless. Scarcely had the assault ceased when horsemen were despatched in various directions to seek for fresh ropes, and by dint of the greatest exertions the machine was placed in position to renew its attack shortly after noon.

By two o'clock several large portions of the damaged wall had fallen, and the debris formed a slope by which an assaulting column could rush to the bridge. As soon as this was manifest the French force formed for the assault and rushed forward in solid column.

Walter had made the best preparation possible for the defence. In the courtyard behind the breach his men had since morning been driving a circle of piles, connected by planks fastened to them. These were some five feet high, and along the top and in the face next to the breach sharp-pointed spikes and nails had been driven, rendering it difficult in the extreme for anyone to climb over. As the column of the assailants approached Walter placed his archers on the walls on either side of the breach, while he himself, with his men-at-arms, took his station in the gap and faced the coming host. The breach was some ten yards wide, but it was only for about half this width that the mound of broken stones rendered it possible for their enemies to assault, consequently there was but a space of some fifteen feet in width to be defended. Regardless of the flights of arrows, the French, headed by their knights and squires, advanced to the assault, and clambering up the rough stones attacked the defenders.

Walter, with Ralph and three of his best men-at-arms, stood in the front line and received the first shock of the assault. The roughness and steepness of the mound prevented the French from attacking in regular order, and the very eagerness of the knights and squires who came first in contact with their enemies was a hindrance to them. When the columns were seen gathering for the assault Walter had scattered several barrels full of oil and tar which he found in the cellars over the mound in front of the breach, rendering it greasy and slippery, and causing the assailants to slip and stagger and many to fall as they pressed forward to the assault. Before the fight commenced he had encouraged his soldiers by recalling to them how a mere handful of men had at Cressy withstood for hours the desperate efforts of the whole of the French army to break through their line, and all were prepared to fight to the death.

The struggle was a desperate one. Served by their higher position, and by the difficulties which the French encountered from the slipperiness of the ground and their own fierce ardour to attack, Walter and his little band for a long time resisted every effort. He with his sword and Ralph with his heavy mace did great execution, and they were nobly seconded by their men-at-arms. As fast as one fell another took his place. The breach in front of them was cumbered with dead and red with blood. Still the French poured upwards in a wave, and the sheer weight of their numbers and the fatigue caused by the tremendous exertions the defenders were making began to tell. Step by step the English were driven back, and Walter saw that the defence could not much longer be continued. He bade one of his men-at-arms at once order the archers to cease firing, and, leaving the walls, to take refuge in the keep, and thence to open fire upon the French as they poured through the breach.

When he found that this movement had been accomplished Walter bade the men-at-arms fall back gradually. A gap had been left in the wooden fence sufficient for one at a time to pass, and through this the men-at-arms retired one by one to the keep until only Walter and five others were left. With these Walter flung himself suddenly upon the assailants and forced them a few feet down the slope. Then he gave the word, and all sprang back, and leaping down from the wall into the courtyard ran through the barrier,

Walter and Ralph being the last to pass as the French with exulting shouts leapt down from the breach. There was another fierce fight at the barrier. Walter left Ralph to defend this with a few men-at-arms while he saw that all was in readiness for closing the door rapidly in the keep. Then he ran back again. He was but just in time. Ralph indeed could for a long time have held the narrow passage, but the barriers themselves were yielding. The French were pouring in through the breach, and as those behind could not see the nature of the obstacle which arrested the advance of their companions they continued to push forward, and by their weight pressed those in front against the spikes in the barrier. Many perished miserably on these. Others, whose armour protected them from this fate, were crushed to death by the pressure; but this was now so great that the timbers were yielding. Walter, seeing that in another moment they would be levelled, gave the word, sprang back with Ralph and his party, and entered the keep just as with a crash the barrier fell and the French poured in a crowd into the courtyard. Bolting the door the defenders of the keep piled against it the stones which had been laid in readiness.

The door was on the first floor, and was approached by a narrow flight of stone steps, up which but two abreast could advance. In their first fury the French poured up these steps, but from the loopholes which commanded it the English bowmen shot so hard that their arrows pierced the strongest armour. Smitten through vizor and armour, numbers of the bravest of the assailants fell dead. Those who gained the top of the steps were assailed by showers of boiling oil from an upper chamber which projected over the door, and whose floor was pierced for this purpose, while from the top of the keep showers of stones were poured down. After losing great numbers in this desperate effort at assault the French drew off for a while, while their leaders held council as to the best measures to be taken for the capture of the keep.

After a time Walter from the summit saw several bodies of men detach themselves from the crowd still without the castle and proceed into the country. Two hours later they were seen returning laden with trunks of trees. These were dragged through the breach, and were, in spite of the efforts of the archers and of the men-at-arms with their stones, placed so as to form a sort of penthouse against one side of the keep. Numbers of the soldiers now poured up with sacks and all kinds of vessels which they had gathered from the surrounding villages, filled with earth. This was thrown over the beams until it filled all the crevices between them and formed a covering a foot thick, so that neither boiling oil nor water poured from above could penetrate to injure those working beneath its shelter. When all was ready a strong body armed with picks and crowbars entered the penthouse and began to labour to cut away the wall of the keep itself.

"Their commander knows his business," Walter said, "and the device is an excellent one. We can do nothing, and it only depends upon the strength of the wall how long we can hold out. The masonry is by no means good, and before nightfall, unless aid comes, there will be nought for us but death or surrender."

CHAPTER XVI
A PRISONER

AS long as it was light an anxious look-out was kept from the top of the keep towards Calais. There was nothing to be done. The besiegers who had entered the walls were ensconced in the various buildings in the courtyard or placed behind walls so as to be out of arrow-shot from above, and were in readiness to repel any sortie which might be made to interfere with the work going on under the penthouse. But no sortie was possible, for to effect this it would be necessary to remove the stones from the door, and before this could be accomplished the besiegers would have rallied in overwhelming force, nor could a sortie have effected anything beyond the slaying of the men actually engaged in the work. The beams of the penthouse were too strong and too heavily weighted with earth to be removed, and the attempt would only have entailed useless slaughter. The penthouse was about forty feet in length, and the assailants were piercing three openings, each of some six feet in width, leaving two strong supporting pillars between them. Anxiously the garrison within listened to the sounds of work, which became louder and louder as the walls crumbled before the stroke of pickaxe and crowbar.

"I shall hold out until the last moment," Walter said to Ralph, "in hopes of relief, but before they burst in I shall sound a parley. To resist further would be a vain sacrifice of life."

Presently a movement could be seen among the stones, and then almost simultaneously two apertures appeared. The chamber into which the openings were made was a large one, being used as the common room of the garrison. Here twenty archers, and the remaining men-at-arms—of whom nearly one-half had fallen in the defence of the breach—were gathered, and the instant the orifices appeared the archers began to send their arrows through them. Then Walter ascended to another chamber, and ordered the trumpeter to sound a parley.

The sound was repeated by the assailants' trumpeter.

"Who commands the force?" Walter asked.

"I, Guy, Count of Evreux."

"I am Sir Walter Somers," the young knight continued. "I wish to ask terms for the garrison."

"You must surrender unconditionally," the count replied from the courtyard. "In ten minutes we shall have completely pierced your walls, and you will be at our mercy."

"You may pierce our walls," Walter replied, "but it will cost you many lives before you force your way in; we will defend the hold from floor to floor, and you know how desperate men can fight. It will cost you scores of lives before you win your way to the summit of this keep; but if I have your knightly word that the lives of all within these walls shall be spared, then will I open the door and lay down our arms."

A consultation took place between the leaders below. There was truth in Walter's words that very many lives would be sacrificed before the resistance of so gallant a garrison could be overcome. Every minute was of importance, for it was possible that at any moment aid might arrive from Calais, and that the table would be turned upon the besiegers.

Therefore, after a short parley among themselves, the count replied:

"You have fought as a gallant knight and gentleman, Sir Walter Somers, and have wrought grievous harm upon my leading. I should grieve that so brave a knight should lose his life in a useless resistance. Therefore I agree to your terms, and swear upon my knightly honour that upon your surrendering yourselves prisoners of war, the lives of all within these walls shall be spared."

A PRISONER

Walter at once gave the order. The stones were removed and the door thrown open, and leading his men Walter descended the steps into the courtyard, which was now illuminated with torches, and handed his sword to the Count of Evreux.

"You promised me, count," a tall knight standing by his side said, "that if he were taken alive, the commander of this castle should be my prisoner."

"I did so, Sir Phillip Holbeaut. When you proposed this adventure to me, and offered to place your following at my command, I agreed to the request you made me; but mind," he said sternly, "my knightly word has been given for his safety. See that he receives fair and gentle treatment at your hand. I would not that aught should befall so brave a knight."

"I seek him no harm," the knight said angrily; "but I know that he is one of the knights of the Black Prince's own suite, and that his ransom will be freely paid, and as my coffers are low from the expenses of the war, I would fain replenish them at the expense of the English prince."

"I said not that I doubted you, Sir Phillip," the count said calmly; "but as the knight surrendered on my word, it was needful that I should warn you to treat him as I myself should do did he remain in my hands, and to give him fair treatment until duly ransomed."

"I should be glad, count," Walter said, "if you will suffer me to take with me as companion in my captivity this man-at-arms. He is strongly attached to me, and we have gone through many perils together; it will lighten my captivity to have him by my side."

"Surely I will do so, Sir Walter, and wish that your boon had been a larger one. The rest I will take back with me to Amiens, there to hold until exchanged for some of those who at various times have fallen into your king's hands. And now to work, men; lose not a moment in stripping the castle of all that you choose to carry away, then apply fire to the storehouses, granaries, and the hold itself. I would not that it remained standing to serve as an outpost for the English."

ST.GEORGE FOR ENGLAND

The horses were brought from the stables. Walter and Ralph took their horses by the bridle, and followed Sir Phillip Holbeaut through the now open gates of the castle to the spot where the horses of the besiegers were picketed. The knight, and his own men-at-arms, who had at the beginning of the day numbered a hundred and fifty, but who were now scarcely two-thirds of that strength, at once mounted with their prisoners, and rode off from the castle. A few minutes later a glare of light burst out from behind them. The count's orders had been obeyed; fire had been applied to the stores of forage, and soon the castle of Près was wrapped in flames.

"I like not our captor's manner," Ralph said to Walter as they rode along side by side.

"I agree with you, Ralph. I believe that the reason which he gave the count for his request was not a true one, though, indeed, I can see no other motive which he could have for seeking to gain possession of me. Sir Phillip, although a valiant knight, bears but an indifferent reputation. I have heard that he is a cruel master to his serfs, and that when away fighting in Germany he behaved so cruelly to the peasantry that even the Germans, who are not nice in their modes of warfare, cried out against him. It is an evil fortune that has thrown us into his hands; still, although grasping and avaricious, he can hardly demand for a simple knight any inordinate ransom. The French themselves would cry out did he do so, seeing that so large a number of their own knights are in our hands, and that the king has ample powers of retaliation; however, we need not look on the dark side. It is not likely that our captivity will be a long one, for the prince, who is the soul of generosity, will not haggle over terms, but will pay my ransom as soon as he hears into whose hands I have fallen, while there are scores of men-at-arms prisoners, whom he can exchange for you. Doubtless Sir Phillip will send you over, as soon as he arrives at his castle, with one of his own followers to treat for my ransom."

After riding for some hours the troop halted their weary horses in a wood, and lighting fires, cooked their food, and then lay down until morning. Sir Phillip exchanged but few words with his captive; as, having removed his helm, he sat by the fire, Walter had an opportunity of seeing his countenance. It did not belie his reputation. His face had a heavy and brutal expression which was not decreased by the fashion of his hair, which was cut quite short, and stood up without parting all over his bullet-shaped head; he had a heavy and bristling moustache which was cut short in a line with his lips.

"It is well," Walter thought to himself, "that it is my ransom rather than my life which is dear to that evil-looking knight; for, assuredly, he is not one to hesitate did fortune throw a foe into his hands."

At daybreak the march was resumed, and was continued until they reached the castle of Sir Phillip Holbeaut, which stood on a narrow tongue of land formed by a sharp bend of the Somme.

On entering the castle the knight gave an order to his followers, and the prisoners were at once led to a narrow cell beneath one of the towers. Walter looked round indignantly when he arrived there.

"This is a dungeon for a felon," he exclaimed, "not the apartment for a knight who has been taken captive in fair fight. Tell your master that he is bound to award me honourable treatment, and that unless he removes me instantly from this dungeon to a proper apartment, and treats me with all due respect and courtesy, I will, when I regain liberty, proclaim him a dishonoured knight."

The men-at-arms made no reply; but, locking the door behind them, left the prisoners alone.

"What can this mean, Ralph?" Walter exclaimed. "We are in the lowest dungeon, and below the level of the river. See how damp are the walls, and the floor is thick with slimy mud. The river must run but just below that loophole, and in times of flood probably enters here."

Phillip of Holbeaut, on dismounting, ascended to an upper chamber, where a man in the dress of a well-to-do citizen was sitting.

"This is a dungeon for a felon," he exclaimed.

"Well, Sir Phillip," he exclaimed, rising to his feet as the other entered, "what news?"

"The news is bad," the knight growled. "This famous scheme of yours has cost me fifty of my best men. I would I had had nothing to do with it."

"But this Walter Somers," the other exclaimed, "what of him? He has not escaped surely! The force which marched from Amiens was large enough to have eaten him and his garrison."

"He has not escaped," the knight replied.

"Then he is killed!" the other said eagerly.

"No; nor is he killed. He is at present a prisoner in a dungeon below, together with a stout knave whom he begged might accompany him until ransomed."

"All is well then," the other exclaimed. "Never mind the loss of your men. The money which I have promised you for this business will hire you two hundred such knaves; but why didst not knock him on head at once?"

"It was not so easy to knock him on the head," Sir Phillip growled. "It cost us five hundred men to capture the outer walls, and to have fought our way into the keep, held, as it was, by men who would have contested every foot of the ground, was not a job for which any of us had much stomach, seeing what the first assaults had cost us; so the count took them all to quarter. The rest he carried with him to Amiens; but their leader, according to the promise which he made me, he handed over to me as my share of the day's booty, giving me every charge that he should receive good and knightly treatment."

"Which, no doubt, you will observe," the other said, with an ugly laugh.

"It is a bad business," the knight exclaimed angrily, "and were it not for our friendship, in Spain, and the memory of sundry deeds which we did together, not without profit to our purses, I would rather that you were thrown over the battlements into the river than I had taken a step in this business. However, none can say that Phillip of Holbeaut ever deserted a friend who had proved true to him, not to mention that the sum which you promised me for my aid in this matter will, at present time, prove wondrously convenient. Yet I foresee that it will bring me into trouble with the Count of Evreux. Ere many days a demand will come for the fellow to be delivered on ransom."

"And what will you say?" the other asked.

"I shall say what is the truth," the knight replied, "though I may add something that is not wholly so. I shall say that he was drowned in the Somme. I shall add that it happened as he trying to make his escape, contrary to the parole he had given; but in truth he will be drowned in the dungeon in which I have placed him, which has rid me of many a troublesome prisoner before now. The river is at ordinary times but two feet below the loophole; and when its tide is swelled by rain it often rises above the sill, and then there is an end of any one within. They can doubt my word; but there are not many who would care to do so openly; none who would do so for the sake of an unknown English knight. And as for any complaints on the part of the Black Prince, King Phillip has shown over and over again how little the complaints of Edward himself move him."

"It were almost better to knock him on head at once," the other said thoughtfully; "the fellow has as many lives as a cat."

"If he had as many as nine cats," the knight replied, "it would not avail him. But I will have no violence. The water will do your work as well as a poinard, and I will not have it said, even among such ruffians as mine, that I slew a captured knight. The other will pass as an accident, and I care not what my men may think as long as they can say nothing for a surety. The count may storm as much as he will, and may even lay a complaint against me before the king; but in times like the present, even a simple knight who can lead two hundred good fighting men into the field is not to be despised, and the king is likely to be easily satisfied with my replies to any question that may be raised. Indeed, it would seem contrary to reason that I should slay a captive against whom I have no cause of quarrel, and so forfeit the ransom which I should get for him."

"But suppose that a messenger should come offering ransom before the river happens to rise?"

"Then I shall anticipate matters, and shall say that what I know will happen has already taken place. Do not be uneasy, Sir James. You have my word in the matter, and now I have gone so far I shall carry it through. From the moment when I ordered him into that dungeon his fate was sealed, and in truth, when I gave the order I did so to put an end to the indecision in which my mind had been all night. Once in there he could not be allowed to come out alive, for his report of such treatment would do me more harm among those of my own station in France than any rumours touching his end could do. It is no uncommon affair for one to remove an enemy from one's path; but cruelty to a knightly prisoner would be regarded with horror. Would you like to have a look at him?"

The other hesitated. "No," he replied. "Against him personally I have no great grudge. He has thwarted my plans, and stands now grievously in the way of my making fresh ones; but as he did so from no ill-will towards myself, but as it were by hazard, I have no personal hatred towards him, though I would fain remove him from my path. Besides, I tell you fairly, that even in that dungeon where you have thrown him I shall not feel that he is safe until you send me word that he is dead. He has twice already got out of scrapes when other men would have been killed. Both at Vannes and at Ghent he escaped in a marvellous way; and but a few weeks since, by the accident of his having a coat of mail under his doublet he saved his life from as fair a blow as ever was struck. Therefore I would not that he knew aught of my having a hand in this matter, for if after having seen me he made his escape I could never show my face in England again. I should advise you to bid three or four men always enter his cell together, for he and that man-of-arms who follows him like a shadow are capable of playing any desperate trick to escape."

"That matter is easily enough managed," Sir Phillip said grimly, "by no one entering the dungeon at all. The river may be slow of rising, though in sooth the sky looks overcast now, and it is already at its usual winter level; and whether he dies from lack of water or from a too abundant supply matters but little to me; only, as I told you I will give no orders for him to be killed. Dost remember that Jew we carried off from Seville and kept without water until he agreed to pay us a ransom which made us both rich for six months? That was a rare haul, and I would that rich Jews were plentiful in this country."

"Yes, those were good times," the other said, "although I own that I have not done badly since the war began, having taken a count and three knights prisoners, and put them to ransom, and having reaped a goodly share of plunder from your French burghers, else indeed I could not have offered you so round a sum to settle this little matter for me. There are not many French knights who have earned a count's ransom in the present war. And now I will take horse; here is one-half of the sum I promised you, in gold nobles. I will send you the remainder on the day when I get news from you that the matter is finished."

"Have your money ready in a week's time," the knight replied, taking the bag of gold which the other placed on the table, "for by that time you will hear from me. I hope this will not be the last business which we may do together; there ought to be plenty of good chances in a war like this. Any time that you can send me word of an intended foray by a small party under a commander whose ransom would be a high one I will share what I get with you; and similarly I will let you know of any rich prize who may be pounced upon on the same terms."

"Agreed!" the other said. "We may do a good business together in that way. But you lie too far away. If you move up as near as you can to Calais and let me know your whereabouts, so that I could send or ride to you in a few hours, we might work together with no small profit."

"I will take the field as soon as this affair of yours is settled," the knight replied; "and the messenger who brings you the news shall tell you where I may be found. And now, while your horse is being got ready, let us drink a stoup of wine together in memory of old times, though, for myself, these wines of ours are poor and insipid beside the fiery juice of Spain."

While this conversation, upon which their fate so much depended, had been going on, Walter and Ralph had been discussing the situation, and had arrived at a tolerably correct conclusion.

"This conduct on the part of this brutal French knight, Ralph, is so strange that methinks it cannot be the mere outcome of his passions or of hate against me as an Englishman, but of some deeper motive; and we were right in thinking that in bargaining for my person with the Count of Evreux it was more than my ransom which he sought. Had that been his only object he would never have thrown us into this noisome dungeon, for my report of such treatment would bring dishonour upon him in the eyes of every knight and noble in France as well as in England. It must be my life he aims at, although what grudge he can have against me it passes me to imagine. It may be that at Cressy or elsewhere some dear relative of his may have fallen by my sword; and yet were it so, men nourish no grudge for the death of those killed in fair fight. But this boots not at present. It is enough for us that it is my life which he aims at, and I fear, Ralph, that yours must be included with mine, since he would never let a witness escape to carry the foul tale against him. This being so, the agreement on which I surrendered is broken, and I am free to make my escape if I can, and methinks the sooner that be attempted the better.

So let us work to plan how we may best get out of this place. After our escape from that well at Vannes we need not despair about breaking out from this dungeon of Holbeaut."

"We might overpower the guard who brings our food," Ralph said.

"There is that chance," Walter rejoined, "but I think it is a poor one. They may be sure that this dishonourable treatment will have, rendered us desperate, and they will take every precaution and come well armed. It may be, too, that they will not come at all, but that they intend us to die of starvation, or perchance to be drowned by the floods, which it is easy to see often make their way in here. No, our escape, if escape there be, must be made through that loophole above. Were that bar removed, methinks it is wide enough for us to squeeze through. Doubtless such a hazard has not occurred to them, seeing that it is nigh twelve feet above the floor, and that a single man could by no possibility reach it, but with two of us there is no difficulty. Now, Ralph, do you stand against the wall. I will climb upon your shoulders, and standing there can reach the bar, and so haul myself up and look out."

This was soon done, and Walter seizing the bar, hauled himself up so that he could see through the loophole.

"It is as I thought," he said. "The waters of the Somme are but a foot below the level of this window; the river is yellow and swollen, and a few hours' heavy rain would bring it above the level of this sill. Stand steady, Ralph, I am coming down again."

When he reached the ground, he said:

"Take off your belt, Ralph; if we buckle that and mine together, passing it round the bar, it will make a loop upon which we can stand at the window and see how best we can loosen the bar. Constantly wet as it is, it is likely that the mortar will have softened, in which case we shall have little difficulty in working it out."

A PRISONER

The plan was at once put into execution; the belts were fastened together and Walter standing on Ralph's shoulders passed one end around the bar and buckled it to the other, thus making a loop some three feet in length; putting a foot in this he was able to stand easily at the loophole.

"It is put in with mortar at the top, Ralph, and the mortar has rotted with the wet, but the bottom lead was poured in when the bar was set and this must be scooped out before it can be moved. Fortunately the knight gave no orders to his men to remove our daggers when we were thrust in here, and these will speedily dig out the lead; but I must come down first, for, the strap prevents my working at the foot of the bar. We must tear off a strip of our clothing and make a shift to fasten the strap half-way up the bar so as not to slip down with our weight."

In order to accomplish this Walter had to stand upon Ralph's head to gain additional height. He presently, after several attempts, succeeded in fixing the strap firmly against the bar half-way up, and then placing one knee in the loop and putting an arm through the bar to steady himself, he set to work at the lead. The sharp point of the dagger quickly cut out that near the surface, but farther down the hole narrowed and the task was much more difficult. Several times Ralph relieved him at the work, but at last it was accomplished, and the bar was found to move slightly when they shook it. There now remained only to loosen the cement above, and this was a comparatively easy task; it crumbled quickly before the points of their daggers, and the bar was soon free to move.

"Now," Walter said, "we have to find out whether the bar was first put in from below or from above; one hole or the other must be a good deal deeper than the iron, so that it was either shoved up or pushed down until the other end could get under or over the other hole. I should think most likely the hole is below, as if they held up the bar against the top, when the lead was poured in it would fill up the space; so we will first of all try to lift it. I must stand on your head again to enable me to be high enough to try this."

"My head is strong enough, I warrant," Ralph replied, "but I will fold up my jerkin, and put on it, for in truth you hurt me somewhat when you were tying the strap to the bar."

All Walter's efforts did not succeed in raising the bar in the slightest, and he therefore concluded that it had been inserted here and lifted while the space was filled with lead. "It is best so," he said; "we should have to cut away the stone either above or below, and can work much better below. Now I will put my knee in the strap again and set to work. The stone seems greatly softened by the wet, and will yield to our daggers readily enough. It is already getting dark, and as soon as we have finished we can start."

As Walter had discovered, the stone was rotten with the action of the weather, and although as they got deeper it became much harder, it yielded to the constant chipping with their daggers, and in two hours Ralph, who at the moment happened to be engaged, announced to Walter that his dagger had found its way under the bottom of the bar. The groove was soon made deep enough for the bar to be moved out; but another hour's work was necessary, somewhat further to enlarge the upper hole, so as to allow the bar to have sufficient play. Fortunately it was only inserted about an inch and a half in the stone, and the amount to be cut away to give it sufficient play was therefore not large. Then at last all was ready for their flight.

CHAPTER XVII
THE CAPTURE OF CALAIS

W HEN the bar was once ready for removal the captives delayed not a minute, for although it was now so late that there was little chance of a visit being paid them, it was just possible that such might be the case, and that it might occur to the knight that it would be safer to separate them.

"Now, Ralph, do you go first, since I am lighter and can climb up by means of the strap, which you can hold from above; push the bar out and lay it down quietly on the thickness of the wall. A splash might attract the attention of the sentries, though I doubt whether it would, for the wind is high and the rain falling fast. Unbuckle the strap before you move the bar, as otherwise it might fall and I should have difficulty in handing it to you again. Now, I am steady against the wall."

Ralph seized the bar and with a great effort pushed the bottom from him. It moved through the groove without much difficulty, but it needed a great wrench to free the upper end. However, it was done, and laying it quietly down he pulled himself up and thrust himself through the loophole. It was a desperate struggle to get through, for it was only just wide enough for his head to pass, and be was so squarely built that his body with difficulty followed. The wall was four feet wide, and as the loophole widened considerably without, there was, when he had once passed through from the inside, space enough for him to kneel down and lowered one end of the strap to Walter. The latter speedily climbed up, and getting through the slit with much less trouble than Ralph had experienced—for although in height and width of shoulder he was his equal, he was less in depth than his follower—he joined him in the opening; Ralph sitting with his feet in the water in order to make room for him.

The dungeon was upon the western side of the castle, and consequently the stream would be with them in making for shore. It was pitch dark, but they knew that the distance they would have to swim could not exceed forty or fifty yards.

"Keep along close by the wall, Ralph, if we once get out in the stream we might lose our way; we will skirt the wall until it ends, then there is a cut, for as you saw when we entered, the moat runs right across this neck. If we keep a bit farther down and then land, we shall be fairly beyond the outworks."

Ralph slipped down into the water, and followed by Walter swam along at the foot of the wall. They had already been deprived of their armour, but had luckily contrived to retain their daggers in their belts, which they had again girdled on before entering the water. The stream hurried them rapidly along, and they had only to keep themselves afloat. They were soon at the corner of the castle. A few strokes farther and they again felt the wall which lined the moat. The stream still swept them along, they felt the masonry come to an end, and bushes and shrubs lined the bank. They were beyond the outer defences of the castle. Still a little farther they proceeded down the stream in order to prevent the possibility of any noise they might make in scrambling up being heard by the sentinels on the outer postern. Then when they felt quite safe they grasped the bushes, and speedily climbed the bank. Looking back at the castle they saw lights still burning there. Short as was the time they had been in the water they were both chilled to the bone, for it was the month of February, and the water was bitterly cold.

"It cannot be more than nine o'clock now," Walter said, "for it is not more than four hours since darkness fell. They are not likely to visit the dungeon before eight or nine to-morrow, so we can rely upon twelve hours' start, and if we make the best of our time we ought to be far on travelling on a night like this through a strange country. I would that the stars were shining. However, the direction of the wind and rain will be a guide to us, and we shall soon strike the road we travelled yesterday, and can follow that till morning."

They were not long before they found the track, and then started at a brisk pace along it. All night they struggled on through wind and rain until the first dawn enabled them to see the objects in the surrounding country; and making for the forest which extended to within a mile of the road, they entered deep into its shelter, and there utterly exhausted, threw themselves down on the wet ground. After a few hours of uneasy sleep they woke, and taking their place near the edge of the forest watched for the passage of any party which might be in pursuit, but until nightfall none came along.

"They have not discovered our flight," Ralph said at last, "or they would have passed long before this. Sir Phillip doubtless imagines that we are drowned. The water was within a few inches of the sill when we started, and must soon have flooded the dungeon; and did he trouble to look in the morning, which is unlikely enough seeing that he would be sure of out fate, he would be unable to descend the stairs, and could not reach to the door, and so discover that the bar had been removed. No; whatever his motive may have been in compassing my death, he is doubtless satisfied that he has attained it, and we need have no further fear of pursuit from him. The rain has ceased, and I think that it will be a fine night; we will walk on, and if we come across a barn will make free to enter it, and stripping off our clothing to dry, will sleep in the hay, and pursue our journey in the morning. From our travel-stained appearance any who may meet us will take us for two wayfarers going to take service in the army at Amiens."

It was not until nearly midnight that they came upon such a place as they sought, then after passing a little village they found a shed standing apart. Entering it they found that it was tenanted by two cows. Groping about they presently came upon a heap of forage, and taking off their outer garments lay down on this, covering themselves thickly with it. The shed was warm and comfortable and they were soon asleep, and awaking at daybreak they found that their clothes had dried somewhat. The sun was not yet up when they started, but it soon rose, and ere noon their garments had dried, and they felt for the first time comfortable. They met but few people on the road, and these passed them with ordinary salutations.

They had by this time left Amiens on the right, and by nightfall were well on their way towards Calais. Early in the morning they had purchased some bread at a village through which they passed; Walter's Norman-French being easily understood, and exciting no surprise or suspicion. At nightfall they slept in a shed within a mile of the ruins of the castle of Près, and late next evening entered the English encampment at New Town. After going to his tent, where he and Ralph changed their garments and partook of a hearty meal, Walter proceeded to the pavilion of the prince, who hailed his entrance with the greatest surprise.

"Why Sir Walter," he exclaimed, "what good saint has brought you here? I have but an hour since received a message from the Count of Evreux to the effect that you were a prisoner in the bands of Sir Phillip de Holbeaut, with whom I must treat for your ransom. I was purporting to send off a herald to-morrow to ask at what sum he held you; and now you appear in flesh and blood before us! But first, before you tell us your story, I must congratulate you on your gallant defence of the Castle of Près, which is accounted by all as one of the most valiant deeds of the war. When two days passed without a messenger from you coming hither, I feared that you were beleaguered, and started that evening with six hundred men-at-arms. We arrived at daybreak to finding only a smoking ruin. Luckily among the crowd of dead upon the breach we found one of your men-at-arms who still breathed, and after some cordial had been given him, and his wounds stanched, he was able to tell us the story of the siege. But it needed not his tale to tell us how stanchly you had defended the castle, for the hundreds of dead who lay outside of the walls, and still more the mass who piled the breach, and the many who lay in the castle-yard spoke for themselves of the valour with which the castle had been defended. As the keep was gutted by fire, and the man could tell us nought of what had happened after he bad been stricken down at the breach, we knew not whether you and your brave garrison had perished in the flames. We saw the penthouse beneath which they had laboured to cut through the wall, but the work had ceased before the holes were large enough for entry, and we hoped that you might have seen that further resistance was in vain, and have made terms for your lives; indeed we heard from the country people that certain prisoners had been taken to Amiens. I rested one day at Près, and the next rode back here, and forthwith despatched a herald to the Count of Evreux at Amiens asking for news of the garrison; but now he has returned with word that twenty-four men-at-arms and fifty-eight archers are prisoners in the count's hands, and that he is ready to exchange them against an equal number of French prisoners; but that you, with a man-at-arms, were in the keeping of Sir Phillip of Holbeaut, with whom I must treat for your ransom. And now tell me how it is that I see you here. Has your captor, confiding in your knightly word to send him the sum agreed upon, allowed you to return? Tell me the sum and my treasurer shall to-morrow pay it over to a herald, who shall carry it to Holbeaut."

"Thanks, your Royal Highness, for your generosity," Walter replied, "but there is no ransom to be paid."

And he then proceeded to narrate the incidents of his captivity at Holbeaut and his escape from the castle. His narration was frequently interrupted by exclamations of surprise and indignation from the prince and knights present.

"Well, this well-nigh passes all belief," the prince exclaimed when he had concluded. "It is an outrage upon all laws of chivalry and honour. What could have induced this caitiff knight, instead of treating you with courtesy and honour until your ransom arrived, to lodge you in a foul dungeon, where, had you not made your escape, your death would have been brought about that very night by the rising water? Could it be, think you, that his brain is distraught by some loss or injury which may have befallen him at our hands during the war and worked him up to a blind passion of hatred against all Englishmen?"

"I think not that, your Royal Highness," Walter replied. "His manner was cool and deliberate, and altogether free from any signs of madness. Moreover, it would seem that he had specially marked me down beforehand, since, as I have told you, he had bargained with the Count of Evreux for the possession of my person should I escape with life at the capture of the castle. It seems rather as if he must have had some private enmity against me, although what the cause may be I cannot imagine, seeing that I have never, to my knowledge, before met him, and have only heard his name by common report."

"Whatever be the cause," the prince said, "we will have satisfaction for it, and I will beg the king, my father, to write at once to Phillip of Valois protesting against the treatment that you have received, and denouncing Sir Phillip of Holbeaut as a base and dishonoured knight, whom, should he fall into our hands, we will commit at once to the hangman."

Upon the following day Walter was called before the king, and related to him in full the incidents of the siege and of his captivity and escape; and the same day King Edward sent off a letter to Phillip of Valois denouncing Sir Phillip Holbeaut as a dishonoured knight, and threatening retaliation upon the French prisoners in his hands.

A fortnight later an answer was received from the King of France saying that he had inquired into the matter, and had sent a seneschal, who had questioned Sir Phillip Holbeaut and some of the men-at-arms in the castle, and that he found that King Edward had been grossly imposed upon by a fictitious tale. Sir Walter Somers had, he found, been treated with all knightly courtesy, and believing him to be an honourable knight and true to his word, but slight watch had been kept over him. He had basely taken advantage of this trust, and with the man-at-arms with him had escaped from the castle in order to avoid payment of his ransom, and had now invented these gross and wicked charges against Sir Phillip Holbeaut as a cloak to his own dishonour.

Walter was furious when he heard the contents of this letter, and the king and Black Prince were no less indignant. Although they doubted him not for a moment, Walter begged that Ralph might be brought before them and examined strictly as to what had taken place, in order that they might see that his statements tallied exactly with those he had made.

When this had been done Walter obtained permission from the king to despatch a cartel to Sir Phillip de Holbeaut denouncing him as a perjured and dishonoured knight and challenging him to meet him in mortal conflict at any time and place that he might name. At the same time the king despatched a letter to Phillip of Valois saying that the statements of the French knight and followers were wholly untrue, and begging that a time might be appointed for the meeting of the two knights in the lists.

To this King Phillip replied that he had ordered all private quarrels in France to be laid aside during the progress of the war, and that so long as an English foot remained upon French soil he would give no countenance to his knights throwing away the lives which they owed to France, in private broils.

"You must wait, Sir Walter, you see," the king said, "until you may perchance meet him in the field of battle. In the mean time, to show how lightly I esteem the foul charge brought against you, and how much I hold and honour the bravery which you showed in defending the castle which my son the prince intrusted to you, as well as upon other occasions, I hereby promote you to the rank of knight-banneret."

Events now passed slowly before Calais. Queen Philippa and many of her ladies crossed the Channel and joined her husband, and these added much to the gaiety of the life in camp. The garrison at Calais was, it was known, in the sorest straits for the want of food, and at last the news came that the King of France, with a huge army of 200,000 men, was moving to its relief. They had gathered at Hesdin, at which rendezvous the king had arrived in the early part of April; but it was not until the 27th of July that the whole army was collected, and marching by slow steps advanced towards the English position.

King Edward had taken every precaution to guard all the approaches to the city. The ground was in most places too soft and sandy to admit of the construction of defensive works; but the fleet was drawn up close inshore to cover the line of sand-hills by the sea with arrows and war machines, while the passages of the marshes, which extended for a considerable distance round the town, were guarded by the Earl of Lancaster and a body of chosen troops, while the other approaches to the city were covered by the English camp.

The French reconnoitring parties found no way open to attack the English unless under grievous disadvantages. The Cardinals of Tusculum, St. John, and St. Paul endeavoured to negotiate terms of peace, and commissioners on both sides met. The terms offered by Phillip were, however, by no means so favourable as Edward, after his own victorious operations and those of his armies in Brittany and Guienne, had a right to expect and the negotiations were broken off.

The following day the French king sent in a message to Edward saying that he had examined the ground in every direction in order to advance and give battle, but had found no means of doing so. He therefore summoned the king to come forth from the marshy ground in which he was encamped and to fight in the open plain; and he offered to send four French knights, who, with four English of the same rank, should choose a fair plain in the neighbourhood, according to the usages of chivalry. Edward had little over 30,000 men with him; but the same evening that Phillip's challenge was received a body of 17,000 Flemings and English, detached from an army which had been doing good service on the borders of Flanders, succeeded in passing round the enemy's host and in effecting a junction with the king's army. Early the next morning, after having consulting with his officers, Edward returned an answer to the French king, saying that he agreed to his proposal, and enclosed a safe-conduct for any four French knights who might be appointed to arrange with the same number of English the place of battle.

The odds were indeed enormous, the French being four to one; but Edward, after the success of Cressy, which had been won by the Black Prince's division, which bore a still smaller proportion to the force engaging it, might well feel confident in the valour of his troops. His envoys, on arriving at the French camp, found that Phillip had apparently changed his mind. He declined to discuss the matter with which they were charged, and spoke only of the terms upon which Edward would be willing to raise the siege of Calais. As they had no authority on this subject the English knights returned to their camp, where the news was received with great disappointment, so confident did all feel in their power to defeat the huge host of the French. But even greater was the astonishment the next morning when, before daylight, the tents of the French were seen in one great flame, and it was found that the king and all his host were retreating at full speed. The Earls of Lancaster and Northampton, with a large body of horse at once started in pursuit, and harassed the retreating army on its march towards Amiens.

No satisfactory reasons ever have been assigned for this extraordinary step on the part of the French king. He had been for months engaged in collecting a huge army, and he had now an opportunity of fighting the English in a fair field with a force four times as great as their own. The only means indeed of accounting for his conduct is by supposing him affected by temporary aberration of mind, which many other facts in his history render not improbable. The fits of rage so frequently recorded of him border upon madness, and a number of strange actions highly detrimental to his own interests which he committed can only be accounted for as the acts of a diseased mind. This view has been to some extent confirmed by the fact that less than half a century afterwards insanity declared itself among his descendants.

A few hours after the departure of the French the French standard was lowered on the walls of Calais, and news was brought to Edward that the governor was upon the battlements and desired to speak with some officers of the besieging army. Sir Walter Manny and Lord Bisset were sent to confer with him, and found that his object was to obtain the best terms be could. The English knights, knowing the determination of the king on the subject, were forced to tell him that no possibility existed of conditions being granted, but that the king demanded their unconditional surrender, reserving to himself entirely the right whom to pardon and whom to put to death.

The governor remonstrated on the severe terms, and said that rather than submit to them he and his soldiers would sally out and die sword in hand. Sir Walter Manny found the king inexorable. The strict laws of war in those days justified the barbarous practise of putting to death the garrison of a town captured under such circumstances. Calais had been for many years a nest of pirates, and vessels issuing from its port had been a scourge to the commerce of England and Flanders, and the king was fully determined to punish it severely. Sir Walter Manny interceded long and boldly, and represented to the king that none of his soldiers would willingly defend a town on his behalf from the day on which he put to death the people of Calais, as beyond doubt the French would retaliate in every succeeding siege. The other nobles and knights joined their entreaties to those of Sir Walter Manny, and the king finally consented to yield in some degree. He demanded that six of the most notable burghers of the town, with bare heads and feet, and with ropes about their necks and the keys of the fortress in their hands, should deliver themselves up for execution. On these conditions he agreed to spare the rest. With these terms Sir Walter Manny returned to Sir John of Vienne.

THE CAPTURE OF CALAIS

The governor left the battlements, and proceeding to the market-place ordered the bell to be rung. The famished and despairing citizens gathered a haggard crowd to hear their doom. A silence followed the narration of the hard conditions of surrender by the governor, and sobs and cries alone broke the silence which succeeded. Then Eustace St. Pierre, the wealthiest and most distinguished of the citizens, came forward and offered himself as one of the victims, saying, "Sad pity and shame would it be to let all of our fellow-citizens die of famine or the sword when means could be found to save them." John of Aire, James and Peter De Vissant, and another whose name has not come down to us, followed his example, and stripping to their shirts set out for the camp, Sir John of Vienne, who, from a late wound, was unable to walk, riding at their head on horseback. The whole population accompanied them weeping bitterly until they came to the place where Sir Walter Manny was awaiting them. Here the crowd halted, and the knight, promising to do his best to save them, led them to the tent where the king had assembled all his nobles around him. When the tidings came that the burghers of Calais had arrived, Edward issued out with his retinue, accompanied by Queen Philippa and the Black Prince.

"Behold, Sire," Sir Walter Manny said, "the representatives of the town of Calais!"

The king made no reply while John of Vienne surrendered his sword, and kneeling with the burghers, said, "Gentle lord and king; behold, we six who were once the greatest citizens and merchants of Calais, bring you the keys of the town and castle, and give ourselves up to your pleasure, placing ourselves in the state in which you see us by our own free-will to save the rest of the people of the city, who have already suffered many ills. We pray you, therefore, to have pity and mercy upon us for the sake of your high nobleness."

All present were greatly affected at this speech, and at the aspect of men who thus offered their lives for their fellow-citizens. The king's countenance alone remained unchanged, and he ordered them to be taken to instant execution. Then

Sir Walter Manny and all the nobles with tears besought the king to have mercy, not only for the sake of the citizens, but for that of his own fame, which would be tarnished by so cruel a deed.

"Silence, Sir Walter!" cried the king. "Let the executioner be called. The men of Calais have put to death so many of my subjects that I will also put these men to death."

At this moment Queen Philippa, who had been weeping bitterly, cast herself upon her knees before the king. "Oh, gentle lord," she cried, "since I have repassed the seas to see you I have neither asked or required anything at your hand; now, then, I pray you humbly, and require as a boon, that for the sake of the Son of Mary, and for the love of me, you take these men to mercy."

The king stood for a moment in silence, and then said:

"Ah ! lady, I would that you had been other where than here; but you beg of me so earnestly I must not refuse you, though I grant your prayer with pain. I give them to you; take them, and do your will."

Then the queen rose from her knees, and bidding the burghers rise, she caused clothing and food to be given them, and sent them away free.

Sir Walter Manny, with a considerable body of men-at-arms, now took possession of the town of Calais. The anger of the king soon gave way to better feelings; all the citizens, without exception, were fed by his bounty. Such of them as preferred to depart instead of swearing fealty to the English monarch were allowed to carry away what effects they could bear upon their persons and were conducted in safety to the French town of Guisnes. Eustace de St. Pierre was granted almost all the possessions he had formerly held in Calais, and also a considerable pension; and he and all who were willing to remain were well and kindly treated. The number was large, for the natural indignation which they felt at their base desertion by the French king induced very many of the citizens to remain and become subjects of Edward. The king issued a proclamation inviting English traders and others to come across and take up their residence in Calais, bestowing upon them the houses and lands of the French who had left. Very many accepted the invitation, and Calais henceforth and for some centuries became virtually an English town.

A truce was now, through the exertions of the pope's legates, made between England and France, the terms agreed on being very similar to those of the previous treaty; and when all his arrangements were finished Edward returned with his queen to England, having been absent eighteen months, during which time almost unbroken success had attended his arms, and the English name had reached a position of respect and honour in the eyes of Europe far beyond that at which it previously stood.

CHAPTER XVIII
THE BLACK DEATH

THE court at Westminster during the few months which followed the capture of Calais was the most brilliant in Europe. Tournaments and fêtes followed each other in rapid succession, and to these knights came from all parts. So great was the reputation of King Edward that deputies came from Germany, where the throne was now vacant, to offer the crown of that kingdom to him. The king declined the offer, for it would have been impossible indeed for him to have united the German crown with that of England, which he already held, and that of France, which he claimed.

Some months after his return to England the Black Prince asked his father as a boon that the hand of his ward Edith Vernon should be bestowed upon the prince's brave follower Sir Walter Somers, and as Queen Philippa, in the name of the lady's mother, seconded the request, the king at once acceded to it. Edith was now sixteen, an age at which, in those days, a young lady was considered to be marriageable, and the wedding took place with great pomp and ceremony at Westminster; the king himself giving away the bride, and bestowing, as did the prince and Queen Philippa, many costly presents upon the young couple. After taking part in several of the tournaments, Walter went with his bride and Dame Vernon down to their estates, and were received with great rejoicing by the tenantry, the older of whom well remembered Walter's father and mother, and were rejoiced at finding that they were again to become the vassals of one of the old family. Dame Vernon was greatly loved by her tenantry; but the latter had looked forward with some apprehension to the marriage of the young heiress, as the character of the knight upon whom the king might bestow her hand would greatly affect the happiness and well being of his tenants.

Sir James Carnegie had not returned to England after the fall of Calais; he perceived that he was in grave disfavour with the Black Prince, and guessed, as was the case, that some suspicion had fallen on him in reference to the attack upon Walter in the camp, and to the strange attempt which had been made to destroy him by Sir Phillip Holbeaut. He had, therefore, for a time taken service with the Count of Savoy, and was away from England, to the satisfaction of Walter and Dame Vernon, when the marriage took place; for he had given proofs of such a malignity of disposition that both felt, that although his succession to the estates was now hopelessly barred, yet that he might at any moment attempt some desperate deed to satisfy his feeling of disappointment and revenge.

In spite of the gaiety of the court of King Edward a cloud hung over the kingdom; for it was threatened by a danger far more terrible than any combination of foes—a danger which no gallantry upon the part of her king or warriors availed anything. With a slow and terrible march the enemy was advancing from the East, where countless hosts had been slain. India, Arabia, Syria, and Armenia had been well-nigh depopulated. In no country which the dread foe had invaded had less than two-thirds of the population been slain; in some nine-tenths had perished. All sorts of portents were reported to have accompanied its appearance in the East; where it was said showers of serpents had fallen, strange and unknown insects had appeared in the atmosphere, and clouds of sulphurous vapour had issued from the earth and enveloped whole provinces and countries. For two or three years the appearance of this scourge had been heralded by strange atmospheric disturbances; heavy rains and unusual floods, storms of thunder and lightning of unheard-of violence, hail-showers of unparalleled duration and severity, had everywhere been experienced, while in Italy and Germany violent earthquake shocks had been felt, and that at places where no tradition existed of previous occurrences of the same kind.

From Asia it had spread to Africa and to Europe, affecting first the sea-shores and creeping inland by the course of the rivers. Greece first felt its ravages, and Italy was not long in experiencing them. In Venice more than 100,000 persons perished in a few months, and thence spreading over the whole peninsula, not a town escaped the visitation. At Florence 60,000 people were carried off, and at Lucca and Genoa, in Sicily, Sardinia, and Corsica it raged with equal violence. France was assailed by way of Provence, and Avignon suffered especially. Of the English college at that place not an individual was left, and 120 persons died in a single day in that small city. Paris lost upwards of 50,000 of its inhabitants, while 90,000 were swept away in Lubeck, and 1,200,000 died within a year of its first appearance in Germany.

In England the march of the pestilence westward was viewed with deep apprehension, and the approaching danger was brought home to the people by the death of the Princess Joan, the king's second daughter. She was affianced to Peter, the heir to the throne of Spain; and the bride, who had not yet accomplished her fourteenth year, was sent over to Bordeaux with considerable train of attendants in order to be united there to her promised husband. Scarcely had she reached Bordeaux when she was attacked by the pestilence and died in a few hours. A few days later the news spread through the country that the disease had appeared almost simultaneously at several of the seaports in the south-west of England. Thence with great rapidity it spread through the kingdom; proceeding through Gloucestershire and Oxfordshire it broke out in London, and the ravages were no less severe than they had been on the Continent, the very lowest estimate being that two-thirds of the population were swept away. Most of those attacked died within a few hours of the seizure. If they survived for two days they generally rallied, but even then many fell into a state of coma from which they never awoke.

No words can describe the terror and dismay caused by this the most destructive plague of which there is any record in history. No remedies were of the slightest avail against it; flight was impossible, for the loneliest hamlets suffered as severely as crowded towns, and frequently not a single survivor was left. Men met the pestilence in various moods: the brave with fortitude, the pious with resignation, the cowardly and turbulent with outbursts of despair and fury. Among the lower classes the wildest rumours gained credence. Some assigned the pestilence to witchcraft, others declared that the waters of the wells and streams had been poisoned. Serious riots occurred in many places, and great numbers of people fell victims to the fury of the mob under the suspicion of being connected in some way with the ravages of the pestilence. The Jews, ever the objects of popular hostility, engendered by ignorance and superstition, were among the chief sufferers. Bands of marauders wandered through the country plundering the houses left empty by the death of all their occupants, and from end to end death and suffering were universal.

Although all classes had suffered heavily the ravages of the disease were, as is always the case, greater among the poor than among the rich, the insanitary conditions of their life, and their coarser and commoner food rendering them more liable to its influence; no rank, however, was exempted, and no less than three Archbishops of Canterbury were carried off in succession by the pestilence within a year of its appearance.

During the months which succeeded his marriage Sir Walter Somers lived quietly and happily with his wife at Westerham. It was not until late in the year that the plague approached the neighbourhood. Walter had determined to await its approach there. He had paid a few short visits to the court, where every effort was made by continuous gaiety to keep up the spirits of the people and prevent them from brooding over the approaching pestilence; but when it was at hand Walter and his wife agreed that they would rather share the lot of their tenants, whom their presence and example might support and cheer in their need, than return to face it in London. One morning when they were at breakfast a frightened servant brought in the news that the disease had appeared in the village, that three persons had been taken ill on the previous night, that two had already died, and that several others had sickened.

"The time has come, my children," Dame Vernon said calmly, "the danger so long foreseen is at hand, now let us face it as we agreed to do. It has been proved that flight is useless, since nowhere is there escape from the plague; here, at least, there shall be no repetition of the terrible scenes we have heard of elsewhere, where the living have fled in panic and allowed the stricken to die unattended. We have already agreed that we will set the example to our people by ourselves going down and administering to the sick."

"It is hard," Walter said, rising and pacing up and down the room, "to let Edith go into it."

"Edith will do just the same as you do," his wife said firmly. "Were it possible that all in this house might escape, there might be a motive for turning coward, but seeing that no household is spared, there is, as we agreed, greater danger in flying from the pestilence than facing it firmly."

Walter sighed.

"You are right," he said, "but it wrings my heart to see you place yourself in danger."

"Were we out of danger here, Walter, it might be so," Edith replied gently; "but since there is no more safety in the castle than in the cottage, we must face death whether it pleases us or not, and it were best to do so bravely."

"So be it," Walter said; "may the God of heaven watch over us all! Now, mother, do you and Edith busy yourselves in preparing broths, strengthening drinks, and medicaments. I will go down at once to the village and see how matters stand there and who are in need. We have already urged upon all our people to face the danger bravely, and if die they must, to die bravely like Christians, and not like coward dogs. When you have prepared your soups and cordials come down and meet me in the village, bringing Mabel and Janet, your attendants, to carry the baskets."

Ralph, who was now installed as major-domo in the castle, at once set out with Walter. They found the village in a state of panic. Women were sitting crying despairingly at their doors. Some were engaged in packing their belongings in carts preparatory to flight, some wandered aimlessly about wringing their hands, while others went to the church, whose bells were mournfully tolling the dirge of the departed. Walter's presence soon restored something like order and confidence; his resolute tone cheered the timid and gave hope to the despairing. Sternly he rebuked those preparing to fly, and ordered them instantly to replace their goods in their houses. Then he went to the priest and implored him to cause the tolling of the bell to cease.

"There is enough," he said, "in the real danger present to appall even the bravest, and we need no bell to tell us that death is among us. The dismal tolling is enough to unnerve the stoutest heart, and if we ring for all who die its sounds will never cease while the plague is among us; therefore, father, I implore you to discontinue it. Let there be services held daily in the church, but I beseech you strive in your discourses to cheer the people rather than to depress them, and to dwell more upon the joys that await those who die as Christian men and women than upon the sorrows of those who remain behind. My wife and mother will anon be down in the village and will strive to cheer and comfort the people, and I look to you for aid in this matter."

The priest, who was naturally a timid man, nevertheless nerved himself to carry out Walter's suggestions, and soon the dismal tones of the bell ceased to be heard in the village.

Walter despatched messengers to all the outlying farms desiring his tenants to meet him that afternoon at the castle in order that measures might be concerted for common aid and assistance. An hour later Dame Vernon and Edith came down and visited all the houses where the plague had made its appearance, distributing their soups, and by cheering and comforting words raising the spirits of the relatives of the sufferers.

The names of all the women ready to aid in the general work of nursing were taken down, and in the afternoon at the meeting at the castle the full arrangements were completed. Work was to be carried on as usual in order to occupy men's minds and prevent them from brooding over the ravages of the plague. Information of any case that occurred was to be sent to the castle, where soups and medicines were to be obtained. Whenever more assistance was required than could be furnished by the inmates of a house another woman was to be sent to aid. Boys were told off as messengers to fetch food and other matters as required from the castle.

So, bravely and firmly, they prepared to meet the pestilence; it spread with terrible severity. Scarce a house which did not lose some of its inmates, while in others whole families were swept away. All day Walter and his wife and Dame Vernon went from house to house, and although they could do nothing to stem the progress of the pestilence, their presence and example supported the survivors and prevented the occurrence of any of the panic and disorder which in most places accompanied it.

The castle was not exempt from the scourge. First some of the domestics were seized, and three men and four women died. Walter himself was attacked, but he took it lightly, and three days after the seizure passed into a state of convalescence. Dame Vernon was next attacked, and expired six hours after the commencement of the seizure. Scarcely was Walter upon his feet than Ralph, who had not for a moment left his bedside, was seized, but he too, after being at death's door for some hours, turned the corner. Lastly Edith sickened.

By this time the scourge had done its worst in the village, and three-fifths of the population had been swept away. All the male retainers in the castle had died, and the one female who survived was nursing her dying mother in the village.

Edith's attack was a very severe one. Walter, alone now, for Ralph, although convalescent, had not yet left his bed, sat by his wife's bedside a prey to anxiety and grief; for although she had resisted the first attack she was now, thirty-six hours after it had seized her, fast sinking. Gradually her sight and power of speech faded, and she sank into the state of coma which was the prelude of death, and lay quiet and motionless, seeming as if life had already departed. Suddenly Walter was surprised by the sound of many heavy feet ascending the stairs. He went out into the ante-room to learn the cause of this strange tumult, when five armed men, one of whom was masked, rushed into the room. Walter caught up his sword from the table.

"Ruffians," he exclaimed, "how dare you desecrate the abode of death?"

Without a word the men sprang upon him. For a minute he defended himself against their attacks, but he was still weak, his guard was beaten down, and a blow felled him to the ground.

"Now settle her," the masked man exclaimed, and the band rushed into the adjoining room. They paused, however, at the door at the sight of the lifeless figure on the couch.

"We are saved that trouble," one said, "we have come too late."

The masked figure approached the couch and bent over the figure.

"Yes," he said, "she is dead, and so much the better."

Then he returned with the others to Walter.

"He breathes yet," he said. "He needs a harder blow than that you gave him to finish him. Let him lie here for a while, while you gather your booty together; then we will carry him off. There is scarcely a soul alive in the country round, and none will note us as we pass. I would not despatch him here, seeing that his body would be found with wounds upon it, and even in these times some inquiry might be made; therefore it were best to finish him elsewhere. When he is missed it will be supposed that he went mad at the death of his wife, and has wandered out and died, may be in the woods, or has drowned himself in a pond or stream. Besides, I would that before he dies he should know what hand has struck the blow, and that my vengeance, which he slighted and has twice escaped, has overtaken him at last."

After ransacking the principal rooms and taking all that was valuable, the band of marauders lifted the still insensible body of Walter, and carrying it down-stairs flung it across a horse. One of the ruffians mounted behind it, and the others also getting into their saddles the party rode away.

They were mistaken, however, in supposing that the Lady Edith was dead. She was indeed very nigh the gates of death, and had it not been for the disturbance would assuredly have speedily entered them. The voice of her husband raised in anger, the clash of steel, followed by the heavy fall, had awakened her deadened brain. Consciousness had at once returned to her, but as yet no power of movement. As at a great distance she had heard the words of those who entered her chamber, and had understood their import. More and more distinctly she heard their movements about the room as they burst open her caskets and appropriated her jewels, but it was not until silence was restored that the gathering powers of life asserted themselves; then with a sudden rush the blood seemed to course through her veins, her eyes opened, and her tongue was loosed, and with a scream she sprang up and stood by the side of her bed.

Sustained as by a supernatural power she hurried into the next room. A pool of blood on the floor showed her that what she had heard had not been a dream or the fiction of a disordered brain. Snatching up a cloak of her husband's which lay on a couch, she wrapped it round her, and with hurried steps made her way along the passages until she reached the apartment occupied by Ralph. The latter sprang up in bed with a cry of astonishment. He had heard but an hour before from Walter that all hope was gone, and thought for an instant that the appearance was an apparition from the dead. The ghastly pallor of the face, the eyes burning with a strange light, the flowing hair, and disordered appearance of the girl might well have alarmed one living in even less superstitious times, and Ralph began to cross himself hastily and to mutter a prayer when recalled to himself by the sound of Edith's voice.

"Quick, Ralph!" she said, "arise and clothe yourself. Hasten, for your life. My lord's enemies have fallen upon him and wounded him grievously, even if they have not slain him, and have carried him away. They would have slain me also had they not thought I was already dead. Arise and mount, summon everyone still alive in the village, and follow these murderers. I will pull the alarm-bell of the castle."

Ralph sprang from his bed as Edith left. He had heard the sound of many footsteps in the knight's apartments, but had deemed them those of the priest and his acolytes come to administer the last rites of the church to his dying mistress. Rage and anxiety for his master gave strength to his limbs. He threw on a few clothes and rushed down to the stables, where the horses stood with great piles of forage and pails of water before them, placed there two days before, by Walter when their last attendant died. Without waiting to saddle it, Ralph sprang upon the back of one of the animals, and taking the halters of four others started at a gallop down to the village.

His news spread like wild fire, for the ringing of the alarm-bell of the castle had drawn all to their doors and prepared them for something strange. Some of the men had already taken their arms and were making their way up to the castle when they met Ralph. There were but five men in the village who had altogether escaped the pestilence; others had survived its attacks, but were still weak. Horses there were in plenty. The five men mounted at once, with three others who, though still weak, were able to ride.

So great was the excitement that seven women who had escaped the disease armed themselves with their husbands' swords and leaped on horseback, declaring that, women though they were, they would strike a blow for their beloved lord, who had been as an angel in the village during the plague. Thus it was scarcely more than ten minutes after the marauders had left the castle before a motley band, fifteen strong, headed by Ralph, rode off in pursuit, while some of the women of the village hurried up to the castle to comfort Edith with the tidings that the pursuit had already commenced. Fortunately a lad in the fields had noticed the five men ride away from the castle, and was able to point out the direction they had taken.

At a furious gallop Ralph and his companions tore across the country. Mile after mile was passed. Once or twice they gained news from labourers in the field of the passage of those before them, and knew that they were on the right track. They had now entered a wild and sparsely inhabited country. It was broken and much undulated, so that although they knew that the band they were pursuing were but a short distance ahead they had not yet caught sight of them, and they hoped that, having no reason to dread any immediate pursuit, these would soon slacken their pace. This expectation was realized, for on coming over a brow they saw the party halted at a turf-burner's cottage in the hollow below. Three of the men had dismounted; two of them were examining the hoof of one of the horses, which had apparently cast a shoe or trodden upon a stone. Ralph had warned his party to make no sound when they came upon the fugitives. The sound of the horses' hoofs was deadened by the turf, and they were within a hundred yards of the marauders before they were perceived; then Ralph uttered a shout and brandishing their swords the party rode down at a headlong gallop.

The dismounted men leaped to their saddles and galloped off at full speed, but their pursuers were now close upon them. Ralph and two of his companions, who were mounted upon Walter's best horses, gained upon them at every stride. Two of them were overtaken and run through.

The man who bore Walter before him, finding himself being rapidly overtaken, threw his burden on to the ground just as the leader of the party had checked his horse and was about to deliver a sweeping blow at the insensible body.

With a curse at his follower for ridding himself of it, he again galloped on. The man's act was unavailing to save himself, for he was overtaken and cut down before he had ridden many strides; then Ralph and his party instantly reined up to examine the state of Walter, and the two survivors of the band of murderers continued their flight unmolested.

CHAPTER XIX
BY LAND AND SEA

WALTER was raised from the ground, water was fetched from the cottage, and the blood washed from his head by Ralph, aided by two of the women. It had at once been seen that he was still living, and Ralph on examining the wound joyfully declared that no great harm was done.

"Had Sir Walter been strong and well," he said, "such a clip as this would not have knocked him from his feet, but he would have answered it with a blow such as I have often seen him give in battle; but he was but barely recovering and was as weak as a girl. He is unconscious from loss of blood and weakness. I warrant me that when he opens his eyes and hears that the lady Edith has risen from her bed and came to send me to his rescue, joy will soon bring the blood into his cheeks again. Do one of you run to the hut and see if they have any cordial waters; since the plague has been raging there are few houses but have laid in a provision in case the disease should seize them."

The man soon returned with a bottle of cordial water compounded of rosemary, lavender, and other herbs. By this time Walter had opened his eyes. The cordial was poured down his throat, and he was presently able to speak.

"Be of good cheer, Sir Walter," Ralph said; "three of your rascally assailants lie dead, and the other two have fled; but I have better news still for you. Lady Edith, who you told me lay unconscious and dying, has revived. The din of the conflict seems to have reached her ears and recalled her to life, and the dear lady came to my room with the news that you were carried off, and then, while I was throwing on my clothes, roused the village to your assistance by ringing the alarm-bell. Rarely frightened I was when she came in, for methought at first it was her spirit."

The good news, as Ralph had predicted, effectually roused Walter, and rising to his feet he declared himself able to mount and ride back at once. Ralph tried to persuade him to wait until they had formed a litter of boughs, but Walter would not allow it.

"I would not tarry an instant," he said, "for Edith will be full of anxiety until I return. Why, Ralph, do you think that I am a baby? Why, you yourself were but this morning unable to walk across the room, and here you have been galloping and fighting on my behalf."

"In faith," Ralph said, smiling, "until now I had forgotten that I had been ill."

"You have saved my life, Ralph, you and my friends here, whom I thank with all my heart for what they have done. I will speak more to them another time, now I must ride home with all speed."

Walter now mounted; Ralph took his place on one side of him, and one of his tenants on the other, lest he should be seized with faintness; then at a hand-gallop they started back for the castle. Several women of the village had, when they left, hurried up to the castle. They found Edith lying insensible by the rope of the alarm-bell, having fainted when she had accomplished her object. They presently brought her round; as she was now suffering only from extreme weakness, she was laid on a couch, and cordials and some soup were given to her. One of the women took her place at the highest window to watch for the return of any belonging to the expedition.

Edith felt hopeful as to the result, for she thought that their assailants would not have troubled to carry away the body of Walter had not life remained in it, and she was sure that Ralph would press them so hotly that sooner or later the abductors would be overtaken.

Lady Edith's last effort.

An hour and a half passed, and then the woman from above ran down with the news that she could see three horsemen galloping together towards the castle, with a number of others following in confused order behind.

"Then they have found my lord," Edith exclaimed joyfully, "for Ralph would assuredly not return so quickly had they not done so. 'Tis a good sign that they are galloping, for had they been bearers of ill news they would have returned more slowly; look out again and see if they are bearing one among them."

The woman, with some of her companions, hastened away, and in two or three minutes ran down with the news that Sir Walter himself was one of the three leading horsemen. In a few minutes Edith was clasped in her husband's arms, and their joy, restored as they were from the dead to each other, was indeed almost beyond words.

The plague now abated fast in Westerham, only two or three more persons being attacked by it. As soon as Edith was sufficiently recovered to travel Walter proceeded with her to London and there laid before the king and prince a complaint against Sir James Carnegie for his attempt upon their lives. Even in the trance in which she lay, Edith had recognized the voice which had once been so familiar to her. Walter, too, was able to testify against him, for the rough jolting on horseback had for a while restored his consciousness, and he had heard words spoken, before relapsing into insensibility from the continued bleeding of his wound, which enabled him to swear to Sir James Carnegie as one of his abductors.

The king instantly ordered the arrest of the knight, but he could not be found; unavailing search was made in every direction, and as nothing could be heard of him it was concluded that he had left the kingdom. He was proclaimed publicly a false and villainous knight, his estates were confiscated to the crown, and he himself was outlawed. Then Walter and his wife returned home and did their best to assist their tenants in struggling through the difficulties entailed through the plague.

So terrible had been the mortality that throughout England there was a lack of hands for field work, crops rotted in the ground because there were none to harvest them, and men able to work demanded twenty times the wages which had before been paid. So great was the trouble from this source that an ordinance was passed by parliament enacting that severe punishment should be dealt upon all who demanded wages above the standard price, and even more severe penalties inflicted upon those who should consent to pay higher wages. It was, however, many years before England recovered from the terrible blow which had been dealt her from the pestilence.

While Europe had been ravaged by pestilence the adherents of France and England had continued their struggle in Brittany in spite of the terms of the truce, and this time King Edward was the first open aggressor, granting money and assistance to the free companies, who pillaged and plundered in the name of England. The truce expired at the end of 1348, but was continued for short periods. It was, however, evident that both parties were determined ere long to recommence hostilities. The French collected large forces in Artois and Picardy, and Edward himself proceeded to Sandwich to organize there another army for the invasion of France.

Phillip determined to strike the first blow, and, before the conclusion of the truce, to regain possession of Calais. This town was commanded by a Lombard officer named Almeric of Pavia. Free communication existed, in consequence of the truce, between Calais and the surrounding country, and Jeffrey de Charny, the governor of St. Omer, and one of the commissioners especially appointed to maintain the truce, opened communications with the Lombard captain. Deeming that like most mercenaries he would be willing to change sides should his interest to do so be made clear, he offered him a large sum of money to deliver the castle to the French.

BY LAND AND SEA

The Lombard at once agreed to the project. Jeffrey de Charny arranged to be within a certain distance of the town on the night of the 1st of January, bringing with him sufficient forces to master all opposition if the way was once opened to the interior of the town. It was further agreed that the money was to be paid over by a small party of French who were to be sent forward for the purpose of examining the castle, in order to ensure the main body against treachery. As a hostage for the security of the detachment, the son of the governor was to remain in the hands of the French without, until the safe return of the scouting party.

Several weeks elapsed between the conclusion of the agreement and the date fixed for its execution, and in the meantime the Lombard, either from remorse or from a fear of the consequences which might arise from a detection of the plot before its execution, or from the subsequent vengeance of the English king, disclosed the whole transaction to Edward.

The king bade him continue to carry out his arrangements with De Charny, leaving it to him to counteract the plot. Had he issued orders for the rapid assembly of the army the French would have taken alarm. He therefore sent private messengers to a number of knights and gentlemen of Kent and Sussex to meet him with their retainers at Dover on the 31st of December.

Walter was one of those summoned, and although much surprised at the secrecy with which he was charged, and of such a call being made while the truce with France still existed, he repaired to Dover on the day named, accompanied by Ralph and by twenty men, who were all who remained capable of bearing arms on the estate.

He found the king himself with the Black Prince at Dover, where they had arrived that day. Sir Walter Manny was in command of the force, which consisted in all of 300 men-at-arms and 600 archers. A number of small boats had been collected, and at midday on the 1st of January the little expedition started, and arrived at Calais after nightfall.

ST. GEORGE FOR ENGLAND

In the chivalrous spirit of the times the king determined that Sir Walter Manny should continue in command of the enterprise; he and the Black Prince, disguised as simple knights, fighting under his banner.

In the meantime a considerable force had been collected at St. Omer, where a large number of knights and gentlemen obeyed the summons of Jeffrey de Charny. On the night appointed they marched for Calais, in number five hundred lances and a corresponding number of footmen. They reached the river and bridge of Nieullay a little after midnight, and messengers were sent on to the governor, who was prepared to receive them. On their report De Charny advanced still nearer to the town, leaving the bridge and passages to the river guarded by a large body of crossbow-men under the command of the Lord De Fiennes and a number of other knights. At a little distance from the castle he was met by Almeric de Pavia, who yielded his son as a hostage according to his promise, calculating, as was the case, that he would be recaptured by the English. Then, having received the greater portion of the money agreed upon, he led a party of the French over the castle to satisfy them of his sincerity. Upon receiving their report that all was quiet De Charny detached twelve knights and a hundred men-at-arms to take possession of the castle, while he himself waited at one of the gates of the town with the principal portion of his force.

No sooner had the French entered the castle than the drawbridge was raised. The English soldiers poured out from their places of concealment, and the party which had entered the castle were forced to lay down their arms. In the meantime the Black Prince issued with a small body of troops from a gate near the sea, while De Manny, with the king under his banner, marched by the sally-port which led into the fields. A considerable detachment of the division was despatched to dislodge the enemy at the bridge of Nieullay, and the rest, joining the party of the Black Prince, advanced rapidly upon the forces of Jeffrey de Charny which, in point of numbers, was double their own strength.

BY LAND AND SEA

Although taken in turn by surprise the French prepared steadily for the attack. De Charny ordered them all to dismount and to shorten their lances to pikes five feet in length. The English also dismounted and rushing forward on foot a furious contest commenced. The ranks of both parties were soon broken in the darkness, and the combatants separating into groups a number of separate battles raged around the different banners.

For some hours the fight was continued with unabating obstinacy on both sides. The king and the Black Prince fought with immense bravery, their example encouraging even those of their soldiers who were ignorant of the personality of the knights who were everywhere in front of the combat. King Edward himself several times crossed swords with the famous Eustace de Ribaumont, one of the most gallant knights in France. At length towards daybreak the king, with only thirty companions, found himself again opposed to De Ribaumont with a greatly superior force, and the struggle was renewed between them.

Twice the king was beaten down on one knee by the thundering blows of the French knight, twice he rose and renewed the attack, until De Charny, seeing Sir Walter Manny's banner, beside which Edward fought, defended by so small a force, also bore down to the attack, and in the struggle Edward was separated from his opponent.

The combat now became desperate round the king, and Sir Guy Brian, who bore De Manny's standard, though one of the strongest and most gallant knights of the day, could scarce keep the banner erect. Still Edward fought on, and in the excitement of the moment, forgetting his incognito, he accompanied each blow with his customary war-cry— "Edward, St. George! Edward, St. George!" At that battle-cry, which told the French men-at-arms that the King of England was himself opposed to them, they recoiled for a moment. The shout too reached the ears of the Prince of Wales, who had been fighting with another group. Calling his knights around him he fell upon the rear of De Charny's party and quickly cleared a space around the king.

The fight was now everywhere going against the French, and the English redoubling their efforts the victory was soon complete, and scarcely one French knight left the ground alive and free. In the struggle Edward again encountered De Ribaumont, who, separated from him by the charge of De Charny, had not heard the king's war-cry. The conflict between them was a short one. The French knight saw that almost all his companions were dead or captured, his party completely defeated, and all prospects of escape cut off. He therefore soon dropped the point of his sword and surrendered to his unknown adversary. In the meantime the troops which had been despatched to the bridge of Nieullay had defeated the French forces left to guard the passage and clear the ground towards St. Omer.

Early in the morning Edward entered Calais in triumph, taking with him thirty French nobles as prisoners, while two hundred more remained dead on the field. That evening a great banquet was held, at which the French prisoners were present. The king presided at the banquet, and the French nobles were waited upon by the Black Prince and his knights. After the feast was concluded the king bestowed on De Ribaumont the chaplet of pearls which he wore round his crown, hailing him as the most gallant of the knights who had that day fought, and granting him freedom to return at once to his friends, presenting him with two horses, and a purse to defray his expenses to the nearest French town.

De Charny was afterwards ransomed, and after his return to France assembled a body of troops and attacked the castle which Edward had bestowed upon Almeric of Pavia, and capturing the Lombard, carried him to St. Omer, and had him there publicly flayed alive as a punishment for his treachery.

Walter had as usual fought by the side of the Prince of Wales throughout the battle of Calais and had much distinguished himself for his valour. Ralph was severely wounded in the fight, but was able a month later to rejoin Walter in England.

BY LAND AND SEA

The battle of Calais and the chivalrous bearing of the king created great enthusiasm and delight in England, and did much to rouse the people from the state of grief into which they had been cast by the ravages of the plague. The king did his utmost to maintain the spirit which had been evoked, and the foundation of the order of the Garter, and the erection of a splendid chapel at Windsor, and its dedication, with great ceremony, to St. George, the patron saint of England, still further raised the renown of the court of Edward throughout Europe as the centre of the chivalry of the age.

Notwithstanding many treaties which had taken place, and the near alliance which had been well-nigh carried out between the royal families of England and Spain, Spanish pirates had never ceased to carry on a series of aggressions upon the English vessels trading in the Bay of Biscay. Ships were every day taken, and the crews cruelly butchered in cold blood. Edward's remonstrances proved vain, and when threats of retaliation were held out by Edward, followed by preparations to carry those threats into effect, Pedro the Cruel, who had now succeeded to the throne of Spain, despatched strong reinforcements to the fleet which had already swept the English Channel.

The great Spanish fleet sailed north, and capturing on its way a number of English merchantmen, put into Sluys, and prepared to sail back in triumph with the prizes and merchandise it had captured. Knowing, however, that Edward was preparing to oppose them, the Spaniards filled up their complement of men, strengthened themselves by all sorts of the war machines then in use, and started on their return for Spain with one of the most powerful armadas that had ever put to sea.

Edward had collected on the coast of Sussex a fleet intended to oppose them, and had summoned all the military forces of the south of England to accompany him; and as soon as he heard that the Spaniards were about to put to sea he set out for Winchelsea, where the fleet was collected.

The queen accompanied him to the sea-coast, and the Black Prince, now in his twentieth year, was appointed to command one of the largest of the English vessels.

The fleet put to sea when they heard that the Spaniards had started, and the hostile fleets were soon in sight of each other. The number of fighting men on board the Spanish ships was ten times those of the English, and their vessels were of vastly superior size and strength. They had, moreover, caused their ships to be fitted at Sluys with large wooden towers, which furnished a commanding position to their crossbow-men. The wind was direct in their favour, and they could have easily avoided the contest, but, confiding in their enormously superior force, they sailed boldly forward to the attack.

The king himself led the English line, and directing his vessel towards a large Spanish ship, endeavoured to run her down. The shock was tremendous, but the enemy's vessel was stronger as well as larger than that of the king; and as the two ships recoiled from each other it was found that the water was rushing into the English vessel, and that she was rapidly sinking. The Spanish passed on in the confusion, but the king ordered his ship to be instantly laid alongside another which was following her, and to be firmly lashed to her. Then with his knights he sprang on board the Spaniard, and after a short but desperate fight cut down or drove the crew overboard. The royal standard was hoisted on the prize, the sinking English vessel was cast adrift, and the king sailed on to attack another adversary.

The battle now raged on all sides. The English strove to grapple with and board the enemy, while the Spaniards poured upon them a shower of bolts and quarrels from their cross-bows, hurled immense masses of stone from their military engines, and, as they drew alongside, cast into them heavy bars of iron, which pierced holes in the bottom of the ship.

Walter was on board the ship commanded by the Black Prince. This had been steered towards one of the largest and most important of the Spanish vessels. As they approached, the engine poured their missiles into them. Several great holes were torn in the sides of the ship, which was already sinking as she came alongside her foe.

"We must do our best, Sir Walter," the prince exclaimed, "for if we do not capture her speedily our ship will assuredly sink beneath our feet."

The Spaniard stood far higher above the water than the English ship, and the Black Prince and his knights in vain attempted to climb her sides, while the seamen strove with pumps and buckets to keep the vessel afloat. Every effort was in vain. The Spaniard's men-at-arms lined the bulwarks, and repulsed every effort made by the English to climb up them, while those on the towers rained down showers of bolts and arrows and masses of iron and stone. The situation was desperate when the Earl of Lancaster, passing by in his ship, saw the peril to which the prince was exposed, and, ranging up on the other side of the Spaniard, strove to board her there. The attention of the Spaniards being thus distracted, the prince and his companions made another desperate effort, and succeeded in winning their way on to the deck of the Spanish ship just as their own vessel sank beneath their feet; after a few minutes' desperate fighting the Spanish ship was captured.

The English were now everywhere getting the best of their enemies. Many of the Spanish vessels had been captured or sunk, and after the fight had raged for some hours, the rest began to disperse and seek safety in flight. The English vessel commanded by Count Robert of Namur had towards night engaged a Spanish vessel of more than twice its own strength. His adversaries, seeing that the day was lost, set all sail, but looking upon the little vessel beside them as a prey to be taken possession of at their leisure, they fastened it tightly to their sides by the grappling irons, and spreading all sail, made away. The Count and his men were unable to free themselves, and were being dragged away, when a follower of the count named Hennekin leapt suddenly on board the Spanish ship. With a bound he reached the mast, and with a single blow with his sword cut the halyards which supported the main-sail. The sail fell at once. The Spaniards rushed to the spot to repair the disaster which threatened to delay their ship. The count and his followers, seeing the bulwarks of the Spanish vessel for the moment unguarded, poured in, and after a furious conflict captured the vessel. By this time twenty-four of the enemy's vessels had been taken, the rest were either sunk or in full flight, and Edward at once returned to the English shore.

The fight had taken place within sight of land, and Queen Philippa, from the windows of the abbey, which stood on rising ground, had seen the approach of the vast Spanish fleet, and had watched the conflict until night fell. She remained in suspense as to the result until the king himself with the Black Prince and Prince John, afterwards known as John of Gaunt, who, although but ten years of age, had accompanied the Black Prince in his ship, rode up with the news of the victory.

This great sea-fight was one of the brightest and most honourable in the annals of English history, for not even in the case of that other great Spanish Armada which suffered defeat in English waters were the odds so immense or the victory so thorough and complete. The result of the fight was, that after some negotiations a truce of twenty years was concluded with Spain.

CHAPTER XX
POITIERS

AFTER the great sea-fight at the end of August, 1350, England had peace for some years. Phillip of France had died a week before that battle, and had been succeeded by his son John, Duke of Normandy. Upon the part of both countries there was an indisposition to renew the war, for their power had been vastly crippled by the devastations of the plague. This was followed by great distress and scarcity owing to the want of labour to till the fields. The truce was therefore continued from time to time; the pope strove to convert the truce into a permanent peace, and on the 28th of August, 1354, a number of the prelates and barons of England, with full power to arrange terms of peace, went to Avignon, where they were met by the French representatives. The powers committed to the English commissioners show that Edward was at this time really desirous of making a permanent peace with France; but the French ambassadors raised numerous and unexpected difficulties, and after lengthened negotiations the conference was broken off.

The truce came to an end in June, 1355, and great preparations were made on both sides for the war. The King of England strained every effort to furnish and equip an army which was to proceed with the Black Prince to Aquitaine, of which province his father had appointed him governor, and in November the Prince sailed for Bordeaux, with the advance-guard of his force. Sir Walter Somers accompanied him. During the years which had passed since the plague he had resided principally upon his estates, and had the satisfaction of seeing that his tenants escaped the distress which was general through the country. He had been in the habit of repairing to London to take part in the tournaments and other festivities; but both he and Edith preferred the quiet country life to a continued residence at court. Two sons had now been born to him, and fond as he was of the excitement and adventure of war, it was with deep regret that he obeyed the royal summons, and left his house with his retainers, consisting of twenty men-at-arms and thirty archers, to join the prince.

Upon the Black Prince's landing at Bordeaux he was joined by the Gascon lords, the vassals of the English crown, and for three months marched through and ravaged the districts adjoining, the French army, although greatly superior in force, offering no effectual resistance. Many towns were taken, and he returned at Christmas to Bordeaux after a campaign attended by a series of unbroken successes.

The following spring the war recommenced, and a diversion was effected by the Duke of Lancaster, who was in command of Brittany, joining his forces with those of the King of Navarre, and many of the nobles of Normandy, while King Edward crossed to Calais and kept a portion of the French army occupied there. The Black Prince, leaving the principal part of his forces under the command of the Earl of Albret to guard the territory already acquired against the attack of the French army under the Count of Armagnac, marched with 2000 picked men-at-arms and 6000 archers into Auvergne, and thence turning into Berry, marched to the gates of Bourges.

The King of France was now thoroughly alarmed, and issued a general call to all his vassals to assemble on the Loire. The Prince of Wales, finding immense bodies of men closing in around him, fell back slowly, capturing and levelling to the ground the strong castle of Romorentin.

The King of France was now hastening forward, accompanied by his four sons, 140 nobles with banners, 20,000 men-at-arms, and an immense force of infantry. Vast accessions of forces joined him each day, and on the 17th of September he occupied a position between the Black Prince and Guienne. The first intimation that either the Black Prince or the King of France had of their close proximity to each other was an accidental meeting between a small foraging force of the English and three hundred French horse, under the command of the Counts of Auxerre and Joigny, the marshal of Burgundy, and the lord of Chatillon. The French hotly pursued the little English party, and on emerging from some low bushes found themselves in the midst of the English camp, where all were taken prisoners. From them the Black Prince learned that the King of France was within a day's march.

The Prince despatched the Captal de Buch with 200 men-at-arms to reconnoitre the force and position of the enemy, and these coming upon the rear of the French army just as they were about to enter Poitiers, dashed among them and took some prisoners. The King of France thus first learned that the enemy he was searching for was actually six miles in his rear. The Captal de Buch and his companions returned to the Black Prince, and confirmed the information obtained from the prisoners, that the King of France, with an army at least eight times as strong as his own, lay between him and Poitiers.

The position appeared well-nigh desperate, but the prince and his most experienced knights at once reconnoitred the country to choose the best ground upon which to do battle. An excellent position was chosen. It consisted of rising ground commanding the country towards Poitiers, and naturally defended by the hedges of a vineyard. It was only accessible from Poitiers by a sunken road flanked by banks and fences, and but wide enough to admit of four horsemen riding abreast along it. The ground on either side of this hollow way was rough and broken so as to impede the movements even of infantry, and to render the manœuvres of a large body of cavalry nearly impracticable. On the left of the position was a little hamlet called Maupertuis. Here on the night of Saturday the 17th of September the prince encamped, and early next morning made his dispositions for the battle. His whole force was dismounted and occupied the high ground, a strong body of archers lined the hedges on either side of the sunken road; the main body of archers were drawn up in their usual formation on the hillside, their front covered by the hedge of the vineyard, while behind them the men-at-arms were drawn up.

The King of France divided his army into three divisions, each consisting of 16,000 mounted men-at-arms besides infantry, commanded respectively by the Duke of Orleans, the king's brother, the dauphin, and the king himself. With the two royal princes were the most experienced of the French commanders. In the meantime De Ribaumont, with three other French knights, reconnoitred the English position, and on their return with their report strongly advised that as large bodies of cavalry would be quite useless owing to the nature of the ground, the whole force should dismount except 300 picked men destined to break the line of English archers and a small body of German horse to act as a reserve.

Just as the King of France was about to give orders for the advance, the Cardinal of Perigord arrived in his camp, anxious to stop, if possible, the effusion of blood. He hurried to the King of France.

"You have here, sire," he said, "the flower of all the chivalry of your realm assembled against a mere handful of English, and it will be far more honourable and profitable for you to have them in your power without battle than to risk such a noble array in uncertain strife. I pray you, then, in the name of God, to let me ride on to the Prince of Wales, to show him his peril, and to exhort him to peace."

"Willingly, my lord," the king replied; "but above all things be quick."

The cardinal at once hastened to the English camp; he found the Black Prince in the midst of his knights ready for battle, but by no means unwilling to listen to proposals for peace. His position was indeed most perilous. In his face was an enormously superior army, and he was moreover threatened by famine; even during the two preceding days his army had suffered from a great scarcity of forage, and its provisions were almost wholly exhausted. The French force was sufficiently numerous to blockade him in his camp, and he knew that did they adopt that course he must surrender unconditionally, since were he forced to sally out and attack the French no valour could compensate for the immense disparity of numbers. He therefore replied at once to the cardinal's application, that he was ready to listen to any terms by which his honour and that of his companions would be preserved.

The cardinal returned to the King of France and with much entreaty succeeded in obtaining a truce until sunrise on the following morning. The soldiers returned to their tents, and the cardinal rode backward and forward between the armies, beseeching the King of France to moderate his demands, and the Black Prince to submit to the evil fortune which had befallen him; but on the one side the king looked upon the victory as certain, and on the other the Black Prince thought that there was at least a hope of success should the French attack him. All, therefore, that the cardinal could obtain from him was an offer to resign all he had captured in his expedition, towns, castles, and prisoners, and to take an oath not to bear arms against France for seven years. This proposal fell so far short of the demands of the French king that pacification soon appeared hopeless.

Early on the Monday morning the cardinal once more sought the presence of the French king, but found John inflexible; while some of the leaders who had viewed with the strongest disapproval his efforts to snatch what they regarded as certain victory from their hands, gave him a peremptory warning not to show himself again in their lines. The prelate then bore the news of his failure to the Prince of Wales. "Fair son," he said, "do the best you can, for you must needs fight, as I can find no means of peace or amnesty with the King of France."

"Be it so, good father," the prince replied, "it is our full resolve to fight, and God will aid the right."

The delay which had occurred had not been without advantages for the British army, although the shortness of provisions was greatly felt. Every effort had been made to strengthen the position. Deep trenches had been dug and palisades erected around it, and the carts and baggage train had all been moved round so as to form a protection on the weakest side of the camp, where also a rampart had been constructed.

Upon a careful examination of the ground it was found that the hill on the right side of the camp was less difficult than had been supposed, and that the dismounted men-at-arms who lay at its foot under the command of the Dauphin would find little difficulty in climbing it to the assault. The prince therefore gave orders that 300 men-at-arms and 300 mounted archers should make a circuit from the rear round the base of the hill, in order to pour in upon the flank of the Dauphin's division as soon as they became disordered in the ascent. The nature of the ground concealed this manœuvre from the enemies' view, and the Captal De Buch, who was in command of the party, gained unperceived the cover of a wooded ravine within a few hundred yards of the left flank of the enemy. By the time that all these dispositions were complete the huge French array was moving forward. The Black Prince, surrounded by his knights, viewed them approaching.

"Fair lords," he said, "though we be so few against that mighty power of enemies, let us not be dismayed, for strength and victory lie not in multitudes, but in those to whom God give them. If He will the day be ours, then the highest glory of this world will be given to us. If we die, I have the noble lord, my father, and two fair brothers, and you have each of you many a good friend who will avenge us well; thus, then, I pray you fight well this day, and if it please God and St. George I will also do the part of a good knight."

The prince then chose Sir John Chandos and Sir James Audley to remain by his side during the conflict in order to afford him counsel in case of need. Audley, however, pleaded a vow which he had made long before, to be the first in battle should he ever be engaged under the command of the King of England or any of his children. The prince at once acceded to his request to be allowed to fight in the van, and

Audley, accompanied by four chosen squires, took his place in front of the English line of battle. Not far from him, also in advance of the line, was Sir Eustace D'Ambrecicourt on horseback, also eager to distinguish himself.

As Sir James rode off the prince turned to Walter. "As Audley must needs fight as a knight-errant, Sir Walter Somers, do you take your place by my side, for there is no more valiant knight in my army than you have often proved yourself to be."

Three hundred chosen French men-at-arms mounted on the strongest horses covered with steel armour, led the way under the command of the Marechals D'Audeham and De Clermont; while behind them were a large body of German cavalry under the Counts of Nassau, Saarbruck, and Nidau, to support them in their attack on the English archers. On the right was the Duke of Orleans with 16,000 men-at-arms; on the left the Dauphin and his two brothers with an equal force; while King John himself led on the rear-guard.

When the three hundred *élite* of the French army reached the narrow way between the hedges, knowing that these were lined with archers they charged through at a gallop to fall upon the main body of bowmen covering the front of the English men-at-arms. The moment they were fairly in the hollow road the British archers rose on either side to their feet and poured such a flight of arrows among them that in an instant all was confusion and disarray. Through every joint and crevice of the armour of knights and horses the arrows found their way, and the lane was almost choked with the bodies of men and horses. A considerable number, nevertheless, made their way through and approached the first line of archers beyond. Here they were met by Sir James Audley, who, with his four squires, plunged into their ranks and overthrew the Marechal D'Audeham, and then fought his way onward. Regardless of the rest of the battle he pressed ever forward, until at the end of the day, wounded in a hundred places and fainting from loss of blood, he fell from his horse almost at the gates of Poitiers, and was borne from the field by the four faithful squires who had fought beside him throughout the day.

Less fortunate was Sir Eustace D'Ambrecicourt, who spurred headlong upon the German cavalry. A German knight rode out to meet him, and in the shock both were dishorsed, but before Sir Eustace could recover his seat he was borne down to the ground by four others of the enemy, and was bound and carried captive to the rear.

In the meantime the English archers kept up their incessant hail of arrows upon the band under the French marshals. The English men-at-arms passed through the gaps purposely left in the line of archers and drove back the front rank of the enemy upon those following, chasing them headlong down the hollow road again. The few survivors of the French force, galloping back, carried confusion into the advancing division the Dauphin.

Before order was restored the Captal De Buch with his six hundred men issued forth from his place of concealment and charged impetuously down on the left flank of the Dauphin. The French, shaken in front by the retreat of their advance guard, were thrown into extreme confusion by this sudden and unexpected charge. The horse archers with the captal poured their arrows into the mass, while the shafts of the main body of the archers on the hill hailed upon them without ceasing.

The rumour spread among those in the French rear, who were unable to see what was going forward, that the day was already lost, and many began to fly. Sir John Chandos marked the confusion which had set in, and he exclaimed to the prince:

"Now, sir, ride forward, and the day is yours. Let us charge right over upon your adversary, the King of France, for there lies the labour and the feat of the day. Well do I know that his great courage will never let him fly, but, God willing, he shall be well encountered."

"Forward, then, John Chandos," replied the prince. "You shall not see me tread one step back, but ever in advance. Bear on my banner. God and St. George be with us!"

The horses of the English force were all held in readiness by their attendants close in their rear. Every man sprang into his saddle, and with levelled lances the army bore down the hill against the enemy, while the Captal De Buch forced his way through the struggling ranks of the French to join them.

To these two parties were opposed the whole of the German cavalry, the division of the Dauphin, now thinned by flight, and a strong force under the Constable de Brienne, Duke of Athens. The first charge of the English was directed against the Germans, the remains of the marshal's forces, and that commanded by the Constable. The two bodies of cavalry met with a tremendous shock, raising their respective war-cries, "Denis Mount Joye!" and "St. George Guyenne!" Lances were shivered, and horses and men rolled over, but the German horse was borne down in every direction by the charge of the English chivalry. The Counts of Nassau and Saarbruck were taken, and the rest driven down the hill in utter confusion. The division of the Duke of Orleans, a little further down the hill to the right, were seized with a sudden panic, and 16,000 men-at-arms, together with their commander, fled without striking a blow.

Having routed the French and German cavalry in advance, the English now fell upon the Dauphin's division. This had been already confused by the attacks of the Captal De Buch, and when its leaders beheld the complete rout of the marshals and the Germans, and saw the victorious force galloping down upon them, the responsibility attached to the charge of the three young princes overcame their firmness. The Lords of Landas, Vaudenay, and St. Venant, thinking the battle lost, hurried the princes from the field, surrounded by eight hundred lances, determined to place them at a secure distance, and then to return and fight beside the king. The retreat of the princes at once disorganized the force, but though many fled a number of the nobles remained scattered over the field fighting in separate bodies with their own retainers gathered under their banners. Gradually these fell back and took post on the left of the French king's division. The Constable and the Duke of Bourbon with a large body of knights and men-at-arms also opposed a firm front to the advance of the English. The king saw with indignation one of his divisions defeated and the other in coward flight, but his forces were still vastly superior to those of the English, and ordering his men to dismount, he prepared to receive their onset. The English now gathered their forces which had been scattered in combat, and again advanced to the fight. The archers as usual heralded this advance with showers of arrows, which shook the ranks of the French and opened the way for the cavalry. These dashed in, and the ranks of the two armies became mixed, and each man fought hand to hand. The French king fought on foot with immense valour and bravery, as did his nobles. The Dukes of Bourbon and Athens, the Lords of Landas, Argenton, Chambery, Joinville, and many others stood and died near the king.

Gradually the English drove back their foes. The French forces became cut up into groups or confined into narrow spaces. Knight after knight fell around the king. De Ribaumont fell near him. Jeffrey de Charny, who, as one of the most valiant knights in the army, had been chosen to bear the French standard, the oriflamme, never left his sovereign's side, and as long as the sacred banner floated over his head John would not believe the day was lost. At length, however, Jeffrey de Charny was killed, and the oriflamme fell. John, surrounded on every side by foes who pressed forward to make him prisoner, still kept clear the space immediately around himself and his little son with his battle-axe; but at last he saw that further resistance would only entail the death of both, and he then surrendered to Denis de Montbec, a knight of Artois.

The battle was now virtually over. The French banners and pennons had disappeared, and nothing was seen save the dead and dying, groups of prisoners, and parties of fugitives flying over the country. Chandos now advised the prince to halt. His banner was pitched on the summit of a little mound. The trumpets blew to recall the army from the pursuit, and the prince, taking off his helmet, drank with the little body of knights who accompanied him some wine brought from his former encampment.

The two marshals of the English army, the Earls of Warwick and Suffolk, were among the first to return at the call of the trumpet. Hearing that King John had certainly not left the field of battle, though they knew not whether he was dead or taken, the prince at once despatched the Earl of Warwick and Lord Cobham to find and protect him if still alive. They soon came upon a mass of men-at-arms, seemingly engaged in an angry quarrel. On riding up they found that the object of strife was the King of France, who had been snatched from the hands of Montbec, and was being claimed by a score of men as his prisoner. The Earl of Warwick and Lord Cobham instantly made their way through the mass, and dismounting, saluted the captive monarch with the deepest reverence, and keeping back the multitude led him to the Prince of Wales. The latter bent his knee before the king, and calling for wine, presented the cup with his own hands to the unfortunate monarch.

The battle was over by noon, but it was evening before all the pursuing parties returned, and the result of the victory was then fully known. With less than 8000 men the English had conquered far more than 60,000. On the English side 2000 men-at-arms and 1500 archers had fallen. Upon the French side 11,000 men-at-arms, besides an immense number of footmen, had been killed. A king, a prince, an archbishop, 13 counts, 66 barons, and more than 2000 knights were prisoners in the hands of the English, with a number of other soldiers, who raised the number of captives to double that of their conquerors. All the baggage of the French army was taken, and as the barons of France had marched to the field feeling certain of victory, and the rich armour of the prisoners became immediately the property of the captors, immense stores of valuable ornaments of all kinds, especially jewelled baldrics, enriched the meanest soldier among the conquerors.

The helmet which the French king had worn, which bore a small coronet of gold beneath the crest, was delivered to the Prince of Wales, who sent it off at once to his father as the best trophy of the battle he could offer him.

Its receipt was the first intimation which Edward III. received of the great victory.

As the prince had no means of providing for the immense number of prisoners, the greater portion were set at liberty upon their taking an oath to present themselves at Bordeaux by the ensuing Christmas in order either to pay the ransom appointed, or to again yield themselves as prisoners.

Immediately the battle was over, Edward sent for the gallant Sir James Audley, who was brought to him on his litter by his esquires, and the prince, after warmly congratulating him on the honour that he had that day won as the bravest knight in the army, assigned him an annuity of five hundred marks a year.

No sooner was Audley taken to his own tent than he called round him several of his nearest relations and friends, and then and there made over to his four gallant attendants, without power of recall, the gift which the prince had bestowed upon him. The prince was not to be outdone, however, in liberality, and on hearing that Audley had assigned his present to the brave men who had so gallantly supported him in the fight, he presented Sir James with another annuity of six hundred marks a year.

CHAPTER XXI
THE JACQUERIE

ON the evening after the battle of Poitiers a splendid entertainment was served in the tent of the Prince of Wales to the King of France and all the principal prisoners. John, with his son and six of his highest nobles were seated at a table raised above the rest, and the prince himself waited as page upon the French king. John in vain endeavoured to persuade the prince to be seated; the latter refused, saying, that it was his pleasure as well as his duty to wait upon one who had shown himself to be the best and bravest knight in the French army. The example of the Black Prince was contagious, and the English vied with each other in generous treatment of their prisoners. All were treated as friends, and that night an immense number of knights and squires were admitted to ransom on such terms as had never before been known. The captors simply required their prisoners to declare in good faith what they could afford to pay without pressing themselves too hard, "for they did not wish," they said, "to ransom knights or squires on terms which would prevent them from maintaining their station in society, from serving their lords, or from riding forth in arms to advance their name and honour."

Upon the following morning solemn thanksgivings were offered up on the field of battle for the glorious victory. Then the English army, striking its tents, marched back towards Bordeaux. They were unmolested upon this march, for although the divisions of the Dauphin and the Duke of Orleans had now reunited, and were immensely superior in numbers to the English, encumbered as the latter were, moreover, with prisoners and booty, the tremendous defeat which they had suffered, and still more the capture of the king, paralysed the French commanders, and the English reached Bordeaux without striking another blow.

Not long after they reached that city the Cardinal of Perigord and another legate presented themselves to arrange peace, and these negotiations went on throughout the winter. The prince had received full powers from his father, and his demands were very moderate; but in spite of this no final peace could be arranged, and the result of the conference was the proclamation of a truce, to last for two years from the following Easter. During the winter immense numbers of the prisoners who had gone at large upon patrol, came in and paid their ransoms, as did the higher nobles who had been taken prisoners, and the whole army was greatly enriched. At the end of April the prince returned to England with King John. The procession through the streets of London was a magnificent one, the citizens vieing with each other in decorating their houses in honour of the victor of Poitiers, who, simply dressed, rode on a small black horse by the side of his prisoner, who was splendidly attired, and mounted on a superb white charger. The king received his royal prisoner in state in the great hall of his palace at Westminster, and did all in his power to alleviate the sorrows of his condition. The splendid palace of the Savoy, with gardens extending to the Thames, was appointed for his residence, and every means was taken to soften his captivity.

During the absence of the Black Prince in Guienne the king had been warring in Scotland. Here his success had been small, as the Scotch had retreated before him, wasting the country. David Bruce, the rightful king, was a prisoner in England, and Baliol, a descendant of the rival of Robert Bruce, had been placed upon the throne. As Edward passed through Roxburgh he received from Baliol a formal cession of his rights and titles to the throne of Scotland, and in return for this purely nominal gift he bestowed an annual income upon Baliol, who lived and died a pensioner of England. After Edward's return to England negotiations were carried on with the Scots, and a treaty was signed by which a truce for ten years was established between the two countries, and the liberation of Bruce was granted on a ransom of 100,000 marks.

The disorganization into which France had been thrown by the capture of its king increased rather than diminished. Among all classes men strove in the absence of a repressive power to gain advantages and privileges. Serious riots occurred in many parts, and the demagogues of Paris, headed by Stephen Marcel, and Robert le Coq, bishop of Leon, set at defiance the Dauphin and the ministers and lieutenant of the king. Massacre and violence stained the streets of Paris with blood. General law, public order, and private security were all lost. Great bodies of brigands devastated the country, and the whole of France was thrown into confusion. So terrible was the disorder that the inhabitants of every village were obliged to fortify the ends of their streets, and keep watch and ward as in the cities. The proprietors of land on the banks of rivers spent the night in boats moored in the middle of the stream, and in every house and castle throughout the land men remained armed as if against instant attack.

Then arose the terrible insurrection known as the Jacquerie. For centuries the peasantry of France had suffered under a bondage to which there had never been any approach in England. Their lives and liberties were wholly at the mercy of their feudal lords. Hitherto no attempt at resistance had been possible; but the tremendous defeat of the French at Poitiers by a handful of English aroused the hope among the serfs that the moment for vengeance had come. The movement began among a handful of peasants in the neighbourhood of St. Leu and Claremont. These declared that they would put to death all the gentlemen in the land. The cry spread through the country. The serfs, armed with pikes, poured out from every village, and a number of the lower classes from the towns joined them. Their first success was an attack upon a small castle. They burned down the gates and slew the knight to whom it belonged, with his wife and children of all ages. Their numbers rapidly increased.

Castle after castle was taken and stormed, palaces and houses levelled to the ground; fire, plunder, and massacre swept through the fairest provinces of France.

The peasants vied with each other in inventing deaths of fiendish cruelty and outrage upon every man, woman, and child of the better classes who fell into their hands. Owing to the number of nobles who had fallen at Cressy and Poitiers, and of those still captives in England, very many of their wives and daughters remained unprotected, and these were the especial victims of the fiendish malignity of the peasantry. Separated in many bands, the insurgents marched through the Beauvoisis, Soissonois, and Vermandois; and as they approached a number of unprotected ladies of the highest families in France fled to Meaux, where they remained under the guard of the young Duke of Orleans and a handful of men-at-arms.

After the conclusion of the peace at Bordeaux, Sir Walter Somers had been despatched on a mission to some of the German princes, with whom the king was in close relations. The business was not of an onerous nature, but Walter had been detained for some time over it. He spent a pleasant time in Germany, where, as an emissary of the king and one of the victors of Poitiers, the young English knight was made much of. When he set out on his return he joined the Captal De Buch, who, ever thirsting for adventure, had on the conclusion of the truce gone to serve in a campaign in Germany; with him was the French Count de Foix, who had been also serving throughout the campaign.

On entering France from the Rhine the three knights were shocked at the misery and ruin which met their eyes on all sides. Every castle and house throughout the country, of a class superior to those of the peasants, was destroyed, and tales of the most horrible outrages and murders met their ears.

"I regret," the Count de Foix said earnestly, "that I have been away warring in Germany, for it is clear that every true knight is wanted at home to crush down these human wolves."

THE JACQUERIE

"Methinks," the Captal rejoined, "that France will do well to invite the chivalry of all other countries to assemble and aid to put down this horrible insurrection."

"Ay," the Count said bitterly; "but who is to speak in the name of France? The Dauphin is powerless, and the virtual government is in the hands of Marcel and other ambitious traitors who hail the doings of the Jacquerie with delight, for these mad peasants are doing their work of destroying the knights and nobles."

The villages through which they passed were deserted save by women, and in the small towns the people of the lower class scowled threateningly at the three knights; but they with their following of forty men-at-arms, of whom five were followers of Walter, fifteen of the Captal, and twenty of the Count de Foix, ventured not to proceed beyond evil glances.

"I would," de Foix said, "that these dogs would but lift a hand against us. By St. Stephen, we would teach them a rough lesson!"

His companions were of the same mind, for all were excited to fury by the terrible tales which they heard. All these stories were new to them, for although rumours had reached Germany of the outbreak of a peasant insurrection in France the movement had but just begun when they started. As far as the frontier they had travelled leisurely, but they had hastened their pace more and more as they learned how sore was the strait of the nobles and gentry of the country and how grievously every good sword was needed. When they reached Chalons they heard much fuller particulars than had before reached them, and learned what the Duchess of Normandy, the Duchess of Orleans, and near three hundred ladies, had sought refuge in Meaux, and that they were there guarded but by a handful of men-at-arms under the Duke of Orleans, while great bands of serfs were pouring in from all parts of the country round, to massacre them.

265

Meaux is eighty miles from Chalons, but the three knights determined to press onward with all speed in hopes of averting the catastrophe. Allowing their horses an hour or two to rest, they rode forward, and pressing on without halt or delay, save such as was absolutely needed by the horses, they arrived at Meaux late the following night, and found to their delight that the insurgents, although swarming in immense numbers round the town, had not yet attacked it.

The arrival of the three knights and their followers was greeted with joy by the ladies. They, with their guard, had taken up their position in the market-house and market-place, which were separated from the rest of the town by the river Marne, which flows through the city. A consultation was at once held, and it being found that the Duke of Orleans had but twenty men-at-arms with him it was determined that it was impossible to defend the city walls, but that upon the following morning they would endeavour to cut their way with the ladies through the peasant hosts. In the night, however, an uproar was heard in the city. The burghers had risen and had opened the gates to the peasants, who now poured in in thousands. Every hour increased their numbers.

The market-place was besieged in the morning, and an hour or two afterwards a large body of the ruffians of Paris, under the command of a brutal grocer named Pierre Gille, arrived to swell their ranks.

The attack on the market-house continued, and the Duke of Orleans held a consultation with the three knights. It was agreed that against such a host of enemies the market-place could not long be defended, and that their best hope lay in sallying out and falling upon the assailants. Accordingly the men-at-arms were drawn up in order, with the banners of the Duke of Orleans and the Count de Foix, and the pennons of the Captal and Sir Walter Somers displayed, the gates were opened, and with levelled lances the little party rode out. Hitherto nothing had been heard save yells of anticipated triumph and fierce imprecations and threats against the defenders from the immense multitude without; but the appearance of the orderly ranks of the knights and men-at-arms as they issued through the gate struck a silence of fear through the mass.

Without an instant's delay the knights and men-at-arms, with levelled lances, charged into the multitude. A few attempted to fight, but more strove to fly, as the nobles and their followers, throwing away their lances, fell upon them with sword and battle-axe. Jammed up in the narrow streets of a small walled town, overthrowing and impeding each other in their efforts to escape, trampled down by the heavy horses of the men-at-arms, and hewn down by their swords and battle-axes, the insurgents fell in vast numbers. Multitudes succeeded in escaping through the gates into the fields; but here they were followed by the knights and their retainers, who continued charging among them and slaying till utter weariness compelled them to cease from the pursuit and return to Meaux. Not less than seven thousand of the insurgents had been slain by the four knights and fifty men, for ten had been left behind to guard the gates of the market-place.

History has no record of so vast a slaughter by so small a body of men. This terrific punishment put a summary end to the Jacquerie. Already in other parts several bodies had been defeated, and their principal leader, Caillet, with three thousand of his followers, slain near Clermont. But the defeat at Meaux was the crushing blow which put an end to the insurrection.

On their return to the town the knights executed a number of the burghers who had joined the peasants, and the greater part of the town was burned to the ground as a punishment for having opened the gates to the peasants and united with them.

The knights and ladies then started for Paris. On nearing the city they found that it was threatened by the forces of the Dauphin. Marcel had strongly fortified the town, and with his ally, the infamous King of Navarre, bade defiance to the royal power. However, the excesses of the demagogue had aroused against him the feeling of all the better class of the inhabitants. The King of Navarre, who was ready at all times to break his oath and betray his companions, marched his army out of the town and took up a position outside the walls. He then secretly negotiated peace with the Duke of Normandy, by which he agreed to yield to their fate Marcel and twelve of the most obnoxious burghers, while at the same time he persuaded Marcel that he was still attached to his interest. Marcel, however, was able to bid higher than the Duke of Normandy, and he entered into a new treaty with the treacherous king, by which he stipulated to deliver the city into his hands during the night. Everyone within the walls, except the partisans of Marcel, upon whose doors a mark was to be placed, were to be put to death indiscriminately, and the King of Navarre was to be proclaimed King of France.

Fortunately Pepin des Essarts and John de Charny, two loyal knights who were in Paris, obtained information of the plan a few minutes before the time appointed for its execution. Arming themselves instantly, and collecting a few followers, they rushed to the houses of the chief conspirators, but found them empty, Marcel and his companions having already gone to the gates. Passing by the hotel-de-ville, the knights entered, snatched down the royal banner which was kept there, and unfurling it mounted their horses and rode through the streets, calling all men to arms. They reached the Port St. Antoine just at the moment when Marcel was in the act of opening it in order to give admission to the Navarrese. When he heard the shouts he tried with his friends to make his way into the bastile, but his retreat was intercepted, and a severe and bloody struggle took place between the two parties. Stephen Marcel, however, was himself slain by Sir John de Charny, and almost all his principal companions fell with him. The inhabitants then threw open their gates and the Duke of Normandy entered.

Walter Somers had, with his companions, joined the army of the duke, and placed his sword at his disposal; but when the French prince entered Paris without the necessity of fighting, he took leave of him, and with the Captal returned to England. Rare, indeed, were the jewels which Walter brought home to his wife, for the three hundred noble ladies rescued at Meaux from dishonour and death had insisted upon bestowing tokens of their regard and gratitude upon the rescuers, and as many of them belonged to the richest as well as the noblest families in France the presents which Walter thus received from the grateful ladies were of immense value.

He was welcomed by the king and Prince of Wales with great honour, for the battle at Meaux had excited the admiration and astonishment of all Europe. The Jacquerie was considered as a common danger in all civilized countries; for if successful it might have spread far beyond the boundaries of France, and constituted a danger to chivalry, and indeed to society universally.

Thus King Edward gave the highest marks of his satisfaction to the Captal and Walter, added considerable grants of land to the estates of the latter, and raised him to the dignity of Baron Somers of Westerham.

It has always been a matter of wonder that King Edward did not take advantage of the utter state of confusion and anarchy which prevailed in France to complete his conquest of that country, which there is no reasonable doubt he could have effected with ease. Civil war and strife prevailed throughout France; famine devastated it; and without leaders or concord, dispirited and impoverished by defeat, France could have offered no resistance to such an army as England could have placed in the field. The only probable supposition is that at heart he doubted whether the acquisition of the crown of France was really desirable, or whether it could be permanently maintained should it be gained. To the monarch of a country prosperous, flourishing, and contented, the object of admiration throughout Europe, the union with distracted and divided France could be of no benefit. Of military glory he had gained enough to content any man, and some of the richest provinces of France were already his. Therefore it may well be believed that, feeling secure very many years must elapse before France could again become dangerous, he was well content to let matters continue as they were.

King John still remained a prisoner in his hands, for the princes and nobles of France were too much engaged in broils and civil wars to think of raising the money for his ransom, and Languedoc was the only province of France which made any effort whatever towards so doing. War still raged between the Dauphin and the King of Navarre.

At the conclusion of the two years' truce Edward, with the most splendidly-equipped army which had ever left England, marched through the length and breadth of France. Nowhere did he meet with any resistance in the field. He marched under the walls of Paris, but took no steps to lay siege to that city, which would have fallen an easy prey to his army had he chosen to capture it. That he did not do so is another proof that he had no desire to add France to the possessions of the English crown. At length, by the efforts of the pope, a peace was agreed upon, by which France yielded all Aquitaine and the town of Calais to England as an absolute possession, and not as a fief of the crown of France; while the English king surrendered all his captures in Normandy and Brittany and abandoned his claim to the crown of France. With great efforts the French raised a portion of the ransom demanded for the king, and John returned to France after four years of captivity.

At the commencement of 1363 Edward the Black Prince was named Prince of Aquitaine, and that province was bestowed upon him as a gift by the king, subject only to liege homage and an annual tribute of one ounce of gold. The prince took with him to his new possessions many of the knights and nobles who had served with him, and offered to Walter a high post in the government of the province if he would accompany him. This Walter begged to be excused from doing. Two girls had now been added to his family, and he was unwilling to leave his happy home unless the needs of war called him to the prince's side. He therefore remained quietly at home.

THE JACQUERIE

When King John returned to France, four of the French princes of the blood-royal had been given as hostages for the fulfilment of the treaty of Bretigny. They were permitted to reside at Calais, and were at liberty to move about as they would, and even to absent themselves from the town for three days at a time whensoever they might choose. The Duke of Anjou, the king's second son, basely took advantage of this liberty to escape, in direct violation of his oath. The other hostages followed his example.

King John, himself the soul of honour, was intensely mortified at this breach of faith on the part of his sons, and after calling together the states-general at Amiens to obtain the subsidies necessary for paying the remaining portion of his ransom, he himself, with a train of two hundred officers and their followers, crossed to England to make excuses to Edward for the treachery of the princes. Some historians represent the visit as a voluntary returning into captivity; but this was not so. The English king had accepted the hostages in his place, and was responsible for their safe-keeping, and had no claim upon the French monarch because they had taken advantage of the excess of confidence with which they had been treated. That the coming of the French king was not in any way regarded as a return into captivity is shown by the fact that he was before starting furnished by Edward with letters of safe-conduct, by which his secure and unobstructed return to his own country was expressly stipulated, and he was received by Edward as an honoured guest and friend, and his coming was regarded as an honour and an occasion for festivity by all England.

At the same time that John was in London the King of Cyprus, the King of Denmark, and the King of Scotland were also there, and the meeting of four monarchs in London was the occasion of extraordinary festivities and rejoicing, the king and his royal guests being several times entertained at sumptuous banquets by the lord-mayor, the ex-mayor Henry Pickard, and several of the aldermen.

Six weeks after John's arrival in London he was seized with illness at the palace of the Savoy, and died on the 8th of April, 1364. The Dauphin, Charles, now succeeded him as Charles V., and the war between the houses of Navarre and Valois was carried on with greater fury than ever. The armies of Navarre were commanded by the Captal de Buch, who was a distant relation of the king; while those of Charles were headed by the Maréchal de Boucicault and Bertrand du Guesclin, one of the most gallant of the French knights. A great battle was fought near Cocherel. Contrary to the orders of the Captal, his army, which consisted principally of adventurers, descended from the strong position he had chosen, and gave battle in the plain. They were completely defeated, and the Captal himself taken prisoner.

In Brittany John of Montford and Charles of Blois had renewed their struggle, and King Charles, seeing the danger of Brittany falling into the hands of De Montford, who was a close ally of England, interfered in favour of Charles of Blois, and sent Du Guesclin to his assistance.

This was a breach of the treaty of Bretigny, and De Montford at once sent to the Black Prince for assistance. The Prince did not treat the conduct of Charles as a breach of the treaty, and took no part himself in the war, but permitted Sir John Chandos, who was a personal friend of De Montford, to go to his aid. De Montford's army, after the arrival of Chandos with 200 spears, amounted to but 1600 men-at-arms and from 800 to 900 archers, while Charles of Blois had 4000 men-at-arms and a proportionate number of infantry. De Montford tried to negotiate. He offered to divide the dukedom, and to agree that in case he died childless it should revert to the family of Charles. Charles, however, refused all terms, even to grant his adversary's request to put off the battle until the morrow, so as to avoid violating the Sabbath; and having given orders that all prisoners taken in the battle should be hung, he advanced upon De Montford.

THE JACQUERIE

Both forces were divided in four bodies. The first on De Montford's side was commanded by Sir Robert Knolles, the second by Oliver de Clisson, the third by Chandos and De Montford, the fourth by Sir Hugh de Calverley. Du Guesclin led the front division of Charles's army, the Counts of Auxerre and Joigny the second, Charles himself the third, and the Lords of Roye and Rieux the reserve. The ducal arms of Brittany were displayed on both sides.

By slow degrees the two armies closed with each other in deadly strife. Both parties had dismounted and fought on foot with lances shortened to five feet. Du Guesclin and his division attacked that of Knolles. Auxerre fell upon De Clisson, while the divisions of the two rival princes closed with each other. After desperate fighting numbers prevailed. De Montford was driven back, but Calverley advanced to his aid, fell upon the rear of the French, threw them into disorder, and then having rallied De Montford's men, retired to his former position in readiness to give succour again where it might be needed.

In the meantime Clisson had been engaged in a desperate struggle with the Count of Auxerre, but was obtaining no advantage. Clisson himself had received the blow of a battle-axe which had dashed in the vizor of his helmet and blinded for ever one of his eyes. He was still leading his men, but the enemies' superior numbers were pressing him back, when Chandos, the instant the assistance of Calverley had relieved De Montford's division, perceiving his danger, drew off a few men-at-arms, and with them fell upon the rear of the Count of Auxerre, and dashing all who opposed him to the ground with his battle-axe, cleft his way to the very centre of the enemy. Pressed by De Clisson in front and broken by the sudden attack of Chandos in the rear, the French division gave way in every direction. Auxerre was desperately wounded, and he and Joigny both taken prisoners.

Chandos then returned to De Montford, who had gallantly followed up the advantage gained by the confusion into which Charles's division had been thrown by the attack of Calverley. Charles was routed; he himself struck down and slain by an English soldier, and the division defeated with great slaughter. De Montford's whole force now gathered round Du Guesclin's division, which now alone remained, and after fighting gallantly until all hope was gone, the brave French knight and his companions yielded themselves as prisoners.

The battle of Auray terminated the struggle between the houses of Blois and Montford. More than 1000 French men-at-arms died on the field, among whom were many of the noblest in Brittany. Two counts, 27 lords, and 1500 men-at-arms were made prisoners. De Montford now took possession of the whole of Brittany, and at the suggestion of King Edward himself did homage to Charles V. for the duchy, which he afterwards ruled with wisdom.

CHAPTER XXII
VICTORY AND DEATH

WHILE the Black Prince was with difficulty governing his province of Aquitaine, where the mutual jealousies of the English and native officers caused continual difficulties, King Edward turned all his attention to advancing the prosperity of England. He fostered trade, commerce, and learning, was a munificent patron of the two universities, and established such order and regularity in his kingdom that England was the admiration of all Europe. Far different was the state of France. The cessation of the wars with England and the subsequent disbandment of troops had thrown upon their own resources great numbers of men who had been so long engaged in fighting that they had no other trade to turn to. The conclusion of the struggle in Brittany after the battle of Auray and the death of Charles of Blois still further added to the number, and these men gathered in bands, some of which were headed by men of knightly rank, and scattered through France plundering the country and extracting heavy sums from the towns.

These "great companies," as they were called, exceeded 50,000 men in number, and as almost all were trained soldiers they set the king and his nobles at defiance, and were virtually masters of France. The most tempting offers were made to them to lay down their arms, and the pope sent legates threatening excommunication, but the great companies laughed alike at promises and threats. At last a way of deliverance opened to France. Pedro, named the Cruel, of Castile, had alienated his people by his cruelty, and had defeated and driven into exile his half-brother, Henry of

Trastamare, who headed an insurrection against him. Pedro put to death numbers of the nobles of Castile, despoiled the King of Arragon, who had given aid to his brother, plundered and insulted the clergy, and allied himself with the Moors.

His quarrel with the clergy was the cause of his ruin. The pope summoned him to appear before him at Avignon to answer to the crimes laid to his charge. Pedro refused to attend, and the pope at once excommunicated him. The King of Arragon and Henry of Trastamare were then summoned to Avignon, and a treaty of alliance was concluded between them, and the pope declared the throne of Castile vacant owing to the excommunication of Pedro, and appointed Henry to it.

These measures would have troubled Pedro little had it not been that France groaned under the great companies, and the French king and the pontiff at once entered into negotiations with them to support Henry in his war against his brother. It was necessary that a leader in whom the companies should have confidence should be chosen, and Du Guesclin, still a prisoner of Chandos, who had captured him at Auray, was selected, and the pope, the King of France, and Don Henry, paid between them the 100,000 francs demanded for his ransom. Du Guesclin on his release negotiated with the leaders of the great companies, and as the pope and king promised them large gratuities they agreed to march upon Spain. They were joined by a great number of French knights and men-at-arms.

The expedition was under the nominal command of John of Bourbon, but the real guidance was in the hands of Du Guesclin. As the army marched past Avignon they worked upon the terrors of the pope until he paid them 200,000 francs in gold. France was filled with joy at the prospect of a riddance of the free companies which had so long been a prey upon them. They were, too, eager to avenge upon the cruel King of Spain the murder of his queen, who was a princess of France. The same feeling animated the people of Aquitaine, and Calverley, D'Ambrecicourt, Sir Walter Hewitt, Sir John Devereux, Sir John Neville, and several other distinguished knights, with a large train of men-at-arms, joined the adventurers. The great army moved through Arragon, whose king in every way facilitated their progress. As they entered Castile the whole people declared in favour of Henry, and Pedro, deserted by all, fled to Bordeaux and besought aid from the Prince of Wales.

Between Pedro and the English court a firm alliance had existed from the time when the former so nearly married the Princess Joan, and immediately the king heard of the expedition against him he issued orders that no English knights should take part in it. The order, however, came too late. The English knights had already marched into Spain with Du Guesclin. As for the English who formed no inconsiderable portion of the great companies, they had already declined to obey the king, when, at the instance of the pope and the King of France, he had ordered them to disband.

On Pedro's arrival at Bordeaux with his three daughters and his son, they were kindly received by the Black Prince, courtesy and kindness to those in misfortune being among the leading characteristics of his nature. Pedro, cruel and ruthless as he was, was a man of great eloquence and insinuating manners, and giving his own version of affairs, he completely won over the prince, who felt himself, moreover, bound in some degree to support him, inasmuch as he, an ally of England, had been dethroned by an army composed partly of English. Pedro made the most magnificent promises to the prince in return for his aid, ceding him the whole of the province of Biscay, and agreeing to pay the British troops engaged in his service when he regained his throne, the Black Prince engaging to pay them in the meantime.

King Edward aided his son by raising an army in England, which sailed for Bordeaux under the command of the prince's brother, John of Gaunt, Duke of Lancaster. Walter formed part of this expedition. The king had issued his writs to him and other barons of the southern counties, and the Black Prince had himself written to ask him to join him, in memory of their former deeds of arms together.

As it was now some years since he had taken the field, Walter did not hesitate, but with thirty retainers, headed by Ralph, joined the army of John of Gaunt.

The Black Prince's first step was to endeavour to recall the Englishmen of the free companies, estimated to amount to at least 30,000 men. The news that he was taking up arms and would himself command the army caused Calverley and the whole of the other English knights to return at once, and 10,000 of the English men-at-arms with the great companies also left Don Henry and marched to Aquitaine. The road led through the territory of the King of Navarre, and the Black Prince advanced 56,000 florins of gold to pay this grasping and treacherous king for the right of passage of the army.

By Christmas, 1366, the preparations were complete, but the severity of the weather delayed the advance for some weeks. Fresh difficulties were encountered with Charles the Bad, of Navarre, who, having obtained the price for the passage, had now opened negotiations with Don Henry, and the governors of the frontier towns refused to allow Sir Hugh Calverley and the free companies, who formed the advance, to pass. These were not, however, the men to stand on ceremony, and without hesitation they attacked and captured the towns, when the King of Navarre at once apologized for his officers, and renewed his engagements. As, however, the Black Prince had received intelligence that he had formed a plan for attacking the English as they passed through the terrible pass of Roncesvalles, he compelled him to accompany the army. The invitation was couched in language which was friendly, but would yet admit of no denial.

On the 17th of February the English army, 30,000 strong, reached the pass. It marched in three divisions, the first commanded by the Duke of Lancaster and Lord Chandos, the second by the Black Prince, the third by the King of Majorca and the Count of Armagnac. The divisions crossed over on different days, for the pass was encumbered by snow and the obstacles were immense. Upon the day when the prince's division were passing a storm burst upon them, and it was with the greatest difficulty that they succeeded in crossing. On the 20th of February, however, all arrived safe on the other side of the Pyrenees. Du Guesclin, who, seeing the storm which was approaching from Aquitaine, had returned to France and levied a French army, was nigh at hand, and kept within a few miles of the English army as it advanced, avoiding an engagement until the arrival of Don Henry, who was marching to join him with the great companies and 60,000 Spanish troops.

Du Guesclin kept up secret communications with the King of Navarre, who was still forced to accompany the English army. The latter accordingly went out from the camp under pretence of hunting and was captured by a detachment of French troops.

On the 1st of April, the Spanish army having joined the French, the Black Prince sent letters to Don Henry, urging him in mild but dignified language to return to obedience, and to resign the throne he had usurped, offering at the same time to act as mediator between him and his brother, and to do all in his power to remove differences and abuses. Henry, confident in his strength, replied haughtily and prepared for battle.

The forces were extremely unequal. The Black Prince had under him 30,000 men; while under Don Henry were 3000 men-at-arms on mail-clad horses, 20,000 men-at-arms on horses not so protected, 6000 light cavalry, 10,000 crossbow-men, and 60,000 foot armed with spear and sword.

The night before the battle the Black Prince lodged in the little village of Navarretta, which had been deserted by its inhabitants. Walter had been his close companion since he started, and occupied the same lodging with him in the village.

"This reminds me," the prince said, "of the day before Cressy. They outnumber us by more than three to one."

"There were greater odds still," Walter replied, "at Poitiers, and I doubt not that we shall make as good an example of them."

"They are more doughty adversaries," the prince replied. "There are nigh 20,000 English in their ranks—all veterans in war—and they are led by Du Guesclin, who is a host in himself."

"Their very numbers will be a hindrance to them," Walter replied cheerfully; "and never did I see a better army than that which you have under you. I would we were fighting for a better man, for Don Pedro is to my mind treacherous as well as cruel. He promises fairly, but I doubt if when he has gained his end he will keep his promises. He speaks fairly and smoothly, but his deeds are at variance with his words."

"It may be, my lord," the prince replied, "that I am somewhat of your opinion, and that I regret I so quickly committed myself to his cause. However, he was my father's ally, and having fulfilled all his engagements had a right to demand our assistance. I am a bad hand, Walter, at saying no to those who beseech me."

"It is so, Sir Prince," Walter said bluntly. "Would that your heart had been a less generous one, for your nobleness of disposition is ever involving you in debts which hamper you sorely, and cause more trouble to you than all your enemies!"

"That is true enough," the Black Prince said with a sigh. "Since I was a boy I have ever been harassed with creditors; and though all Aquitaine is mine, I verily believe that there is not a man in my father's dominions who is so harassed and straitened for money as I."

"And yet," Walter said, smiling, "no sooner do you get it than you give it away."

"Ah!" the prince laughed, "I cannot deny it. It is so much pleasanter to give than to pay, that I can never find heart to balk myself. I am ever surrounded by suitors. Some have lost estates in my cause, others have rendered brilliant services in the field, some have burdened themselves with

280

debts to put their retainers in arms—all have pleased to urge, and for the life of me I cannot say them nay. I trust, though," he added more seriously, "that Don Pedro will fulfil his promises to pay my army. I have bound myself to my soldiers for their wages, besides advancing large sums to Pedro, and if he keeps not his engagements I shall indeed be in a sore strait."

"There is one thing," Walter said; "if he fail to keep his promises, we will not fail to oblige him to do so. If we win a kingdom for him, we can snatch it from him again."

"We have not won it yet," the prince said.

"We will do so to-morrow," Walter rejoined confidently. "I hope the fortunes of the day may bring me face to face with Du Guesclin. I am thrice as strong as when I fought at Cressy, and I should like to try my hand against this doughty champion."

The next morning the two armies prepared for battle, the Black Prince dividing his army as before. The divisions were commanded as in the passage of the Pyrenees, and each numbered 10,000 men.

Don Henry had also divided his force in three parts. In the first division, commanded by Du Guesclin, were 4000 veteran French knights and men-at-arms with 8000 foot-soldiers; the second was led by the prince's brother, Don Tillo, with 16,000 horse; while he himself commanded the third, in which were a multitude of soldiers, making up the gross total of 100,000 men.

As on the night preceding the battle of Poitiers, the English army had lain down supperless. Soon after midnight the trumpets sounded, and the troops soon moved forward. At sunrise the prince and his forces reached the summit of a little hill, whence was visible the approaching host of Spain. The first division, under the Duke of Lancaster and Lord Chandos, immediately quickened its pace and charged the division of Du Guesclin, which received it with great steadiness, and a desperate conflict ensued. The Black Prince charged the division of Don Tillo, which gave way at the first attack, and its commander, with 2000 horse, at once fled. The remainder of the division resisted for some time, but was unable to withstand the steady advance of the English, who without much difficulty dispersed and scattered it from the field. The King of Majorca now joined his division with that of the Black Prince, and the two advanced against the great division led by Don Henry.

The Spanish slingers opened upon the advancing force and for a time annoyed them greatly, but when the English archers arrived within bow-shot and opened fire they speedily dispersed the slingers, and the men-at-arms on both sides advanced to the attack. The conflict was long and desperate, and both sides fought with great gallantry and determination. Don Pedro—who, although vicious and cruel, was brave—fought in the ranks as a common soldier, frequently cutting his way into the midst of the Spaniards, and shouting to Don Henry to cross swords with him. Henry on his part fought with great valour, although, as he had the burden of command upon him, he was less able to distinguish himself by acts of personal prowess. Though fighting in the thickest of the press, he never lost his grasp of the general purpose of the battle. Three times, when his troops wavered before the assaults of the Black Prince and his knights, he rallied them and renewed the fight.

While this battle was raging, a not less obstinate fight was proceeding between the divisions of Lancaster and Du Guesclin. For a long time victory was doubtful, and indeed inclined towards the side of the French. The ranks of both parties were broken, and all were fighting in a confused mass, when, in the midst of the mêlée, a body of French and Spaniards poured in upon the banner of Chandos. He was struck to the ground, and a gigantic Castilian knight flung himself upon him and strove to slay him as he held him down. Chandos had lost sword and battle-axe, but drawing his dagger, he held with one hand his opponent's sword-arm, and at last, after repeated strokes with his dagger, he found an undefended part of his armour and pierced him with his dagger to the hilt. The Spaniard relaxed his hold, and Chandos, throwing him off, struggled to his feet and rejoined his friends, who had thought him dead. They now fought with more enthusiasm than ever, and at last, driving back the main body of the French knights, isolated a body of some sixty strong, and forced them to surrender. Among these were Du Guesclin himself, the Marshal D'Audenham, and the Bigue de Vilaines.

As these were the leaders of the division, the main body lost spirit and fought feebly, and were soon completely routed by Lancaster and Chandos. These now turned their attention to the other part of the field where the battle was still raging, and charged down upon the flank of Don Henry's army, which was already wavering. The Spaniards gave way at once on every side, and ere long the whole were scattered in headlong rout, hotly pursued by the English. The greater portion fled towards the town of Najarra, where they had slept the previous night, and here vast quantities were slaughtered by the English and Gascons. A number of prisoners were taken, and the palace and town sacked. The pursuit was kept up the whole day, and it was not until evening that the leaders began once more to assemble round the banner of the Prince of Wales. Among the last who arrived was Don Pedro himself. Springing from his charger he grasped the hand of the Prince of Wales, thanking him for his victory, which he felt would restore him to his throne.

"Give thanks and praise to God, and not to me," the prince replied, "for from Him, and not from me, you have received victory."

About 8000 men fell in the battle, the loss of the English, French, and Spaniards being nearly equal; but many thousands of the latter fell in the pursuit, and as many more were drowned in endeavouring to cross the river Ebro. Don Henry escaped after fighting till the last, and reaching the French territory in safety took refuge in the Papal court of Avignon.

Upon the morning after the battle Don Pedro requested the Black Prince to give him up all the Castilian prisoners, in order that he might put them to death. The prince, however, was always opposed to cruelty, and asked and obtained as a boon to himself that the lives of all the Spanish prisoners, with the exception of one whose conduct had been marked with peculiar treachery, should be spared, and even induced Pedro to pardon them altogether on their swearing fealty to him. Even Don Sancho, Pedro's brother, who had fought at Najarra under Don Henry, was received and embraced by Pedro at the request of the Prince of Wales. The city of Burgos at once opened its gates, and the rest of the country followed its example, and resumed its allegiance to Pedro, who remounted his throne without further resistance.

As Walter had fought by the side of the Black Prince his desire to cross swords with Du Guesclin was not satisfied; but his valour during the day won for him the warm approbation of the prince. Opposed to them were many of the great companies, and these men, all experienced soldiers and many of them Englishmen, had fought with great stubbornness. Walter had singled out for attack a banner bearing the cognizance of a raven. The leader of this band, who was known as the Knight of the Raven, had won for himself a specially evil notoriety in France by the ferocity of his conduct. Wherever his band went they had swept the country, and the most atrocious tortures had been inflicted on all well-to-do persons who had fallen into their hands, to extract from them the secret of buried hoards or bonds, entailing upon them the loss of their last penny.

The Knight of the Raven himself was said to be as brave as he was cruel, and several nobles who had attempted to oppose his band had been defeated and slain by him. He was known to be English, but his name was a mystery; and the Black Prince and his knights had long wished to encounter a man who was a disgrace alike to chivalry and the English name. When, therefore, Walter saw his banner in the king's division he urged his horse towards it, and, followed by Ralph and some thirty men-at-arms, hewed his way through the crowd until he was close to the banner.

A knight in gray armour spurred forward to meet him, and a desperate conflict took place.

VICTORY AND DEATH

Never had Walter crossed swords with a stouter adversary, and his opponent fought with as much vehemence and fury as if the sight of Walter's banner, which Ralph carried behind him, had aroused in him a frenzy of rage and hate. In guarding his head from one of his opponent's sweeping blows Walter's sword shivered at the hilt; but before the Gray Knight could repeat the blow Walter snatched his heavy battle-axe from his saddle. The knight reined back his horse for an instant, and imitated his example, and with these heavy weapons the fight was renewed. The Knight of the Raven had lost by the change, for Walter's great strength stood him in good stead, and presently with a tremendous blow he beat down his opponent's axe and cleft through his helmet almost to the chin.

The knight fell dead from his horse, and Walter, with his band pressing on, carried confusion into the ranks of his followers. When these had been defeated Walter rode back with Ralph to the spot where the Knight of the Raven had fallen.

"Take off his helmet, Ralph. Let me see his face. Methinks I recognized his voice, and he fought as if he knew and hated me."

Ralph removed the helmet.

"It is as I thought," Walter said; "it is Sir James Carnegie, a recreant and villain knight and foul enemy of mine, a disgrace to his name and rank, but a brave man. So long as he lived I could never say that my life was safe from his machinations. Thank God, there is an end of him and his evil doings!"

Walter was twice wounded in the fight, but upon neither occasion seriously, and he was soon able to take part in the tournaments and games which the Prince of Wales instituted partly to keep his men employed, partly for the amusement of the citizens of Burgos, outside whose walls his army lay encamped.

The prince was now obliged to remind the king of his promise to pay his troops; but nothing was farther from the mind of the treacherous monarch than to carry out the

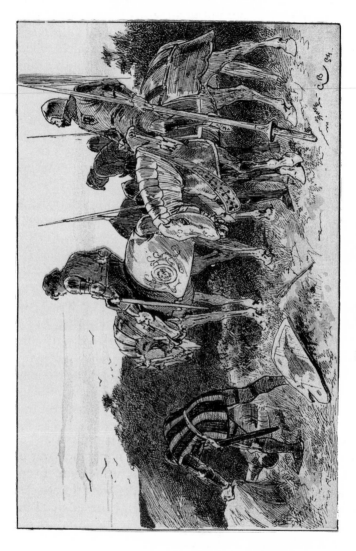

The end of a recreant knight.

promises which he had made in exile. He dared not, however, openly avow his intentions; but, trusting to the chapter of accidents, he told the prince that at Burgos he could not collect a sufficient sum; but if the army would march into Leon and take up their quarters near Valladolid, he himself would proceed to Seville, and would as soon as possible collect the money which he had bound himself to furnish. The plan was adopted. Edward marched his troops to Valladolid, and Don Pedro went to Seville.

Some time passed on without the arrival of the promised money, and the prince was impatient to return to Aquitaine. Don Henry had gathered a force in France, secretly assisted by the French king, and had made an inroad into Aquitaine, where he obtained several successes, and was joined by many of the disinterested nobles of that province.

"You were right," the prince said to Walter one day; "this treacherous king, who owes his kingdom to us, intends to break his plighted word. I know not what to do; my men are clamorous for their pay, and I am unable to satisfy them. Don Pedro still sends fair promises, and although I believe in my heart that he has no intention of keeping them, yet I can hardly march against him as an enemy, for, however far from the truth it may be, his pretext that the treasury has been emptied by his brother, and that in the disturbed state of the kingdom no money can be obtained, may yet be urged as valid."

Scarcely had the army encamped before Valladolid when a terrible pestilence attacked the army. For a while all questions of pay were forgotten, and consternation and dismay seized the troops. Neither rank nor station was of avail, and the leaders suffered as severely as the men. Every day immense numbers died, and so sudden were the attacks, and so great the mortality, that the soldiers believed that Don Pedro had poisoned the wells in order to rid himself of the necessity of fulfilling his obligations.

The Black Prince himself was prostrated, and lay for some time between life and death. A splendid constitution enabled him to pull through, but he arose from his bed enfeebled and shattered, and although for some years he lived on, he received his death-blow at Valladolid. His personal strength never came to him again, and even his mind was dulled and the brightness of his intellect dimmed from the effects of the fever. When he recovered sufficiently to inquire into the state of his forces, he was filled with sorrow and dismay. Four-fifths of the number were either dead or so weakened as to be useless for service again. The prince wrote urgently to Don Pedro for the money due; but the king knew that the English were powerless now, and replied that he had not been able to collect the money, but would forward it to Aquitaine, if the prince would return there with his army. Edward knew that he lied, but with only 6000 or 7000 men, many of whom were enfeebled by disease, he was not in a position to force the claim, or to punish the base and ungrateful king. Again, therefore, he turned his face north.

Charles of Navarre had now allied himself with Don Henry, and refused to allow the remnants of the army to pass through his dominions, although he granted permission to the prince himself and his personal attendants and friends. The southern route was barred by the King of Arragon, also an ally of Don Henry; but with him the prince was more successful. He had a personal interview with the monarch, and so influenced him that he not only obtained permission for his troops to pass through his dominions, but detached him from his alliance with Don Henry, and induced him to enter into a friendly treaty with Pedro.

A greater act of magnanimity was never performed. In spite of the base ingratitude with which he had been treated, and the breach of faith which saddled him with enormous liabilities and debts, which weighed him down and embittered the rest of his life, Edward remained faithful to the cause of his father's ally, and did his best to maintain him in the position which English valour had won for him. He himself with a few companions passed through Navarre, and arrived safely in Bordeaux, where his wife awaited him, and where he was received with rejoicings and festivities in honour of his glorious campaign in Spain.

His health was now irreparably injured. Troubles came thick upon him in Aquitaine, and he had no longer the energy to repress them. Risings took place in all directions, and the King of France renewed the war. In addition to his own troubles from the debts he had incurred, and the enemies who rose against him, he was further shaken by the death of his mother Philippa, whom he tenderly loved. His friend Chandos, too, was killed in a skirmish. Unhappily, while thus weakened in mind and body the treachery of the bishop and people of Limoges, who, having bound themselves by innumerable promises to him, surrendered their city to the French, caused him to commit the one act of cruelty which sullied the brightness of an otherwise unspotted career, for at the recapture of the town he bade his soldiers give no quarter.

This act, although common enough at the time, is so opposed to the principles of mercy and humanity which throughout all the previous acts of his life distinguished the conduct of the Black Prince that it cannot be doubted that his brain was affected by the illness which was fast hurrying him to the grave. Shortly afterwards he returned to England, and busied himself in arranging the affairs of the kingdom, which his father's failing health had permitted to fall into disorder. For the remaining four years of life he lived in seclusion, and sank on the 8th of June, 1376.

Walter, Lord Somers, returned home after the conclusion of the campaign in Spain, and rode no more to the wars.

Giles Fletcher and his wife had died some years before, but the good citizen Geoffrey the armourer, when he grew into years, abandoned his calling, and took up his abode at Westerham Castle to the time of his death.

In the wars which afterwards occurred with France Walter was represented in the field by his sons, who well sustained the high reputation which their father had borne as a good and valiant knight. He and his wife lived to a green old age, reverenced and beloved by their tenants and retainers, and died surrounded by their descendants to the fourth generation.

THE END